Praise for Gerry Boyle

Straw Man
2017 Winner Maine Literary Award Best Crime Fiction
"This hypnotically suspenseful, beautifully written novel is impossible to put down!"
—Gayle Lynds, bestselling author of *The Assassins*

Random Act
2020 Winner Maine Literary Award Best Crime Fiction
"Five stars for a first-rate, fast-paced yet intelligent murder-suspense-mystery. Add it to your summer reading list."
—*The Miramichi Reader*

"This may be the most insightful book Boyle has written. It may also be his best."
—*LJ's Mystery Reviews*

Once Burned
"Plot, characterization, atmosphere—everything works in Boyle's excellent 10th Jack McMorrow mystery."
—*Publishers Weekly*

Deadline
"*Deadline* is a fast, lively and exceptionally well written mystery by a new author in the genre."
—*Midwest Book Review*

STRAW MAN

A JACK McMORROW MYSTERY

Other books by Gerry Boyle

Jack McMorrow Mystery Series

Deadline
Bloodline
Lifeline
Potshot
Borderline
Cover Story
Pretty Dead
Home Body
Damaged Goods
Once Burned
Random Act

Brandon Blake Mysteries

Port City Black and White
Port City Shakedown

STRAW MAN

A JACK McMORROW MYSTERY

GERRY BOYLE

ISLANDPORT PRESS

STRAW MAN
A Jack McMorrow Mystery

First Islandport Edition November 2017
2020 printing

ISBN: 978-1-944762-45-2
ISBN: 978-1-939017-94-9 (ebook)
Library of Congress Control Number: 2015945356

Islandport Press
P.O. Box 10
Yarmouth, Maine 04096
www.islandportpress.com
info@islandportpress.com

Publisher: Dean Lunt
Cover Design: Tom Morgan, Blue Design
Interior Book Design: Teresa Lagrange, Islandport Press
Cover image courtesy of iStock.com/sakhorn38

Printed in the USA

For my growing family. Life is good.

ACKNOWLEDGMENTS

Heartfelt thanks go to my editor, Genevieve Morgan, whose insights on *Straw Man* were spot-on; to Punch, who read the manuscript closely (It takes a village . . .); and to Melissa Hayes, for her eagle eye. Lastly and especially, thanks to Vic, who made this book possible. As always.

STRAW MAN

A JACK McMORROW MYSTERY

1

—∿—

The sun slipped behind the ridgetop to the west, the woods darkening at midday like Waldo County, Maine, was Alaska in winter.

Mosquitoes were stirring, deerflies backing off. Crows harried something high in the trees, and I saw the flash of a hawk's silhouette, then wing-flapping shapes in pursuit. And then the crows were gone and it was the buzz of bugs and the snap of Clair's lunchbox latch.

Our break was over.

Clair climbed up and into the cab of the skidder, under the roll cage. He got situated and I started his big Ford pickup, waited for Louis to hoist himself up onto the seat. We pulled out, the truck lurching over the ruts we'd worked into the forest floor. Clair started the skidder and it clacked to life with a puff of diesel smoke, and he followed us up the rough path through the dark, dappled trees.

We'd been hired to do a careful cut of forty acres of hardwood—maple and oak, mostly—for sawlogs. The parcel was part of more than a thousand acres owned by Mrs. Hodding, who was eighty-seven and in assisted living in Rockport, twenty-five miles to the east. Mr. Hodding, who was ninety-one, and for a quarter century had had Clair look after these woods like they were the king's forest, had suffered a stroke. In the time it took for the blood clot to move to Mr. Hodding's brain, assisted living turned to acute care.

Mrs. Hodding needed money, and fast.

She called Clair. He called us. We put down everything we were doing and loaded up our gas and oil and chain saws. In my case, that meant temporarily trading writing newspaper stories for dropping sixty-foot trees. Louis came up from his hideaway in the deep woods near Sanctuary, twenty miles to the south. Clair left his tractor at home, loaded up the skidder, and we went to work.

Cutting massive trees, their crowns crashing to the forest floor. Limbing them until the trunks looked like the torsos of dismembered bodies. Wrestling heavy steel cable around the logs and jumping back as Clair skidded them away to the wood yard. Stepping up to the next trunk with a chain saw, leaning into the spume of chips and exhaust.

This was the third day in the late-September heat and we were bone-tired. Dirty. Smelled like oil and gasoline. The truck lurched and rocked.

"Iraq, women used to spend a whole morning looking for wood, come back with this pathetic little bunch of sticks," Louis said, looking out the truck window at the wall of trees.

"What a few thousand years of human habitation will do for a place," I said.

"It isn't all desert," he said. "There's farms and orchards and groves of these weird olive trees. Not what people think."

"Most things aren't," I said.

"You'd think you'd figured it out, even a little," Louis said, "and it would change in an instant. Kaboom."

And then he was quiet. We drove on.

The logging road was blocked by dead trees, the debris of ice storms and lightning, the passage of time. With Clair following on the skidder we stopped every twenty yards or so and got out and hacked our way through brambles, sawed the skeleton-dead limbs and tossed them to the side of the trail. We could have rammed the stuff out of the way with the skidder but this was cleaner, the way Mr. Hodding liked it.

The trail eventually emerged in Hyde on the other side of the hardwood ridge, the northeast corner of the Hoddings' land. We drove a quarter mile and crested a rise—and there was a wall of fresh slash.

It was a pile of branches ten feet high and it blocked the trail forty yards ahead. We heard the sound of distant chain saws and the roar of a diesel, saw blue smoke wafting through the green-brown woods to the right, like the wrong color in a painting.

"The old lady hire two crews?" Louis said.

"No way," I said.

"Then what—"

"Outlaws," I said. "Figure nobody will notice."

Louis and I turned as Clair rumbled up behind us on the skidder and climbed down, leaving the motor running. He walked up and Louis said, "We're not—"

"At the end of the parcel?" Clair said. "Not even close."

"There must be some confusion," I said.

I smiled. Clair smiled back.

"Well, let's go see if we can't straighten that confusion out," he said.

Clair took point, then Louis and me, the two Marines moving easily in single file. I tromped along like a reporter and tried to keep up. We passed the brush piles, the leaves shriveled at the edges but the centers still pale green.

"Two days," Clair said.

We kept walking, down the trail to the left, and eventually came on a truck, a dented primer-black Ford one-ton with dual rear wheels and ratty stake sides. Up close we saw a red dump sticker from Monroe, a couple of towns to the west. The truck bed was full of prime oak sawlogs, twelve-footers someone had winched up a makeshift steel ramp. There was a stack of logs off to the side. Thirty yards beyond the truck, a battered flatbed trailer was parked to the side of the path.

And just beyond the trailer, a small bulldozer was rumbling out of the woods.

The bulldozer was painted camouflage green, like army surplus, and it was dragging a foot-thick log, leaves dragging at the end of a jagged limb. The driver's back was to us, as he turned to watch the tree. He dragged the trunk out onto the trail and then reversed to slacken the cable, and jumped down.

Looked up.

Saw us.

Froze.

2

He was six six, maybe taller. Wide shoulders over a catcher's pad of a gut. A black beard and a shock of dark wild hair. His barrel chest was swathed in a black T-shirt, sweat stained at the armpits. Steel showed through the toes of his worn logger's boots. His eyes darted back and forth, and I could see him trying to peg us: friend or foe, looking for help or trouble. He turned back to the clacking dozer and reached over the seat and shut it off. We heard chain saws from the woods.

The guy turned back to us while the cooling motor ticked.

Clair strode up, stopped six feet short. "How you doing?"

The big guy nodded.

"Working this parcel from the south," Clair said. "Taking out some hardwood."

He looked at the log cinched to the end of the steel cable.

"Nice piece of oak you got there," Clair said. He smiled, but there was something very hard behind it, and I could see the guy stiffen, eyes narrowing. Trouble it was.

"Looks like your crew is doing the same," Clair said, glancing toward the oak log.

"Yup," the big guy said.

"But you know, you're either not where you think you are, or there's some"—Clair paused—"misunderstanding." He let the words float a bit, like diesel smoke.

The guy reached for the back pocket of his jeans, pulled out a pack of Marlboros. He shook one out and took a lighter from a front pocket. The flame flickered, he sucked, and then he blew a cloud of smoke in Clair's direction. Clair didn't flinch.

"Maybe you boys are the ones with the misunderstanding," the big guy said.

"I don't think so," Clair said. "We were hired to cut from the Prosperity line straight through to the Hyde line. Been working this woodlot for ten years, maybe more. You sure you started in the right place? Where you boys from?"

"Around," the guy said.

"Who hired you?"

"A friend of mine."

"Is that right?" Clair said. "Well, you're either on the wrong land or have the wrong friend. 'Cause I talked to the owner day before yesterday. There aren't two crews working this parcel."

"Well, you better talk to him again, old man. 'Cause I know we're working here."

"No doubt about that. Question is, are you lost—"

A pause.

"—or are you just helping yourself?"

The words lay across the big guy's cheek like a slap. He tilted his head back, thrust his chest out. Spat to the side and turned to the bulldozer. I braced myself, expecting a wrench, but he picked up an air horn from under the seat, the kind in an aerosol can. He held it up and blew it, two long, loud blasts. One chain saw shut down. He blew the horn again and another saw went quiet. A third blast and the third saw went quiet. I could hear the guy breathing, huff and puff.

He put the horn back behind the seat, turned back.

"Don't care much for being called a thief," the big guy said to Clair.

"Something tells me it isn't the first time," Clair said. "But if your feelings are hurt too bad, we can just get the sheriff and he can sort it out."

There was a crashing from the woods and three other guys emerged, saws in hand. We waited as they drew closer.

One of the loggers was a younger version of the big guy, chubby like a bear cub. He was flanked by an older guy, lean and hard, his whiskered face flushed and sweaty. His T-shirt was emblazoned with a skull, his arms smeared with grease that blurred jailhouse tattoos.

The fourth guy was just a high school kid, maybe a little older, tall and lanky, big hands dangling from long sinewy arms. His head had been shaved, but not recently. His eyes were set in deep sockets, and he looked like a boot-camp recruit. They put their saws on the ground and stood beside the big guy, a united front.

"What's the problem, Beefy?" the jailhouse guy said to the tall one.

"Nothing we can't handle," Beefy said.

The lanky kid—camo T-shirt and greasy jeans—was facing me. The lean, hard guy lined up across from Louis. Baby Fat stood alongside his dad.

"These guys is calling us thieves," Beefy said.

The others looked at us and scowled. Up close the older one had a jagged scar on his neck, like he'd been slashed with a broken bottle. There was a long knife in a sheath on his belt. Next to him Baby Fat was clenching and unclenching his fists so his biceps flexed and his knuckles cracked.

Clair grinned.

"Oh, I know. It's a little awkward. But the thing is, the old couple who owns this land, they're good people, worked hard all their lives. She's logging some of it off so she can pay his hospital bills. So I'll be damned if I'll let some two-bit yahoos take their money."

A long pause.

"Nothing personal," Clair said.

"Kiss my ass," the big guy said.

We stood there, guys with their hands on their hips. Deerflies buzzed but nobody swatted. Clair took a deep breath and let it out slow. He looked at the big guy, nobody else.

"Not worth getting hurt over," Clair said.

"Then turn around and go back the way you came," the big guy said.

"You tell him, Pa," Baby Fat said.

"You gonna let 'em go, Beefy?" the lanky kid said.

Clair smiled, reached up, and slipped his Stihl hat off, then back on. "My fault for not speaking more precisely," he said. "I meant it's not worth *you all* getting hurt over. So collect your gear and go back the way *you* came, and we'll just call it a day."

The big guy was silent, calculating what they'd gotten into.

It was the lean guy who took a step forward, chin out, hands low, palms spread. A half-smile. A guy who loved a fight.

"Come on, chickenshit," he said to Louis. "I know one when I see one."

Louis didn't answer, just stood and stared, an emotionless gaze that slowed things way down. The lean guy said, excited now, "I'm gonna tear your head off."

Still Louis stared, no tension showing. Placid. Calm.

"You deaf?" the guy said. "I'm saying I'm gonna tear your friggin' face off."

"I got this guy, Billy," the lanky kid said. He moved toward me like we were playing pickup basketball. Shirts and skins.

"And I got this one," Billy said, his eyes alight, wired like a meth head but probably all adrenaline. "Chickenshit here—cat got his tongue."

"Listen, old man," Beefy said to Clair. "Why don't you just get the hell out of here while you can still walk."

The voice of reason, Beefy seeing something in Clair and Louis that made him hesitate.

"Too late," Billy said, eye to eye with Louis. "Call me a thief? You only do that once."

He wanted this. The crazy one. Louis still said nothing, stood stock-still.

"Too scared to talk, you son of a bitch?" Billy said, his eyes bright, smile locked on.

From the trees, a woodpecker's drumroll. A pileated. Billy snorted phlegm and then spat. The skinny kid said, "I think they're all chickenshits."

"You got that goddamn right, Semi," Billy said. And then he took two quick steps, shoved Louis with two hands. Louis staggered backwards a step, then another. Billy was smiling now, then laughing, his bared teeth yellow like a dog's. He kept coming. Another shove. Louis staggered. Another shove and he backed up again. Rope-a-dope. Luring the guy away, where it would be one-on-one, plenty of room to—

The skinny kid rushed me, grabbed my shirt, his right arm swinging, hitting my ear, the top of my head. I bulled him back. The big guy grabbed for Clair's shoulders and swung and Clair twisted right and elbowed him in the throat. The guy coughed and grunted and Clair jammed his palm under the guy's nose. Blood spurted. The son waded in to help.

Semi was still punching my shoulder—my neck, my eye. The eye stung and blurred and he kept swinging, long arms windmilling. My temple, my mouth, my neck. And then I pulled back and he missed and I caught his forearm, held on and spun him around. I tripped him and he fell backwards and I rode him to the ground, a knee driving into his groin. We hit and he gasped, mouth open, and I punched him once in the teeth, again in the belly. He blew air again, the smell of tobacco and vomit. His fingernails clawed at my face, and I ducked low and hit him in the mouth, felt teeth jabbing into my hand. He was still raking at my eyes when I hit him, the soft part just under his rib cage. One, two, three.

His arms went limp. He was sucking air as I rolled off.

The big guy was on his hands and knees, gasping, blood running down his chin. His son was on the ground, too, and he scrambled up and threw himself at Clair, who sidestepped, kicked the kid's legs out from under him, dropped him onto his back like it was a drill at Special Forces school, which it had been. The kid bounced back up again and charged and Clair absorbed a wild punch, stepped inside another, and wrapped his arms around the kid's shoulders. He spun the kid loose, backhanded him across the face. More blood. Twice more, forehand and backhand, hard slaps, bone on bone. A quick step in close and Clair hit him hard in the belly.

The chubby kid staggered, wavered, crumpled. Semi started crawling for the truck.

I started after him, then glanced back. Louis was on top of Billy, arms pumping like pistons. Billy's face was all black blood, his eyes and nose and mouth. He flailed weakly and then he fell back. Louis kept punching, a smacking sound like he was pounding meat on a board. I ran to him, said, "Enough, man. Just stop."

I grabbed Louis by the shoulders, but his arms kept pumping up and down like an oil rig. I pulled him and he kept punching, blood spattering. I put an arm around his neck and yanked, couldn't move him. Finally I just held on and backed away, dragging him off. His expression hadn't changed from the first exchange, placid and emotionless.

Over by Clair, the father and son were still on the ground, spitting blood. Semi was at the truck, fumbling with the door handle. And then Billy was up, moving behind us.

He was standing in a swaying crouch, smiling through the blood, knife held out in front of him. He moved three steps and lunged toward Louis, slashed the air, the blood spraying from his chin. He whirled toward me and slashed and I jumped back. Clair leaned down for a tree limb, started toward us.

"You're a fucking dead man," Billy said, grinning with his splattered lips, eyes on Louis now. He waved the knife again and missed and Louis darted in, and spun backwards. He clamped Billy's knife arm under his armpit. Louis dug his fingers into the guy's forearm, finding nerves. Billy bellowed and Louis elbowed him in the face, spun, and kicked his legs out from under him.

The knife slashed weakly at the air.

And Louis dropped knee-first onto Billy's right forearm.

There was a crack, like a branch snapping, and Billy screamed. Louis, back on his feet, had the knife and flung it into the woods, a silver spinning thing. Billy was turned on his side, writhing, holding his right arm and moaning.

"You asshole! You busted his arm," Semi said from the truck, and when we turned we saw the shotgun. He raised it, aimed at Louis, but Clair was running toward him, shouting, "Hey, hey." The kid swiveled the gun toward Clair, and I ran at him, screaming, "Me, me," and he started to swing back toward me and then Clair was on him.

He bulled Semi back, got a hand on the barrel, men and gun going over, the gun booming as they hit the ground, the blast ripping the leaves above us as Clair punched him hard in the face, a slapping sound.

The kid was mumbling, "Get offa me," but after the second punch he stopped. I wrenched the shotgun from his hands, jacked the shells out.

One, two, three, four.

Stepped to the oak log and raised the gun by the barrel, brought it down like an ax. Once. Twice. On the third swing the stock splintered, and I dropped the shotgun to the ground, stomped it into the mud.

The woods were quiet. Again.

They glowered at us as they helped Billy to the truck, stepping on the broken gun. Billy, his arm swinging at his side like a dead animal, slid onto the passenger's side, butt first. Semi, his mouth bloody, got in the driver's seat and started the truck while Beefy went and started the bulldozer. Truck and bulldozer moved to the flatbed. Baby Fat backed the truck up and got out and hitched it to the trailer. Beefy drove the bulldozer onto the trailer, hooked up the chains.

They traded spots, according to hierarchy. Beefy drove, his son and Semi in the middle, Billy hunched over in pain against the passenger door, face swelling, maybe going into shock. The truck and trailer pulled into the slashed tote road, crushing branches and brush, and then backed out. The kid flipped us off as they pulled away. Billy revived enough to raise his head to bellow, "You're dead. You're all motherfucking dead."

And they rumbled off. We stood in the clearing, the oily diesel smoke hanging. Louis shook his head like he'd just awakened, looked down at his bloody hands. "I would have killed him," he said.

"A knife comes out, it changes things," I said.

"And all that training kicks in," Clair said. "Becomes automatic."

"Then what about you?" Louis said to him.

Clair took a step toward the skidder, turned and smiled, said, "Guess I've lost a step."

3

It was deep dusk when I pulled into the driveway. Roxanne's Subaru was there, a new blue Tacoma pickup parked beside it. I got out, winced as I stepped down, my knee sore, my face, too. I reached back into the cab of the truck and retrieved a six-pack of Ballantine ale, sixteen-ounce cans. I yanked one of the cold cans from the plastic web and pressed it against my swollen cheekbone. Lowered it and popped the top, took a long swallow. Looked at the Tacoma, the matching cap on the back with gold lettering that said

HEAVEN SENT FARM
Organic Chevre

"Needs a hyphen," I said. "And a freakin' accent."

I turned to the back of my old Toyota truck and lifted my chain saw out, then my toolbox. Walked to the shed door and slid it open. Went inside and put the saw and toolbox on the bench. Took another drink of ale. Pressed the cold can against my face.

Drank.

When I opened the door to the kitchen, I heard voices. Laughter. Welt.

"Just what I need," I said.

I crossed the kitchen and stepped through the opened door to the deck. He was sitting in an Adirondack chair. Roxanne was in the other one, her legs crossed, her shorts hiked up. Her feet were bare, her sandals tossed off. Her face was flushed with wine and her shirt was open, tank top underneath. Welt—rumpled white button-down shirt with the sleeves rolled, frayed khaki shorts, a belt embroidered with faded sailboats, blond hair raked back—was smiling, leaning toward her.

"You were great," he was saying. "I mean, when you said that her jaw just—"

He leaned forward, put his hand on her knee. I squeezed the can and it crackled. They turned toward me.

"Jack," Roxanne said. "What happened?"

The hand slipped off.

"A branch," I said. "Sometimes they spring loose."

"My God, your face," Roxanne said.

"I'm fine," I said.

"Just a flesh wound, huh?" Welt said.

He grinned.

"Your hands, Jack," Roxanne said. "That doesn't look like—"

The words trailed off as the picture became clear.

"How's the tree doing?" Welt said.

"Fine," I said. "Cut into twelve-foot logs."

"That'll teach it, huh?" he said. "Next tree will think twice before it picks a fight with you."

Another grin.

Roxanne sat up, tugged the hem of her shorts down. "Jack," she said. "You remember Welt Remington. From the school? Salandra's dad."

"Sure," I said.

I reached out and he did, too, and we shook hands. Welt's were soft, for a farmer. Must be cashmere goats.

"Welt came by to pick up Salandra. She and Sophie have been upstairs, just giggling away."

She paused.

"Are you sure you're all right? Your eye looks—"

"It's fine. Be back to normal by morning," I said.

I looked at the tray on the table. A bottle of wine, a half-inch left. Cheese and crackers and a cheesy knife. A sprig of flowers, yellow and white.

"Welt brought this delicious goat cheese from his farm," Roxanne said.

"From the LaManchas," Welt said.

I glanced at the plate.

"That's a kind of goat. I have Alpines and Kinders, too. And we grow our own herbs. I'm sorry to say the wine isn't local."

"That's okay," I said.

"But I got it from these wonderful friends of mine who own this vineyard in Napa. Canter and Trot?"

He said it like I should have heard of it.

"They're also into horses, obviously. My wife—we're separated— she did the label for them."

He said it like being separated was a happy and expected outcome. Then he reached and took the bottle off the table, held it up to me. There was a picture of two rearing horses, silhouettes against an orange sun.

"Handsome," I said.

"Grab a glass, Jack," Welt said, glancing at the beer can. "I brought another bottle. It's this perfect little chardonnay, just a hint of citrus and then this subtle waft of oak that follows. You almost think you imagined it. Kip and Chloe won all kinds of awards for this."

"Good for them," I said. "But I'm all set."

He looked at me, then at the green can, and then back at Roxanne. I moved away from the table, leaned against the railing of the deck, put my boot up. Welt sipped his wine, reached across to Roxanne to top off her glass. She leaned toward him and held out the glass, cleavage bared, the smooth white skin beyond her tan line, the curve of her breasts.

He poured slowly. No surprise. I touched my hand to my forehead and came away with a bit of dried blood. I flicked it over the rail. My right eye was swollen almost shut.

"My God, Jack," Roxanne said.

"It's okay."

"How 'bout ice?"

I held up the beer can and smiled.

"Well, the girls are still playing upstairs," Roxanne said. "We were just talking. About the peace project."

"Peace is a good thing," I said. "Quiet is, too."

A flicker of annoyance, and then Roxanne said, "We worked on the mission statement today."

Welt spread some cheese on a cracker and held it out. At least he didn't feed it to her.

"You and the little kids?" I said.

"They really contributed," Welt said. "I mean, it really made you think there was some hope. For a world without conflict. Of course, I know it's just a start. An elementary school in Prosperity, Maine. But you know the old saying—'Think globally. Act locally.'"

"Gandhi had to start somewhere," I said.

The look from Roxanne again. My eye was nearly shut. Behind it my head was starting to throb.

"It was just so heartening," Welt said. "They're learning that there's no disagreement that can't be resolved peacefully, as long as you have mutual respect and understanding."

"They're learning that? Six years old?"

I caught Welt in midsip, so Roxanne filled in.

"They are," she said. "I mean, they really are getting it."

"We underestimate children," Welt said. "As a result, we actually lose their most formative years, when they're forming as people. Six is almost too late."

"Studies say that many social patterns are established by three years old," Roxanne said. "That's why the kids, the older ones, were so hard to change. The agency would try, bring in every expert we could find. But by the time they're eleven or twelve . . . "

"You were so courageous to do that work," Welt said.

I bit my tongue. He prattled on.

"Most people would just run the other way. But there you were, on the front lines, working so hard to make a difference. Really. I have so much respect for you. Makes my work in the school look kind of—"

"Piddly," I said.

They both looked at me. I smiled and it hurt. Roxanne's lips were pressed tight, her eyes slightly narrowed.

"No, it's not piddly," she said. "It's important. It shows what a difference we can make if we all take responsibility for the way we live."

That seemed to be directed at me. I finished my ale and walked to the kitchen and got another. This time I pressed the can to my eye. It felt good. I walked back to the deck, popped the can, and drank. That felt good, too.

"We did these exercises," Welt said.

His face was tanned but his skin was smooth. His eyes were ice blue like cough drops and his teeth were gleaming ivory. He'd crossed his legs and was dangling his shoe, a vintage boat shoe.

"Role play, for one thing," he said. "We had each child play both the bully and the victim. The idea is to help them put themselves in the place of others, see somebody else's point of view. Did you know that sociopaths aren't as much violent as totally lacking in empathy?"

"Glad to hear the little skinny kids finally got in some whacks," I said.

"Jack," Roxanne said. "There's no need to be disparaging."

"No, it's okay," Welt said. "Skepticism is part of the process, remember? Stage three? It's a sign that the change agent is being taken seriously. It becomes threatening."

"I've already been threatened today," I said. "Believe me, this isn't threatening."

"Jack," Roxanne said. "Please."

"So what were you doing?" Welt said. "Duking it out with the local lumberjacks?" He gave me the smug grin again. He needed a good slap.

"Resolving a dispute," I said.

"You couldn't have found another way, establish some common ground?" Welt said. Like I needed his advice.

"There was common ground, but they stepped across it. This one guy, he was named Beefy. He was six six, two-eighty. But you know what they say. The bigger they are . . . "

"Oh, but that's another thing we're working on," Welt said. "The male reflex to see conflict as a chance to prove manhood, or at least some antiquated notion of it. Not lose face. That's just what we're trying to teach these boys not to do. But they model their fathers, who instead of reasoning with someone, finding a way to compromise, just lash out. Why talk things out when you can just smash somebody in the face?"

I looked at him.

"You're right there, Weltie," I said. "That's exactly what they do. And if you don't hit 'em back, they move on from your face and start on the rest of you."

I lifted the can and drank. Put it back on my face and smiled.

"I'll leave you two to your meeting. See if I can clean off some of this blood."

4

I peeked in on the girls. They had all of Sophie's dolls and stuffed animals lined up in pairs on the floor. Sophie was seated at the head of the line. She was holding an invisible steering wheel. Salandra, blonde and catalog-ready like her dad, was seated by Sophie.

Sophie made a hissing noise and reached to open the door. Salandra looked up at me and froze.

"We're playing school bus," Sophie said. "I'm the driver and 'Landra is the monitor—"

She paused.

"Daddy, you hurt your face," Sophie said.

"I bumped into a tree," I said.

"You should be more careful."

"I will be," I said.

Salandra said, "We're not supposed to fight."

She looked at me, her six-year-old face full of judgment, just like her dad's.

"You're right," I said. "Fighting is a bad thing."

I moved to Sophie, patted her head, and told her I'd see her later. I told Salandra I was glad she had come to see us. She looked up at me with unveiled suspicion.

"I'll let the bus keep rolling," I said, and I backed out and closed the door. I started down the hall, stopped at the window over the deck, and listened.

Their voices were just murmurs, soft and low. Welt, then Roxanne, then Welt again. And then he spoke up in a staged voice, and said, "Well, I guess I'd better gather up the child and head home."

"Thanks for bringing her," Roxanne said. "Sophie just loves it when you come. And I do, too."

I wondered what there was to love—Mr. Organic Pretty Boy or his scold of a daughter.

I scowled, hobbled to the bathroom. Took off my boots and T-shirt and jeans and stood in front of the mirror. My right eye was purple, tinged with fiery red. My upper lip was swollen, the left side scabbed over where it had split. There were claw marks on my left cheek from Semi's fingernails.

"We won," I said.

I stepped into the shower and let the hot water drum on my back, then fill my hair. There were scrapes there, too, and they stung. I took a washcloth and dabbed at my mouth and eye and cheek and the cloth turned rosy red. I stood there as the bits of dried blood swirled in the water at my feet, and then I turned the shower off, toweled myself dry, and headed for the bedroom.

I put on clean boxers and shorts and a faded blue polo shirt from some long ago *New York Times* gathering. Then I stepped to the window and glanced out.

Welt's truck was still in the driveway. Roxanne was standing at the driver's door on the far side. Salandra was in the backseat on my side.

Roxanne said, "Good-bye, guys," and Sophie, out of sight, said, "See you tomorrow."

The truck slipped into gear, the backup lights snapping on. Roxanne seemed to reach through the window, to what? Give Welt a pat? A squeeze on the shoulder? The truck started to pull out. I turned and walked down the stairs and into the kitchen. I was opening another beer when Roxanne came in the door.

"Hey," I said.

No reply. She took the kettle from the stove, moved past me to the sink. Filled the kettle and slammed it back down on the burner. Past me again, to the cupboard where she took out a box of herbal tea, shook out a tea bag. Took out a mug, dropped the tea bag in, put the mug down on the stove. The kettle began to quiver. I heard Roxanne take a deep breath, her hands on her hips.

"Where's Sophie?" I said.

After a long moment she said, "She went home with Salandra. She begged. They were having so much fun."

"I didn't know that."

"You were in the shower," Roxanne said.

"I would have said good-bye."

"Sorry. They had to go. Welt had milking to do."

"I'm sure," I said. She turned to me, her eyes dark and angry and hard.

"What the hell does that mean? And what the hell was that all about?"

"That's what I was about to ask," I said.

"You were absolutely hostile."

"No I wasn't. I was skeptical. He said so."

"Don't you ever treat my friends like that," she said.

"Is that all he is?"

"Don't be ridiculous, Jack."

"You're dressed to impress. And believe me, it was working," I said.

"He's just a friend. I have a right to have friends. Men or women."

"Of course you do. It's just a little awkward when your friend is looking down your shirt."

"Oh, stop it."

"It's true," I said.

Roxanne poured her tea. Slammed the kettle back down. Dipped the tea bag up and down in the water. Hard. Water splashed and I could see her jaw clench. She picked up the mug and turned to me.

"You were totally rude to him."

"I don't like being patronized," I said.

"He wasn't patronizing."

"Oh, come on. The whole thing about fighting?"

"You goaded him, Jack. You backed him into a corner."

"If I hadn't he would have been all over you."

"Oh, Jesus Christ. Just stop with the jealousy thing."

"You're telling me you didn't see it? You'd have to be blind. I mean, he's divorced, right?"

"Separated."

"Well, he's got his sights set on number two."

"Oh, please."

A pause. Roxanne lifted the tea bag from the mug and swung it into the sink. I smelled orange and spices. She sipped, then lowered the mug.

"And another thing," she said.

"Bring it on," I said.

Roxanne took a deep breath, looked up from the mug, and said, "I'm worried about Sophie."

"Why? She seemed fine."

"It's about you."

"What about me?"

"What about you? Did you look in the mirror, Jack? Your face, your hands. What the hell happened?"

"There were some guys poaching wood off the Hoddings' land."

"So you beat them up?"

"Clair told them to leave and they wouldn't. They started it."

"Oh, don't tell me," Roxanne said. "And you finished it."

"Well, me and Clair and Louis."

"You had a brawl in the woods?"

"There were four of them. And they had a knife and a shotgun."

"My God, Jack. Don't you get it? You can't do this anymore. You have a daughter."

"That's why we made sure we won."

Roxanne was shaking her head. She turned and put the mug down on the counter, then picked it up, her mind apparently churning about more than the fight. Without looking at me she said: "This isn't right for Sophie to see. It's not a good example."

"Standing up for an old lady in a nursing home? Kicking some dirtbags off her land? Defending ourselves when they attacked us? The guy went right after Louis with a knife."

"Who's got issues to begin with," Roxanne said. "I know. The war and all, and he's good in so many ways, but still he's—"

"He's just processing what he's been through."

Roxanne turned and picked up a sponge, started wiping the counter with quick and angry swipes. And then she turned to me and her eyes were red rimmed and wet with tears. She hesitated and then said, "I'm not having an affair."

The words stunned me. Had she considered it? I'd been angry, thought this guy was a lecher, maybe Roxanne was flirting. But not that they were actually playing around. I fumbled for a response.

"Good to know," I said. "Because I'd kick his sorry ass down the road. Cram his chardonnay bottle down his—"

"Please, Jack. Just stop it. The violence."

"I don't ask for it."

"I know. And Clair doesn't either. But it finds you guys. Or you attract it, with the way you work and think and act."

I waited.

"I've been thinking about things. In a different way."

"Okay."

"Welt is a really nice guy. What he's doing is good. He wants to make the world a better place."

"So did Mother Teresa. Doesn't mean he gets to jump your bones."

Roxanne paused, sipped the tea. The anger had subsided, but it had been replaced by something deeper, more ominous.

"I know this is going to come out wrong."

I reeled inwardly. "You're right about the wrong part," I said.

"Sometimes I feel like I'm not getting your full attention. But when I'm talking to Welt, about our project—"

She hesitated. "—I don't know, it just feels like he's fully engaged."

That top would do it, I thought. The hint of makeup.

"I'm sure."

"Jack," Roxanne said. "You're never around."

"I'm working," I said. "Things are going great. The *Times* has me booked for the next three months. The story for *Outland* is a go. I'm making money, what, six grand in the last month? Another six under contract. It's taking off. And we talked about this. You working at the school and me stepping up the writing."

"But I hardly see you."

"I've been on the road."

"But Sophie hardly sees you. And she's growing up. She needs her dad. She needs you to be present and not be all—"

"You've got to jump on this when you're hot," I said. "I mean, turn down an assignment and all of a sudden you're off the list. The A-list, I mean. And there's no guarantee that you'll ever—"

"But then this Mrs. Hodding person calls and off you guys go. These were supposed to be the days you said you'd be home. You said—"

"She needs help," I said.

"So do I," Roxanne said. "I need your help with Sophie. I need your help in our relationship. I need your help to keep us together. Really together, like we've always been. And we're not. I feel so—"

She paused. I waited.

"—alone."

So she had considered it. A roll in the hay with Mr. Goat Cheese. She sipped her tea, formulating something more. I waited.

"And another thing," Roxanne said.

"That wasn't enough?"

"The peace project."

"Uh-huh."

"I really believe in this. I spent seven years trying to put kids and families back together. And sometimes it worked. But the problem is, they were already so broken. This way you intervene earlier and have a chance to break the cycle before it starts. And you could duplicate it anywhere. You could make real generational change on a big scale."

"Great," I said. "I hope it's a success."

"So what I'm saying is, you should know I'm going to be spending time with Welt. Working. We're applying for grant funding. We're a good team for this. I have hands-on experience with troubled kids and he has these fresh new ideas."

"A match made in heaven," I said.

She paused for another sip. A deep breath.

"Jack."

"Yeah."

"This is very important to me."

"I understand that."

"Please respect what I'm trying to accomplish here."

"I do. Really."

"And think about what I said. About being here for us. About you as a role model. We talked about it. After the last time. How hard that was on Sophie. And on me. On all of us."

"I know. It was tough all around. They were bad people. Sanctuary was a bad place."

"The fire and the shooting."

"I know," I said.

"So here we go again, Jack. I love you. You know I do. But we can't keep doing this. Not to our daughter. Not to me."

"You want me to start turning the other cheek."

"That's one way of putting it. I mean, you're a reporter, right? Was the newsroom in New York full of people with cuts and black eyes? Of course not. So there's a way to do your job without all of this, I don't know, this aggression. Someone threatens you, just walk away."

My turn for a deep breath.

"Welt tells the kids it takes real courage to be a peacemaker."

I took another breath.

"He says the real sign of weakness is to give in to that impulse. Anger and violence."

I clenched my teeth. Breathed.

"Welt says if you want to be a real man, you—"

"God almighty. The places I go, they'd chew him up and spit him out. Easy to spout all this stuff when you're off in friggin' la-la land, with your goats and your chardonnay and your inheritance or whatever it is he lives on. And your friends have a vineyard in Napa and have I heard of it? No, I haven't heard of some goddamn vineyard or seen their label designed by your goddamn ex-wife or separated wife or ex-whatever the hell she is who is now your best friend."

A breath.

"Because you know what I was doing? I just got pretty much punched out by some redneck kid, another one tried to stab Louis, then one of them goes for a shotgun and Clair comes at him from the left and I'm coming from the right and the guy can't decide, so he ends up in between and Clair takes him down. Now there's a crazy guy out there with a broken arm, another guy who probably still can't breathe, all of 'em swearing to get even. And this happens because we're helping a sweet old lady whose husband, a real gentleman, had a stroke and can't talk or walk, and taking care of him costs twenty grand a month that they don't have. But they do have trees."

I paused. Roxanne stared, clenched the mug.

"So I'm sorry if I'm not setting a good example for our daughter, or if I'm Exhibit A for your buddy when he thinks about what's wrong with the world. Or if my face looks like crap next to Mr. Spray Tan. And you're kidding yourself if you don't think he has the hots for you."

Roxanne still stared; tears were welling fast. I hurried.

"This project sounds great. I'm serious, honey. Go for it. I hope it works in spades, I really do. And I understand why you're good at it, and how you give Welt there—what kind of name is that?"

"Welton."

"The third, I'm sure. So yeah, you give him some street cred. And good for him, putting his time into something like this. Really. But don't patronize me. And don't say that I'm what's wrong with men. And do not try to scoop my wife."

I stopped. Swallowed. Roxanne was really crying now, tears running down her cheeks, one clinging to her chin. She wiped the drip, then her eyes. Then she said, "Are you here tomorrow? I need to plan."

Her voice was cool and distant.

"I'm working. Starting to report a couple of stories."

"How long will you be gone?"

"Just for the day," I said. "I'm starting the Mennonite farmers for the *Times*. Or maybe the *Outland* story."

"Where's that one?"

"I'm not sure. I have to go shopping. For guns."

She looked away.

"Nice," Roxanne said, and she put the mug on the counter and walked out of the room. I listened to her footsteps on the stairs, heard the bedroom door slam shut.

5

—〰—

Roxanne slept curled in a fetal position on the edge of her side of the bed, her back to me. I was awake most of the night, the argument replaying in my head. At 3:45 a.m., I said, "I'm sorry." She didn't answer.

At 4:30 I collected my clothes from the floor by the bed, went downstairs, and got dressed in the kitchen. While the kettle heated, I put bread in the toaster, poured a glass of orange juice while I waited for both.

Roxanne's mug from the previous night was on the counter. I put it in the dishwasher, as though that somehow would erase what had happened. Ditto for the four Ballantine empties, placed quietly into the bin. I scowled as I poured my tea, grimaced as the first sip touched my scabs.

When I was done, I put the glass and plate in the dishwasher. Took my tea and went to the study. Opened my laptop and went to mainesbestdeals.com, clicked on GUNS.

Roxanne's reaction replayed in my mind. I sighed, pressed on.

I had a few items bookmarked. A Mossberg tactical shotgun in matte-black finish. Body armor, approved for law enforcement use. A couple of AR-15 assault rifles, one a Czech replica with a fifteen-round clip. Two Glock handguns, a nine-millimeter, and a .40, the latter offered with a laser sight.

Seven hundred dollars. Cash.

I fired off e-mails, asking if the items advertised were still available. I figured I needed to look at a dozen to give a representative idea of what was available. The editor at *Outland*, Josh Clifford, had tacked $1,000 onto my $5,000 fee to buy a handgun, a rifle, and ammo for both. I'd have to dicker.

Clifford had gone for the pitch inside an hour, the way things had been falling for me of late. He said he was hooked after the first two sentences: *Gun control? Not in Maine, where the Second Amendment is alive and well and doing a very brisk business, cash on the barrelhead.*

But not at five a.m.

I packed my satchel with notebooks, pens, my iPad. The house was still: the hum of the refrigerator, a wood frog croaking outside. Taking out a pad and ripping out a page, I wrote Roxanne a note. *Hey, honey. Headed out early. Very sorry about last night. I think you're doing a good thing. I love you and I'll call around 10. Give Sophie a hug for me when you see her.*

I stuck it to the refrigerator with a magnet photo of Sophie at nursery school. She was smiling and her eyes sparkled. I wondered how much she'd sensed from the previous night, whether Salandra had kept up the lecture. Or maybe the girls got together with Welt, talked about an intervention.

I scowled. Grabbed my satchel and pushed out the door. Locked it behind me.

It was dark, the morning sky tinged with blue-black, stars showing faintly to the west. A robin cackled on its roost as I crossed to the truck, and I looked to the woods. There was a rustle but it was the wind in the trees. The birds were still, the wood frogs quiet now. Billy and company were probably sleeping in.

I started the truck and, with lights out, eased out of the driveway. Snapping the lights on, I went left, the tires crackling on the gravel road. Approaching Clair and Mary Varney's house, I slowed and looked back toward the barn. It was dark. Passing the house, I saw the kitchen light on, Clair probably up and making coffee. I thought about stopping, but knew he'd sense my mood and ask what was bugging me. I wasn't ready to talk about Welt—even less ready to talk about Welt and Roxanne.

He just gives me something I don't feel like I'm getting from you.

"What the hell does that mean?" I said.

Maybe I should have seen it coming, hearing Welt's name in passing, then more as Roxanne talked about the school. Some guy who volunteered a lot. His kid was Sophie's friend. He had a farm or something. There probably had been more. I hadn't been paying attention.

Clearly.

In my head I'd pictured some big Mainer, manure on his boots and tongue-tied in front of women. Who knew the guy was more Marin County than Waldo? That the cheese probably had gotten a spread in *Bon Appétit*?

Welt says if you want to be a real man . . .

Jesus.

I drove down the road, headlights picking up red eyes that blipped out as a deer sprang for the woods. A half mile farther I braked as a skunk waddled across, then threaded its way into the brush. And then it was clear sailing on the main road, allowing me to stew for the five miles to the top of the ridge. The sky was pale to the east, more blue than black. At the Belle View restaurant, the lights were on and there were a half-dozen trucks in the lot out front. I added mine to the line, grabbed a notebook and the iPad, and walked in.

The place smelled like coffee and bacon. Belle and Kathy said, "Morning, Jack" in unison from behind the counter. A couple of older guys looked up from their coffee and nodded. I said, "Morning" and nodded back and went to a booth by the far window. It was number six. Like Wyatt Earp in the saloon, I liked a clear view of the door.

Belle brought my tea and, peering at my face, said, "What happened to you?"

"Working in the woods," I said.

"Uh-huh," she said knowingly. "Don't ask, don't tell, huh?"

I smiled, ordered scrambled eggs, home fries, toast. I sipped as Kathy worked up the eggs and home fries, opened the iPad to the gun list to see if there was anything new. A bunch of deer rifles, another Glock. An interesting .22 rifle with a high-powered scope. I'd read somewhere that there were assassins who liked .22 rifles because they were quiet and accurate. I bookmarked that one and closed the screen as Kathy brought my eggs and ketchup in a plastic squeeze bottle—and Baby Fat and Billy came through the door.

Billy's arm was in a sling, a cast from his wrist to above his elbow. The sling was dark blue and the cast was dirty white. He held the arm in front of him like he was asking someone to waltz. His face was swollen, his eyes squinting behind bulging purple flesh.

Baby Fat was wearing unlaced work boots, baggy shorts, and a big flannel shirt, a baseball cap on backwards. He had a bill in his hand and he flicked it onto the counter as Belle stepped forward.

No smile. No greeting.

"Two coffees. Sugar and cream."

Belle turned and reached for paper cups. Baby Fat stood with his hands on his big hips, turned and scanned the restaurant. The old couples. A guy whose hat advertised animal feed. Me.

Baby Fat froze. Elbowed Billy. Billy turned and looked over. His scowl hardened. They both stared and I stared back, gave them a slow salute. Smiled and looked away.

Belle put the coffee cups down on the counter and scooped up the bill. Slapped their change down and Baby Fat swept it into his hand and dumped it in his pocket. No tip. I eased closer to the edge of the seat of the booth in case I had to get up fast, but they took their coffees, gave me a last look, and turned and walked out the door.

I kept eating. Belle came over and said, in her cheerful morning voice, "How you doing, dear?"

"Great," I said. "Delicious."

She leaned closer.

"You know those two?"

"A little," I said.

"Trouble. Won't serve 'em inside here. Older one, Billy, beat hell outta my sister-in-law's niece."

"Why don't I know him?"

"From Monroe, the kid's Junior. Father they call Beefy. I don't know their real names. Pretty much outlaws. Other one, Billy, he's poison. My sister-in-law's niece lived in Monroe, out by Brooks. Met him there."

"Good taste in men," I said.

"Makes bad choices," Belle said. She looked back, leaned close to me. "Story is Billy met Beefy in jail. Went and looked him up when he got out. He's from Lewiston area. Sabattus, I think. Pretended to be Mr. Nice Guy at first. Taking the kids fishing."

"What was he in for?"

"Assault. Beat up his ex's new boyfriend with a pipe. Story is the ex got him locked up for aggravated domestic assault. He thought she was fooling around so he burned her with cigarettes and threw her out in the yard, naked."

"Nice. Why doesn't this niece send him away again?"

"Won't testify. Scared to death of him," Belle said. "She took her kids, moved to Manchester, New Hampshire. But she could tell you some stories."

"I'd talk to her," I said. A story about the unreported toll of domestic abuse. Add it to the list.

Belle glanced over toward the exit, where the pair of them slouched against the wall, just outside the door. She leaned close as she wiped the table with a cloth.

"What are they doing in Prosperity?"

"I guess they ran outta people to burn over there. Word going around is somebody busted his arm for him. Wish they'd busted the other one, and his legs, too."

"Maybe next time."

"Guy like that, you don't give him a chance to come back at you," Belle said, leaning closer, and then it was the loud cheery voice again. "Well, you enjoy your breakfast."

I did, the eggs and the home fries with onions and homemade wheat toast. Belle brought me another cup of tea and I went through the gun list one more time. I drank half the tea and Belle brought my check. Leaving money on the table, I headed for the door.

Kathy told me to have a good day. Belle said, "Take care of yourself, Jack," like she meant it. I walked out into the parking lot and looked both ways. The sun was coming up. Billy and Baby Fat were to the right at the end.

They were sitting in a copper-colored Dodge pickup with a homemade flatbed. The truck was backed up against the orange snow fence, and they were facing the door and me.

I walked to my truck and got in, took the lug wrench from the floor, and put it on the seat next to me. Started the truck and pulled out of the lot and went left. There was a flashing light at the corner, and I took another left, and drove slowly west, watching the mirror, squinting at the glare of the rising sun. After a few seconds, the Dodge swung into view, but Baby Fat hung back.

The road was two lanes, the main highway to places like Troy and Plymouth. There were farms on both sides, fields of late-season corn turned tanned and crisp. The road climbed and fell, crossing one ridge after another. The Dodge kept up with me, a steady quarter-mile back, like now that they knew my truck, they were following me home.

Fat chance.

I crested a ridge, floored the truck on the downhill side, hit eighty going into a long corner, braked hard, and slung off onto a dirt road, downshifting and climbing. The gravel spattered the underside of the truck as I skidded into the corners, woods on both sides. An oncoming car swerved right and I slipped past it, still climbing. There were farms ahead, on the hilltop, but first there were ramshackle cabins tucked into the trees.

I slowed, swung into a dirt track into the woods, passed orange signs that said POSTED—NO TRESPASSING. Thirty yards in, a red SUV was pulled into a turnaround. The truck was covered with leaves. I backed in on the far side of it, shut off the motor. I didn't want steam rising from the exhaust. I took my foot off the brake so no lights would show. And I sat.

A blue jay called. The cooling motor ticked. The sun dappled the leaves, yellow in a stand of maples. I began to relax, thinking the Mennonite farmers were up on the hill to the northwest, that I could make my way over there. Maybe go in the bakery, strike up a conversation, make my pitch.

I didn't think the Mennonites were as publicity-shy as the Amish, but then again, these were Old Order Mennonites, and—

The Dodge rolled slowly past the head of the driveway. I counted to ten, and started the motor and pulled out. I didn't want to get cut off back in the woods. At least in the road there would be cars coming along and—

Then the Dodge rolled back, in reverse, Billy with his head hanging out of the passenger window looking at the ground. I braked and stopped. The Dodge rolled to a halt. Billy looked up. He smiled.

I stopped the truck and opened the door. Slid off the seat, slipping the lug wrench into the back of my jeans. I went to the front of my truck and stood. Billy eased his way out and down and Baby Fat came around the back.

Baby Fat grinned. Billy stared.

"Fuckin' A," Baby Fat said. "You're a hard man to keep up with."

"A lot to do," I said.

"We decided to take a day off," Billy said. "Do some hunting."

"What?" I said. "Birds? Deer isn't for another couple months."

"Getting ready," Baby Fat said, still grinning. "Following trails. You know you oughtn'ta gone so fucking fast. On the gravel, tires slew up the rocks and shit. Leaves a trail like deer in mud."

"Sorry," I said. "I thought you were as dumb as you look."

The grin fell away and he took a half-step forward, hand going back and out of sight. I slipped the wrench out and held it in front of me, the screwdriver end pointed at him. Baby Fat's hand came around, a hunting knife held low.

"Easy, boys," Billy said, a new side of him, a peacemaker. "Let's not jump too fast-like."

His turn to grin, the carnivorous yellowed teeth bared.

"You see, buddy," Billy said, "we're scouting. We ain't up for shooting just any deer. We're waiting for a trophy buck. One with a big rack. To get a big buck, when the doe walks outta the woods, even if it's a fat one, you take your finger off that friggin' trigger."

"And you're a doe, asshole," Baby Fat said.

"We're gonna keep watching. And waiting," Billy said.

"And your buddy there, bustin' his arm—"

"He's the big buck," Billy said. "Eight-point rack on that son of a bitch."

"He's nobody to mess with," I said.

"We're nobody to mess with," Baby Fat said.

"You kidding? You guys are chump change," I said. "I don't care if you were in prison, county jail, whatever. You're way, way out of your league."

"Guy got lucky," Billy said.

"No, you were the one who was lucky. If you're smart, you'll just walk away. Really. You don't know what you're getting into."

"An old guy and some deaf-mute whack job," Baby Fat said.

I looked at him and smiled, shook my head.

"The two of them could have killed all four of you. With their bare hands. In fifteen seconds."

"Bullshit," Billy said.

I turned and started for my truck. Over my shoulder I said, "Trying to tell you, but you won't listen. This isn't like beating up some girl."

Billy took a step toward me, then stopped.

Took his finger off the trigger.

6

I backed down the drive away from the road, shut off the motor, and sat for a minute, the birds flitting through the undergrowth, the sun climbing beyond the trees.

The tracks of the tires. Something to remember—that driving slow leaves less of a trail. The other thing was that I'd underestimated both of them, especially Billy. Nasty and violent I'd understood. Patient and persistent I hadn't counted on.

Questions: In this place of small towns, where somebody's vehicle proclaimed their presence like a banner, how long would it take before they tracked me to my house? How long would it take them to figure out that Clair lived on the same road? Would they track down Louis Longfellow as well?

If they found him in Sanctuary, God help them. A guy who spent six months shooting his way through Fallujah wouldn't have any trouble with these yahoos. Or would he? And even if he didn't, at that point it might be too late for Louis as well, explaining the two dead bodies on his front porch. I made a mental note for another stop for the day: Clair's, for a briefing.

I started the truck and drove up to the road, hesitated for a moment. Right was down and through the hills, where I could start calling and e-mailing the gun sellers for the *Outland* magazine story. Left was north to the Mennonite farms, the story for the *Times*. Peaceful, God-fearing folks right out of the nineteenth century.

I went left. Needed something to renew my faith in humanity.

The background for my story ran through my mind as I drove. Asking around town, I'd learned that the Mennonites had come from Ontario in late spring, two years earlier. First they were a rumor; somebody had bought the Prentiss place, all three hundred acres, give or take, and paid cash. And then they'd arrived, three guys in a U-Haul truck. Word was that two of them had beards and were wearing white shirts and baggy black trousers. The third guy, the driver, was wearing jeans. He helped them unload some old suitcases and toolboxes, table saws, and a horse-drawn wagon, just like the Old West. And then that guy got back in the truck and left.

The women came by car a couple of weeks later. They were wearing long skirts with aprons and cloth bonnets. Their driver was a lady who stopped at the store on the way out of town. She had on jeans and a sweatshirt that said NIAGARA FALLS. Someone asked if they were Amish. No, she said. Old Order Mennonites. There's a difference.

The distinction was lost on the locals. We did note that they cleaned out the house and barn, stripped out the electric lights and appliances. They bought pulling horses and dairy cows, and the horses pulled a wagon around the perimeter so the Mennonites could put up new fences. Kids and another couple came not long after that, and some people in town started saying it was a cult. But then the Mennonites planted corn and wheat. They opened a little bakery, just off the main house. And they sold eggs and milk. They were quiet but polite, and they worked hard. Always paid cash.

First, the Prentiss farm. Then a half-abandoned spread next door, from a couple from away named Greta and Dave. After that, the Geberth place next door, another two hundred acres, with fields across the ridge on top of Hanley Hill, which is where I found them.

There were two Mennonite girls leaning against a fence at the side of the road. They were watching two teenage guys working a horse-drawn harrow to turn over a field of squash and pumpkins. The squash and pumpkins were piled by a gate. The girls, in skirts and aprons and bonnets, looked over the gate at me when I pulled up and got out of the truck.

"Good morning," I said, smiling. "How are you?"

"Good morning," the older one said. The younger one looked at me warily, and then away. The younger one looked sixteen or so, the other one a year or two older. The older girl smiled right back. She was blonde and very pretty.

"I'm Jack," I said. "I live in town."

The friendly one nodded; the younger one took two steps back. Beyond them, in the field, the guy on the plow seat shouted something at the horses and they pulled up. He slid down off the seat, handed the reins to a younger boy who had been riding on the frame of the plow, started walking across the field toward us.

"So I've driven by ever since you and your family have been up here," I said. "Never took the time to stop."

"It's a nice day to be out and about," the older girl said. Her accent was faintly German. Or maybe it was just Canadian. I leaned on the top rail of the gate and saw that there were wicker picnic baskets on the grass by the fence. I noticed again that the blonde girl was strikingly pretty, like an actress playing an Amish character. Except she was neither.

"That your brother?"

"Yes."

"He's the farmer?"

"One of them," she said. "But he works, too. For money. We all do. Except for my father. He's the bishop. He does the services, mostly."

"Huh," I said. And then the guy approached, his boots leaving tracks in the furrowed ground. He was lanky with sinewy arms and a noncommittal expression that I took for encouraging.

"Hi there," I said.

He nodded. "Can we help you?"

Same accent. More than Canadian.

"Jack McMorrow," I said. "I live in town."

"I'm Abram Snyder. I live right here."

A real smile. I pressed on.

"I'm a writer. I write for newspapers. I'm wondering if you'd let me do a story on your settling here. Coming all the way from, where was it—"

"Canada," Abram said.

"Abram," the younger girl scolded. "You can't."

"We're just talking here," I said. "Not for a story. I just wanted to introduce myself."

"Do you write for the newspaper in Galway?" Abram said. "Because our father, he told them already. We don't do articles. Or pictures."

"I don't write for them."

"Which one, then?" Abram said.

I hesitated, then smiled and took the plunge. "Different places," I said. "But mostly the *New York Times*."

The younger girl turned and trotted off across the field toward the kid with the horses.

"I've seen it," Abram said. "Your newspaper."

"You subscribe?"

He shook his head.

"I worked in a toy shop. Busy season. Before Christmas. They had their toys in an advertisement."

"So you do get out," I said.

"We aren't hermits," Abram said. "You live in New York?"

He moved closer, and the older girl did, too.

"Many years," I said. "I grew up there. But I like it here more."

"Why?" he said. The girl watched. Up close she had blue eyes and fine skin, a faint smattering of freckles across the bridge of her nose.

"New York's fun," I said. "But loud. And crowded. If Prosperity is like a pond, New York is like a rushing stream. You step into the water and it sweeps you away. Get caught off balance and you drown."

"I've been to Buffalo," he said. "We drove through."

"Think taller," I said, turning to the girl. "What's your name?"

She glanced at the guy before replying. "Miriam," she said. "Abram is my brother. And Sarah, that's my sister."

"And the guy on the plow?"

"That's Victor," she said. "He's not our brother."

"Got it," I said.

"The subways must be cool," the guy said, like he'd been waiting for a place to break in. "I read about people living down there. Some of them even had beds and chairs and stuff."

"Yeah, some people actually settle in in the tunnels. It's pretty spooky, when you go to find them."

"You've done that?" he said.

"Many years ago. For a story."

"Maybe we should do the article on you," he said.

Again the accent.

"Sure," I said. "Glad to talk. I could come and talk at your school or whatever."

"Father would never," the girl blurted.

"Is he the teacher?" I said.

"He's the Bishop," the guy said.

A flicker of something in their eyes, a look exchanged. Rebellion?

"So I'd have to talk to him to do a story? On the Mennonite community in Prosperity?"

"He'd say no," Abram said.

"Can't hurt to ask," I said.

"Have you been to Ground Zero?" he asked.

I looked at him. Who was this Mennonite guy?

"Before and after," I said.

"What about the Bronx?"

"Sure," I said.

"A lot of murders there," Abram said.

"Some," I said. "But that's exaggerated. Like saying everybody in Maine is a lobsterman. Mostly good people in the Bronx."

"I'd like to see it," he said.

"You could take the bus down from Portland," I said.

The look exchanged again.

"Yeah, well," he said. "We have work to do here."

Miriam looked like she was gathering herself up to say something. I looked at her, smiled, and waited.

"I'd like to see Ellis Island," she said.

A monument to immigrants, I thought. Just like them.

"Definitely a must-see," I said, and then Sarah came running back, jumping the rows, her skirt billowing, sneakers digging into the clumps of soil.

"Victor needs Abram," the younger girl said. She moved close to her sister and whispered, "We have to go back."

"We brought their meal," Miriam said to me. "Second breakfast."

There was something endearing and earnest about her, like she was eager to engage but wasn't sure how to begin.

"What did you make?" I said.

"There's bread and butter and pie and—"

"Miriam," Sarah said, pulling at her sister's arm. "Now."

The girls turned, Sarah leading Miriam like a calf on a rope. Abram stayed put, hands in the pockets of his trousers.

"Let's talk again," I said.

"Yeah, Mr. McMorrow," Abram said, and then stepped closer. "But not here."

Worried about their father, the Bishop?

"Okay. We could have coffee," I said.

"Yeah," he said, turning and moving away. Victor had come off the rig, was headed our way. When he was ten feet from us, he stopped and stared at me. Hard.

"This is Victor. We work the horses together."

"Hi there," I said. "I'm Jack."

Victor hesitated, then nodded.

"Just talking to Abram about the big city," I said. "I'm from New York."

Victor nodded again, then moved close to Abram, covered his mouth to talk. What was he saying? Don't talk to the—what was it that Amish called non-Amish? English? Was there an Old Order Mennonite equivalent? Would the Bishop tan their hides?

The huddle broke up and Abram smiled, said, "We have to work."

"Me, too," I said. "Plow well."

"We'll talk," Abram said.

"Abram," Victor urged, grabbed him by the arm, and started to pull him back toward the horses.

"Good meeting you, Victor," I said.

"Yeah, sure," he said.

And then they were back at the plow. Abram waved back, climbed up on the seat, and gave the reins a shake, said something that sounded like *Yap*. The horses shook their heads in their harnesses and dug their hooves into the loam. Victor hopped up on the plow frame, looked back at me and scowled.

The seed had been sown, the foundation laid. Abram hadn't shut the door. I'd pushed the door open a crack—that is, if Victor didn't rat him out.

I got back in the truck, got out my notebook, and started writing in a rapid scrawl. My impressions. The conversation. Every comment I could remember. The subways. Ground Zero. *I'd like to see Ellis Island.* Did that come out of left field or what? Who were these kids, and what was their life like? How did they fend off everything around them?

"This," I said, "could be a damn good story."

If I worked it right, didn't push too hard, too soon. If the Bishop didn't slam the door shut. If Sarah didn't stand up from her hard pew in church and ask for forgiveness for talking to the reporter. If Abram didn't lose his nerve.

If Billy and Baby Fat and the rest of them didn't try to take me out.

Tossing the notebook down on the passenger seat, I picked up my phone and went to mainesbestdeals.com, the bookmarked guns. The Glock with the laser sight. Thought I might buy it even without the story. What did Billy and Baby Fat do when they had time to plot? Pull up beside you on the road and fire away? Break your legs and arms with a bat? Tie you to a tree and leave you to die of thirst?

I started the truck and, with a last glance at the distant horses and plow, headed for home. I took a circuitous route, lefts and rights. Just short of the Dump Road I pulled over and waited. After two minutes had passed with nothing in sight, I turned in.

Roxanne's Subaru was gone, probably gone to pick up Sophie. I kept going, pulled into the yard in front of Clair's barn. His truck was there, Louis's Jeep, too. The lights were on in the shop.

Music was playing: Beethoven's Piano Concerto No. 3, one of Clair's favorites, not mine. I preferred Vivaldi. Clair said I liked classical music lite, that he'd educate me if it was the last thing he did.

He was bent over the workbench, cutting a length of hydraulic hose from a big coil with a clamp sort of thing. Louis was at the other end of the bench, the bar of his chain saw clamped in the vise. He was running a file over the chain. Louis's big dog, Friend, was stretched out on the barn floor behind him. The dog didn't get up or wag or bark, just tracked me with his big black eyes.

Louis was saying, "That's the thing about an army of martyrs. You can't apply any principles of warfare that are based on self-preservation. There was a little of that in Ramadi, but nothing like—"

Louis looked up and stopped. Clair snapped the cutter through the hose, glanced at me, and said, "Had enough of your tippy-typing? Ready to do some real work?"

"If I find any, I'll call you," I said. "I can see you guys are resting up."

Clair smiled. Louis did, too, barely. He put the file down and moved the chain on the bar. Bent to the next tooth.

"Speaking of martyrs," I said, "does stupidity count? Or having nothing to lose?"

I told them about my conversation with Billy and Baby Fat, how they said I was the doe and Louis was the big buck. I said I didn't know where that put Clair. A six-pointer, maybe.

Louis showed nothing, just kept filing. The dog took a deep breath and sighed. Clair said, "Huh."

"I told them they didn't know who they were messing with," I said.

"Probably true," Clair said. "Not sure whether that makes them less dangerous or more."

"All that matters is saving face," Louis said, face to the saw.

"Not patient enough to wait for his arm to heal," I said. "I picture him sitting in the woods, leaning a rifle across his cast, peering into a scope."

"You think he's that calculating?" Clair said, snapping off the hose.

"Enough to pass on me this morning," I said. "Then follow me onto the back roads. Track me by my tire marks in the gravel. Said they were looking for Louis. I was supposed to lead them there."

Clair lined the two pieces of hose up side by side, reached for the coil, and pulled another length out. Louis was filing, the rhythmic sound of metal on metal cutting the quiet between sections of Beethoven. And then he said, "Problem is, if you win, you lose. It's like the war. Better to win, but even then you're diminished. You're not the same person you were. That's why I think this idea of 'self-defense' is a little off. Yeah, you defend yourself, but you get hurt, too."

He paused. Pulled the chain a few inches, and said, "I shouldn't have kept on with the guy. Disarm him, leave it. I lost it, and now you guys are paying for it."

"Something that was thrust on you by circumstances," Clair said. "They had their chance to walk away."

"So did I," Louis said.

"You deal with what's presented to you," Clair said. "And right now, it's this guy obsessing about what was done to him. And he has to go around with his arm in a cast, everybody knowing somebody kicked his butt. And he's a guy whose self-worth is built on being tough and nasty and violent."

"I picture a guy raised not to cry," Louis said. "He cried, the old man hit him harder."

"And the worst thing in his eyes is to back down," I said.

"Shoot you in the back before he does that," Clair said. He turned from the bench and said, "Jack, what do you have in that truck of yours, anyway?"

I knew what he meant.

"Nothing," I said. "A lug wrench. I got that out today. I could put a rifle in the rack."

"Kinda hard to maneuver a thirty-thirty in that Toyota, " he said. "You want something smaller?"

At the very least, Clair had a couple of Glocks, a Smith & Wesson .38 revolver. He'd recently picked up a Kimber .40, said it was a fine weapon.

"That thirty-eight, short-barrel," he said. "Nothing more dependable than a good revolver."

I considered it, thought of Roxanne. Would I be protecting her or defying her?

"Roxanne's got this thing about guns right now," I said.

Clair looked at me. Louis glanced over, too, then turned back to the saw chain and started filing.

"Don't blame her," he said. "And I don't blame you. Ever shot anybody?"

My mind went to a time with Clair, behind his barn. The guy, a survivalist nut job obsessed with Roxanne taking his kids, was shooting from the edge of the woods. Clair saying, "Take him," me firing a round and then hearing the shot returned, the slug hitting the wall above our heads. Clair taking the gun from me, pressing his eye to the scope.

A pause. A squeeze. The boom of the rifle, and then silence.

"No," I said. "I missed."

Louis looked at Clair, but Clair showed nothing. The dog watched and listened.

"My experience, it takes a piece out of you, shooting a man," Louis said. "Or maybe it adds one. I think of it in different ways. Are you missing something, or are you carrying something extra? No matter what, it stays with you. One second it's a human being, some guy has a mother and father and maybe some kids, likes to smoke and drink and watch sports. And in an instant he's just a pile of guts, like some animal you just ran over, splattered in the middle of the road."

He caught himself, leaned close to the saw.

"We do what we have to do," Louis said. "But just know it all comes with a price."

The file began to stroke the chain, the rasping sound, and then the piano, a brisk beginning to the passage, the notes flung high in the rafters.

"So what is it, Jack?" Clair said.

"Allegretto?" I said.

7

I didn't take the handgun. Not yet. I did drive past my house, where there was still nobody home, and kept going for a half mile until I reached the crest of a rise that gave me a clear view back past my house and Clair's. I pulled over and watched the road in the mirror. It was empty behind me, a gravel strip between the crimson bleeding trees. It was empty in front, the fifty-yard stretch before it turned and descended. I watched in the mirror another full minute, then pulled out, drove between the big maples down to the end of the road.

Nobody left. Nobody right. Nobody behind me.

I turned and headed north toward the two-lane highway. I did the same check at that intersection, then took a right and headed east. The road climbed past occasional houses, mobile homes, gave way to pastures where cows were grazing, all turned in the same direction. The road flattened out, passed a fallen-down chicken barn, a trailer with kids' toys strewn on the lawn like somebody had been abducted.

Past the Prosperity post office, a shingled shack with cars parked out front, the road dipped and went left. Glancing at the mirror, I took the first right past the Prosperity Grange Hall, shut up since nearly all of the members had died of old age. The road followed along the banks of the Swift River, past a fallen-down sawmill, climbing into the hills where there were pastures lined with stone walls, big trees shading the hedgerows.

I drove on, headed southeast now. And then I saw a sign hanging from a tree limb. Up close, I could see it was handpainted, two goats' heads with curving horns, just below the words *Heaven Sent*, beside the word *Farm*.

There was a driveway with stone walls on both sides, a farmhouse set back, a porch wrapping two sides. Beyond the house there were barns and sheds, tractors and wagons. Just beyond the tractors was Welt's Toyota pickup—and Roxanne's Subaru.

I slowed and rolled past the end of the driveway, looking at the car.

She'd gone to pick up Sophie, I knew, but where were they? The girls playing somewhere and Roxanne and Welt having a nice strategy session about conflict resolution?

I drove a hundred yards, turned around, then backtracked until the farm came into sight. It was a very pretty place, the white house with green shutters, rope swing in a big maple.

And people coming out of one of the barns. Sophie and Salandra, Salandra pulling a goat on a lead. I reached to the glove box and took out a pair of binoculars. The goat was wearing a straw hat, holes cut for his horns. Sophie was adjusting the hat, giggling. Behind her was a young woman, college age, one of Welt's interns. She was slim and blonde, hair tied back under a baseball cap. After her another young woman, this one dark haired, wearing jeans and a plaid flannel shirt.

Sophie turned to her and the blonde woman took off her hat and put it on Sophie's head. They laughed and disappeared behind the house, and Welt and Roxanne appeared from the barn and they were smiling and joking, too. He was a happy farmer, Welt was, with his bevy of beauties. He said something to Roxanne and reached over and took her by the shoulder and drew her to him, then she looked at the ground and he said something and guided her along.

Don't step in the goat poop? Are you sure we can't end up in the sack?

I watched as they made their way to the car, Sophie and Salandra walking the goat to the center of the barnyard. There were chickens here and there, a couple of white geese. The chickens fluttered and one of the geese raised up and flapped its wings.

I lowered the binoculars. Looked out to see the copper-colored Dodge parked beyond the driveway on the far side of the road. I raised the binoculars. It was Baby Fat and Billy, and their eyes were on the farm, the drive, the cars, Roxanne.

I glanced back. She was at the car, leaning in, bending over to fasten Sophie's seat belt. I put the binoculars on Billy and Baby Fat, saw Billy mouth something to Baby Fat.

Baby Fat smiled and replied. Billy, watching Roxanne with a lewd smile, said something that I couldn't make out. He licked his lips. Baby Fat smiled.

I didn't have to hear the words. Baby Fat nodded and reached for the ignition and started the motor. As Roxanne's car came down the drive, they started to ease out of the grass.

I slammed the truck out of the brush and floored it, ramming through the gears, speeding past the farm entrance as Roxanne and Sophie approached. Billy and Baby Fat were wide-eyed as my truck skidded in the gravel, nearly hit them head-on. I was out of the truck as the dust still billowed, yanked the passenger door open, grabbed Billy by his broken arm.

"What the—," he began, but then he was sliding off the seat, grabbing for the door frame. He hit the ground and I shouldered him up against the cab, Baby Fat saying, "What the fuck?" and Billy howling as I jammed his broken arm against his belly.

"You son of a bitch, what the hell you think—"

I punched him hard in the cast and he said, "Owww—Jesus," and I grabbed him by the throat and stood him up against the truck. Baby Fat was heaving himself down out of the cab, saying, "You crazy son of a bitch," but I had Billy pinned and I got close to his face and said, "If you ever go near my family again, I'll blow your head off. You got that, you piece of shit?"

Billy writhed, kicked at my shins, and I jammed the cast upward and he gasped. Baby Fat was coming around the front of the truck, a sawed-off baseball bat in his hand. I turned Billy so he was between me and Baby Fat. He stopped six feet away, the club held low.

"You, too, you piece of crap. If you ever come near my family again, or my house, or anywhere close, you're dead."

"We're just looking for somebody to lead us to your friend," Baby Fat said. "Somebody pointed out your old lady, so we—"

"No talk. No argument. Come near my family, I kill you."

"You're the one who's dead, asshole," Billy said, and he started to laugh, a maniacal cackle that gave me a chill. I fought the feeling off by ramming the cast upward but he kept laughing through the pain, even as I shoved his broken arm.

"Dead man, McMorrow," he said, still laughing. "It's gonna be sweet to watch you die. 'Cause then we're gonna bang your old lady."

I slammed his arm up, practically broke it again, heard him gasp, then Baby Fat moved closer. I watched him, my hand still clenched around Billy's throat, saw the car come out of the driveway and turn toward us. Roxanne braked in the road and leaned on the horn. It blared and she kept it on, then started pounding the steering wheel with one hand, punching her phone with the other.

Baby Fat turned, said, "Calling the cops, the fucking bitch." Billy flinched and I yanked his broken arm again, took a step back, and shoved him against the truck. Baby Fat trotted for the cab, dropping the bat as he hauled himself in. Billy had squirmed back up on the seat, pulling with his good arm. Baby Fat revved the motor and reached for the shifter. To ram her?

I picked the bat up, smashed the windshield, then the passenger window, then the windshield again.

"Back up," I shouted at Roxanne, waved my arm.

Baby Fat fishtailed in the weeds in reverse, the back end of the truck hopping out onto the road and away from me. He whipped it around, flooring it, and the rear tires screeched and the truck roared off, trailing tire smoke.

The horn stopped.

Roxanne looked at me from behind the wheel, then turned to Sophie. I looked over, saw Welt standing a hundred yards up the driveway, fiddling with his phone.

I looked down, saw my hand was bleeding, and dropped the bat on the road. Ran to the car, saw Sophie in the backseat. She had her fingers in her ears and her eyes scrunched shut. Roxanne was out of the car, opening the door on the far side. I opened my side and reached in and started to undo Sophie's seat belt. Roxanne said, "I've got this," and slapped my hand aside. She undid the belt, pulled Sophie out, away from me.

"Honey," I said to her. "It's okay."

"I'm sorry, honey," Roxanne was saying. "I know it was loud and scary."

Sophie started to cry, said, "Are the bad men gone?"

"They're gone," I said. "There's nothing to worry about."

Roxanne glared at me over Sophie's shoulder, patted her back. "It's okay, honey."

"They were just some people Daddy knows from his work," I said.

I was looking at them through the backseat of the Subaru, and I backed out and came around, wiping my right hand on my jeans, putting my left arm around Sophie. She was still being held by Roxanne, who was rubbing her back, and Sophie's feet were hanging, her sneaker laces dangling.

"It was two of them from the woods," I said, and Roxanne said, "I saw that truck on the highway. They must have seen me driving over—" She looked down and saw that Sophie was listening. Roxanne shook her head. Later.

As I straightened up, Welt came around the truck. He had his phone in his hand and a look of concern.

"Is everyone all right?" he said. "I called the police."

"All over but the shouting, Weltie," I said. "But thanks for being there when we needed you."

"Who were those guys? Did they follow you here?"

"They followed Roxanne."

"Why? What did they want?"

"Payback," I said. "What else?"

The cop was a sheriff's deputy, a woman with dark wavy hair pulled back. She came out of the cruiser, a brown Charger, slipped the baton in its holder, came toward us and said, "Who called?"

Welt held up his hand, like the annoying kid in the front row of class.

"There was the horn blowing and shouting and yelling," Welt said. "Jack was arguing with the other guys, and then there was glass breaking and then the other fellows left."

The deputy looked at me, my hand, the bat, my truck, Roxanne's car.

"What glass breaking?" she said.

"Their windshield," I said. "And the passenger window."

"These other guys were the assailants?" she said.

"Sort of," I said. "They were following my wife."

"Why?"

"It's a long story," I said.

She said, "You come with me. Everybody else, just stay put."

Her nameplate said she was D. M. Staples. She was wiry under the flak vest and had a broad, open face with sun spots and crow's-feet. Maybe thirty-five—old for a patrol deputy; second career? I told her my name and the story, from the woods to the restaurant to the back road near the Mennonite farm. I described the four of them, then the two of them. I said I knew one as Billy and the other I called

Baby Fat, but I didn't know Baby Fat's real name. I described the big Dodge pickup.

"Wesley Rowe, Jr.," she said. "Dad is Senior, goes by 'Beefy.' "

"You know him."

"Know a lot of people around here."

"You didn't know me," I said.

"Do now," Staples said. "And Billy. Scar on his neck?"

"Yes. Jagged."

"Billy Sloban."

"I figured it for a bottle," I said. "Bar fight. Fourth guy was called Semi, like the truck. Or the gun."

"Bates Cropley. Lightweight compared to the other three. But give him time."

She looked at me a little harder and said, "You the one put Sloban in the cast?"

"Friend of mine, actually."

"He a reporter, too?" she said.

"No, a disabled combat veteran."

"Couldn't have been too disabled."

"For some of these guys, it's like riding a bicycle," I said. "Hand to hand, I mean. He was defending himself, by the way."

Staples looked at me like she was starting to figure me out.

"You know, Mr. McMorrow, in my experience most reporters don't ride quite so close to the edge," she said.

I felt Roxanne behind me; Welt, too.

"Wusses," I said.

I waited by the truck while Staples talked to Roxanne and then, briefly, Welt. After a minute, Roxanne gave Sophie a kiss and sent her over to me. I picked her up and held her and she put her chin on my shoulder and was quiet as I patted her back. She felt very small, tucked into me. Finally, she whispered, "I want to go home and see Pokey."

"We will," I said. "Have you had lunch? I can make you mac and cheese."

"I'm not hungry. Welt made us French toast," Sophie said. "With their own eggs and syrup from their own trees."

Of course, I thought.

"Sounds yummy," I said.

Welt, standing twenty feet away by the farm entrance, must have sensed that he was being talked about, and he smiled sympathetically. I looked through him and held Sophie closer. She said, in a muffled voice, her chin pressed against my collarbone, "Are the bad men coming back, Daddy?"

"They're gone," I said, dodging the question. "And the police lady is going to find them and tell them to stay far, far away."

Sophie was silent for minute, her arms around my neck, and then she said, "What if they disobey?"

When Roxanne was done, she came over and held out her arms and Sophie swung over to her. Roxanne patted her back and avoided my gaze and we stood, the whole family, and said nothing.

Welt and Staples stood and talked, the cruiser out of place in front of the HEAVEN SENT FARM SIGN, the white rail fence, the crimson-leafed maples lining the drive, the dappled goats grazing in the pasture.

The police radio squawked. A goat baahed. What were they—LaManchas?

After a long five minutes, Welt and Staples approached. Staples was putting a small notebook in the breast pocket of her uniform. Welt looked puffed up by the attention, like he'd saved the day.

Roxanne put Sophie down. Welt took her hand and led her over to the fence and they started picking black-eyed Susans.

"We'll pick them up and talk to them about why they were out here," Staples said. "We could summons them for stalking, but it's hard to justify that with just one incident. There's also the question of who was the aggressor. Mr. McMorrow, they'll probably claim your attack on them was unprovoked—that they didn't know Mrs. McMorrow was here."

"And they'll be lying," I said.

"Doesn't matter," she said. "I'm just saying I can warn them, but I probably can't lock them up. Not for this."

"So we're at their mercy?" Roxanne said. "They can just follow me around? Wait for their chance to do . . . whatever?"

"I'm not gonna let these assholes come near my family," I said.

"So you're saying you can't do anything," Roxanne said.

"If you see them again, if they seem like they're following you, let's say, or if they drive by your house over and over in the middle of the night—"

"There'd be no over and over," I said.

Staples pointed her finger at me. "Leave it to law enforcement," she said. "Call 911."

"And you'll be there in what? Twenty minutes?"

"I'm strongly advising you, Mr. McMorrow," the deputy said. "Do you have firearms in the house?"

I didn't answer, which she took to be a yes.

"You don't want to shoot somebody unless it's a total last resort. It's a can of worms."

There was an awkward moment where nobody talked. Sophie had a bouquet in one hand and she and Welt were crouched down, looking at a caterpillar. "And then when it comes out, it will be a beautiful monarch butterfly," Welt was saying.

"Call me if you have any questions," Staples said, and she held out her card. Roxanne took it, then walked over to Welt and Sophie and took Sophie by the hand. They walked to the car and Roxanne said as they passed, "See you at home."

She got Sophie buckled in the backseat, got in the car, backed into the drive. Roxanne pulled back out and drove off down the road and the deputy followed. Welt had walked over from the fence and the flowers, and we watched as the two cars drove over a rise and out of sight.

"She's right, you know," he said.

"About what?" I said.

"These guys are violent, and if you match their violence, you're the one who loses."

"Spare me the lecture, Weltie. Where were you when he was coming around the truck with a baseball bat? Diddling with your phone and staying as far away as possible."

"I was calling 911," he said.

"While my wife gets in their face with the car."

"We needed the police."

"*We* didn't need anything," I said. "You needed to get off your cowardly ass and step in."

"Oh, come on, Jack. I know you're upset, but—"

"Sure I'm upset. A couple of dirtbags following my wife and kid, watching Roxanne and licking their lips."

"I understand why you'd get emotional," Welt said, like he was my therapist. "But I think the lesson here is, don't engage. That only gets you entangled. It's like Rox and I were telling the kids: Two wrongs not only don't make a right; most of the time they make three wrongs, because—"

"Rox?"

He looked startled.

"Yeah. I mean, that's what I call her. I say it with the utmost respect, Jack. She's one of the most amazing people I've ever met. I'm sure you know that."

"I know you like her. Sometimes I think you like her too much," I said.

He went wide-eyed. Shocked.

"Jack. I think Roxanne is a lovely person, and I love working with her. But that doesn't mean I have, I don't know, designs on her."

"Good to know, Welt," I said. "But I'm not stupid. I know when some guy is looking down my wife's shirt. Can't keep his hand off her leg."

He looked aghast, mouth hanging open.

"Jeez, Jack. That's just nuts. I mean, you've got it all wrong. I have total respect for the institution of marriage. You don't know this, but that's why Cassie and I decided to split. We knew that we both had such high expectations of marriage that when we started to grow in different directions, both of us, we were preventing each other from achieving the intimacy and oneness that marriage deserves. Look, I know you and Roxanne are going through a bit of a rough patch right now, but—"

"Who told you that?" I said.

"Nobody told me. I mean, I know Roxanne has been unhappy, not her usual self. When you spend a lot of time with a person, you can read their moods, and—"

"Then read this mood. I don't like guys pawing at my wife. I don't like guys who run away from a fight. I don't like guys who lecture me about how I do my job, how I live my life."

Welt's expression hardened, his ice-blue eyes turning icier.

"I'm truly sorry if you and Roxanne are unhappy. But I wouldn't give up."

A pause.

"Not yet," he said. He grinned, the real Welt showing through.

I felt anger well up, my muscles tense. And at that instant when I wanted to hit him, hit him hard, I knew that would play right into his hands, push Roxanne closer to him.

"You don't know what sorry is," I said. "And you'd better pray you don't find out."

I turned and walked to the truck, got in, and started the motor. As I pulled away I saw him smile, maybe even chuckle, as he watched me pass.

8

Roxanne and Sophie were on the couch. *The Jungle Book* was playing on the TV, animals dancing and singing, Mowgli swinging through the trees. There was a bowl of popcorn on the table, barely touched. Sophie was asleep, her head snuggled against Roxanne's chest.

Roxanne held a finger up to her lips. I nodded and walked back to the kitchen, opened the refrigerator.

There was egg salad, probably from Welt's eggs. I took out the milk and a jar of strawberry jam, from the supermarket. The peanut butter was from the supermarket, too. I took down a loaf of home made wheat bread. Welt didn't sell bread, that I knew, but I checked the label. A bakery in Galway. I opened the bag and took two slices out and made a sandwich.

I was leaning against the counter eating the sandwich when Roxanne came in.

"She's asleep," she said.

"Late night at the sleepover?" I said.

"And she was upset. When she's upset, her defense is to go to sleep."

I took a bite of sandwich and a swallow of milk.

"It was upsetting," I said.

Roxanne went to the refrigerator and took out the egg salad. She spooned a mound onto a plate and added some lettuce, then went to the table and sat. We ate in silence until Roxanne said, "How did they know where I was, or who I was?"

"They were following me this morning. Somebody pointed you out as my wife."

Roxanne's fork scraped the plate. The animals were singing again in the living room. I finished the sandwich and wiped peanut butter from my mouth.

"Well, they know me now. Why were you coming to Welt's?"

"Wanted to get a look at the place, if my daughter is going to be spending so much time there."

"And your wife?"

I paused.

"Yes."

"I was embarrassed, Jack. For all kinds of reasons."

"I'm sorry. I didn't know they'd show up."

"And I didn't know *you'd* show up. Why didn't you just drive up and say hello? Welt would have given you the tour. He's very hospitable."

I didn't answer.

"Do you feel like you have to spy on me?" Roxanne said, her voice cold and calm.

"I'm worried," I said.

"I told you that you didn't have to be."

"You're not the one who worries me."

"It takes two, right? So if I say it's nothing, then it's nothing."

I waited.

"Do you think I'd lie to you?"

"No."

"Then what?"

"I don't trust him. He's very persuasive."

"What—you think Welt will seduce me or something?"

"I sure as hell think he'd try," I said.

Roxanne took a deep breath. I heard her exhale.

"We have a problem then, Jack."

"I think we do," I said. Baloo, the bear from *The Jungle Book*, was talking.

I hesitated, then said, "I sort of called him out. After you left."

She turned, looked up from the table. "You did what?"

"I told him I thought he should have stepped in with those guys."

"He was calling the police."

"Standing still, a hundred yards away. I think he may have backed up."

"My God, Jack. I can't believe this. And after we talked?"

My turn for a deep breath. Snarling from the television. The evil tiger, Shere Khan.

"I told him I thought he had inappropriate feelings toward you."

"What!"

"He said I was nuts. He knew we were going through a rough patch, as he put it. He gave me some therapy-speak. And he said he was sorry our marriage was on the rocks. Or something like that."

"What the hell?"

"I think it was his way of getting a shot in," I said.

"No, I mean—what the hell were you thinking? This is my friend."

She was simmering now, about to boil over.

"I'm sorry if I embarrassed you, but that's how I feel."

"Embarrassed me, Jack? I'm mortified. And Sophie is traumatized, seeing her daddy grappling with some thugs and the police coming. My God."

"What did you expect me to do—let them follow you home?"

"You could have called me in the car. Told me to go to the supermarket or something. Call the police then. Instead you rush into this huge confrontation."

"They needed to know," I said.

"Know what?"

"That they'd crossed the line."

"They're not the only ones, Jack. God almighty. Calling him a coward. Accusing him of having an affair with me. Did I say anything when you were hanging around with that sculptor lady?"

I didn't answer.

"You were smitten with her," Roxanne said.

I shrugged.

"And she was infatuated with you," she said.

"She was just lonely," I said.

"Whatever. But I didn't go over there and say, 'Hands off my man.' No, I trusted you, no matter what her intentions were."

A pause.

"And then today, grabbing that guy by the throat."

"It's not like it's the first time this sort of thing has happened," I said, "that I've had to step up. The guys from Sanctuary, they could have—"

"Okay. So I appreciate that you've protected us. I really do."

A momentary softening.

"But I'm seeing things differently now. There's got to be a way to break the cycle, not just fighting battle after battle."

"Somebody points a gun at you, it's a little late to talk about role models," I said.

"But we can be role models. For our daughter."

"I thought I was. Would you rather have somebody like me or Clair or somebody like Welt, asking these dirtbags to share their feelings?"

"Goddamn it, Jack," Roxanne snapped. "Don't you see? You're turning into one of them."

Her eyes filled with angry tears, her cheeks pale, teeth clenched. She walked past me to the sink, put her plate in the dishwasher. Walked past me again and out to the living room. I heard Sophie murmur, Roxanne say, "It's okay, honey. We were just talking."

I stood in the kitchen for ten minutes, all of it playing and replaying in my head. Then I walked out to the living room, saw Sophie asleep on Roxanne's shoulder again. Roxanne was staring at the movie. She didn't look up.

"I'm going out," I said.

No response.

"To talk to Clair."

Roxanne stared.

I went out to the truck, started it, drove down the road and into the barnyard. Clair's truck was there but Louis's Jeep was gone. Good. This was private.

I went into the barn and the music and lights were on but Clair wasn't there. I walked through and out the side door at the rear and saw him out by the paddock. He was moving fence railings, letting Pokey out into the near pasture. Pokey waited for the gap to open and then ambled out, long tail flicking. Clair looked up.

"I'd ask you how things were going," he said, putting the railing back in place, "but I think I can tell."

"The last of the great mind readers," I said.

Clair crossed the paddock, let himself out, and came over to lean on the fence beside me. He waited, and after a minute of watching Pokey graze, I started in. The farm. Billy and Baby Fat showing up. Them eyeballing Roxanne, then pulling out to follow her. The rest of it, right up to Roxanne on the couch.

We leaned. Clair took his hat off and smoothed his silver hair, put his hat back on. Pokey started walking in search of better grass. I waited. Pokey stopped and lowered his head.

"You can't lose her," Clair said.

"No," I said.

"But everything you're doing is driving a wedge."

"I know."

"Shouldn't have gone out to that farm."

"I just don't like the smarmy bastard. He's working this, knowing Roxanne likes the conflict-resolution stuff and that it's a way to get us apart."

Clair looked across the pasture.

"I don't doubt he's got some sort of crush on her. Infatuation or whatever. Who wouldn't? But you have to trust her. And talk things out. Communication keeps you close."

"I didn't know we weren't communicating. Really, I'm not sure where it all went wrong. I mean, I thought things were great. I'm getting good stories. Best stories in years. Making good money. I've been busy, but I thought we were fine. Sophie is fine. And then we meet those guys in the woods."

"Went off track before that," Clair said. "You just weren't paying attention."

"I thought she was okay. Maybe a little lonely because I was away so much."

"Big difference between lonely and neglected, Jack. You got all caught up in your stories, the big magazines calling you up. You weren't seeing her, even when you were around."

I grimaced.

"And our outlaw friends, they're complicating things. Roxanne, working on this peace project, is sensitive to strife and violence, and that's just what these guys are about."

"Yes," I said.

"And they're a real threat," Clair said.

"That, too."

"Shut them down and things might get back on track."

"Or it could just exacerbate things," I said.

"Those are the choices," he said.

We leaned some more, watched wasps moving in and out of a nest at the peak of the barn.

"How 'bout I step in," Clair said. "Mary gave up trying to fix me years ago."

"But you guys do fine."

"Only two things she asks: Don't get hurt, and don't stay out late." I smiled.

"Feel like it's my battle, them coming after my family."

"I'm not thinking of a battle," he said. "More like establishing a no-fly zone. This road and wherever the girls go."

"You think they'll get it?" I said.

"One way or the other," Clair said, his flat tone a statement of absolute fact.

He pushed away from the fence and I followed him back through the barn to the shop. He went to the metal cabinet at the end of the workbench, fished a key out of his pockets, and bent to the padlock.

"I'm picturing them doing some sort of drive-by," Clair said. "They pull up beside you on some back road, a shotgun out the window."

"Sounds about right."

He swung the heavy doors open. There were rifles, shotguns, handguns in brackets on the inside of the door.

"You want that Glock now?" Clair said.

I hesitated, thought of Roxanne, a handgun confirming her worst fears. And wouldn't Welt have a field day with a Glock.

"The nine millimeter," he said. "Accurate, and pretty good stopping power."

I still hesitated. Roxanne. Sophie.

"You're no good to them dead, Jack," Clair said. "Or in a coma. I'm serious. And these boys are, too. I've seen Billy's type before. You saw how he wanted that fight. Guys like him, they're time bombs."

I nodded.

"Okay."

Clair reached to the cabinet door and took out a black handgun. He slid a drawer open and took out two extra clips, a box of ammo, put it all down on the bench. I opened the box and started thumbing cartridges into the spring-loaded clips.

"I'm all for pacifism," Clair said. "But I'm not gonna die for it."

9

I walked out to my truck and put the Glock under the seat. I was locking the truck when I heard Sophie's burbling voice. She was trotting down the path, Roxanne trailing after her. Sophie saw me and called, "Daddy, we're going to see Pokey." I waved and walked back to the barn.

The pony was at the door to the paddock, poking his head out like a dog in a doghouse. Clair was paring slices of apple and handing them to Roxanne, who was holding Sophie up so she could feed them to Pokey. Pokey was gumming them off Sophie's small hand, chewing in his deliberate way. He was a pony who had seen everything before and preferred to take things slow.

"Pokey was starvalating," I said.

"Yes, he has to eat or he'll get skinny," Sophie said.

"That's right, honeybun," Clair said. "Don't want him wasting away."

Roxanne smiled coldly, said nothing.

That was the tone of the afternoon and evening. Clair saddled Pokey and Sophie rode him around and around the paddock, Pokey walking at his stately pace and Sophie making clicking sounds that kept him from stopping. Roxanne and I stood by the paddock fence. I tried to begin a conversation and got the smile back. No more.

After Pokey we went back home, Sophie running in front of us. They went inside and I walked around the house from the back deck, slipped into the woods, and picked my way up to the road. From behind the screen of small yellowing maples, I looked right and left.

No Dodge truck. Nobody in sight.

I stood there for five minutes, watching. A white Chevy sedan came from the direction of Clair's, but it was Mrs. Fortin, the white-haired widow who lived a half mile up on the right.

A few more minutes and I went back to the house, making my way through the woods at the perimeter of the yard. Chickadees flitted around me, nuthatches, too. A red squirrel scolded from a tree, alerted by the crunching of my boots in the dry sticks and forest duff.

Good, I thought. Nice and noisy.

I went inside and Roxanne and Sophie were making dinner. There was salmon cooking in the microwave and Roxanne was cutting zucchini into slices and dropping them into a pan of boiling water. Sophie was standing on a chair, stirring a pot of macaroni and cheese with a wooden spoon.

She said, "It's turning bright orange."

Roxanne said, "Sophie, you are an excellent cook."

We chatted woodenly while we ate, the conversation revolving around Sophie. She talked about Salandra and her doll Chiquita, which Salandra's mom had gotten her in Mexico. Chiquita had black hair in braids. Sophie was glad she had brown hair because it was the same color as Pokey's. Welt had said he liked Sophie's curls. Salandra's hair was blonde like her mom's, but her mom lived in a different house. That gave Salandra two houses. She had toys at each house, but some special toys she took back and forth. Like Chiquita.

Then Sophie asked to be excused and slid down. Roxanne popped up and started to clear the table. I got up and started to help but she said, "That's okay, I'll do this," and took the plate from my hand and put it in the sink. She loaded the dishwasher and started in on the pans, her back to me.

I gave Sophie her bath, a sudsy, sloshy one that left water all over the floor. I mopped up while she got into her pajamas and we went to the window seat in her room and waited to see if deer would show up at the edge of the woods. Sophie chattered until, on cue, a doe emerged. We stayed still, staring through the window screen, until a husky fawn picked its way out of the woods, too.

"Hello, mommy and baby deer," Sophie whispered. And then Roxanne closed a cupboard door and the deer spooked, vaulting back into the underbrush.

We went downstairs and sat on the couch and read books. Roxanne poked her head in and said five minutes until bedtime, and five minutes later came back and scooped Sophie up. I kissed her good night and she said, "I'm glad you scared away the bad guys, Daddy."

Attagirl, I thought. "Me, too," I said.

Roxanne didn't come back downstairs. I heard her moving around, then the squeak of a chair in our bedroom. I walked to the hallway and looked up and the bedroom door was closed, so I went to the study at the back of the house and opened my laptop. I read about Old Order Mennonites—how they were founded by a guy named Menno Simon in Germany in the 1500s, which makes them a hundred years older than the Amish, an offshoot.

Five hundred years later, still going. Abram and Miriam, Victor and Sarah, out there in the field with the plows, the girls in their white bonnets. How did they not get sucked away by Twitter and hip-hop and YouTube? Or maybe some of them did.

I leaned back in my chair. The room had grown dark and the laptop glowed. Tomorrow was Sunday, and I assumed the Mennonites would be in church, probably on hard benches, probably for a long time. The forecast was for rain, heavy at times, which would keep us from going back into the Hoddings' woods.

That left two choices: Stay home and endure hours of the big chill, or ask Clair to keep an eye on things, and go and do some work.

Did gun sellers take Sunday off?

I fired off a few e-mails and called it a bad day.

Roxanne was asleep when I went up, curled up on her two-foot strip of bed. I slept badly, had a dream that Welt had moved in with us and kept wearing my clothes. As Roxanne said, my dreams were as impenetrable as air.

I got up with Sophie at six, grilled blueberry pancakes after she stirred the blueberries into the batter herself. When Roxanne came down, the coffee was made and I was sipping a cup of tea. Sophie had saved her mom two pancakes but nibbled away half of one.

Roxanne poured a cup of coffee. Sophie skittered upstairs to get dressed. Roxanne ate the pancakes, drank her coffee, read the *New York Times* online. I took a shower and got dressed and when I came back down, Roxanne hadn't moved and still hadn't said a word to me.

"I think I'm going to do some work," I said.

"Okay."

"I'll talk to Clair on the way out. He knows the situation. He'll be on duty."

"Right."

"Are you staying home this morning?"

"Yes."

"Would you call him if you decide to go out? And I'll have my phone on."

"Okay."

"And I'll be back after lunch. I'm just hitting a few gun sellers. I won't be far."

"Right."

"So I'll see you."

"Yup."

I gathered my stuff—notebooks, recorder, GPS, and the $1,000 in cash from *Outland* magazine. Grabbing my rain jacket from the hook in the shed, I walked quickly to the truck. A dense mist was falling, and the air was heavy. I leaned down, felt the cold metal. The Glock was under the seat.

Louis's big-wheeled Jeep was parked at Clair's barn. I went in and they were standing in the shop talking. When I came in they nodded and paused, like whatever they were discussing was private. Louis looked a little ragged, like he'd been up for hours. A bad night.

"Hey, Jack," he said, like it was an effort.

"Louis," I said. "How you doing?"

"Oh, you know," he said.

"Still bugging him, the way that argument escalated," Clair said, always straightforward. "I told him that guy and the chubby one were nosing around Roxanne and Sophie yesterday."

"Deserved everything he got and more," I said. "I wouldn't lose a minute's sleep over it."

Louis smiled like it was easy for me to say, and he was right. I wasn't carrying his baggage, wasn't haunted by his memories.

"Going out," I said. "Two or three hours. Would you mind—"

"On it," Clair said. "They staying put?"

"Yes," I said.

I left, heard their voices as their conversation resumed.

There was nobody in sight on the drive out. I went east up to the first intersection, then turned around and drove west to the main road. A car passed with an old couple dressed up, probably headed for church. An SUV with some college kids, driving east toward the coast. Me, I was bound for a guy in a small town called Davidson, fifteen miles to the northwest. Gene had advertised a Taurus nine-millimeter handgun, fifteen cartridges in the clip and one in the chamber. A hundred rounds of ammo. Five hundred dollars. Cash, no checks. And the buyer had to have a Maine driver's license, and no felony convictions.

I was golden.

Davidson was on the edge of the Dixville hills, a long ridge that ran north-south. There had been farms on the ridges, but most were gone now, woods creeping into the pastures, barns sinking into the ground. Everywhere I looked there were reminders that nearly everything we did was for naught.

I'd plugged Gene's address into the GPS and it guided me off Route 202, the main road, and up and over the ridge. On the east side of the ridge, where the road dropped into marshy hollows, I zigzagged through the woods, past trailers and farmhouses, home-built cabins ringed by broken-down pickups and cars and snowmobiles.

And then the GPS went blank. I slowed, looked down each driveway through the rain. One led to a ramshackle trailer that looked like it hadn't seen $500 cash in many years. The next was posted with signs nailed to trees: PRIVATE PROPERTY—NO TRESPASSING.

I turned in.

The house, a neat log cabin, was in a clearing at the end of a long right-hand turn. The pickup in the driveway was big and new, a $40,000 Ford. There was a life-size deer target on the lawn and a chain-link kennel out back. A Rottweiler was barking at me through the fence.

I got out and went to the side door. There was a sign that said FORGET THE DOG. BEWARE OF OWNER. Before I could knock, the door swung open.

The guy on the other side was in his seventies, short and trim, with a gray beard and cropped hair the same length. He pushed the storm door open and held it, and I said, "Gene?"

He had a handgun in a holster on his hip.

"Yes, but you missed it."

"The gun?"

"Just sold it. Woulda called you off, but it was too late. Surprised you didn't see him on the way in."

"Didn't see anybody."

"Yeah, sorry. Paid cash. Nice kid."

"Well, that's the way it goes," I said. "So, you sell a lot of guns?"

"When I have something I don't need."

The rain fell. The dog barked. Gene's arm wasn't getting tired, holding the door open.

"Listen, Gene, I'm a writer."

His eyes narrowed, face tightened.

"For magazines. Live down the road in Prosperity. I was interested in the Taurus. I have a Glock nine millimeter in the truck, but it only holds ten rounds."

"Fifteen's a sight better," Gene said.

"Sure is. Listen, I'm thinking of doing a story on gun sales in Maine. How we go about our business here, same as ever."

"Not exactly," he said.

Gene called it as he saw it, writer or no writer.

"That right?"

"People aren't the same. Druggies and thieves and every other kind of bum. Nobody works. Why should they, handing out the welfare hand over fist. Sucking off the government tit, all they do. Heads down in the public trough."

"Huh," I said. "So how does that affect you selling a gun?"

"I suss 'em out before I sell them anything. I'm not having some shitbum buying my guns, going out and holding up a goddamn drugstore."

"I see."

"Before I sell you a gun, I want to know you're on the right side of the equation."

"Of course."

"Worked hard for a living."

"What did you do?"

"Concrete work. Slabs, foundations. Forty years. My own business. Poured enough concrete to go from here to goddamn Bangor and back."

"No kidding."

"So don't come here looking to buy a firearm with your money from welfare and thieving and drugging," Gene said.

"So what was the kid like who bought the Taurus?"

"Farm kid," Gene said. "Very polite."

"Paid cash?"

"Cash money."

"What was he going to do with the handgun?"

He looked at me like the question was a bit irrelevant, but said, "He said he and his father hunt bear. Need a handgun, you get in close with one of them big boys. You can get in trouble real fast if one of 'em charges and you can't bring your long gun to bear."

"I'm sure."

"Sold him a holster, too. Fits under your jacket, keeps the gun out of the weather."

I looked at his sidearm.

"This holster's okay for around the house," Gene said.

"Looks like it," I said.

The rain had picked up since I was standing at the door. The dog had found a rhythm, hitting the fence and barking.

"How you like that Glock?" Gene said.

"Serves the purpose."

"Glock's a good firearm. I went to a Kimber, though. Light, quick, lots of punch. And made in the U.S.A."

"That right," I said.

"You bust in here, be the last thing you do."

"Who'd be crazy enough to do that?"

"Drugs turn them into animals," Gene said. "They don't know what they're doing."

"True," I said. "Listen, Gene, you think I could use your comments in my story?"

"I don't give a damn."

"What's your last name?"

"Lisbon. Like the town near Lewiston."

Not Portugal.

"Gotcha," I said, and I slipped my notebook out and wrote that down. Like I'd forget.

"Federal government doesn't want us to be strong. Wants us to be weak so we can be ruled. The absolute truth. Only democracy we're going to have left is the one we fight for."

"Right."

"You come in my home and threaten my family, you better be prepared to pay the consequences."

The rain fell. Gene stood guard at the door.

"You have a family here, Gene?" I said.

"No, just me and the dog. Wife passed a few years back, and my boy, he works in the Gulf. On oil rigs. See him once a year. Christmas."

"I see. But if somebody did come here in a threatening way . . . "

"I can't guarantee that man's safety," Gene said.

I wrote that down. The quote about the feds. The one about the consequences.

"But the farm kid, he was okay?"

"Oh, yeah. And I can smell scum a mile away," he said. "He was a good kid."

"So I passed the test?" I said.

"If you didn't, we wouldn't be standing here," Gene said.

I smiled and thanked him. The dog had stopped barking. He liked me, too.

10

I sat in my truck at the end of the driveway and went over my notes, filling in where words were missing or the ones that were there were illegible. I liked this guy, screening the kids who bought his handguns. But I wondered what kind of bear would take fifteen rounds to bring down.

I put the notebook on the seat, tapped my phone, and started off. The call dropped and I tapped it again as I came off the top of a rise near the main road. As I waited for a tractor-trailer to pass, Roxanne answered. The truck roared. She waited.

"Hi," I said. "How you doing?"

"Fine," she said, but didn't elaborate.

"Good. How's Sophie?"

"She's fine, too."

"What's she doing?"

"Playing upstairs."

"Oh, good. So she's okay?"

"Okay."

"Seen Clair?"

"No, but . . ."

The words trailed off.

"Right," I said. "That doesn't mean he isn't there."

"No," Roxanne said.

A long pause. A pickup pulled up behind me, a big Dodge, but this one was black. I swung out onto the road, holding the wheel with my knees as I shifted.

"So everything's okay there?" I said.

"Fine. You can go do what you have to do."

"I thought I'd hit another gun seller or two, make a loop. East to Bangor, then shoot down to Winterport, then home."

"Okay."

"As long as all's well on the home front."

"I don't know about that, Jack," Roxanne said. "But we're fine. See you when you get home."

She rang off. I swerved as I punched in another number.

"Hey," Clair said.

"How are things there?"

"Quiet. Nobody."

"You watching the house?"

Silence.

"Sorry," I said. "I know I don't have to ask. Can you stay there another couple of hours?"

More silence.

"Okay. I'll be back by eleven-thirty. If they show up—"

"Jack," Clair said.

"Right," I said, and put the phone down.

It was twenty miles to Bangor, the road running east and skirting a ridge so that there were hills close on the right and in the distance on the left. The foliage was brightest along the bogs, flares of red-orange from the swamp maples. I noted the colors but didn't let my eyes linger, just drove fast and hard, passing on the straights, crowding impatiently on the curves, blasting past when slower cars moved right on the upgrades.

I needed the interviews. I needed the story. I needed to be home.

In Newburgh I cut north to the interstate, hammered the last eight miles into Bangor. At the base of the exit ramp I typed the address into my GPS, waited, and started off. The route wound through nondescript streets lined with drab houses, left, right, left. My destination, the GPS said, was on the right.

It was a red ranch house with peeling white trim and beat-up snowmobiles on a trailer beside the driveway. There was a FOR SALE sign on the tongue of the trailer, a blue tarp bunched up on the pavement. There was no car or truck in the driveway, but the garage was closed, the shades on the house lowered tight.

I parked and walked to the side door. A wooden sign to the right of the door said PROTECTED BY SMITH & WESSON. I didn't care. I was there for the shotguns.

Hesitating for a moment to listen, I knocked. Waited and then knocked again. My arm was raised for a third try when the door swung open. A man was standing there, short and skinny and maybe thirty, but it was hard to tell because his head was shaved. He had on baggy jeans and unlaced work boots and a sweat-stained T-shirt that said AC/DC.

"Angus Young," I said.

"What?" he said.

"The singer. I called about the shotguns. My name's Jack."

"Got cash?"

"Sure do."

He flicked his bald head toward the room behind him and turned away. I followed.

It was dim inside and it took a moment for my eyes to adjust. The blinds were closed, the flowers in the vase on the kitchen table dead and crisp. A cat scurried out from under the table and disappeared into the depths of the place, which smelled like litter box. The guy walked around the table and bent down and lifted the guns from the seats along the wall. He put them down beside the dead flowers.

"These are them," he said.

There were two shotguns, a standard Remington 870 pump, and an old Sears single-shot, like a kid would get for Christmas circa,1950.

"Good working order?" I said.

"Fine."

"You don't use 'em?"

"My old man did. Shot ducks," he said.

"He give up hunting?"

"He died," the guy said.

"Sorry," I said.

He shrugged. "Two seventy-five for the pump, hundred and fifty for the single. Four hundred for both. Cash."

I picked up the pump and opened the chamber. It was empty. I racked the pump, pointed it at the floor, and pulled the trigger. It clicked. I picked up the single-shot and snapped the bolt back and forth. Pulled the trigger. Another click, this one fainter. Both guns were dirty, and the action on both felt rough.

The guy, sensing my hesitation, said, "I got a lot of ammo I can throw in. Birdshot, buckshot, slugs."

"I thought he hunted ducks," I said. "What were the slugs for?"

"Protection."

"From what?"

"Assholes," he said.

I hesitated, put the single-shot back down on the table.

"Listen," I said. "I'm buying guns but I also write stories. For magazines, mostly. I'm doing a story on private gun sales in Maine—how there have been crackdowns in other states, but for us, the tradition lives on."

He looked at me and frowned, wrinkles appearing on his stubbled skull.

"A fucking reporter?" the guy said.

"Magazines usually call us writers. Reporters are more for news-papers, typically."

The frown turned into a scowl and the scowl turned into a snarl.

"No reporter is gonna set foot in this house," he said.

"Oh, yeah?" I said. "Why's that?"

"Out," he barked.

I put my hand on the table, crossed my legs at the ankle.

"What?" I said. "Somebody spell your name wrong in the police log?"

"Out," he snapped, spittle flying.

"Your guns are dirty. I don't think you'll get more than five for the pair."

He pulled his right arm back and cocked it. His bicep barely showed and flab hung from under his arm. I straightened up, half turned toward the door. I could see his fist trembling.

"Just missed your chance to be in *Outland* magazine," I said.

"Get the fuck outta here," he shouted.

"Your mom here? Shouldn't use that language around a lady. And the only way to get away with punching a reporter is to kill him after. And you're way too out of shape for that."

I started for the door, which was still open, the cold, clean air cutting the cat smell.

"What was it—child pornography or something? Figure it had to be something embarrassing to get you this upset."

"It wasn't me, you son of a bitch," he said, edging along behind me. "It wasn't even my computer."

Still walking, I said, "So your buddy was the perv and you got nailed for it? Doesn't matter if there's no conviction. One story like that and you're done. All you can do is hide in the house."

I looked around the dingy cave of a kitchen, pictured Mom off working at a convenience store to support her son, steeling herself to the stares, real or imagined.

"Or move someplace where nobody knows you," I said, and then it clicked. "Which takes money. So you need to sell stuff."

"Out," the guy bellowed, more spittle flying, his head starting to sweat.

"If you're innocent, I'm sorry for you," I said. "And I'm sorry I gave you a hard time. If you're guilty, go to hell."

I stewed all the way out of town, along the Penobscot River. The perv, Welt . . . Roxanne and I as far apart as I could remember . . . it all draped over me, pushing me down into the truck seat, making every shift a labor. I didn't see the river, the trees along the roadside barely registering. I could feel myself sinking into a deep funk, something I'd avoided even with the arguments. It was like the exchange with the pasty pervert had been the last straw.

In the town of Winterport, I almost missed the turn to head west toward home, stomped the brakes, and swerved right and straightened out. I drove under my personal cloud past Monroe, then to a crossroads called Brooks. I looked at my phone, read the directions, swung north to my last stop. The guy had said 2.5 miles north, on the left. Mailbox was red, the number 239 spray-painted on the boulder by the driveway.

I watched the odometer, counted off the tenths of miles. At 2.3 I slowed and watched the woods, passed a trailer with a wishing well, then saw the boulder, numbers plain as day. I braked, looked right, saw the driveway threading into the spruce and birch. As I started to turn in, I saw a pickup coming out. I stopped and reversed, turning around to check traffic when I pulled back out. I waited for a delivery truck, eased out onto the road, and stopped.

The pickup, an older red Chevy with black spoke rims and loud exhaust, swung out and the driver gave a wave. As I waved back, our eyes met.

Semi—the kid from the woods. His head pivoted as he passed. I turned and tracked with him, glimpsed another guy with him, riding shotgun. It didn't look like Baby Fat or Billy, but beyond that I couldn't tell.

"Huh," I said. I watched the truck head west, back toward Hyde and the farm. "Huh," I said again.

I pulled back into the driveway, drove through the woods for a hundred yards, popped out in a clearing with a new log house, a dug pond, ducks swimming along the cattailed shoreline. The guy had advertised a Ruger Mini-14 rifle, a military-style .223, for $600.

I pulled up to the garage where a new Jeep Grand Cherokee was parked. As I got out, a guy poked his head out of one of the garage doors. Forty, dressed in fleece vest and flannel shirt and jeans. Good-looking with an expression that said self-made success. I walked toward him and he smiled, said something to somebody inside the garage who turned out to be a black Lab. The Lab trotted out of the garage, bounded to me, and nuzzled my hand. Probably smelled cats.

"I called about the Mini-fourteen," I said.

"You missed it by five minutes," he said. "Just went out the door."

"Those guys in the red pickup?"

"Saw the pickup," he said. "Only one guy."

"Guy driving, baseball hat, maybe nineteen?"

"I guess. Said he was going to give it to his dad for Christmas. Real family oriented."

"Works in the woods?"

"Could be; I didn't ask. But he was very polite. Good, direct eye contact. You know how half these young guys won't look you in the eye. This guy, good handshake, real stand-up kid."

"Where was he from?"

He looked at me.

"Why? You want to buy the gun from him?"

"Just curious. Want to know where the competition is."

"Said he was from Hyde."

The dog was sniffing my leg. The guy said, "Red. Cut that out." He turned back to me and said, "You ask a lot of questions."

"Yeah, well . . . , " I began, and I went through my magazine-writer pitch. The guy listened, no expression either way. The dog sat down next to us and wagged his tail across the concrete floor. The guy cleared his throat like he was about to make a statement, which he proceeded to do.

"I sell the occasional firearm. If I get a good deal, I turn around and try to make a small profit. I believe firmly in the right to bear arms. I also believe that guns belong in the hands of the law-abiding, not criminals. I ask for buyers to identify themselves. I interview them, in a way, to determine what sort of people they are. I think I'm a good judge of character, so that's the extent of my background check."

"Did that buyer provide identification?"

"He identified and described himself—how long he's lived there, and so on. I saw no reason to think that the firearm would be used inappropriately. I go with my gut, and my gut's rarely wrong."

"So who was he? What did he do for work?"

The guy held up his hand to stop me.

"That's my statement."

"May I ask your name?"

"John."

"Last name?"

"Just John."

Damn, I thought. I looked down at the dog, his tongue lolling.

"So this is Red?"

"He prefers to remain anonymous," John said.

"What did the kid say his dad was going to do with the rifle?"

"Varmints," the guy said, and, like the president walking away from the podium, he strode across the garage and through a door and into the house.

11

More scribbling, my truck pulled over by the side of the road. I got the dialogue down, not sure if I'd need it for the story. *I go with my gut, and my gut's rarely wrong.* And when it was wrong, what then?

I put the pen and notebook down, picked up my phone just as a white work van rolled past slowly, the guy at the wheel turning to give me a once-over.

As the van continued on I called Roxanne. Six rings and it went to voice mail. "Hey, call me," I said. I was calling again when the phone buzzed and Roxanne's number showed.

"Hi," I said. "You okay?"

"Fine," Roxanne said, and I heard girls laughing in the background.

"Where are you?"

"We're at the school."

More chattering, Roxanne putting her hand over the phone and saying, "Sophie, quiet."

"I thought you were staying home," I said.

"Sophie wanted to come over and go on the swings and the tree house. And Salandra was going to be here."

It was becoming clearer.

"And your friend?"

"Welt?" Roxanne said, her public voice on. "He's here. The girls are playing and we're watching them and going over some things."

"Things?"

"We're working on a presentation for the administrative team. They're a tough audience, and we need to be ready."

"Don't farmers have to farm? Like all the time? Like never get a vacation? How does he have time for all this?"

"Oh, he has the interns."

I didn't reply.

"The students from the college," Roxanne said.

"I see," I said. "So they run the place and he does his peace work."

"Right. But we want to be sure we're ready for their questions."

"Right," I said.

The phone covered again, muffled voices, Roxanne saying, "Okay, but be careful, you two." Then Welt's voice, unintelligible.

"After our conversation I thought he might want to give you some distance," I said.

"No, he's fine," Roxanne said. "We're going over our talking points. We want to have every base covered."

It was the public voice again.

"You know how I feel," I said.

"Yeah."

"About him."

"Right. And I told you."

"That I was nuts, and you have a right to have friends?"

"Exactly."

The same van passed, from the other direction. There was a sign on the driver's door. A & G PLUMBING SUPPLY. The same guy at the wheel, the same slow once-over. Baseball hat, goatee, sunglasses. Didn't look like a plumber.

"What about Clair?"

"I told him where we were going."

"And?"

"He followed us over."

"Is he still there?"

"I think so. He brought a book."

"And he's in his truck?"

"He said he might take a walk."

Clair taking a walk meant he had a clear view of the playground, an open line of fire.

"Okay," I said.

"It's fine, Jack," Roxanne said.

Welt's voice, calling to the girls. Something about knowing their limits.

"Christ," I said.

"What?"

"Nothing."

"Jack, please."

"When are you gonna be home?"

"An hour or two. We're halfway through the PowerPoint."

"Call me when you're leaving, okay?"

"Have you seen those guys again?" she said.

"No. Just a bunch of gun sellers."

"How was that?"

"Fine. All good."

"Then I'll see you," Roxanne said.

"Right."

I waited. She didn't come back. No long good-bye.

I put the phone down, scowled, started the truck. There was a trailer across the road, a woman draping laundry on the railing of a rickety deck. A dog was around her legs and it spotted me and shoved its muzzle between the railings and started to bark. I put the truck in gear and pulled away, headed east toward home, an empty house. The road climbed past a shingled barn, chickens scratching in the yard, a rust-red tractor for sale. I had my head in my hand, a scowl on my face. I glanced up at the rearview, saw the van fifty yards back.

Two guys showing now. I sped up, then slowed and took a quick left. It was a long right-hand turn, the hump of a culvert, and then the road straightened out. Nothing out here but bog and brush, roads named after dead men. Butler, Aborn, Webb, the signs passing as I went right, right, left, zigzagging past woods, fields, logging roads blocked by steel cables.

The van followed.

What, had Billy and Baby Fat subbed out the job? Hired somebody to break my legs? Whoever it was, I wasn't leading them home.

I watched the mirror as I descended a long hill, spruce and pine woods streaming by. The van kept pace, didn't gain or fall back. I rounded a right-hand curve, hit the gas. We were in Hyde, my turf. I saw the logging road coming up on my left, one Clair and I had used to check out a woodlot. I braked, made sure the van was in sight behind me, slowed, and swung in.

The truck jounced over ruts, slashed through tall grass as I missed the tracks. I pulled in fifty yards, skidded to a stop, slammed the truck into reverse, and whipped it into an overgrown turnaround, backing as the bumper flattened the brush and branches scraped underneath me.

I stopped. The motor idled. And then the van drove past, the driver peering deeper into the woods. I counted to ten and pulled out, put my truck across the road. Stopped and shut off the motor.

Reached for the Glock and racked a shell into the chamber.

Got out and put the gun behind me in my waistband.

Stood and waited.

The road went a hundred yards deeper before there was a wood yard, only a skidder trail beyond that, too rough for the van to negotiate.

I pictured them stopping and staring at the opening before deciding to turn around. Backing around the slash piles, taking a last glance down the trail, then heading back my way. Coming slowly up the rise.

And there they were.

The van slowed to a roll as they saw me, my truck—no exit. Then the driver continued on, stopped twenty feet from me. The motor ticked. They stared. The white guy with the goatee and the baseball hat. The other, black, maybe Caribbean, head shaved clean. No expression, either of them.

And then, simultaneously, they opened their doors and got out. Closed the doors, the motor still running. Walked toward me and stopped six feet away.

Jeans. Black T-shirts. Bulked up, but not overly so. An air of authority that is the hardest thing to disguise.

"Cops," I said.

"ATF," the Caribbean guy said.

"ID?"

He pursed his lips, on the verge of telling me to screw off. Then he reached into his jeans, took out a leather ID holder, and flipped it open. He stepped forward and held it up. I peered at it, then at his face.

Ramos, Joseph R.

Special Agent.

The other guy moved up and put his ID in my face.

O'Day, Terrence G.

Special Agent.

He had more hair in the photo, no goatee.

"Pleased to meet you, Mr. McMorrow," Ramos said.

They'd run the plate.

"Likewise," I said. "And just so you know, I've got a gun."

"Where?" O'Day said.

"Waist. Behind me. I didn't know who you were or why you were following me."

"Got a carry permit?" Goatee said.

"Yes."

"Produce it. After you put the gun on the hood of your truck, just so there's no misunderstanding," he said.

He moved around and behind me, and I heard his gun slip out of a holster somewhere. I turned, lifted my shirt, eased the Glock up and out with two fingers. Moving to the truck, I laid the gun on the hood. I turned back, took my place in front of them. O'Day was putting his gun back into his waistband. I slowly held out my wallet and showed my card. They handed it back and forth.

"You always carry a loaded firearm?" Ramos said.

"This is Maine. It's a gun culture."

"So we noticed," O'Day said.

The accent was Boston, the pieces falling into place. The Bureau of Alcohol, Tobacco, and Firearms checking on private gun sales in rural Maine. Massachusetts was a destination for Maine guns. They stake out some sellers and see the same blue Toyota pickup making the rounds.

"I'm a reporter," I said, cutting to the chase.

"For who?" Ramos said.

I told him.

"This magazine issues firearms to its reporters?"

"I'm freelance," I said.

"Uh-huh," O'Day said.

"I've had some run-ins of late."

A red squirrel chittered somewhere in the trees above us. A blue jay called. It was their move, and they had to decide how much to tell me, how much to ask.

"So you must know what we're up here for," Ramos said.

"I'm thinking a Maine gun was picked up at a Boston homicide. You came up to see how that might have happened."

"Dorchester," O'Day said. "Intervale Street. And then we see you. Keep turning up at private sellers."

"I'm mostly just talking," I said.

Ramos looked toward the Glock on the hood of the truck.

"I borrowed that from a friend. For protection. I'm going to buy two or three guns, but I haven't found the right ones yet."

"This is for your story?" O'Day said.

"Right. So if you have a few minutes, I'd love to know about the homicide that triggered your investigation. I'd like to know if this is a trend. How many hands the guns go through from Maine to Boston. If it's an organized thing or just random. If it's an organized thing, how much profit is made by the time the gun gets down there. And why are you in Waldo County."

"That's all?" Ramos said.

"My turn for questions," O'Day said. "Guy making the rounds looking at handguns. Has connections to New York and is carrying a loaded Glock. Decides somebody's following him, so he lures them into the woods and then blocks the road so they can't get out. What kind of reporter is that?"

"Thorough?" I said.

"Move your vehicle," Ramos said.

I did, after I gave Ramos my card and asked who I should talk to in Boston. He gave me a name, Brenda Gleeson, said if I called the main number, they'd get a message to her. And then I took my gun and put it back in the truck, backed into the woods to let them pass.

They did, Ramos giving me a two-fingered salute. I saluted back, and followed them out to the road. They went left, I went right. Fifty yards down the road, I'd decided: This story was getting better by the minute. But at a cost.

It all swirled around in my head: Billy and Baby Fat, Welt and his goddamn PowerPoint, the gun sellers and their varied sense of right and wrong, Semi picking up an assault rifle. For what purpose? Target shooting? To join a militia? To pick me off from a hundred yards? Or would it be Clair? Or Louis?

It had clouded up, matching my mood, weather rolling in from the west like the dust cloud over an invading army. I thought of driving out to the school, but would that just inflame matters more? Besides, Clair was there, on sentry duty. I slowed, picked up my phone, and punched him in. His cell buzzed and then he said, "Yessuh."

"How are things out there?" I said.

"Quiet," he said. "Kids are on the swings. Roxanne and the other dad are sitting at the picnic table, doing stuff on their computers."

"PowerPoint," I said.

"Good times," Clair said. "Sometimes I think we can't see the forest *or* the trees."

"Will you call me when they leave?"

"Roger that."

"What's Louis up to?"

"Lying low, I think. This thing's still bugging him."

"We shouldn't forget that he's the one they'd target," I said. "Though they'd have to find him first."

"Not forgetting," Clair said. "Not for a second."

The clouds had darkened to the west, and I put the phone down and turned on the radio, fiddled until I found a weather report. Thunderstorms moving in, possibly with hail. I drove north, vaguely headed for the Mennonite farms on the hills north of Hyde, thinking I might meet someone out there, might move a step closer to getting this promised story actually under way. I wove my way on back roads, climbing toward the ridgetop, my mind flitting. The Boston cops. Billy and Baby Fat. Roxanne and Welt. Around and around.

I crossed parallel to the ridge, took a right, and bounced over the ruts in the gravel road. The farms were a half mile up, the fields here spiked with seven-foot-high Mennonite corn. The road curved and, lost in thought, I had to yank the wheel to get the truck out of the oncoming lane. And then there was someone walking. I slowed, started to wave. Saw Abram and stopped.

He had been walking toward me, away from the farm. I got out of the truck, waited as he turned around and approached. He looked somber, troubled.

"Hey," I said. "Everything okay?"

He looked at me, and, with an odd directness, said, "No."

"You want to talk about it?"

"I don't know," Abram said.

"Where you headed?"

"Just away. Everybody's at service."

"Not you?"

"I said I was sick."

"Not true?"

"No," he said. "It was a lie."

He said it like a lie was a big deal. Mennonite boy, let me introduce you to the rest of the world.

We stood there, an odd sort of pair in an unlikely place, a ridgetop in a forgotten corner of a forgotten county. The clouds were billowing and the new leaves were turning over, showing their pale undersides. Storm sign.

"Do you drink coffee?" I said.

"Sure," Abram said.

"Hop in."

He seemed to think about it, turned back toward the farm as though to make sure nobody was watching. And then he came around, opened the door. I moved my notebooks and pens from the passenger seat.

We rode in silence for the six miles to the restaurant. I figured I wouldn't push him. He'd either want to talk or he wouldn't.

He didn't say anything for the first few minutes that we sat in the booth at the Belle View. Belle put down placemats and Abram appeared absorbed by the advertisements: trucking, excavation, a dog groomer. The coffee came and he looked up and then around the table. He spooned in sugar, opened two creamers. Stirred the milky concoction with his spoon and said, "What if he's wrong?"

I sipped my coffee, put the mug back down.

"Who?"

"The Bishop. My father."

"Wrong about what?"

"Everything," he said. He raised the mug in both hands and slurped. Wiped his mouth with the paper napkin.

"We're Old Order Mennonite, which is pretty strict. Pretty hardcore even for Old Order. The Bishop, my dad, he came to Maine because he thought the Ontario folks were sliding. It's God and the Bible for the Bishop, and how you have to do it a certain way so you don't go to hell. But I don't know."

I looked at him. Waited.

"Lately, it keeps sort of getting into my head. This last time I was reading a *National Geographic*. It was in the break room at work."

"Where's work?"

"The toy factory. In Thornhill."

"Uh-huh."

"And there was this story about this tribe way out in the jungle in Borneo. They have some religion, worshipping rain gods or whatever, and they think they have it all figured out."

"Well, for their purposes they do," I said.

"The Bishop, I was telling him about them, about how they had never heard of Jesus, and he said they were lost and they'd burn in hell. I said, 'But how are they supposed to believe in something they never heard of?' He said he'd have to think about that, but there was no way they were going to heaven."

"Luck of the draw," I said.

Abram took a nervous gulp of coffee. His hands clenched the mug tightly, fingers flexing. Belle came up and asked if we wanted refills, and he held his mug out. She poured and he set to adding his sugar and cream.

He stirred, gathering himself up.

"It's just that, those people in the jungle, they probably have a Bishop guy, too. He's probably saying you have to do this and that, sacrifice a goat or whatever, to get into heaven, or whatever they call it. So why should they go to hell? It makes me wonder if the whole thing is . . . I don't know."

He paused, deciding whether to say it.

"Just made up."

He drank some more coffee, looked down at the table, and shook his head.

"You must think I'm weird, going on about all this stuff, and me hardly knowing you. It's just that—"

"You had to let it out," I said. "And you can't do that when you're with your family."

"No way."

"Do you know people your age who aren't Mennonite?"

"Yeah, from work. But they're not into talking about religion and all that. They just talk about sports and hunting and getting loaded, and their trucks and hot babes and stuff."

"Hard to jump in with your crisis of faith."

Abram looked at me and smiled.

"If you want to talk about your truck, feel free," he said.

I smiled back and sipped my coffee. He was a good kid, smart and thoughtful, and that was never easy. Belle swung by again and asked if we wanted menus. Abram said no, he had to go.

"It's natural to question things," I said.

"Not in my world," he said. "Not natural at all."

"Does your family know you're having a hard time?"

"They think it's because I'm hanging out with these guys at the shop. Sinners and everything. They want me to just work on the farm, settle down. There's a girl in Ontario, we're supposed to be getting set up."

"To have a date?"

"To get married," Abram said.

"Big step," I said.

"I know. I mean, farming's fine, but if I do that I'll be right here the rest of my life. The Bishop, he'd rather write sermons than run the farm, really. So he needs me to help work the place. But I want to get out and try some things. I don't know, just experience stuff."

"Don't you get that year where you go out and see the outside world?"

"That's Amish," Abram said. "We don't have Rumspringa."

"So for you to break loose, you really have to break loose."

"Exactly. Because of the Bishop being my father and all."

"You always call him 'the Bishop'?"

"It's what he is."

"He's your dad, too. And being a bishop is his job. I don't expect my daughter to call me 'the reporter.' "

"It's different," Abram said. "It's not like it's his job. It's more like it's his—"

"Identity?"

"Right."

"Does he love you?"

Abram looked taken aback, like it was a weird question.

"Sure," he said. And then he looked away. "But it's like he treats me like everybody else. He's the Bishop, so he cares about everybody."

"Huh."

My turn to look away. Belle swished by, coffeepot in hand.

"So it's hard to confide in him?"

"About this? I'd have forty people praying for my soul, trying to keep me out of hell. The Bishop did a whole talk on hell last week. 'Wide is the gate, and broad is the way that leadeth to destruction.' "

"You must know all this by heart," I said.

"My whole life, it's been drilled into me," Abram said. "Thessalonians. 'The Lord Jesus shall be revealed from heaven with his mighty angels, in flaming fire taking vengeance on them that know not God, and that obey not the gospel of our Lord Jesus Christ.' "

He grinned, gave a little snort.

"The flaming fires. With the 'abominable and murderers and whoremongerers and sorcerers and idolaters and all liars.' That's Revelation twenty-one, eighteen. And the doubters."

"If you believe in all that."

"And if I don't," Abram said, "that's the worst sin of all."

He drank the last of his coffee, lifting the mug up so I could see the trademark on the bottom. Put the mug down and wiped his mouth again with the paper napkin. Folded the napkin and placed it neatly next to the mug, like he didn't want any evidence that he'd been there.

"I'm sure it's tough," I said. "But this is the way I look at it: I don't think God let all these billions of people set up all of these religions so he could pull the rug out from under them. 'Hah. You thought you were doing the right thing your whole life, but you know what? You're wrong.' "

Abram looked halfway interested, so I kept going.

"I think we have different versions of pretty much the same thing. You do the best you can, and you're kind and you try to help other people, and you do the good things that Jesus or Mohammed or whoever showed you. And then maybe you go to heaven. Or you don't. But, in the meantime, you made the world a little better place."

He looked at me skeptically.

"Right. Like that's gonna fly at my house," Abram said. "We believe, or they believe, that the Bible is the only truth. But how do you know that?"

"That's why they call it faith, I guess," I said.

Abram dug in his pockets.

"I got it," I said.

He stood, said, "Thanks. Sorry to dump all this on you."

"It's fine. I hope it helped."

"My sisters, they'd freak if they knew. They think I'm this perfect brother. That's the thing. If I go one way or the other, they're gonna want to follow. Miriam, at least. She thinks I'm just great."

He shook his head, said, "Thanks again," and started to walk away.

"I'll give you a ride back," I said.

"That's okay," Abram said, over his shoulder. "I like to walk."

He pushed out the door. I left money on the table, said thanks to Belle as she came and picked up the mugs. She said, "We don't get the Mennonites in here much."

"Well, if you get any of them, it will be Abram," I said.

"The rebel of the crowd?"

"No, he just thinks a lot."

I left the restaurant and walked to my truck. It was starting to rain in spattering gusts, so I figured I'd ask Abram again if he'd like a lift, at least to somewhere close to home. I looked down the road and saw him walking, but as I pulled out, a truck passed me, moving fast.

It was a red pickup. *The* red pickup, the Chevy Semi had been driving. I followed, slowed as the truck pulled over. It was Semi behind the wheel, and he waited as Abram climbed in. I glanced over as I passed them, saw Semi reach over and give Abram a slap on the shoulder.

Semi was smiling. Abram, I couldn't tell.

12

Semi caught up to me a mile down the road, passed me on a curve, the truck exhaust blaring. Abram didn't look over. As the truck went by I saw a decal on the back window, the figure of a naked woman and the words *Country girls do it in the mud*.

If Abram was stepping out with Semi, it was a big step indeed.

I mulled it over as I took the back roads, checking the mirror the whole way. The Mennonite story had the potential to be even better than I'd envisioned, if Abram would talk on the record. *For twenty-first-century Mennonite youth, a culture clash . . .*

The gun story could be way better, too, if there was a real homicide for a hook. So things were looking up on the writing front. Now if Roxanne would only realize that Welt was a smug, patronizing, lecherous bastard, and Billy and Baby Fat would get locked up for ten years, all would be well with the world.

If only . . .

Roxanne's car wasn't in the driveway, so I continued on to Clair's. He wasn't back either, but Louis's Jeep was parked by the barn. I swung in, saw the lights on in the shop, and went inside. The music was on, some Celtic dirge. Louis was leaning on his elbows on the workbench, reading a book. His big dog was stretched out on the floor by the woodstove. They both looked up.

"Hey," I said.

"McMorrow," Louis said.

"How you doing?"

"Fine," he said. "Or close enough to it. How you doing?"

"Not so fine," I said.

"Yeah, well, that makes two of us, I guess."

I walked over and he flipped the book closed. It was *Walden* by Henry David Thoreau.

"Enjoying it?" I said.

"Clair gave it to me. Turns out me and old Henry have some things in common," Louis said.

Thoreau's cabin. Louis's house in the woods.

"Just stopping the roller coaster and trying to come to some real conclusions," he said. "He was a very smart guy."

"Yes," I said. "Boiled it down to the essentials."

"Right. Essential truths. The stuff you should be thinking about but most people don't."

"Like what, do you think?"

"Like why we prey on each other. Why we're such a violent species."

"Survival, I guess," I said.

"Kill or be killed?" Louis said. "But how do we get in that position to begin with?"

"Too many people, too few resources?"

"Christ, McMorrow. Look around you. This country is drowning in resources. We're choking on our own prosperity. And still—"

He trailed off. I hesitated, realizing that he and I hadn't talked much, not one-on-one. When we'd met in Sanctuary, when that town was targeted by an arsonist and Louis was the suspect "troubled veteran," I'd brought Clair to break trail. He and Louis had war in common. I was the third wheel.

So how was I doing, Louis had asked. Louis, a guy who had been so ridden by guilt at the things he'd done and witnessed in the war that for months he'd only come out of the woods at night. Louis, who, until he met Clair, had lost faith in humanity and only trusted one friend, his vigilant Baskervillian hound.

What would he think of my problems? Was it even worth trying to explain?

"Not so great," I repeated.

Louis looked up, his dark, brooding eyes fixed on mine. The dog was watching me, too.

"How so?" he said.

I took a deep breath and unloaded on him, as they say. I told him about the ATF guys, but that wasn't a bad thing. I told him about my conversation with Abram.

"Hard when your beliefs start to fall apart," Louis said, from experience.

I told him about Abram and Semi, and he looked pained.

"They'll eat that kid up and spit him out," Louis said. "Naive and vulnerable, and guys like them, they're predators by instinct. Saw it in the Marine Corps. Some people just sense weakness. They can smell it."

He shook his head.

"Use him for whatever they can get out of him, and then they'll dump him by the side of the road."

"Use him for what?" I said. "Start a new Bible study?"

"You said Semi bought a rifle from one of these guys."

"Right. I saw him leaving. A Mini-fourteen."

"Kind of a popgun, but nice little nine-millimeter," Louis said. "Maybe this Abram kid has cash. Mennonites, Amish—they operate cash-only, right? Maybe they get him to start skimming the family strongbox."

"Front them money? For what?"

A piece snapped into place. Semi. Ramos and O'Day, the ATF agents. But Semi and Abram in Boston, roaming around the 'hood? That would be like Jed and Granny in Beverly Hills.

"I don't know," Louis said. "What do people like them usually do with money? They buy booze and drugs, right? Maybe sex to go with the other two."

"Abram's not into any of that," I said.

"Yet," Louis said.

It was all troubling, and it got worse the more I thought about it. Abram was smart, but he was a total naïf in the outlaw world of Semi and friends. Billy and Baby Fat? Abram would be like a goat staked in a lion's cage. He'd be in over his head so fast that he—

"Where's Clair?" Louis said.

I formed the words in my head.

"He should be back soon. He's doing me a favor."

Louis waited for the real answer. I told him about Billy and Baby Fat following Roxanne, our confrontation. I didn't tell him about Welt and what he added to the mix.

"So Clair pulled security detail?"

"He volunteered," I said.

"So those guys were stalking your wife and daughter?"

"Yeah. At least watching her. Thinking she'd lead them to me."

"And you'd lead them to me," Louis said.

"Probably," I said.

"You can put me on the roster for that detail."

"You don't have to do that."

"I started it," Louis said. "I'll finish it if I have to."

It was his martyr tone, the soldier ready for a suicide mission. We were talking about a scuffle in the woods of Prosperity, Maine, but his mind was steeped in killings in the dusty villages of Anbar Province.

"They track you down yet?"

"Not to here, that I know of. Somebody tipped them off that Roxanne was my wife, pointed her out. So then they see her, spot her driving by. Follow her to the farm."

"Semi must know your truck by now, too. Seen it twice—first at the gun sellers', then probably by the restaurant. And your Mennonite buddy there, if they're friends, he'll tell him about you. Town this size, nowhere to hide, at least for long."

I didn't answer, just took in the bad news.

"Thing is, I'm the one they're really after, not you or your wife and daughter," Louis said. "I did the worst damage to the worst guy."

"I'm sure they'd settle for whoever they can find," I said.

"A slippery slope, this kind of violence," Louis said. "Back and forth. Prisal and reprisal. Before you know it, everybody's fighting but nobody knows what the war was about."

"Hatfields and McCoys," I said.

"Shia and Sunnis."

"Catholics and Protestants."

"Buddhists and Muslims," Louis said. "But we got one advantage."

"We're on the side of right?" I said.

"That," Louis said, "and two of us are professional killers, trained by the United States government."

He looked at me and suddenly smiled—an eerie, black, and humorless grin.

I heard Clair's truck coming first. When I pulled up to the house, his truck was parked next to her Subaru. Roxanne and Sophie were waiting in the car while Clair went into the house. I was at the car when Clair came out, gave them a thumbs-up. I popped the door open and Sophie slid out, said, "Hey, Daddy. Clair's looking for you."

"Well, he was looking for me here, but I was at his house," I said.

"Well, he was down here looking for you when you were looking for him," Sophie said brightly. "We went to school and I played with Salandra on the playground and Mommy and Salandra's daddy did their work."

Roxanne was taking her bag out of the backseat. She looked across the top of the car and gave me a brittle smile. Clair came up and stood, hands on his hips.

"That's nice," I said.

"What did you do?" Sophie said.

"I talked to a boy named Abram who lives on a farm and has lots of horses."

"Maybe we can take Pokey there to visit," she said.

Roxanne came around the corner and Sophie told her, "Daddy's friend Abram has horses, so we're going to take Pokey there to play with them."

"That's quite a plan," Roxanne said.

"I want to go tell Pokey about it," Sophie said, and she started to run toward the side of the house and the trail to Clair's.

"No," Roxanne said, scrambling after her, grabbing her by the arm. "You stay with us."

"But Clair's here," Sophie said. "The bad men aren't gonna bother us."

Roxanne patted Clair on the shoulder as she led Sophie inside. The door shut and I looked up at the sky—overlapping layers of gray, the clouds sailing in different directions. As I gazed upward, raindrops ticked at my face. The rain started to fall heavier and Clair pulled at his hat.

"Thanks," I said.

"No problem. All quiet."

"You can't keep doing this. And I can't not work," I said.

"Maybe oughta call 'em out, get it over with."

"Louis is up at the barn," I said. "Wants to take the lead on this one."

"How are his spirits?"

"Okay at first, but then he got dark when I told him about Billy and Baby Fat watching Roxanne and Sophie."

"Gonna go light 'em up, is he?" Clair said.

"Thinks it's his fault. And he says you guys would have an advantage in a firefight."

"Probably right, but we don't want him committing some sort of suicide by thug," Clair said.

"No," I said. "We don't."

"Better go see that boy. Always on the precipice. Doesn't take much to send him over the edge."

He started for his truck. "He can fill you in," I called after him. "I've been talking to this Mennonite kid, for a story. He's having doubts about their religion. And he's started hanging out with Semi."

"Not somebody you'd be talking theology with."

"You never know," I said. "Maybe after trucks, guns, and girls."

"Always see the good in people, don't you, McMorrow," Clair said.

"No," I said. "I don't."

13

The rain had paused but the clouds had darkened. The wind was gusting out of the south, birds were flying low and fast into the trees, and there was a guttural rumble of thunder from the distance. I took my stuff out of the truck, rolled up the windows, and went inside to see if another storm was brewing.

It wasn't, not with Sophie up. She'd brought all of her stuffed animals down from her bed and lined them up on the couch in the living room. "I'm the teacher, Daddy," she said, when I walked in. "They are the children."

"What are you going to teach them?" I said.

"To always hold your mommy or daddy's hand when you cross the road," Sophie said. "And never talk to the bad men because they will hurt you because they like to fight and fight."

"They do, honey," I said. "But you don't have to think about that. They went back to their town."

"Where the bad men live?"

"Yes," I said. "Where the bad men live."

"I hope they don't live happily ever after," Sophie said.

I looked at her—six years old, and already thinking in terms of justice.

The next step would be revenge, unless the peace plan took hold and nipped her budding notions of an eye for an eye, a tooth for a tooth.

"Where's Mommy?" I said.

"She's upstairs. Talking on the phone."

I went up the stairs. Our bedroom door was half closed and Roxanne was inside, talking. I paused in the hallway as she said, "No, I'll work on the draft tonight, and I'll see you in the morning." A beat, and she added. "You, too."

As she hung up the phone, I started back down the stairs.

I was at my desk in the study when Roxanne came down and started dinner. She didn't come in, didn't ask me about my day. I got up and went to her, taking a Ballantine ale out of the refrigerator. She was filling a saucepan. She put it on the stove and turned the burner on and then went to the refrigerator and opened the door and rummaged inside. I was standing four feet from her but it was like I was invisible.

"How was the school?" I said.

"Fine," she said, taking out a bundle of asparagus and turning away, the refrigerator door closing behind her. She went to the counter and cut the ends off of the asparagus, put them on the stove by the pan.

"How's the planning coming?" I said.

"Good."

Back to the refrigerator, this time for some cooked chicken breasts. Back to the counter, where she started cutting the chicken into small pieces and dropping the pieces into a bowl.

"Chicken salad?"

"Yes."

She took grapes from a bunch on the counter and started chopping those, too, adding them to the chicken.

"I met some gun sellers," I said. "And two ATF agents. One was out of Boston."

She turned to the refrigerator, took out the mayonnaise, and turned back.

"A gun from around here turned up at a Boston homicide," I said. "Or so it appears."

Nothing.

"I met a Mennonite kid, too. He's doubting his faith, which is hard, because his father is the bishop of the outfit."

Still nothing.

"I bought the kid a coffee at Belle View."

Roxanne slipped past me. Celery. Turned back. Started ripping and chopping.

"I think he needed somebody to talk to," I said.

Roxanne put the uncut celery back in the bag and whipped around to the refrigerator again. Her mouth was clamped shut, her jaw clenched, but leaning into the refrigerator she took a deep breath through her nose and said, "I'm glad you were there for him."

And that was it.

Sophie chattered at dinner, about Salandra and taking Pokey to visit "Abraham"s' horses at his big farm, and about how she was going to tell Mrs. Brown about going to the school on a Sunday.

"Bonus points," I said.

"Everything isn't a competition," Roxanne said, then caught herself and started speaking to Sophie directly. I sat and ate and listened and drank another beer and when everyone was done, I got up and cleared the table.

Roxanne said it was bath time, and would I hold off on the dishes so there would be hot water. I stacked the dishes next to the sink and put away the food. They went upstairs and I slipped outside and stood in the growing darkness.

The thunderstorm was passing to the east, lightning showing through the trees and the thunder rumbling, but faintly. I walked to the end of the shed, then crossed to the truck. I unlocked the driver's door

and took the Glock from under the seat. With the gun in my waistband, I circled the property, stopping every thirty feet or so to listen.

Voles and mice scuffled in the duff of the woods. A robin cackled
as it shifted on its roost. At the east side of the property I could hear
music from Clair's barn, and when I strained, the faintest sound of
men's voices. Clair and Louis having a heart-to-heart.

I turned and crossed the back of the lawn, stopped at the northeast corner. Standing in the darkness, I breathed slowly and listened.
Wood frogs in the brush, the last of the peepers from the big marsh
across the road. And then a long metallic creak, followed by a *thunk*.

A door closing on a car.

Or a truck.

I slipped the gun out, racked a shell into the chamber. The noise
had come from the east, up the road. There was a turnoff there, a
woods road that was mostly overgrown, passable for maybe fifty feet.
And there was a path.

I eased along the tree line, searching for the opening. And then
there was a gap in the brush, showing as a lighter shade of gray. I
paused and listened, and then stepped in, putting one foot down,
then the other.

It was dark in the woods, no moon with the storm. There were no
lights on the east side of the house, our bedroom dark. I stared into
the blackness, walked slowly like it was a procession.

Step. Stop. Listen.

Step. Stop. Listen some more.

Again.

And then I was navigating by memory, peering into the trees,
the Glock clenched, snugged along my leg. Leaves brushed my face.
Spiderwebs. Mosquitoes buzzed my eyes, my ears. The trail curved
left and then, I knew, it bent to the right and began to climb. And
then it came out at the clearing, an elevated hummock sort of space
in the woods.

A low metallic click, like a door latch opening. A creak, like the one before. A distant hiss and spatter. Urine splashing leaves.

I kept my finger outside of the trigger guard. Shoot somebody while they were pissing? No, but I'd sure as hell make them keep their hands up.

Another forty feet, maybe. I smelled car exhaust, saw the glimmer of chrome through the trees, a dark blocky shape. I kept moving, the urination done, a figure standing at the edge of the trees.

Step. Stop. Listen.

Wait.

And then I could see it, the shape of a pickup. The figure moving back toward it, the door creaking and shutting with another *thunk*. The brake lights glowing on, a garish red light. The starter motor cranked, the motor coughed and then revved. I started to move faster, a walk, a trot. The lights were off and I could hear the truck moving, brush crushing under the tires.

It was down the path, onto the road. I was running, the branches slashing at my face. As I sprinted into the clearing, I heard the motor roar, and when I hit the road, it was a black shape receding into the distance.

I raised the gun. Sighted the shadow.

Let my finger fall away, and then the gun, slowly.

I walked back into the woods, used the light on my phone to check the tire marks. Four deep troughs where he had parked. The grass singed by his exhaust. I looked for cigarette butts or beer cans but found none. But then I did find a place where he had urinated, another spot where he'd stood, and the grass was trampled. I stood there and looked toward the house.

Our bedroom light came on. Roxanne stood in the window for a moment, a clean shot.

14

—m—

"I don't know," I said. "I heard it more than I saw it. Big guy, maybe alone, but maybe not. A V-8, loud exhaust but not as loud as Baby Fat's flatbed. Probably stock pipes, but old. Not new, but not a beater, either."

Clair stood with his arms crossed, looking across the yard at the house. The bathroom light was on now, Sophie out of the tub. Roxanne's figure flitted back and forth and then was gone.

"Could have been one of the outlaws," Clair said. "A truck you haven't seen. Or maybe your ATF boys have another vehicle."

He paused.

"Or maybe it was just somebody stopped to take a leak. And you almost shot him."

I looked at him.

"I aimed but I didn't fire," I said.

"You gotta know your target," Clair said.

"That's why I held off."

"Hell, if it had been Billy, would you have shot him in the back?"

I started to answer, stopped.

"No," I said.

"I'm worried about Louis, but I'm thinking maybe I should be worried about the two of you. He's self-destructing, and you're getting so worked up that you're trigger-happy."

Roxanne crossed in front of the window, the bathroom this time. I heard Sophie's chatter, the trill ringing across the yard.

"I won't have them threatening my family," I said.

"I don't think they have," Clair said.

"It's implied. Following Roxanne around town. Already told us—you, me, and Louis—that we're dead."

"Idle threats. That's what the judge will say when you're up on a manslaughter charge."

"You'd fight back. Of all people."

"I pick my fights. I pick my target. I pick my situation. I fire only when fired upon, or close to it. And, Jack, I control my emotions. You're too wound up."

I was silent.

"I told Louis it was time for him to get back to work. Be good for you, too. When the girls get to school tomorrow, come out and we'll finish up a chunk of the Hoddings' lot. Be back by the time they get out."

"I've got stories to work on," I said.

"I know. And potholders to crochet, I'm sure," Clair said. "But a few hours working in the woods will be good for what ails you. Come out to the lot after you get them squared away."

He turned away, started back toward the path to his barn. And then he stopped and turned back.

"Jack," he said.

"What?" I said.

"Get in there and get to work on your marriage. I'll keep an eye on things out here."

I tried. But Roxanne was reading to Sophie, and then she fell asleep on Sophie's bed, books scattered around them. I rattled around the study and the kitchen, even went in and patted her shoulder. She curled herself tighter. I went to bed. Lay there in the dark and listened. Got up in the night every two hours and stood at the window.

I peered at the watching spot, or the place where it was, hidden in the darkness. Was he back? Clair had said he'd keep an eye out, which for him meant more than a glance. I told myself that if the guy came down the road, if I missed it, Clair would be there. If the guy parked in the woods again, Clair would be standing behind him with a gun at his head.

It was what he did, after all. Force Recon in Vietnam. Crawling through the jungles with the enemy all around him. Silent and deadly and endlessly patient. And if he could do that, he could track one dirtbag in the Maine woods.

Reassured, I went back to the bed. Climbed in and lay on my back and then turned and reached up to the slot behind the headboard. The Glock was there. More reassurance, still.

And then it was morning, 4:45, and the sky turning blue-gray from black. I looked to my right, saw the empty space. Soured, I heaved myself up, reached for the gun. Even in the pale light, the threat seemed diminished, the cold, hard pistol somehow out of place. I thought of Clair's admonition, and wondered if he was right.

I got up and pulled on my jeans and T-shirt and, the gun in my waistband, padded down the hall. I peeked through the door into Sophie's room and saw Roxanne and Sophie sleeping, Roxanne's arm thrown over Sophie's hips. Mother and cub.

Closing the door, I went downstairs and slipped on moccasins and stepped outside. It had rained in the night and the ground was wet. To the south there were clouds—quiet; not the gunmetal storm front, but still heavy and dense.

I reached for my phone to check the forecast: 50 percent chance of showers through noon, 60 percent the rest of the day. We didn't cut wood in rain, the muddied ground too slick underfoot to be safe with a chain saw. But I had a feeling Clair was going to want us out there, for the therapeutic value if not the cordage.

Putting the phone away, I stepped around to the far side of the truck, glanced at the house, and slipped the Glock out of my jeans. I opened the door and put it back in place under the seat. Safety on.

Who said I was losing it?

Back inside, I made a silent breakfast: Cheerios and juice, and a cup of tea, the kettle's whistler lifted off. Then I made two peanut butter and jelly sandwiches for the woods, the ten o'clock break. I put the sandwiches in my lunch bag with a banana and an orange, filled my water bottle, and set them out on the counter.

I went to the study with my tea and checked my e-mail. There were messages from my editors at the *Times* and *Outland*, both checking on my progress, both reminding me of looming deadlines, both hoping things were going well.

My love life? Not really. Local dirtbags? Jury was still out. The stories? That was the only good news.

I wrote back, said my reporting was moving ahead. The gun story had the potential to be even stronger than I'd envisioned, I said, with a real-life homicide to hang it on. The Mennonites in Maine story could be stronger, too, with one of the potential subjects questioning his faith and his father's authority.

Sometimes you get lucky.

It was 5:35, the sun rising somewhere behind the clouds. I went out on the deck, saw the perimeter of brush and woods I'd walked the night before. I circled the yard, went out to the road, and walked across to the mailbox. I flipped the door open, peered inside. There was a flyer, something from a tanning parlor, first session free. I pulled it out and another piece of paper fluttered to the ground.

It was small, with ripped holes on one side, a page torn from a coil-bound notebook. I picked it up and turned it over. It said, in neat penciled script:

A lady at the store told me where you live. I can't talk to

you anymore, and nobody else will either. There is no story.
Abram

I turned it over. The back side was blank. Flipped back and read it again.

Short and sweet. Good-bye, Mennonites. Good-bye, three grand.

"Damn," I said.

I started back across to the house, and by the time I'd hit the driveway I'd decided I wouldn't give up, not after pumping the story up. I'd worked sources hard before, spent weeks and even months trying to persuade someone to talk to me. I could change his name, not that that would help him at home. I could set some parameters. Talk about Mennonite life more than his personal crisis. Give the Bishop every opportunity to talk about his congregation. Tell them the story would say how well received the Mennonites were in the larger community. Hard workers. Good farmers. Cute little kids, girls in bonnets. Let them think it was going to be a real Mennonite lovefest.

But I needed Abram, goddamn it.

Back in the house, I went to the study and put the note on my desk. I stared at it for a moment . . . the handwriting. It was cursive, carefully drawn. Was this how they were taught, in their one-room schoolhouse or whatever? Did they learn to write with chalk on slates?

I picked the note up and sniffed. A distinct odor of tobacco. Mennonites smoked, right? I pictured men with wide-brimmed hats and corncob pipes. But how did they get here? Clip-clop the ten miles in a buggy? Or get a ride from a cigarette-smoking English in his pickup?

And another question: Who the hell had been in the woods last night?

The sun was hardly up and things were starting to go off the rails. I had an urge to drive right over to the farm, see if I could start working on Abram first thing.

Or was the note from him at all? Did Semi tell him I was trouble? Did Semi not want me poking around in his business?

There was a stirring upstairs, Roxanne's footsteps headed to the bathroom. I went and refilled the kettle and put it on the burner. The shower came on as I filled the coffeemaker: her favorite vanilla roast. The water started to drip, and I heard the shower go off, the bathroom door open.

I went to the cupboard and got out flour and oil, then milk and butter from the refrigerator. I mixed the stuff up in a bowl, grabbed a bag of frozen blueberries from the freezer, poured them in, too.

When Roxanne came down, dressed in jeans and flats, a white open-necked blouse, Sophie tagging behind her, sleepy-eyed and dragging her stuffed lamb by the neck, the pancakes were sizzling. Sophie brightened. Roxanne didn't.

"Daddy made my favorite," Sophie said. I grabbed her and swung her up and gave her a hug. I gave the lamb a squeeze, too, and then put the two of them down in the chair at the table. I turned and flipped the pancakes; Roxanne poured herself coffee.

"Want some?" I said.

"No, thanks," she said. "I'll just have toast."

I sat with Sophie and ate pancakes with her, poured the syrup. Roxanne stood at the counter and checked her e-mail on her phone. Sophie ate two pancakes before Roxanne said, "Go easy, honey," like she'd been chugging beer.

I got up and cleared the plates, said, "I'm working in the woods this morning. I'll head over when you go to school."

"Okay," Roxanne said, and then, "Honey, time to get dressed."

"Once you're inside, I'll head out."

Sophie dashed down the hallway and up the stairs. Roxanne was pouring another cup of coffee as I said, "So how long is this going to go on?"

She put the carafe back on the machine, poured milk in her mug. Stirred. Turned to me.

"I'm sorry, Jack," she said. "It's hard to go from more mortified than I've ever been in my life to hugs and kisses."

"I'm sorry," I said.

"You're sorry about the result," Roxanne said. "Not sorry you said those things to Welt. Or fought with that man. Or have a gun in your truck."

Yes, I thought. That about summed it up.

"I've got to get Sophie ready," Roxanne said, and she was gone.

I loaded my truck with gas, saws, oil, tools. They came outside and I gave Sophie a big hug and put her in the back of Roxanne's car and buckled her in.

"Salandra's daddy's truck has a backseat," she said.

"Good for him," I said.

"She said I could ride with them when Mrs. Robinson's class goes to see the goats."

"Oh, fun," I said. "When's that?"

"Today," she said, holding up her bag. "We have to bring our mud boots."

I said, "Well, don't let the big billy goats bonk you in the butt."

Sophie laughed. I closed the door, looked across the roof of the car at Roxanne. "Have a good field trip," I said.

"We will, I'm sure," Roxanne said, and she got in the car and closed the door.

I followed them out of our road, glancing at the place where the mystery truck had been parked. I wondered whether we should leave the house unattended all day, but then figured I'd go in first when we got home. And maybe by then Roxanne would have thawed a bit. An afternoon with Welt at the farm . . .

I kept the Subaru in sight as we made our way to Prosperity Primary, a cozy brick complex with a bright blue roof, set in a former pasture. Roxanne parked in the staff lot and I pulled the gun out from under the seat, laid it on my lap as I watched. She and Sophie gathered their bags and hurried to the door, which Roxanne keyed open with her ID. The door closed behind them and I made a loop around the parking lot.

Teachers and parents, backpack-toting kids bailing out of minivans like paratroopers. I looked for the red work van, the ATF soft car, but didn't see it. Maybe they were on Semi today. Worse yet, maybe they'd gone home.

Louis and Clair had already unloaded when I got to the wood yard. The skidder was off the flatbed and Clair was sitting in the seat as the diesel idled. He saluted me as I pulled in and stopped and Louis came over to my Toyota and put his saws and gear in the back with mine. And then the big black hound jumped up into the truck bed, claws scratching at the metal.

The dog sat. Louis climbed in. Clair revved the skidder motor and there was a burst of blue smoke as the big orange machine lurched forward, chained tires digging into the mud.

I followed, easing along in low gear, the truck jouncing down the trail.

"How you doing?" I said.

"Fair," Louis said.

"Me, too."

"So I heard. Clair said you called out some guy's been hitting on your wife. And you torqued on Billy's broken arm with your little kid watching."

"When you're on a roll," I said.

Louis was quiet, then said, "Billy backed off?"

"With a promise to get even."

"And the other guy?"

"He gave me a lecture about male machismo and violence and treating women like property."

"You restrained yourself?"

"Yeah. But too late. Damage is done."

"Everybody's got something," Louis said.

"Except your dog," I said.

"Don't think he doesn't have his cross to bear."

"What's that?"

I looked at Louis and he looked back at me.

"Right," I said.

We were going to the north end of the parcel, where we'd left off before we'd scrapped with the other crew. It was about a mile in, fifteen minutes at this speed. I waited two or three, then said, "You shouldn't make all of this personal. It's not your fault."

Louis shrugged.

"I take responsibility for all my actions, good and bad," he said. "It's the only way to confront evil, to acknowledge it, and your part in it. But if you pretend evil doesn't exist inside you, then you allow it to flourish."

I considered that.

"But mistakes aren't evil," I said. "Sometimes they're just mistakes."

"There's black on one end, white on the other," Louis said. "In the middle there's one long stretch of gray. And it keeps pitching back and forth. If you're weak, you let the dark side prevail, not necessarily in one action but in a bunch of little ones. Evil grows in very small increments."

"Baby steps," I said.

Louis nodded. The truck rolled along, the skidder roared and lurched and smoked. The woods around us looked like rain forest, something primeval.

"So breaking Billy's arm?" I said.

"That tipped the balance," Louis said.

"And now you're tipping it back?"

"Trying, McMorrow. Always trying."

"And if breaking one guy's arm was something, then what about the whole Iraq war?" I said.

"Wasn't the whole war," Louis said, half to himself. "It was one day. One minute. One second. Won't live long enough to earn that back."

The dog was on his feet now, sniffing the forest air. Deer, coyotes, raccoons, and foxes—he probably saw them in the scent, like ghosts.

"Serious damage to the karma," he said. "Some things you can't make up."

"It was war," I said. "Most of it's out of your control."

I downshifted and we rocked over ruts. The dog scrabbled to stay upright. When the truck had righted, Louis said, "He was fifteen, sixteen, McMorrow. Just a child."

"He was blowing up your buddies," I said, looking over at him. "You're a good person, Louis."

"Good people on the other side, too," he said. "All of us good people, blowing each other to bits."

He smiled, shook his head, started to slip away to a place I imagined was dark and guilt-ridden and suffocating. As I drove, passing fresher slash piles where we'd logged last, I tried to pull him back.

"Christians would say that God can wash away your sins," I said. "It's all about redemption. I met this Mennonite kid up here, he was talking about it. Old Order Mennonite, kind of like Amish. He's trying to figure it all out."

"He has sins he needs to have washed away?"

"He's been hanging around with Semi," I said.

"Ah," Louis said. "Then he will." He turned away, staring out the window at the woods.

But what were they? I thought about it as we worked, Louis and me, felling and limbing trees, Clair in full work mode: moving the machine into position, waiting at the controls as we affixed the chains, dragging the logs to a new wood yard. The rain held off but the cloud cover and fog coated everything with a fine mist. In the still, damp air the mosquitoes homed in, and we kept wiping ourselves down with repellent, our hands streaking our faces and arms until we were camouflaged with mud and blood.

I tried to concentrate, but when I was limbing, hauling the slash into piles, Abram crept in. Abram trying to find his way. Abram racked with guilt about being a bad son, a bad brother, a bad Mennonite. Abram trying to figure out where he fit in a world that had people like Billy, but people like Miriam, too. Abram hanging with Semi.

Why him? I thought of Semi in the fight—part jock, part outlaw. What did he offer Abram? I dropped an oak, pondered it as I started cutting. Abram was with family all the time. Miriam. Victor. Younger kids. His parents. Semi would have a crowd. With Semi, Abram could, for the first time, be one of the guys.

Would that be enough? I pictured a lot of backslapping, drinking cheap beer, Abram being called "dude." It would be novel, comfortable, somehow supportive. But how long would it take for Semi to show his violent side, the kid who went for the gun?

We'd paused for the skidder to do its work when Louis came up to me. He put his saw down, then stood looking away for a moment, the way he did when he had something to say.

"You like this Mennonite kid, huh?"

"Yeah," I said. "He reminds me of myself, way back when."

"You should tell him to hang on to his faith. Sometimes it's all you got. And once you lose it, it's pretty damn hard to get it back."

"I'll pass that on," I said.

He looked away again, then said, "I thought good reporters weren't supposed to get attached to people in their stories."

"Who said I was a good reporter?" I said.

Louis looked at me, picked up his saw, and walked away.

Problem was, even if Abram didn't want to talk to me, I wanted to talk to him, story or no story. I wanted to keep him from going too far off course, so far he wouldn't ever get back.

So when it began to rain, the sound a growing hiss from high in the forest canopy, I knew where I was going. When the rain came harder and broke through the trees, I had a plan.

We drove back to the first wood yard, the dog, who had waited all morning in the bed of my truck, up front now, draped across Louis's lap. He was a hundred pounds of muscle, his brown eyes alert like a snake's. The dog was quiet, and Louis was, too. The three of us were dirty and wet and smelled of oil and gas and exhaust. When we got to the yard, Clair rumbling up behind us, then driving hard up onto the trailer, Louis opened the door and the dog leapt out. Louis followed and I slid down, too. He transferred his stuff to Clair's pickup, and then he came back and leaned on the side of the bed of my truck. The dog went to the wheel of the trailer and peed.

"You have a good day, McMorrow," Louis said, and I felt like we'd gotten closer somehow, with our talk of good and evil.

"You, too, Louis," I said.

"I'll be bunking in at Clair's for a bit, doing some work up here," he said.

"Good. Then I'll see you."

He nodded, like he was agreeing with himself, and then he said, "This Mennonite kid."

"Abram," I said.

"I'd like to meet him," Louis said. "I think me and him, we may not be wrestling in the same class, but we're in the same sort of fight."

I looked at him, waited, and hoped for more.

"Trying to figure out who the good guys are, wondering if we're one of them. On the right team, you know what I mean? You think you have it all figured out and then you start to get these doubts creeping in. And you know that if the thing starts to unravel, all of it comes apart. And then where are you? I mean, what's left, if you can't believe you're doing the right thing?"

"Sure," I said, getting it. "You and Abram, I think you'd have a lot to talk about."

Same quandary, one guy going into battle unarmed, the other armed to the teeth.

15

The horses were pulling some sort of mowing bar, cutting six-foot swaths of corn. The team was at the far end of the field, and I could see the white-shirted figure at the reins. I parked under the shade of a big roadside oak and shut off the motor, the rain pattering on the truck roof. The horses were still headed away from me, not yet at the far end of the cornfield. I settled back into the seat to wait.

As I watched, the team came to a halt. I saw the driver, presumably Abram, slip down from his seat and bend over the machinery. I reached to the glove box and fished out a pair of binoculars, rolled down my window, raised them, and focused.

It was Abram. He was yanking on something on the bar, maybe freeing some sort of jam, the wet cornstalks bound up. I wondered if he'd be calling it quits.

"Come on, Abram," I said to myself. "Come on down this way."

And I felt something at my left shoulder. A puff of air, a whiff of tobacco.

I turned. A big man with a dark ruff of a beard was staring at me. He was dressed like Abram. His expression was stern and foreboding.

"You must be the Bishop," I said.

"You must be the reporter," he said. "We need to talk."

I opened the door and slid out and stood, and he still had three inches on me. His eyes were black-brown and intense. His chest was big under the white shirt, and his muscled arms were farmer-tan against his white shirt.

I held out my hand. He kept his hands behind his back.

"I've met your son," I said. "We had coffee at the—"

"I know you did," the Bishop said. "I ask that you not do that again."

His accent the same, Canadian, a hint of German thrown in.

"It was off the record, if that's—"

"There is nothing here for you. There is no story for your newspaper. We don't seek attention. We just want to be left alone."

I smiled, mollifyingly, I hoped.

"Oh, I understand. The story I was thinking of wasn't as much about you as it was about your reception here. How this old-fashioned way of living and farming has reinvigorated the community. How you and your Mennonite friends and relatives are bringing back farmland that had been fallow for decades. How—"

"No one in our community will talk to you."

"I understand, Bishop, but this is a free country. They can decline, but you can't prevent me from asking—"

"And you are forbidden from talking to Abram."

I hesitated. His expression hadn't changed, and his position, arms behind his back like a bodyguard, hadn't either.

"I'm not part of your church, sir," I said.

"Stay away from my son."

This time it was an order, and I wondered if his hands were clenched behind his back to keep from breaking a Mennonite edict against physical violence. I held my hands out to calm him.

"I understand what you're saying, but you don't have authority over me. And I like your son. He's a good guy. I mean, I don't want to bother him. We were just—"

"I'm speaking to you as his father."

"I see that."

"He isn't himself," the Bishop said. "I think there are bad influences, wicked influences, that are trying to lure him away from God's path. It's always the way. It's a narrow path we walk."

"Well, that's not me, just so you know. I don't want to lure Abram away from anything. We were just having a conversation."

"He told me you told him about New York."

"Yeah. I lived there for a long time. I grew up there. He was asking; your daughter Miriam, she was asking, too. They were just curious."

The hands came out from behind his back, the right clenched into a fist. He put it in front of my face and shook it.

"You are forbidden to talk to my daughter."

"Okay, okay," I said. "Easy. I spoke to her once, in a group of young people. Right here on the edge of the field. I was just curious about the community here, and they were curious about me."

"You're Jack McMorrow," the Bishop said.

"That's right."

"I've been told that you're a violent person."

I looked at him.

"Well, it's all relative, I guess. But I don't consider myself—"

"Do you know the way to hell, Mr. McMorrow?"

"Uh, doing very bad things?"

" 'Wide is the gate, and broad is the way that leadeth to destruction, and many there be which go in thereat,' " the Bishop said.

"I'm sure," I said. "No lack of bad people in the world. Sometimes it seems like evil is the rule, not the—"

"The wicked shall be turned into hell, and all the nations that forget God. The fearful, and unbelieving, and the abominable, and murderers and whoremongerers and sorcerers and idolaters, and all liars, shall have their part in the lake which burneth with fire and brimstone."

His eyes were burning, too, his voice cracking with emotion.

"I try to tell the truth," I said.

"I do not want my son to go to hell," the Bishop bellowed. "I will not let him be led astray."

A big finger flicked out of the fist like a switchblade and pointed at my nose. "Stay away from my son. Stay away from my family. Stay away from our farm. Stay away from this community."

I reached out and took his wrist and pushed the fist away from my face. His tendons flexed and I could feel his arm start to cock, but then he relaxed and let his arm fall to his side.

The other cheek turning.

I started to form the words that would warn the Bishop about the likes of Semi and Billy, but I caught myself.

"How old is Abram?" I said.

"He's nineteen."

"And his sister? Miriam?"

"She's eighteen."

"Then they're legal adults, adults in most other ways. If you've done your job, then you shouldn't have anything to worry about."

"Don't tell me how to do my job," the Bishop said. "The Lord tells me how to do my job."

There was a pause, no logical rejoinder to make to that. I heard the clinking of chains and turned to see the horses and Abram starting back toward us, the cutter bar clanking and the corn falling flat.

"They've been told not to speak with you," the Bishop said. "There is no story here. Go."

He pointed to the horizon, like I was being cast out of the Garden of Eden. I half turned back toward the truck, then stopped and turned back. His arm was still raised, as if in some sort of trembling salute.

"With all due respect, sir, for your faith and your position," I said, "this is a public road, and I can stay here all day if I choose to. And any story I'd write? That's the least of your problems."

I got back in the truck, and with a last glance at Abram approaching with the horses, I started the motor and drove off. As I rattled down the road, I thought, And the least of mine.

It was a short drive back down to the main road, black clouds rolling over the treetops to the east. As I zigzagged my way south, I glanced at the shrouded driveways that burrowed into the woods: a rusty chain strung between trees, a sign that said KEEP OUT!!!, a faded yellow school bus, tires flat and saplings grown up all around it. A leaf-littered pickup blocking a road, its windshield riddled with bullet holes.

Who were these people, hidden away in the Maine woods? Idolaters and fornicators? Sorcerers and whoremongerers? How did he wall himself off? How did the Bishop expect to keep his community—and his children—pure?

I guess you just prayed.

It was five miles to the Belle View. Time for a cup of tea and, with the Mennonite story mired, some serious regrouping. I followed an old couple in an old pickup, their two white heads bobbing on the bumps. They drove below the speed limit, no rush at their age, and pulled into the restaurant lot in front of me. They parked and I pulled in next to them, watched as the old guy got out and hobbled around and opened his wife's door.

Chivalry isn't totally dead, I thought, but the wife said, "You keep saying you're gonna fix that door."

I watched them in the mirror as they crossed the lot to the restaurant. He held the door and she toddled through. I smiled, got out, was at the end of my truck when the big Dodge flatbed pulled in.

Baby Fat at the wheel. Billy in the middle. Beefy on the far side. The truck slid to a halt. Baby Fat smiled and waved for me to cross. I hesitated, then started, and he floored the accelerator, then the brakes again, stopping six inches from my right hip.

"You done?" I said.

They were out of the truck on both sides, grinning as they approached me. I turned and stood my ground. They stopped just short of me, Billy saying, "Just want to clear the air."

He was red-faced and unshaven, the bottle scar showing on his neck, tobacco stains on his teeth and the corner of his mouth. Baby Fat had his chin thrust out, his camo hat on backwards, a roll of flab circling his waist. Beefy was a step back, closer to the truck.

He had a chew going, too, and he spat at my feet.

"Cancer of the mouth," I said. "Couldn't happen to a nicer bunch of guys."

"Shit, McMorrow," Billy said. "Just when we try to make up, you go getting all ornery."

I didn't answer, the three of us facing each other like it was the O.K. Corral.

"So, nothing to say?" Beefy said.

I shook my head.

"Think you're a real tough guy, picking on a guy with a busted arm," Billy said. "Buncha witnesses to take your side."

I tried to stay calm, but the words welled up and out.

"Takes a real tough guy to follow a woman around. You have something to say to me, just say it. Right now. You want to go, we can do that, too. Right here. Right now."

I looked at Billy, then at Baby Fat, then back at Beefy. Their grins were sagging. Baby Fat took a shuffling half step toward me and turned, ready to swing. "You sorry son of a—"

Billy reached out with his good arm.

"I see what you're doing, reporter boy," he said. "Get him to throw the first punch, old farts watching out the window. Get us locked up and you go on your pussy-ass way."

He leered.

"No worries, McMorrow. We ain't here to beat the shit outta you."

He pulled Baby Fat back and they both moved past Beefy toward their truck.

"We was just gonna talk, you know?"

They were moving away now, by the truck doors. They got in, slammed the doors shut. I moved toward my truck, the Glock under the seat. Baby Fat revved the motor and spun the tires, stopped beside me. Billy leaned over Baby Fat toward the driver's window, spat on the ground at my feet.

"What I was gonna say, reporter boy, is you got one sweet old lady. Pretty as a picture, and that ass? That ass is to freakin' die for."

"You come near her again, I'll blow your head off," I said.

Billy gave a snort, wiped spittle from his chin with his forearm.

"There you go again. Just when I try to pay you a compliment, you go making threats."

"Not a threat. A fact," I said.

Beefy smiled now, showing stained teeth, dark grit in his gums. "She don't want to be looked at, McMorrow, she oughta close the curtains," he said.

"Or maybe she likes being looked at," Billy said. "Lotta chicks get off on it. Hey, maybe that goat farmer, he likes looking at her, too. Maybe does more than look."

Billy fell back into the truck as Baby Fat hit the throttle. Gravel sprayed and the exhaust blared. And then the truck slid to a halt again. Billy called, "We're coming, reporter boy. We're coming for you. We bang your old lady, that's fucking gravy."

The truck lurched forward and peeled out of the parking lot, headed east.

I sat in the booth and sipped my tea. Put pen to notebook paper but wrote nothing. Belle came over and asked me if I was okay. I said I was, but not much more.

"My sister-in-law's niece, I talked to her," she said. "She said she can't talk to you. If Billy found out, he'd come and kill her."

She paused, bent toward me, wiping the edge of my table with a cloth.

"She said he's a psychopath and a predator. A sex predator. She thinks he molested their babysitter, but she won't talk either."

"Why is somebody like that even loose?" I said.

Belle tucked the cloth in the back of her jeans. "Because nobody's taken him out," she said.

16

The first gun seller was a place called Frankie's Gun Traders, in the town of Dixville, fifteen miles north. I drove fast, porpoising over the Dixville Hills. There were mist-covered mountains rising on the distant horizon, but I saw little of the view, my hands clenching the wheel, eyes on the road. My neck was stiff as I craned for the landmarks the guy had described: a fieldstone signpost, a chicken barn turned into apartments, an abandoned church with no steeple.

And then I turned. Drove the prescribed half mile down a side road. Saw the sign and then the shop, a converted garage appended to a ranch house in the middle of a field.

The guy's name was Darrell, not Frankie. He was neatly bearded, my age, brisk. He was making money on volume, selling Czech knock-offs. New semiautomatic pistols in three calibers: .380, .40, and .45. The guns ranged in price from $155 to $210. He lined up all three on the counter for me to inspect. "What you got here is pretty much protection guns," he said. "Does the same job as a Glock but for hundreds less."

The guns looked lethal but cheap, like they might kill somebody or they might just blow up in your hand. I pulled out my wallet and some of *Outland*'s cash, and bought a .45 and a box of ammunition. He asked for my driver's license and I laid it on the counter. My name went on the bottom of a very long list of names.

When he turned to put the gun in a box, I ran quickly down the list.

"What happens if you don't have an ID?" I said.

"No deal," Darrell said. "Maine license or carry permit."

"That happen very often?"

"Once in a while. It's in the ad, but they figure they'll sweet-talk me. I tell 'em to take their money and hit the road."

And with that, our business was done.

It was 12:55. The next stop was another ten miles northwest: Detroit, which the locals pronounced *DEE-troit*, to differentiate it from its beleaguered namesake. Detroit, Maine, while not exactly downtrodden, wasn't in its prime, either. The town's heyday was when small farms filled the countryside, or maybe when egg farmers had built chicken barns. The chickens were gone, most of the farms, too, pastures grown up with poplar. But commerce went on, in this case being transacted by a guy named Sam, who, according to the ad, was selling a Marlin .308 caliber rifle with a Bushnell scope, and a Smith & Wesson nine-millimeter handgun with two holsters and four seventeen-round magazines.

The rifle was sold. The handgun was still available.

Sam was older, maybe seventy, thinning white hair tied in a ponytail, the whole thing tied back by a Sylvester Stallone–style headband. He had a bull's-eye tattoo on his left forearm, a military insignia—an eagle clutching a rifle in its talons—on the right. His expression was vigilant, eyes narrowed.

"You in the service?" I said.

"Yeah, but the fighting ended before I could get over to 'Nam."

"Too bad."

"I was ready," Sam said.

"I'm sure."

"Didn't know I'd end up fighting for my rights back home the rest of my life."

"How's that?"

"Liberals," he said.

"Ah," I said.

"A lot of good men died, too, get old Georgie off our backs. Read much about the Revolution?"

"Some."

"I've got a whole room full of books about that war. Hell of a fight, outgunned and outnumbered. Total miracle we pulled it off. Now, with the liberals, it's no guns for civilians. No God in schools. All the power to the central state? What does that sound like?"

I thought.

"Soviet Union?"

"Or Communist China. Take your pick."

"Right."

"Democracy isn't something you're given. It's something you have to earn. Every day."

"I see," I said.

"That's why I sell firearms. Every time I put a firearm in the hands of a law-abiding citizen, I uphold and defend the Second Amendment."

I nodded, picked up the S&W. It was solid and comfortable compared with the cheap knockoff.

"What do you do when you're not selling firearms, Sam?" I said.

"Diesel mechanic. Taught me in the army. But I'm retired. You?"

"I work for one of the other freedoms. The press."

He tensed.

"Reporter?"

"Right."

"You working now?"

"On a story about the firearms business in Maine. Would you mind talking on the record?"

He looked at me from underneath the headband.

"Mind? Hell, no. Free speech—I exercise that all the time, too."

So he did, repeating most of what he'd said, a little more. I scribbled in my notebook. When he was starting to slow, I thought of the ATF guys, and said, "How would you feel if one of the guns you sold was used in a homicide?"

"I'd feel like crap," Sam said. "But there's only so much I can do."

"Like what?"

"You got a permit to carry a concealed weapon in the state of Maine?"

"Me, personally?"

"Yeah."

"Yeah, I do," I said.

"Then I'd sell to you. No valid permit, no handgun deal. Proves you're not a criminal or a nut job."

"I see," I said. "What about long guns?"

"I gotta like the cut of your jib."

"So who bought the rifle, Sam?"

"Lawyer from Augusta, this one. Kind of a city type. Said his buddy offered to take him hunting and he didn't want to show up empty-handed. Usually I get the locals. Before him, a coupla farm boys, from down the road a piece," he said. "Nice kids. Getting ready for deer season. One of 'em, he was interested in a handgun, but no dice. Like I told you."

"He didn't have a permit?"

"Nah. One buying the rifle didn't even have a driver's license. I said, 'How you get around?' He says, 'Good Samaritans.' I said to myself, 'Any boy knows the Bible, he's good people.' "

I paused.

"So you interested in the handgun?" Sam said.

"I think I'll pass."

"How do I see this story?"

"I'll call you when it comes out. You can read it online."

"Deal."

"So, Sam," I said, "what did the Samaritan kid look like?"

"Oh, I don't know," he said, putting the S&W back in its case. "Nice-looking kid. Your height, in shape like farm kids are. Aren't sitting on the goddamn couch in front of goddamn video games all day."

"Right."

"Kind of old-fashioned-acting. Polite. Respectful. Even had kind of an old-fashioned haircut, like he cut his hair himself."

"Where'd you say he was from? Maybe I could talk to him?"

Sam looked at me.

"I didn't say. But it was one of those towns down around Hyde, past Posterity."

"Prosperity?"

"Yeah, that was it."

"Huh. That's where I live. Maybe I know them. The other guy? What did he look like?"

"Jeez, you reporters got a million questions, don't you."

I smiled.

"A little rougher around the edges. Bigger kid, built like a basketball player. Didn't say too much, except he wanted the handgun. Had a bruise on his cheek, a scrape. I asked him how he got it, and he said mixed martial arts—you know, where they punch and kick each other? I guess I got the basketball part wrong."

"Huh," I said. "So he was the designated driver?"

"Yup. Put the rifle behind the truck seat. Said they'd e-mail me a photo when they got their deer. Then they said they had to get back. Smaller kid said his dad would be missing him on the farm. And then went roaring off."

"Roaring."

"Right. Kids like that loud exhaust."

"Was this pickup a red Chevy? Older truck, black spoke rims?"

"Yeah. So you do know them?"

"Pretty well," I said. "One more than the other."

I mulled it over all the way back to Prosperity, and kept coming up with the same conclusion: Abram was buying guns with Semi, and in pretty sizable volume, the way our paths kept crossing. He was the wholesome one, the farm boy with the innocent smile. Why couldn't Semi pull it off himself? Maybe he didn't want his name tied to the guns, if, as in the Boston case, they were tied to a crime. Maybe some people were suspicious of him, his outlaw feel. Maybe he had felonies on his record. Maybe sellers didn't always like the cut of Semi's jib.

But who wouldn't like Abram, who looked like John-Boy Walton and could quote the Bible?

It was after 2:15 and Sophie got out of school at 2:30. Roxanne was usually there for another hour, so that gave me just enough time to make the twenty-mile trip back to Prosperity, provide an armed escort from the school to home. When I thought of Billy's leering threats, I picked up the pace.

I rolled into the parking lot at 2:50, shut off the truck, and reached for the Glock, left the knockoff .45 in its box. I placed the Glock on the passenger seat, covered it with a notebook, and sat back and waited.

The rain had stopped, the sky had lightened. The school was quiet, the buses gone, but a handful of parents were sitting in their cars. The field trip was late.

I picked up a notebook and went over my notes from the gun guys, filling in the words where they'd been skipped or were illegible. It was good stuff, and once I had the law enforcement side, I'd be ready to write. I wondered if I could get the family of the homicide victim in Boston, see what they had to say about guns in Maine.

I Googled *homicide* and *Boston* on my phone and came up with dozens of hits, including the last one of 2014, a black teenage guy who was number fifty-two. I put the phone back down.

Still quiet. I looked at my watch. It was 3:05. I called Roxanne. No answer. I texted, *Hey, where are you?* Waited a minute. No reply.

Sophie had said she was going to ride in Salandra's daddy's big truck. Did that mean Roxanne, too? Well, she wouldn't be taking the bus. I heard Billy's sneering voice. *Maybe that goat farmer, he does more than look.*

I scowled, scanned the nearly empty lot. Took a deep breath and picked the notebook up off the Glock. It was my Mennonite notebook, initialed "OOM" on the front cover. I flipped past my notes of my conversation with Abram and Miriam and their friend Victor. Past the notes from my chat with Abram at the restaurant. At the next blank page I wrote what I recalled of my conversation with the Bishop, if it could be called that.

Do you know the way to hell, Mr. McMorrow?

How had he said it? *Wide is the gate, and broad is the way that leadeth to destruction.*

Leadeth.

I sat back in the seat. I felt for him, as he truly believed that Abram might be straying from the righteous path. What would you do if you thought someone was sending your child to spend eternity in hell? Kill that person and take the rap yourself? Would I kill to save Sophie's soul?

In a heartbeat.

A strange thought to have, sitting in the parking lot of an elementary school. I looked out at the playground, the peace garden, the frog pond with its wire safety fence. When the kids went to collect tadpoles they wore life jackets. What we did to protect our children from the world. Buckled them in, held their hands when they crossed the street.

Sat in school parking lots, handguns locked and loaded.

At that point a minivan rolled in, a woman at the wheel whom I recognized as a mom from Sophie's class. Then a Toyota pickup, a dad driving and two boys in the backseat. An Audi station wagon, a mom and two more of Sophie's classmates.

The field trip was back.

Mrs. Robinson, Sophie's teacher, was with a mother in an SUV. She got out, stood in the parking lot in her tall rubber boots. She had a clipboard and she was checking kids off, noting that they had returned from the goat farm. The cars rolled out one by one, and finally Mrs. Tracy went into the school.

No Roxanne. No Sophie.

I waited, the good Jack and the bad Jack jostling for position. *Maybe that goat farmer likes to do more than look.* Roxanne saying, *I've never been so mortified in my life.*

Tell him again to back off. Or be conciliatory, give old Welt a big smile, ask about the goats. Make Roxanne happy. Or, at least, happier.

And then the shiny Tacoma wheeled down the entrance road and into the lot. Welt was driving, Roxanne in the passenger seat. They were smiling, laughing. When was the last time Roxanne had laughed with me?

I choked back my resentment and got out of the truck, locking it behind me, the Glock on the seat. Sophie saw me from the back of the cab and waved as they passed. I followed them to the door and walked up as Welt got out.

He smiled.

"Jack. You missed a great day."

I smiled back.

"I'm sure."

Roxanne came around the rear of the truck, opened the back door. Sophie slid out and down and beamed as she ran to me.

"Daddy," she said. "I milked a goat. All by myself."

"Wow, honey. Did you bring me some goat's milk?"

"No, but we brought you some cheese."

Salandra ran up, handed Sophie a brown paper bag, the Heaven Sent Farm label printed on it. The cheese.

And then Roxanne.

"Hey," she said.

"I was driving by," I said. "Thought I'd see how the day went."

"I had to get the milk out of the udder," Sophie said.

"Which one?" I said. "This one or the udder one?"

"No, Daddy," she said, laughing.

"Gonna make a farm girl out of her," Welt said, and for a moment I thought he meant Roxanne.

"Thanks for having the whole crew, Welt," I said.

"Oh, my pleasure, Jack," he said, bygones clearly being bygones in the Welt Prescription for Peace. "It was a great time, didn't you think, Roxanne?"

Their eyes met and there was a pause, a moment of connection. Some sort of understanding, a shared experience. I felt like a third wheel, fought it off.

"Daddy," Sophie said. "You should learn to milk the goats. It's really warm and it comes squirting out."

"Did you drink some?"

"It has to be—"

"Pasteurized?" I said.

"We sell raw milk," Welt said, "but I wouldn't give it to the kids without their parents' permission."

"Of course not," I said. "That would be—"

I looked at him.

"—overstepping your bounds."

Roxanne gave me a look, and then the girls were hugging good-bye and Welt gave me a pat on the shoulder, said he'd see me around. Roxanne got a finger wave from him—for my benefit?—and then she was getting into the car with Sophie.

The truck rolled out. Then Roxanne's Subaru. I was the rear guard in the motorcade, the Secret Service car packed with weapons.

Billy was out there. Baby Fat, too. I reached over and touched the gun.

17

That afternoon Roxanne went upstairs to finish preparing her presentation for the school board. I went to the barn with Sophie. She chattered about goats and udders and teats, not to me, but to Pokey as she rode him around the paddock.

Pokey plodded and appeared to listen patiently. Clair came out of the house and waved and then stood beside me. After I told him about my day, he said, "Could talk to them."

"Break more of their limbs?" I said.

"Couldn't hurt."

"Legs this time," I said.

"Been done," Clair said.

I told Clair about the Bishop, and he disagreed that I was violent. "Maybe by Old Order Mennonite standards," Clair said. "Compared to the rest of the world, you're a librarian."

I smiled.

"Louis told me he's going to be staying with you more."

"Seemed like a good idea. He has trouble being alone."

"The demons come when it's just him and his thoughts?"

"That's why he's such a vampire, roaming all night, sleeping all day. He said he has fewer nightmares when it's light out."

"What's he going to do here, out all night?" I said, but I'd barely uttered the words when I knew the answer. "He can patrol until these guys are in jail or gone," I said.

"It's what he does," Clair said. "Or did, in Iraq."

"That won't bother him?"

"It wasn't fighting that got to him. He's one tough son of a bitch."

From Clair, high praise.

"It was fighting with no purpose," he said. "Seeing his best buddies, dearest friends die, often horribly, and then handing the territory back to the enemy. Fallujah. Helmand. Just a shameful waste of brave soldiers."

"The underlying cause wasn't just," I said.

"The intention was. Analysis and implementation was flawed."

"This is simple to analyze. The guy threatened to assault Roxanne."

"No confusion about who the enemy is," Clair said.

"None whatsoever," I said.

Sophie had stopped talking and was making faint clucking noises. They were enough to keep Pokey from skidding to a halt. And then he was past us, a live carousel horse marching to the music in his head, Sophie waiting to grab for the brass ring. Where would she be if Billy ever . . .

I shuddered at the thought, as, like a ghost, Louis materialized beside us. Friend, the big dog, was beside him. Louis leaned. Friend sat.

"Hey," I said.

Louis nodded. His hair was mussed, like he'd been sleeping. His black T-shirt was wrinkled, his camo pants, too.

"She's quite the equestrian," he said.

"Olympics-bound," I said.

"I think the horse is ready," Louis said.

"Peaking at the right time," Clair said.

Pokey passed for the fiftieth lap, looking like he'd seen it all.

"I don't think he'll be rattled by the occasion," I said.

Louis smiled, but darkly. And then he said to me, "How you been?" I shrugged. Started to explain, then stopped. Clair stepped in, told the story in hushed tones. Semi and Abram and the guns. Billy and Baby Fat. Louis listened intently. And then the story was done. He waited for Pokey and Sophie to pass and said, "In Iraq, out in the boonies, the Taliban raped women so they could plant enemy seed in their wombs."

We looked at him and he continued.

"And then the women would be shunned, or worse, because they'd disgraced their families."

He took a long breath, watching the pony, but his mind a million miles away.

"And then we had our own guys, they started thinking that way. That women were something to plunder or loot or something. I didn't know anyone who actually did it, not in my unit. But one guy, he started making comments. 'Like to get her veil off.' That kind of thing, except worse."

Another pause for Pokey and Sophie to pass, Louis waiting, his eyes dark. The dog watched Louis, not the horse.

"I called him on it. I'd seen enough, you know Iraqi women tortured by insurgents, bodies dumped in the street. They said they were prostitutes, like that made it okay. So I took it out on this guy, all of it. We fought and I put him down and if they hadn't stopped me, maybe I would've killed him. But it wasn't him I was fighting. It was everything, you know? These women, girls, all of it. Like half of humanity was devouring the other half. Like cannibals."

The word hung, and there was a long silence. Louis breathed in, blew a breath out in something like a sigh.

"So what are we fighting for?" he said. "Here, I mean."

I considered it. It was simple, right? To protect my wife and daughter. To beat back the forces of evil, which sometimes seemed all around us. Then I thought of the Bishop, corralling his clan of God-fearing folks, building a spiritual fort to keep out marauders. Were he and I the same in some way? Maybe so.

I looked to Louis. "Because we can't let them win," I said. "Not now. Not ever."

The pony clumped past. Louis watched him, then turned to me. "I'm in," he said.

"You don't have to be," I said.

"Yes," he said. "I do."

So Louis said he and Friend would patrol the woods at night, starting at dusk. Clair said he'd be around—keep an eye on the west end of the road, behind the barn. They'd communicate by radios, which Clair had.

"Nobody will get in," he said.

"And nobody will get out," Louis said.

I said I'd be around, too, but first I had to tell Roxanne of the plan, and the problem.

She was sitting cross-legged on our bed, papers strewn around her, typing on her laptop. She glanced at me when I walked in, then back down at the screen.

I said we needed to talk. She said she was listening. I said we had a problem. She said she knew that. I said it wasn't the same problem, it was a different one. Roxanne looked up and I told her about Billy and Baby Fat in the parking lot, what Billy had said.

"These people are disgusting," Roxanne said. "Let's talk to the deputy. Staples."

"We can but I don't think that's enough."

"But, Jack, what am I supposed to do? Hide in the cellar? I have a life. I have things I have to do."

"I know. Just be aware of this, until it's taken care of."

Her eyes narrowed.

"So you all are going to go after this pathetic Peeping Tom?"

I said nothing.

"Jack," Roxanne said.

"Honey, I can't just—"

"Can't the police handle it? Read him the riot act or whatever it is they do."

"He tried to stab Louis," I said. "Belle, at the restaurant—he burned her sister-in-law with cigarettes, threw her out in the yard, naked."

Roxanne gasped.

"This is not some harmless creeper," I said.

"I get it," she said, quiet now.

I waited. Roxanne looked at me, then at the papers, then at the computer screen. "I was going to say, this presentation we're doing— you all could be Exhibit A. This is exactly the pattern we're trying to break in boys. That every slight has to be followed by an even bigger retaliation. That violence is the solution to every problem."

"Not every," I said. "Just some."

Roxanne looked at me long and hard. And then she put her laptop aside, got up from the bed, and walked to the east-facing windows. She reached out and yanked the curtains together, then climbed back on the bed and picked up her laptop.

"If we call the police," she said, "then maybe you can stay out of it, right? Right?"

I didn't answer.

Dinner was scrambled eggs, Sophie's favorite. Roxanne added kale and cranberry salad, with chopped walnuts. I added ketchup. Roxanne and I talked through Sophie, like our daughter was an interpreter. The mortification remained.

After dinner, Sophie had a bath and Roxanne went back upstairs to finish her presentation. I went to the study to work on my gun story, while Sophie, stretched out on the study floor, did drawings of goats and goats being milked, and a barn full of goats standing on little milking stands, like dogs at the groomer's. In another series, all of her classmates were lined up waiting their turns to step up to the udders. Sophie drew each of them as likenesses, with distinctive ears and hair and glasses and clothing.

Off to the side were two adults, standing together and smiling.

"Who's that?" I said.

"That's Mommy and Salandra's daddy," Sophie said.

I looked closer. Salandra's daddy's arm, a long jointless appendage like a skinny balloon, was looped around Roxanne's shoulders.

"What are they doing?" I said. "Hugging?"

"Yes," Sophie said. "Because Salandra's daddy doesn't have a wife."

At eight, Sophie went to bed. She ran into our bedroom and gave Roxanne a hug and a kiss, and then went with me to her bedroom and started hauling out her books. We read for a half-hour—*One Morning in Maine*, *Blueberries for Sal*—and then she was nodding. I kissed her good night and tucked her in, and she was asleep before I turned out the light.

I looked in on Roxanne and asked how it was going. She said fine. I said I was going down to work on my gun story and she said okay. Looked back down.

So I did, introducing *Outland* readers to Dicker & Deal, and how one went about buying a gun in Maine, should one need one. It was a fun piece, or should have been, describing the landscape, the characters, the guns. I wrote it straight as an arrow, with respect for all concerned. I had liked the gun sellers, except for the doofus with his dead dad's shotguns. Most of the people I knew kept firearms, and I liked most of them. But if Maine guns were being used to kill people—ex-wives, and abused women, and teenagers and innocent bystanders and little kids who have the bad break to live in neighborhoods where there's little hope—then there's the rub.

I flipped through my notebook pages until I found the name of the ATF spokesperson in Boston. I'd call her first thing in the morning. In fact, a good number to keep on hand. I was reaching for my phone when it buzzed.

The ID said B. Porter. It took me a second. Belle from the restaurant. It was 9:10 p.m.

I answered.

"Jack," she said.

"Belle," I said. "Everything okay?"

She said she was sorry to bother me so late, which it was, if you got up at four a.m. I said it wasn't a bother.

"It's that guy?" Belle said.

"Billy?"

"No, the Amish guy. Or whatever he is."

"Mennonite," I said. "What about him?"

"I came by to check on the freezer and the fridges. The breaker popped yesterday and we caught it, but if I hadn't, we'd have lost a lot of food."

"I see."

"So the guy. Your friend, there."

"Abram?"

"He was standing just around the corner, at the end of the parking lot. Him and another guy and a girl. I drove past them. At first I didn't recognize him, 'cause he had on regular clothes. Not the black-and-white thing and the baggy pants."

"No?"

"No, all three of them looked like normal people. They had on jeans and sweatshirts and sneakers, and you wouldn't have known they were Amish at all. Or whatever."

"Huh," I said.

"So I thought, and maybe this is crazy, but I thought maybe they were running away from the Amish. Or whatever. Taking off. Because they were carrying bags. Big paper bags, filled with something."

"Their clothes," I said.

Belle paused. I heard a faint sucking sound. A drag on a cigarette.

"So I looked out at them, from the restaurant. They were standing there like they were waiting for a ride."

"How did they get there?"

"I don't know," Belle said. "And then when I locked up and went out to the car, they were walking down the road toward Thornhill. I said, 'I have to call Jack. Something weird's going on.' "

"Thanks," I said. "When was all this?"

"Right now. They're still walking. In the dark. I passed them and now I'm stopped beside the road. To call you."

"Thanks."

"Don't the Amish—I saw something on TV—don't they have this thing where the kids go off and sort of go crazy?"

"Rumspringa," I said. "But these guys aren't Amish."

"Oh, yeah."

"And I don't think they do that."

"Well, they're doing something. And, I don't know, it just made me worried. Like, they're not quite ready for the real world. Maybe I'm not saying it very well."

"No, Belle," I said. "You're saying it just fine."

After she rang off, I looked at my watch: 9:12. Hyde Corner was ten minutes away. I could take a quick ride up there, see what they were up to. Leaving the Bishop? Running away to New York? Talk about babes in the woods.

I went to the sliding doors, pulled the curtain back, unlocked the latch, and stepped out. It was dark but a little gray still showing to the west. I called Clair and he answered and I asked if he could watch the house closely, Louis, too. I was going to pop out for a half-hour, I said, and told him why.

"We got this," Clair said.

I went upstairs and poked my head in. I told Roxanne I was going out for a few minutes, that Abram, the Mennonite Abram, was walking out by Hyde and might need a ride. Roxanne looked up from her laptop and papers and said, "Fine."

In ten minutes I was on the Ridge Road, my headlights scanning the roadside. Minutes later I had them in sight, three figures, reflective patches on their shoes moving like fireflies in the roadside grass.

I slowed. They turned, squinted into the lights. It was Abram, Miriam, and Victor. They were, indeed, wearing jeans and sweatshirts. Abram even had a Red Sox ball cap. They looked like very bad undercover cops.

Pulling over in front of them, I got out and walked to the back of the truck. Abram looked alarmed. The others hung back.

"Hey," I said. "You guys should be careful. Hard to see you in the dark. You want a lift home?"

Abram looked away for a moment. The other two looked at him. "We're not going home," he said. "I mean, not right now."

"Where are you going?"

He hesitated, seemed to be gathering himself up.

"A party," Abram said.

"Really."

"Yeah, these guys from work are having it. It's in the woods. With a bonfire and everything."

A bonfire. Beer. Maybe some weed. The Bishop's worst fears realized. And not just Abram tilting toward the gates of hell, but his sister and friend, as well. They looked at me, uncomfortable in their disguises. It was the first time I'd seen Miriam without her bonnet, and she seemed even prettier, her blonde hair loose, but somehow exposed. Victor looked nervous, hiding under his hoodie, like he was afraid he'd be recognized.

"Where is it?" I said.

"Powell Road," Abram said.

It was two miles up the main road, at least two miles off in the hills.

"You gonna walk up there?"

"We can do it."

"I don't know," I said, the chaperone in me kicking in. "It's awful dark, walking out here. And you have those dark clothes on. How 'bout I drop you off?"

They looked at each other. The motor idled. I waited. Finally Abram said, "Okay."

I got in first, slipped the gun back under the seat, then unlocked the passenger door. The truck wasn't built for four, but they squeezed in: first Abram, then Miriam, then Victor. The shift lever was against Abram's leg and when I shifted, he leaned to the right against his sister.

We drove two miles north, then swung off into the trees. The narrow blacktopped road climbed and meandered, and I took a right at the first intersection and continued on. A mile east, I slowed at the Powell Road intersection, moths flinging themselves at the headlights.

"We shouldn't go," Victor said. "We should go home."

"It's okay," Abram said.

"Come on, Victor," Miriam said. "It's only once."

"You heard what the Bishop said. 'Every sin will receive its reward.' "

"We're not sinning," Miriam said. "We're just going to watch."

"Listen to music," Abram said.

"If you are dishonest or a scoffer at the truth of God, you're damned to hell," Victor said.

"Nobody's scoffing," Miriam said.

"But this is dishonest," Victor said.

I slowed, started to pull over.

"So what do you want to do, guys?" I said.

"Go right," Abram said, and I did, driving slowly, braking for pot-holes. They rode in silence. When a deer bounded across in front of us, vaulted a stone wall, and disappeared into an overgrown orchard, I said, "That was cool."

They didn't reply, just peered into the narrow swath of light.

Abram was watching the road. Up ahead we saw a truck parked in the ditch, taillights reflecting. Then a car, and then another pickup and a Jeep. When I looked closer, I could see other vehicles pulled into the trees.

"This is it," Abram said, and I slowed, passed the vehicles, stopped at the entrance to a logging road, a rusty steel cable stretched across the opening. People were barely visible, walking up the road. I pulled into the ditch and the truck leaned right and the three of them piled together.

"I don't know," Victor said, but he unlatched the door and half tumbled out.

They gathered by the truck, still clutching their bags. I asked them if that was their food and drinks and Abram said no, which answered my question. They were carrying their Mennonite clothes, probably had changed in the woods. Ducking under the cable, they started up the road. I followed, walked behind Abram. Victor stayed by Miriam's side, like marauders might spring from the dark woods. Crickets were chirping and mosquitoes hummed, and fifty yards in I called softly, "Abram."

He turned.

"I need to talk to you," I said.

I caught up and we walked side by side, the others forty feet ahead.

"Who's having the party?" I said.

"Some guys from the wood shop," Abram said.

"Good guys?"

"Yeah. I mean, sure."

"Great. I hope you have fun. But listen."

We kept walking, picking our way along the trail in the dark, but I could tell he was.

"This guy Semi," I said.

No reply.

"I know what you've been doing with him. The guns."

"It's nothing," Abram said. "Just helping him out. He fixes them up and sells them to hunters, guys who come up here from out of state."

"What's he need you for?"

"He's been in trouble. A while ago, I mean. So some people don't like to sell to him."

"But they will sell to you?"

He hesitated.

"Yeah."

"What do you get out of it?"

"Twenty dollars per gun. And a deer rifle. I got a Remington seven hundred."

"Nice," I said. "But how would you feel if one of those guns you bought found its way down south and was used to kill someone?"

He walked. One step. Two. Three. Four.

"Terrible," Abram said. "But these are for hunters."

"Says who?"

"Semi."

"How does he know? And do you believe him? Why should a hunter buy a gun from him? They can go to Cabela's. Or their local gun shop. Why some guy from Maine with a felony record?"

"He knows guns."

"Do you get great deals?"

"I don't know. Sometimes. Maybe."

"If he's making a good profit, it isn't from hunters," I said. "It's from criminals. Sell them on the street and make two or three hundred per gun. Or more."

"We're not doing that," Abram said.

"ATF is up here right now," I said. "From Boston. Know what ATF is?"

"No."

"Gun cops. Feds. They're here because a handgun sold around here was used to murder a kid in Dorchester. That's part of Boston. You buy handguns?"

"Sometimes. But a lot of hunters carry handguns. For if the deer or bear isn't dead or whatever."

"Or if you need to spray a car in a drive-by," I said.

"It's not like that, Jack," Abram said. Miriam and Victor turned and looked back.

"Abram, I'm telling you. Cut loose from this thing while you still can. You get in too deep, you may not be able to extricate yourself. And if Semi goes down, you know he'll take you with him. Or try to pin it on you."

"He wouldn't do that," Abram said.

"He's bad people, Abram. Believe me. I know a few, and he's one. Not the worst, but definitely not somebody you want to hang out with."

We walked. Abram looked angry, eyes fixed to the ground.

"I just want to see some things," he said. "I want to see real life."

"Real life could end up being a prison cell. I'm not exaggerating. Federal firearms charges? You could go away for a long time. The ATF doesn't screw around."

He didn't answer, seemed to be wrestling with it all. Miriam and Victor, dim figures in the darkness, had slowed, waiting for Abram to catch up. We walked on and I began to smell smoke. Then hear music. Voices.

"One last thing," I said. "You know what you've been taught. Right and wrong and heaven and hell. And I know you're struggling with some of that. But, Abram, selling guns to murderers? That's gotta be something that will send you directly to hell."

He turned and looked at me, his eyes dark and unblinking.

"I get it, okay?" he snapped. "I get it."

"Is Semi going to be at this party?"

Abram hesitated.

"I don't know. He was supposed to pick us up but he never came."

"You know a guy named Billy? Another guy, kind of heavy? Semi cuts wood with them?"

"Met 'em once. They're like one side of Semi and I'm the other."

"They're serious trouble."

Abram didn't reply.

"How are you getting home?"

"I'll figure it out."

"Abram, listen to me. You be careful," I said. "I don't know any other way to say this, but I think you're in way over your head."

I slowed.

"And look out for your sister," I said.

Abram kept walking.

18

I stood on the path and watched them move around a bend. I checked the time: 9:52. Louis and Clair were on duty, so maybe I could afford to stay a few more minutes.

I moved down the path, followed it to the left and up a grade, and then I could see firelight up ahead, smelled the smoke. I walked carefully, staying close to the woods, and then a clearing opened up, an old wood yard, probably. There was the smell of freshly cut brush where they had widened their party spot. I moved off the path and between the trees, bending under branches, pushing them aside. When I was close enough to see, I crouched and stayed still.

There was a bonfire at the center of the clearing, flames ten feet high, silver-gray smoke billowing upward, the fire crackling. I could see twenty people, but there may have been more on the other side of the fire. Everyone was drinking, and there was music coming from speakers propped up on a parked ATV, one of three parked off to the side. The music was country. I searched in the shadows for Abram and Victor and Miriam.

She was in a group of five or six girls—late teens, early twenties—and they seemed to be gathered around her. There was a lot of laughing and excited girl voices. Another girl joined them, carrying two cans of something. She opened one and handed one to Miriam and they raised the cans and touched them.

Someone said, "You go, girl."

There were twice as many guys, some of them standing at the fire, throwing in sticks, cigarettes glowing. A few more were by the ATVs. There was a lot of whooping, talking, some shouting and shoving. Someone moved and I spotted Abram, standing by the fire with a beer in his hand. He raised it and drank, a long chug. Then he lowered the can, flung it to the ground, and moved to a cooler and took another. He drank like a new drinker, and the night was very young.

I looked for Victor, found him standing at the edge of the group. He was holding a beer to his chest like someone would try to steal it. The can, reflected in the fire, was blue. Bud Ice.

There was the flare of a lighter, a flame in front of a guy's face. He puffed, passed the joint to the guy next to him. That guy, baseball cap on backwards, took a long toke and offered the joint to Abram. I could see him hesitate, heard the first guy say, "Come on, Amish. It ain't gonna kill ya."

"It's the sacred weed, Amish," the other guy shouted. "Toke up."

Abram pulled back for a moment, eyed the joint, then tentatively reached out and took it. He held it awkwardly in front of him for a moment, waved a hand through the smoke.

"Come on, Amish," the same guy said. "It's natural. God made reefer, dude."

Abram suddenly lifted the joint to his lips and inhaled. The joint glowed and then he coughed and a cloud of smoke billowed out of him, the group guffawing. "Amish is stoked," somebody shouted. Abram took another toke, and this time didn't cough. He offered the glowing joint to Victor, but Victor shook his head and took a step back. Abram blew out a cloud of smoke and it hung in the damp air. He took another drag and handed the joint back.

The girls were dancing now, moving like wraiths in the firelight. One put her hands on the shoulders of another and they fell in, snaking their way toward the guys like it was a wedding reception. Miriam was fourth in line, and when she passed close to the fire I saw her face, happy and excited.

So this was the other world.

When the girls reached the guys, the line fell apart and a couple of the guys started dancing with the girls. Some of the girls knew the words to the song and were singing along. One of the singers slipped her sweatshirt off and swung it around her head. Miriam was laughing, like the whole thing was wonderful and amazing.

A guy walked up to her and handed her a beer. She opened it and drank. The guy tapped cans with her and stayed there, and they started to talk.

Voices behind me.

I turned slowly to see three guys coming up the path. As they moved into the light, I saw it was Semi. With him were two African-American guys. Semi had a can of Bud in one hand, the rest of the six-pack in the other. The other guys were carrying liquor bottles. Absolut.

They were wearing sweatshirts, one red, one black, hoods up. Brims of baseball caps stuck out from under the hoods. The taller guy was wearing white basketball shoes, bright in the dim light.

"Whoa," he said. "Buncha white people dancing around a fire in the woods? What's this shit? The Ku Klux fucking Klan?"

They all laughed, the guy going on.

"Man, this ain't a party. Yo, this is a bunch of devil worshippers. What do you do up here in fucking Maine? Sacrifice fucking animals?"

Semi laughed, slapped the guy on the shoulder.

"Just chillin' in the woods, bro," he said. "Crank up the tunes, have a few beers, smoke a little weed."

"Yo, these bugs is in my face," the smaller guy said, as they passed to my right.

"What's the matter with you Maine people?" the bigger guy said. "Never heard of fucking houses? They got bears out here? What kinda party's that, you might get eaten by a bear. Or a mountain lion. You got mountain lions out here?"

Everybody laughed. Semi handed the two of them beers, said, "Boys, this is Trigger and AJ, for Air Jordans. Trigger is what he pulls."

He turned to the group. "Trigger and AJ, this is the boys."

Raised beers, a couple of joints, someone saying, "Yo, dude."

And then they moved to the other side of the fire, out of the smoke, a couple of guys coming up to give Semi a fist bump, Semi making more introductions.

Rednecks, meet the gangstas. One part of Semi's world, meet the other.

I watched for a few more minutes, Semi's Boston friends circulating, the bigger guy gravitating toward the girls, the braver girls sidling up, Miriam and the others hanging back. I heard the bear line again, more laughter as I turned away, eased my way through the trees. I was back on the path when I heard someone call.

"Hey, you."

I turned. Three guys were trotting toward me from the clearing. I stopped, stood my ground. They slowed as they approached, the one who had handed Abram the joint, two more just behind him.

"Who the hell are you?" the first guy said.

"You a cop?" one of the others said. " 'Cause we got permission to be here. My uncle owns this land, the whole hill."

"Not a cop," I said. "I know Abram. I gave him a ride."

"And then you were watching? You some friggin' creeper?"

More people coming down the path, Semi with them, not the black guys.

"I wanted to make sure they were all right," I said.

"What, like you're the freakin' chaperone at the freakin' school dance," the stoner guy said. "Like we're gonna hurt your little Amish friends?"

Now another four guys were on us, and they formed a circle, me in the center. Semi saw me, said, "Hey, I know you."

"How you doing?" I said.

"Who's he?" somebody said. "A cop?"

"He's a reporter," Semi said, slurring. "But he works in the woods. His buddy busted my friend Billy's arm."

To me he said, "What the hell you doing here?"

"He said he brought the Amish up. Wanted to make sure they were okay."

Semi looked at me more closely.

"How do you know them?"

"Same way I know you. Work."

"I think he's a cop," the stoner said.

"Let's beat the shit out of him," a big curly-haired guy said.

"Let's bring him up to the fire," one guy said. "Drop some hot coals down his pants. That'll get him talkin'."

I shook my head. "All good ideas, boys. If you want to end up doing seven to ten."

They looked at me, the bearded guy recovering first.

"Who's gonna arrest us?" he said. "You?"

I tensed to run, located a tree limb on the ground that might inflict some damage. I remembered Clair's advice on hand-to-hand combat: Number one, always stay on your feet. Number two, go for the eyes.

Semi turned. The rest of the group was watching from the clearing, his city friends standing way in the back. They made no move to approach. I could see Abram and Victor, but not Miriam. Semi was looking to the Boston guys like a quarterback waiting for the play from the sidelines.

One of the guys, AJ, the bigger one, shook his head. Semi seemed to freeze. Turned back to me.

And smiled.

"Listen, dude," he said. "No problem. Bygones be like bygones and all that. Thanks for giving my man Amish a lift. I got held up, you know?"

I nodded.

"And that thing in the woods, that was, like, getting off on the wrong foot. Billy, he gets a little hotheaded, is all. I mean, none of it should have happened. We all just oughta move on."

He held out his hand, no fist bump for the old guy. I hesitated, then reached out and we shook. His hand was big, with long fingers, and his grip was strong. We gave it two shakes and separated.

"No problem," I said.

"Just having a few beers, chillin'," Semi said.

"Right."

"So we'll catch you later."

"I'm sure," I said. "Small town."

He turned away. The others looked disappointed that there was no fight, not even an argument. I turned away and they all did, too. I started down the trail, using my phone to light the way. Then I stopped and, standing in the dark with the mosquitoes buzzing around me, texted Roxanne.

Got held up. Home in 15.

And as I walked back to the truck, I ran over it all again.

Semi the peacemaker. And a drunk Semi at that. What, had he taken Welt's training? This was a guy who tried to bring a shotgun to a fistfight. Who actually pulled the trigger. When had he turned reasonable?

I was coming out of the woods when it clicked.

I'd been given the bum's rush because a fight would have drawn attention to his guests. A fight could have brought the cops, if I survived and called 911. And Semi didn't want cops. His city friends didn't either; they'd hung back as far as they could.

Were they up here to pick up a load of guns? If so, I'd bet their instructions didn't include partying with the locals. But the locals included the guy who was a key part of their operation. Had they met Abram before? Had he met them? If he connected them with the guns, the selling-to-hunters cover would be blown. Abram, I hoped, would want out.

I came out of the woods, walked to my truck, unlocked it, and got in. I fished the Glock out from under the seat and laid it down beside me. When I hit the headlights, I saw cars and trucks poking out of the woods, all older, beat-up. A new Toyota 4Runner, black with orange New York plates—the VIP guests' ride. A white van parked on the other side of the road, listing in the ditch.

I pulled out, drove slowly past it. There was nobody showing at the wheel. The sign on the door: A & G PLUMBING SUPPLY.

"Oh, no," I said.

The ATF agents, tracking Semi and his buddies. What did that mean for Abram? It all flashed through my mind: Abram the Mennonite up on federal gun charges. Abram in the newspaper, the Mennonite doing the perp walk. Abram in jail, then in federal prison.

A crisis of faith? The least of his problems.

I slowed a quarter-mile down the road and pulled over, shut off the lights. Could I bushwhack back to the trail, get up there in time to warn him? If he was buying guns for gangs, did he deserve to be warned at all?

I pulled back onto the road. Did a U-turn, lights still off. Eased back the way I had come. A hundred yards behind the van, I let the truck roll into the ditch and stop. As I watched, someone got out of the van on the passenger side and came around the back. Ramos or O'Day? The figure crossed the road and moved into the woods beside

Semi's truck, then to the Toyota. He disappeared for a minute, maybe two. Then he came out, crossed the road, and got back into the van.

The brake lights flared red. The headlights came on. The van pulled out and started up the road, headed south. I counted to fifty and followed.

The television was on in our bedroom, a blue-gray glow behind the curtain. There was light showing through to the front hall, but it was the kitchen light. Roxanne was in bed. Sophie was asleep. Louis was . . .

Standing at the rear of the truck when I shut off the motor. I saw him in the side mirror, an assault rifle at his side, muzzle pointed at the ground. I got out as Clair came out of the cedars at the side of the shed, a shotgun in the crook of his arm like a shepherd's staff.

"Hey, guys," I said. "How's everything?"

"Quiet," Louis said. "But it's early."

"I can take over now," I said.

"No, you can't," Louis said.

I looked at him, mildly offended.

"It's okay, McMorrow," he said. "I can't write a newspaper story, but I can sure as hell do this."

"Not bad considering your training," Clair said.

Louis smiled.

"Damn short-timer Marine," he said.

"So," Clair said to me. "What's going on outside the wire?"

We moved away from the driveway to the back lawn, away from Sophie's bedroom window. Standing in the darkness, stars dim behind the haze, I told them the story, from the three Mennonites on the roadside to the ATF.

"Your kid's in trouble," Louis said.

"Sounds to me like they're tightening the noose," Clair said.

"Setting the hooks," Louis said.

"He's got one chance," Clair said. "Go in and tell the whole story."

"Before he gets scooped up, too," Louis said. "Four a.m., kicking doors in."

I thought of the Bishop, lying there in bed, knowing at that moment that all his prayers had been for naught.

"He didn't know what he was getting into," I said.

"He'll have to say that," Clair said. "Sit down with the recorder running and tell the whole story, start to finish. Full disclosure."

"ATF, they think he's trying to hide something, they'll come down on him like a ton of bricks," Louis said. "Feds, they do that. Might makes right."

"I'll tell him," I said. "I'll go find him in the morning."

"What do you think they were doing with the cars?" Clair said.

"Tracking. Listening. Both," I said.

"Building their case," Louis said. "Make it so airtight at this level that the Maine guys flip, nail the Massachusetts side, get somebody down there to trade the homicide for two, three years reduced."

We looked at him.

"My dad was a deputy US attorney," Louis said. "Before he went private. Still wondering where I went wrong."

There was a long pause, the three of us standing there on the grass, crickets chirping in the brush, something rustling in the trees.

"The kid," Louis said.

"Abram," I said.

"Where's he now?"

"Probably still at the party."

"Get up early, these farmers?" Louis said.

"Very," I said. "Work to do."

"When you go talk to him, I'd like to go. Maybe I can talk sense into him, growing up with this stuff."

"I'll go along," Clair said.

"Maybe take Louis's Jeep? The Bishop, he knows my truck."

"Deal," Louis said.

"Once Roxanne and Sophie are at school," I said.

"Done," Clair said, and he and Louis turned away and started walking carefully, in different directions, toward the black wall of the woods. I went back to the truck, took out the guns, and went in the house. A single light was on in the kitchen, the counter wiped, dishes put away, Sophie's lunchbox set out, ready to be filled in the morning.

I walked up the stairs, poked the bedroom door open. Roxanne was in bed, the television off. I stood and listened and heard nothing, no breathing, no sounds of sleep.

"Hey," I said.

No response. I moved closer, my heart starting to race. Could they have . . .

"Hi," Roxanne said, her voice coming from the shadows.

"You asleep?"

"Not quite."

"How was the night? How was Sophie?"

"Fine. Tired. A long day."

I could see her now, the blanket pulled up under her chin, dark hair against the pillowcase. That image locked on to other associations: Roxanne with her head thrown back as we made love, her expression of joy and love and lust. It seemed like years ago.

"Sorry to take off."

"It's all right. I was working anyway."

"How's it coming?"

"Fine."

"Ready for the presentation?"

"Ready as we'll ever be."

We.

A pause, and I said, "You know the Mennonite guy. Abram."

"Yeah."

"He's in trouble."

I told her about the party, the ATF stakeout.

"He's in too deep," I said.

"I don't think you should have gone there," Roxanne said.

"I wanted to make sure they were okay."

"Yeah, well, just make sure you don't get swept up in it. All this gun stuff."

"It's for a story."

"It's the feds," Roxanne said. "My experience with them—taking a child across state lines, human trafficking—they suck everybody up like a vacuum cleaner. Let the minor players plead out later."

"I'm not any kind of player," I said.

"You've got a family to support."

"I know that. That's what I'm doing."

"Trying to save this kid from himself?" she said. "It's his problem."

"It's not that simple," I said.

"It never is with you, Jack. I just wish you'd walk away, for once. Think of yourself. Think of us, me and Sophie."

"I am but Abram's a good guy. He really is. He's just naive, got caught up with the wrong people. Think of where he's coming from, how he's been raised. And then he's thrown into the outside world, his whole world the Bishop and this little community and then there's somebody like Semi, and everybody partying and listening to hip-hop and country and whatever. And he's trying so hard to have it all make sense. It's really difficult but he keeps trying, just trying to figure things out."

"Let him figure it out, then," Roxanne said.

"In federal prison?"

"Not your problem."

I felt anger welling up, again. Closed my mouth hard but then it came out, bubbling over.

"Kind of a hard attitude for somebody who wants to save the world one boy at a time," I said.

I regretted it even as the words came out, even more as they hit the target. Roxanne didn't reply, and I thought I could see her sadden in the dim darkness. I heard her exhale softly, not quite a sigh.

"Do you disparage what we're doing because of Welt?" she said, her tone calm and composed. "Or do you really think it's silly?"

I considered it.

"I think what you're doing is fine," I said. "Very worthwhile. It's Welt, I guess. I don't trust him."

"Well, I do, Jack," Roxanne said. "And that's all that matters."

She turned over, her back to me. She didn't say good night.

19

I slept in fits, heard great horned owls woofing at 3:30, robins cackling before dawn. As the sky lightened, I was wide awake, listening to crows in the oaks east of the house. They were cawing hard and long, probably mobbing a hawk or owl. I closed my eyes and listened to Roxanne's rhythmic breathing, the faintest of snores. I reached over and put my hand on her hip. She didn't stir and I left my hand there, as though I could put a spell on her, make things good again.

If only.

At 5:30 I got up and showered and pulled on jeans and a shirt and went downstairs to make tea. While the tea steeped I went out and got the *Bangor Daily News* out of the box. The wind had shifted to the northwest overnight and the air was cool with a bite of fall. Small maples were turning crimson across the road, the leaves reddening at the tips like blood was being squeezed from them. I looked up and down, saw nobody, no vehicles, and turned and went back inside.

At 6:15 Roxanne was up, the shower running upstairs. The shower stopped and I heard Sophie's footsteps, out of her room and into ours and then into our bed. I sipped my tea, read the crime stories, finished my toast. And then Sophie came skipping downstairs, her lamb in tow. She asked me what I had for breakfast, and I said toast and tea, and she said that sounded good, but with peanut butter.

She sat while I made the toast, served it up with orange juice and apple slices. Sophie was eating, peanut butter all over her mouth, when Roxanne came down. She was wearing khaki slacks, her dressy ones, and heels and a red cardigan sweater. Underneath the sweater was a black lace camisole. Above the camisole was a tourmaline pendant I'd given her for the fifth anniversary of our meeting.

"You're wearing the pendant," I said.

"My A game," Roxanne said, with no acknowledgment of the occasion. She went to make coffee and then scrambled eggs. I went upstairs with Sophie, helped her wipe peanut butter off her face. She got dressed and then sat on the edge of her bed as I helped tie her sneakers. Double knots.

And then it was down to the kitchen, where Roxanne was eating, folders and her laptop on the table beside her. I could see the slides for her presentation flashing by, so I went over and looked, saw something about empathy being the foundation.

"Looks good," I said. Sophie pulled at my arm, and as I turned I glanced down. On one of the folders someone had written, *You are a rock star!!*

A man's handwriting. Not mine.

Sophie pulled again and handed me my jacket, pulled hers on, and we went out the sliding door.

It was Pokey's morning feeding: hay and a small scoop of oats and an apple. Sophie had the apple in her hand as she skipped in front of me, skipping being her new trick. I followed, and as we reached the opening of the path to Clair's, heard a loud motor, turned to see the big Dodge—Baby Fat's truck—speed by. The passenger window was down and an arm came out. It was Billy and he waved, slowly, like a beauty queen.

And then the brake lights came on. The truck went out of sight, but I heard the tires sliding on the gravel road.

But Sophie was off down the path and I followed. At Clair's barn, I looked left and glimpsed the Dodge stopped in the middle of the road, Clair on one side, Louis on the other. Louis had his assault rifle; Clair had his shotgun. They were talking to Baby Fat and Billy like it was a checkpoint.

"Come on, Daddy," Sophie said, and she slipped under the paddock fence, ran to the open side door to the barn. I glanced back as I followed her, saw Clair step back from the truck. He was smiling, the warning delivered, no doubt. Louis was standing on the far side of the road, rifle at forty-five degrees. And then the truck drove away.

I opened the gate to Pokey's stall, gave his nose a pat. He snuffled and turned to Sophie, who always had the good stuff. She held out the apple half and he chomped and chewed. I put grain in his bin, some hay in the rack. Sophie had the brush out and was running it across his side, as high as she could reach. I told her it was good enough, time to go to school. Then I held her up and she gave Pokey a kiss on the side of his hairy head. He blinked his big dark eyes and I put Sophie down and we headed out.

Clair and Louis still were out at the road, conferring. They looked up and gave me a wave and I waved back. Sophie and I kept walking, and then she broke into a skip again and I followed.

We got to the house at 7:15. Roxanne was loading up her bag.

"Let's go, honey," she said, and handed Sophie her lunchbox. They went out the side door and I followed. At the car, Roxanne said, "The meeting is at six at the school. Sophie and Salandra can play in the gym. Welt said one of his intern girls will come along and babysit."

Were there any intern boys? I thought not.

"Sounds like a plan," I said. "Good luck."

She got in the car, no kiss good-bye. When they drove off down the road, the car packed with materials for the peace project, I was right behind them, the Glock on the seat beside me.

The ride across town to the school was uneventful. The sky was blue with fast-scudding clouds and the sun was out. No Billy or Baby Fat, or Semi, for that matter. No ATF or Boston gangbangers. When Roxanne and Sophie were safe inside, I turned around and retraced my route, one eye on the mirrors.

All quiet. When I got to Clair's, Louis's Jeep was running.

I got in the back with the dog and the firearms. The dog watched me, Louis drove, and Clair rode, appropriately, shotgun.

"So," I said.

"They said they were just cutting through," Clair said.

"Told them to find another route," Louis said.

"Did they get it?" I said.

"As much as they get anything," Louis said.

"Nothing like the sound of a pump shotgun," Clair said.

Louis pulled out onto the road and hit the gas.

We drove north toward the town of Thornhill, woods alternating with cornfields, the fields almost ready to mow. The corn, stalks and all, would be ground into silage for dairy cows, which lumbered across pastures and lined up in pole barns. At Thornhill we turned off the main road and began tacking up the hills, more woods here, until we emerged at the Mennonite farms, laid out across the ridgetops.

When we neared Abram's farm, I told Louis to slow and we crept past the driveway between the fields. There was a horse team at the far end, but I couldn't tell if it was Abram.

Louis reached into the storage space between the front seats and took out binoculars. He handed them to me and then eased to a stop. I raised the binoculars and focused and it was Abram on the seat, reins in hand.

"But how do we get to him?" I said.

"Sign back there says fresh bread and eggs," Clair said.

"Fresh eggs," Louis said. "Beat hell out of store-bought."

He circled back and pulled into the driveway and drove on. The drive was long and straight and it led past a big new pole barn with solar panels on top. There were windmills behind the barn, then more solar panels atop a big farmhouse. The bakery was a small cedar-shingled building next to the farmhouse. Young girls, bonneted with long skirts, were sweeping the porch of the house. A boy—black trousers, white shirt, barefoot—led a horse and buggy out from a shed. To our right, on the far side of a cornfield, Abram was urging the team along.

Louis pulled the Jeep up to the bakery building and got out and went inside. The dog raised his head and watched him go, looked at me, and whined softly.

Clair said, "Road continues on out the back side, looks like. We go out that way, come up through the woods." Which we did once Louis returned, the Jeep now smelling like fresh-baked bread.

The driveway passed the house and some sort of community building or church. The Bishop came out of the front door and watched us go by. Louis gave him a wave. I was invisible behind the tinted windows.

At the end of the road, we went right. Beyond the end of the cornfield there was a tractor path, and Louis checked the mirror and pulled in. We drove into the trees and continued on, the trail rough and rutted. Louis put the Jeep in four-wheel and we bounced along until I could see the horses and Abram through the trees.

I told Louis to stop. He did.

He shut off the motor and we got out. I slipped into the brush and between the trees, mostly small ash and alders. This side of the cornfield had been cut, and I stood at the edge of the trees and waited for Abram and the team to get close.

When he did, I looked down the field and then walked quickly across the furrows and spikey stalks. Abram looked up, startled, and yanked the reins. The pair of horses stopped, stamped their feet, gave me a look, and settled.

"Hey," I said.

"Yeah," he said, taking off his straw hat.

"How you doing?"

"Okay."

"You look like crap," I said.

He shrugged.

"How was the party?"

"Fine," Abram said, but in a troubled sort of way. "Thanks for the ride."

"No problem," I said. "Listen. We need to talk."

"We are talking."

"No, we need to really talk. I'm with my buddy Clair."

Abram nodded.

"And a guy named Louis. They're good people. The best, in fact. Can you, like, park the horses for a minute?"

Abram looked at the team, hesitated, then reached for a lever that set some sort of brake. He hung his hat on the rig and slid down off the seat. I turned and he followed. I pushed through the bushes and made my way back to the path. Clair and Louis were leaning against the Jeep. The dog was lying at Louis's feet. They stood up and smiled. The dog came over to Abram and sniffed.

"This is Abram. Clair and Louis."

Abram nodded, hesitated, then held out his hand. They shook and we stood back, the four of us.

"I can't leave the horses long," Abram said. "Long as it takes to pee. If I'm too long, they get nervous."

"Then we'll get right to it," I said. "You're in trouble. The ATF is on to Semi and those guys from Boston. They had the entrance to that party staked out last night. Whatever this game is that Semi has going, it's about to end in a very bad way."

Abram looked at me.

"I haven't done anything—"

"Doesn't matter," Louis said. "You'll go down with the whole bunch of them."

"Unless you cooperate voluntarily," Clair said. "Right now."

"What do you care what I—"

"Jack says you're a good guy," Clair said. "I hate to see the good guys get hurt."

"Heard you've been going through some hard times," Louis said. "With your beliefs and all. I know what it's like to have that rug yanked out from under you. I went to Iraq, I thought God was on my side. Then I realized he'd left the premises. Only way that particular hell could exist."

He paused.

"I guess what I'm saying is, I know what it's like to feel sort of lost. And when you're lost, sometimes you make a wrong turn."

"These guys know the ropes, Abram," I said. "They're right. The only way to stay out of jail is to come clean now."

Abram looked at me, then at them, then at the dog. Suddenly he looked stricken, pained.

"I can't," he said.

"Nobody will hurt you," Clair said. "We won't let them."

Abram shook his head.

"I'll go with you," I said. "We'll go talk to the assistant attorney general, or whoever is in charge of the investigation. Once they talk to you, they'll know—"

"No," Abram said.

"What do you mean, 'No'?" I said. "Don't you get it? You could be going to prison for years. Far away. Think of how your father and mother will feel. And Miriam."

"I can't," Abram said, almost shouting. "Because of her."

There was a silence, the three of us waiting, the dog's ears pricked up.

"What do you mean, Abram?" I said.

"They'll hurt her," he said. "They'll hurt Miriam."

"These guys threatened your sister?" Louis said.

Abram looked around, like somebody might be listening.

"I can't talk about it," he said.

"Abram, you have to. Nobody's going to hurt Miriam. Tell us what happened."

He paused. Looked at the ground, and then in a soft voice that was almost a whisper, said, "He has pictures."

"Pictures of Miriam?" I said.

Abram nodded.

"And a video."

I thought of Miriam, innocent and a little scared on her way to the party. How could that Miriam be in—

"Last night," Abram said. "I didn't know where she was. It was loud, and I'd been drinking and smoking pot and somebody had this bottle of something. Brandy or something. And I had some of that."

He paused.

"After I talked to you, I'd really decided. I was done. I started to tell Semi when he first got there, after you and them, you had that argument. And then the party was going on and there were all these people and it was loud and everyone was drinking, and I lost track of her."

He clenched his jaw, started to tremble. Put both hands on top of his head and pushed, like he wanted to crush his own skull.

"I forgot about her. I forgot about my sister."

Clair moved closer, put a big hand on Abram's shoulder, and said, "Just tell us what happened."

Abram hesitated. Breathed. Swallowed. Sighed.

"It was later. I finally got Semi, kind of pulled him away from the fire and everybody. I said I was done. I said I wasn't going to be part of something that might hurt people. Like that murder you were talking about."

He paused.

"And what did Semi say?" I said.

"He didn't say anything. He just held up his phone and . . . and it was on there."

He closed his eyes.

"What was on there, Abram?" I said.

He opened his eyes and looked around, away from all of us. The horses moved and their harness jingled. We waited. A band of chickadees tumbled through, flitting from tree to tree, branch to branch, and still Abram said nothing.

And then he said, "She was at the party. But in the woods someplace."

Another pause.

"Miriam—she'd never had alcohol before. I mean, it was only my third time. But Miriam, it hit her really hard."

A long, deep breath.

"Two of the guys there, I didn't know them. Some guy named Rod. And another one they call Nub. They did things. She was almost passed out. They—"

He stopped. Swallowed hard.

"They what?" I said.

"They, I don't know. They took off her shirt and touched her chest and then they—"

Eyes closing again, opening.

"They took their private parts out and touched her with them and took her jeans off and looked at her and touched her there, too. With their fingers."

"And where was Semi during all this?" I said.

"He was taking the pictures, the video. And saying stuff."

Abram paused. We waited.

"Saying things like, 'This is a genuine Amish virgin. This is the hottest Amish chick ever. So this is what's under those Amish skirts.' "

I felt sick to my stomach, choked it back.

"And he told you that if you didn't stay with the gun thing, he'd show people the video?" I said.

"Yeah," Abram said. "He said there was this place, on the Internet, where people put videos of themselves and other people. And anybody all over the world can look at them. There was a name for it. An animal's name. Ferret. Or weasel. But with Xs."

"And he said he'd post this video?"

"He said he'd put it on there and then he'd send the link thing to everybody he knows. He said, 'Amish.' He calls me Amish. He said, 'Amish, your sister will go viral. Every perv in the world is going to be . . . is going to be looking at her.' Except he said something worse than that."

There was silence there in the clearing in the trees, nothing filling it, not even the birds. The three of us stood motionless, the dog, too, and then Abram broke the silence, saying, "I wanted to kill him. I started to reach for the phone and he jerked it back, said he'd already e-mailed it anyway. He said it was on his laptop now.

"I still want to kill him. But that would be a sin. It would be a terrible thing, another terrible thing I've done."

We stood and then it was Louis speaking up. "Your sister. What does she say about this?"

"That's the only good thing," Abram said. "In the video, she's sort of half conscious. Now she doesn't remember anything. She just knows she feels horrible. She says she'll never drink alcohol again."

"How did you get home?" I said.

"The black guys drove us. In this big fancy car. Semi was there, too. All laughing and joking like nothing had happened."

"Who put her clothes back on?" I said.

"Me and Victor," Abram said. "They just left her there on the ground, like a piece of trash."

"What did Victor think?"

"He's praying for her. Praying hard. He's praying for me, too."

The horses started to whinny. Abram turned and took a step toward them, then turned back to us and said, "You can't talk to anybody about this."

"We won't talk to anybody," Clair said, "who doesn't already know."

20

We were back in the Jeep. Louis put the key in the ignition. Clair, sitting up front, said nothing, just stared out the window at the trees. I'd seen that look before, when he was locked in. It was like he was somewhere else, some sort of killing zone. I couldn't see Louis's face, but felt the same cold resolve from him.

"Tell me about this girl," Clair said.

"Sweet," I said. "Pretty, but doesn't know it. Blonde, with a spray of freckles across the bridge of her nose. She told me she wanted to go to New York City and see the Statue of Liberty and Ellis Island. When they were going to the party you could tell she was excited, and a little scared. She wanted to experience it. She was dancing, but like it was junior high. She wanted to see what was out there. It's like, I don't know—she's too innocent for this world."

"Got it," Clair said. "Location?"

It took me a second, but then I knew what he meant.

"Wait," I said. "Let me check something."

I had my phone out, scrolled down the phone list. I tapped DEPT OF PUBLIC SAFETY, waited. A dispatcher answered. I asked for the Cyber Crime Unit. A couple of clicks, and then it rang and a man answered. He said he was Sergeant York. I identified myself and said I was a reporter.

"McMorrow," he said. "Heard of you."

"All good, I hope," I said.

He didn't answer.

I said I had a question. It had to do with posting explicit videos online without the subject's permission. Sergeant York listened, said, "Hang on."

More clicks. I waited. A woman answered, said she was Lieutenant Beck.

More introductions. I said I'd seen her name in the paper. "Likewise," the lieutenant said. She didn't say I deserved a Pulitzer, but she didn't hang up, either. So I gave my spiel, said I needed to know if it was illegal to post such videos.

"How old is the victim?"

"Eighteen," I said.

"Then no," she said. "Unless it's an ongoing thing, really extreme. Naming the victim, putting her phone number out there. Ex-boyfriend sort of thing. Then you might get in under the stalking law."

"Huh," I said. "What if the threat of posting the video was used to keep someone involved in a criminal activity?"

"Like blackmail?"

"Right."

"Maybe," she said. "But before we arrest somebody, we need to have some confidence a prosecutor will try the case. That could be an uphill battle."

"You wouldn't arrest that person?"

"Only if I got a DA or an assistant AG to sign on."

"What are the chances of that?"

"These days?" she said. "Slim."

"But it's wrong."

"Who is in the video? What state of mind was she in?"

"Not really any. She was drunk."

She made a game-show buzzing sound.

"DA may say she probably shouldn't have put herself in that position to begin with," the lieutenant said. "You're an adult and you go and get inebriated and get yourself on video, that's hard to make a case."

"What if the sexual activity wasn't consensual?" I said.

"That's different. But you still have to prove it. Violent sexual assault?"

"Fondling. Sexual contact."

"Getting stronger. But we have 250 cases backlogged. Child porn, you name it. Toddlers. Babies, even. Those cases have a pretty good chance of moving forward, federal or state."

"So how long would it take to get to something like this?"

"This unit? Weeks. Months," she said. "That's why we tell people to go to the local PD first."

"What would they do?"

"First thing? Interview the complainant, the victim. Then view the video."

Interview Miriam. Deal breaker.

I thanked Lieutenant Beck and lowered the phone, looked to Clair and Louis.

"One more call," I said.

I tapped the number. It buzzed and I waited for someone to pick up. Finally Belle answered, restaurant chatter in the background.

"Hey, Belle, it's Jack," I said. "Listen. You know this guy Semi. You know where he's living?"

Belle said she wasn't sure, but she'd ask. I heard clatter and muffled voices and then she was back. Semi was living in a house on 220, half a mile south of Hyde Corner. Big ramshackle place. There was an old rusty Cadillac out front in the field, just the roof showing above the grass. You couldn't miss it.

I thanked her.

"Anything for you, dear," Belle said, and rang off.

I sat back in my seat, put the phone down. And said, "It's a go."

The rusty Cadillac was barely visible, its peeling roof showing like a swamped boat in a sea of green. There were a few other cars junked out front, a couple of dismantled snowmobiles, too. Semi's red Chevy pickup was parked by the front door.

The driveway was two ruts where Semi drove his truck, the exhaust scorching a trail in the grass. The house was a homebuilt place, three stories, torn plastic sheeting hanging in tatters from the lower four feet, a remnant of a past winter. There were sheets over the windows for curtains. The front of the place looked out at the mobile home directly across the road, where a guy on a lawn tractor was mowing.

Louis drove past once, turned around a half mile up the road, and came back by again. The mower was headed for his back forty. Nobody was stirring at Semi's, probably sleeping off the party.

We pulled over and Louis opened the back of the Jeep and came back with two rolls of duct tape and a long lead for the dog. We switched places and I drove. Louis and the dog rode in the back. He said to put the passenger side of the Jeep close to the door. He'd go in first with the dog. The dog would find occupants. If there were more than one, Clair and I would neutralize them until Semi was located. Louis would bring Semi out and put him on the floor of the backseat. Clair would cover the rear.

"Are we ready?" I asked.

"You bet your ass," Louis said.

Clair said, "Let's go do the right thing."

I slowed when the house came into sight. Pulled off and bounced over the ruts until I came to Semi's truck, then swung through the tall grass around it and pulled alongside the door. Clair and Louis were out before the Jeep stopped, the dog bounding after Louis.

The door was locked but Louis hit it once with the butt of the AR and it shuddered open. The dog slipped past, Louis trotting in behind him. I could hear the click of the dog's nails as we moved down the hallway.

It was dank inside, smelled of spoiled food and dirty laundry. The place had been chopped up into little rooms and the dog sniffed at the door to each before moving on. There was a kitchen, beer bottles everywhere, then a staircase going up. The dog climbed the stairs in long leaps, Louis running behind him. At the top was another corridor, three doors off of it. The dog plunged into the first. Louis followed, and we heard voices, somebody saying, *What the hell?*

Then Clair and I were in the room, one of the Boston guys. Clair put the shotgun on the guy, who put his hands up. The guy had the sheet pulled up over his chest, and he started to reach under it but Clair ripped the sheet back, showing the butt of a handgun sticking out of the side of the bed. I snatched the gun away, popped the clip, and put it in my pocket. I tossed the gun—a Ruger 9 millimeter—onto the floor as Clair kept the shotgun on the guy.

"Where's your buddy?" Clair said.

"I left, he was still partyin'. Musta went home with those other hillbillies," the guy said.

I grabbed it, popped the magazine, put it in my pocket.

"Where's your buddy?" Clair said.

"Went home with some hillbilly chick," the guy said.

"On the floor on your knees," Clair said.

The guy hesitated and Clair motioned to me. I yanked him out of the bed. Clair trained the gun. I taped, the guy saying, "You the motherfucker from the—" before I sealed his lips.

And then we were down the hallway, the next room empty, growling coming from the third. We moved in, saw Semi on the floor on his belly, the dog crouched on the floor facing him. Louis had the muzzle of the rifle pressed to the back of Semi's skull.

"Phone on the floor in the blankets," Louis said. "Laptop on the bureau by the window."

"You can't do this," Semi was saying. He turned his head, said, "McMorrow. You fucking crazy? Are you out of your fucking mind?"

Clair reached down, slapped him hard on the ear, wrapped the tape twice around his head. "Watch your language," he said.

The dog growled louder.

Clair did Semi's wrists while I found the iPhone in the blankets, went to the table and grabbed the laptop.

And then Clair and Louis yanked Semi to his feet, hustled him out the door and down the corridor. In the bedroom, the guy was still on the floor. We moved past him, down the stairs, Clair and Louis lifting Semi up and dragging his feet.

I moved ahead of them, cracked the door, and looked out. No traffic on the road, nobody showing. The guy on the lawn tractor had moved behind the mobile home. I opened the door wider and they rammed through and shoved Semi face-first onto the floor in front of the backseat.

I got in, put the Jeep in gear. The dog hopped onto the backseat, Louis beside him. Clair climbed into the front passenger seat, doors slammed shut, and I backed around Semi's truck, into the grass, and out via the ruts to the road.

Nobody spoke. The dog was bright-eyed, still giving Semi the death stare. A quarter mile north, I swung off, started climbing the hills. Retracing my route from the previous night, I took two rights, drove two miles down, then pulled off into the trees. This time I ran the Jeep up the trail for fifty yards, lurched off into a space in the trees.

Clair and Louis were out. Louis pulled Semi out by his arms, Semi wincing in pain under the tape, his eyes bulging. And then we started to walk, the dog coursing in front of us. When Semi stumbled, his socks tearing on rocks and roots, Louis yanked him upright. Nobody spoke until we came to the clearing, the ashes of the bonfire cold, the grass littered with bottles and cans.

"I guess it's true," I said. "Criminals do return to the scene of the crime."

Clair handed me the shotgun. There was a milk crate upended by the remains of the fire and he flipped it upright. Louis forced Semi down onto it, then told him to cross his legs. Semi looked at him, started to shake his head. Louis kicked Semi's legs into the crossed position so he couldn't leap to his feet, then reached down and ripped the tape off Semi's mouth.

"Yowww," Semi howled. "You are all so dead. Do you know who that was in the house? Have you heard of G-Block? Fuckin' A, they're gonna—"

A slap across the face from Clair rocked Semi to the side. When he rocked back up, Clair grasped Semi's jaw in his big hand and squeezed.

"We ask. You answer. Got it?"

Semi glared.

"The video of the girl," Clair said. "Where is it?"

"I don't know shit about—"

Clair swung again, a backhand, and Semi's head rocked the other way and back. I held out the phone.

"What's the number to unlock it?" I said.

"That's not even my phone," Semi said. "That could be—"

Another smack from Clair and Semi's nose started to bleed, a red rivulet across his lips and down his unshaven chin.

"Twenty fourteen," he said.

I tapped the numbers and the phone unlocked. I went to photos, scrolled down. Drunk guys aping for the camera, white wannabe gangsters making gang signs. People leaning on pickups.

And then Miriam, hands pulling at her tank top.

I tapped the screen shot, and the video started to play. I turned up the volume. Semi's voice: "Yeah, dude. Let's see what she's got." Another voice, "Whoa, look at those nice little perkies."

The guy leaned into the shot, cupping Miriam's breast in his hand. The camera moved up and focused on her face, her eyes half open, unfocused. Semi kept up his narration. "I think she likes it, the Amish girl. Probably doesn't get any at home on the farm."

It continued, got worse. When I finally stopped the video, Clair and Louis were grim faced, solemn.

Semi looked at them, then at me. He managed a bloody grin.

"Hey, we were just fooling around. It's not like we hurt the girl. Just felt her up. She was so drunk, she probably doesn't even remember it. I don't see—"

The punch came fast, a left jab that knocked Semi over backwards. Clair stood while Louis propped him back up. Blood was running out of his mouth and he looked groggy.

"Where are the other copies of this?" Clair said.

"There ain't any," Semi said. "Just that one."

"Not on the laptop?" I said.

He shook his head.

I flipped the screen open, said, "Password."

He hesitated, then looked at Clair and said, "Colt underscore forty-five."

I typed it in and the screen flickered. A picture of his pickup, lathered in mud.

"Not on there?" Clair said.

"No, I told you," Semi said.

Clair nodded to Louis, who reached for his belt, took a combination tool out of its sheath. He flipped the knife open.

"Fair enough," Clair said. "But if we find it, we cut off one of your fingers."

"You freakin' crazy. You can't—"

Louis moved to the other side of the fire pit and picked up a stump. He brought it to Semi's side and thumped it down. Then he reached behind Semi and slashed the tape. Yanked Semi's arm out by the wrist and slapped his hand down onto the stump. Put the serrated blade to Semi's little finger and started to saw.

"No," Semi screamed.

Louis stopped.

"I downloaded it. Onto iPhoto."

"Who else did you send it to?" Clair said.

"Nobody. Just me. I'm the only one that has it."

Louis started cutting, blood beading along the blade.

"No," Semi screamed. "I swear."

Louis stopped.

"What's your Gmail password?"

"Mudneck. One word."

I typed it in, opened his e-mail. Jokes and junk. I went to Sent Mail, scrolled through. Nothing recent with a video attached.

"You're telling me you took this and downloaded it to this machine. So it only exists on your phone and this laptop?"

"Yeah. That's right. I mean, it was late, dude. I'd been drinking for, like, six hours. I was beat."

"I don't believe you," Clair said. He nodded to Louis, who started to cut again.

Semi shrieked. "But it's true. I didn't send it to anybody."

"You posted it online," Clair said. "Some porn site."

"No," Semi said. "No, I didn't. I just said I would. I mean, I've barely looked at the website, all these gross old people and shit. Billy, he's the one into that. Me, it was just leverage, you know? If I actually did it, I wouldn't have the leverage anymore, so why the hell would I do that? Not if Amish was still in. I mean, when he saw his sister, no way was he gonna not do what I said. But if he's got nothing to lose, then—"

Clair hit him again, a right this time, knocking him off the crate onto the ground. Louis yanked him back up and shoved him down. There were dirt and leaves stuck to the blood.

"That was for Miriam," Clair said. "What you put her through."

"What is wrong with you people?" Semi shrieked. "Wasn't like we raped her or nothin'."

I braced for it, the sound of the blow. It came, harder than the others, knocked him onto his back. Louis put him back upright. Semi looked woozy now, concussed. Clair leaned close, looked Semi in the eyes.

"I think you're lying," he said.

Semi roused, his eyes widened.

"No, I'm telling the truth," he said. "I swear."

"To who," I said. "God?"

"The gun," Clair said.

"No," Semi said.

I handed him the shotgun. Louis pulled the tape roll from his sweatshirt pocket, tore off a piece, and did up Semi's wrists again. Clair nodded toward Semi's legs and Louis kicked them out.

"Number-four buckshot," he said. "Some shooters prefer double-aught at very close range but I always figure you need a little bit of spread. Not that it matters here."

He put the muzzle of the gun on the instep of Semi's left foot.

"No," Semi screamed.

"Who else was filming this?" Louis said.

"Nobody. They were just in it. Just the three of us in the woods there. Really. Everybody else was out by the fire, at the party."

Clair racked a shell in the chamber.

"Last chance," he said.

"No," Semi screamed again. "I swear. I didn't even have the idea until I saw how out of it she was, and Amish trying to back out and all. Those guys didn't know anything until I showed her to them. They didn't even have their phones out."

"No selfies with the naked Amish girl?" Louis said.

"No, I swear to God."

Clair shook his head.

"Way up here, you'll probably bleed out," he said. "Sorry."

"My God, I'm telling you everything. I swear it. No. Please don't."

And Semi started to cry, a whimper at first, and then racking hard sobs.

It was sickening, and I gritted my teeth. Clair and Louis looked unaffected, Clair lifting the gun barrel up and then jamming it back down onto Semi's foot. He blubbered, tears running down his cheeks, mixing with the blood, turning it pink.

The gun still in place, Clair said, "You have sisters?"

"Two," Semi said. "Step."

"How would you like it, some guys got them drunk, stripped their clothes off, and molested them? And took pictures of the whole sordid, disgusting episode."

Semi shook his head. "I wouldn't," he said.

"Ever heard of the Golden Rule?"

Semi looked puzzled and then nodded desperately. "Sure. It's like, do unto others like they would like you to do unto them back?"

"Very good," Clair said. "Now if you'd lived by that, look at all the trouble you would have saved yourself. Am I right?"

Semi nodded, blood and tears dripping off his chin. And Clair moved the gun barrel six inches left and fired.

The boom reverberated and Semi screamed like he'd been shot. And then the boom echoed away, the dust settled around the crater in the ground, and Semi's scream lapsed into sobs.

Clair looked at Louis.

"We're done," he said.

Louis said, "He's spent."

"Then let's go," I said.

So we did, the four of us and the dog.

Semi stared straight ahead, the blood drying on his face and hands. Nobody talked until we were approaching his house and I slowed and the Jeep rattled onto the gravel shoulder and came to a stop. Clair got out and opened the left passenger door and leaned in. He snatched a fistful of Semi's T-shirt and yanked him up straight so their faces were six inches apart.

"Listen to me, because what I'm about to tell you is absolute fact," Clair said. "You bother Abram, you're dead. You bother his sister, you're dead. You go near his farm or his family, you're dead. Your buddies come back to Waldo County, they're dead. And if they're dead, you'll be dead, too."

He said it without menace, as though all of it were as inevitable as the sunrise.

"Is that clear?" he said.

Semi nodded. Clair pulled him out of the Jeep by the shirt and let him go. He took a couple of wobbly steps, turned back, and said to me, "When can I get my phone back?"

When I didn't answer, he started lurching down the road toward the driveway, the bottoms of his socks brown and torn.

On the drive back to Clair's we were quiet, the dog taking a deep breath on the seat beside me, letting it out with a harrumph. I had Semi's computer on my lap, his phone in my pocket. We were descending from the hills, almost to the main road, when the phone buzzed against my leg. I took it out, saw a text.

YO WTF? U DED?

Semi's partners? It meant the ATF hadn't pulled the trigger. I texted back:

CLUSTR BUT OK

I waited. The phone buzzed.

WHO THOSE FCKN GUYS? DELTA FUCKN FORCE?

I smiled.

SOMETHING LIKE THAT

A beat and a buzz and then,

—SLICK SAYS LOAD UP N GET OUTTA HERE

—RIGHT

—HIS BITCH BITCHIN BIG TIME

—SHE SHOULDA COME TO THE BONFIRE

—GUCCI? SHE SAYIN MAINE FCKN APPALACH. AINT
BOTHERN ME, KILR WEED @ THAT BOY SCOUT CAMP
OUT.

—WHILE IM FIGHTIN THE US ARMY

—SUX 2 B U, SON. OUTTA HERE.

Louis drove the speed limit, the Jeep wheeling around a bend in the tree-lined road. After five minutes Louis said, "Good to have it not be ambiguous."

"Pretty damn clear," Clair said.

"Good and evil?" I said.

"That's all that I want," Louis said, the Jeep whizzing down the yellow-dappled road. "For everything to be black and freakin' white."

21

The Dump Road was clear, nobody showing. Louis pulled the Jeep up to Clair's barn and swung it close to the door to the shop. We got out, reached back in for the firearms, and went inside. I still had the laptop and the phone, but the phone had gone still.

Clair jacked five shells out of the shotgun, one spent, four live, and put the shotgun on the workbench. He put the live shells in a steel ammo box. Louis snapped the clip out of the AR-15 and laid both gun and clip on the bench.

"Coffee?" Clair said. "Cup of tea? Mary would make us lunch."

I looked at my watch. It was 10:40. "I gotta go," I said. "Work to do."

Clair nodded. Louis went to the faucet on the wall and filled a bowl for the dog. He put it down and the dog gulped like he was a camel and had just crossed a desert.

"That last part," I said. "Before we dropped him off."

Clair was putting the shotgun in a long aluminum case. Louis was wiping the AR-15 with a rag. I stood with the computer under my arm, like a Mafia accountant.

"Telling him he'd be dead," I said. "Did you really mean that?"

"The only reality is in that boy's head," Clair said.

"So as long as he thinks the threat is real," I said.

"Sometimes war is tactical," Louis said. "Sometimes it's psychological."

They put their weapons down and went to the sink to wash their hands, Clair first. He dried them on a towel that was kept on a hook, handed it to Louis.

"Sure you don't want lunch," he said to me.

"No, I'm good," I said. "And thanks. For everything. You, too, Louis."

Clair sniffed. "That girl just needs somebody to stick up for her. Even though she doesn't know it."

"And hopefully she never knows it," Louis said. "Just goes on with her life. Problem solved."

I nodded. We all moved to the door and outside, the dog leading the way. They headed for the house, walking side by side, Clair's silver hair contrasting with Louis's black hair and beard. But they were the same, the way they moved, the way they carried themselves.

They were warriors. I was a reporter. The difference had never been so clear. I headed home to write.

The house was quiet, the breakfast mess still on the counter. I started the kettle, put cereal away, dishes in the dishwasher. Then I took a sponge and wiped the counter, then the table. I scrubbed the wood, picked flecks of dried food off with my thumbnail. And when it was clean, I wiped it dry with a towel. The water was starting to boil and I got a mug from the cupboard, dropped in a tea bag. Barry's Irish Breakfast. The water boiled and I poured.

I took Semi's laptop and phone and placed them on the kitchen table. I tapped the phone on, went to the list of recent calls. Took a photo of the screen with my phone and e-mailed it to myself. Then I put both phones down.

I opened the laptop and clicked through to the video. I dragged it to the trash. Did the same with the photos. Then I emptied the trash folder. Did the same with the phone. Then I went to Gmail, deleted the e-mail Semi had sent to himself.

I scrolled through the photos on the phone. Trucks, guys drinking beer, girls drinking beer. A party with young women grinning and pulling tank-top straps off their shoulders. A party at a lake, everybody in shorts and bikinis, guys holding girls up over their shoulders. Nothing like the video of Miriam.

When I hit winter, the trucks were replaced by snowmobiles. When I hit fall, there were four-wheelers, Semi with a dead deer, its tongue lolling. I thought of Semi's open-mouthed screams when Louis started to slice.

I sipped the tea. Went back to the laptop. The folder marked Photos was mostly trucks and motorcycles, four-wheelers and snowmobiles. Amid the pickups was a folder marked SENZIB. I looked at it. BIZNES backwards. I opened the folder, saw that it contained a single Word document, slugged SNUG.

Semi was a lot of things. Cryptographer wasn't one of them.

It was a list of guns. There were twenty-two of them, mostly handguns, three rifles, four shotguns. Next to each entry was the price paid. In the third column was something less intelligible, but I assumed it had to do with drugs: OC, 50. SK, 80g. CC, and numbers like 2 and 5 and 8.

Oxycodone? Cocaine? Ounces? SK, I didn't know.

The third column was all figures, hundreds, two thousand. Semi's drug income? The profit after he sold the drugs, figured in the cost of the guns?

This was the business he'd brought Abram into. This was the business he was protecting by blackmail. All of it pretty crude. All of it deadly. Drugs to end lives slowly. Guns to snuff lives out in an instant.

I sat back in my chair. The laptop was chock-full of evidence, would have to go to the ATF. I'd have to invent some sort of story as to how it had come to be in my possession. The phone, too. He'd left them in my truck? But as it unraveled, would the Miriam video come out?

I hit PRINT, enabled the wireless printer, heard the pages come whirring out. Two of them—more insurance. I reached for the phone, pulled up the list of recent calls. Most were numbers, not names, the callers showing various area codes. TracPhones. I got out a legal pad and copied the numbers for the past week.

Then I scrolled through iPhoto again. More trucks and drunk guys. I went through the hard drive. Nothing jumped out. No folder of videos of women at parties. But he knew where to post the video of Miriam, and maybe he already had. Maybe he was a better liar than we had given him credit for.

What was the website Abram had mentioned? Ferret something. With Xs.

I went to the browser, typed it in. Pulled up an artist. Then an actual ferret site, saying the animals required a high-protein diet, like kitten food. I tried XFerret, got the same pages. Tried XXXferretXXX—and the website appeared.

It was a home page of thumbnails, naked people of all shapes and sizes. Most of them were having sex, some shot from a distance, some showing only the most private of parts, like something out of a perverted anatomy book.

There were women with stage names—Candy von Lyck, Arianna Luste—who apparently had followings among the viewers. Men and women in every conceivable human perambulation. Clips of old porn movies. *Debbie Does Dallas 2*. Other titles in French, Italian, German. Fuzzy three-minute clips, filmed in somebody's bedroom, by a swimming pool.

I scrolled down, and it continued, an endless X-rated newsreel, explicit to the point of looking like something from a medical textbook. People posted them by the dozens every day. There were abbreviations and acronyms that meant something to people who frequented this world, lists of categories on the side of the page. Top rated. Most viewed. Most commented.

What on earth did they say? Who were these people?

But in the last two days there had been no Miriam video posted, that I could tell. But there was a search box.

I hesitated, then typed. AMISH.

The wheel turned and I felt myself holding my breath. If Miriam were on here, all of what had happened that morning would be for naught. Semi would have won. Evil would have triumphed.

The wheel rotated and the page reloaded. Two hits: a movie, one of the porn actors named Jeremy Amish; some sick joke. Another movie, *Amish Buggy Whips*. I didn't want to know.

And that was it.

I paused. Would Semi have used Miriam's real name?

I searched. More this time. A German woman. A clip called "vintage," the women in the thumbnail with eighties bangs and leg warmers, nothing else. A movie: *Molly & Miriam Frolic Down Under*.

No Mennonite Miriam from Prosperity, Maine.

I was relieved, but it was too soon. I went back a page, wondering what Semi might have called it, if he had posted it. *Amish Chick. Amish Babe. Party Babe?* There would be thousands. Something to do with Maine?

I tried *Maine Party Babe*. Got blurry photos of three naked women, none under forty. Back to the home page.

And one of the photos caught my eye.

It was a young woman, blonde like Miriam, pretty like Miriam, maybe in her late teens, like Miriam. But not Miriam. She was in what looked like a dorm room, grappling with a much bigger guy. Her expression could have been passion or it could have been terror.

Could they do that? Post videos of sexual assaults?

It didn't seem possible, in this public website with hundreds of thousands of viewers. But how could you really tell the difference? How would you know that Miriam would die of humiliation if she knew what had happened? How would you know that it would be a shame from which she might never recover?

How many of these people had been filmed as they were being damaged, sentenced to depression and ruined marriages and alcoholism and drug addiction?

I put the cursor on the blonde woman in the dorm room, hesitated, then clicked. A video came up, a hissing audio. A television on in the background, a sportscaster talking about baseball. The guy, pale and hairless with a pendulous gut, was on top of the woman who was not Miriam. Her head was thrown back and she looked like she was being suffocated by his weight. The guy was moving. The woman's mouth was open and she continued to stare at the ceiling. The guy moved faster and was grunting, then panting, short of breath. The woman closed her eyes and clamped her mouth shut, like she was trying to transport herself to someplace far, far away.

And then she said, "Oh my God"—not like she was in the throes of passion, but like she couldn't believe what was happening.

I felt sick. Clicked off the website. Closed the laptop and sat back in my chair. It was like I'd been swept into some funhouse of perversion, filled with naked men who hated naked women. It was graphic violence without blood, although if I'd dug deeper on the website, I probably could have found that, too.

I looked around the room. The daisies that Roxanne had picked and arranged in a vase on the kitchen table. Sophie's drawings on the refrigerator door: princesses and ponies. A photo of Sophie on Pokey, excited and proud. How many of the young women on the website had come from homes with photos just like these? At what point did things go wrong?

When I looked back at the laptop screen, I felt disoriented, like the porn site had shaken my foundation. The computer itself seemed different, a portal to a dark and cruel and sinister place.

I reached out and quit the browser, like I was sealing the opening to a dangerous mine shaft. But the threat wasn't to me. It was to a sweet young woman and her good but misguided brother, who, at that moment, was probably desperately afraid, overwhelmed by guilt, racked by self-loathing.

That was something I could help with.

The ATF could wait.

It was 12:20 when I drove past the south end of the farm. The sun was high, the sky was a vivid September blue, the remaining corn was trembling in the breeze.

Abram wasn't in the field. I eased to the roadside under the oak trees and parked, got out binoculars, and scanned the farmyard. There were women and children around the bakery, a horse coming from the barns pulling a wagon.

I focused.

It was Victor driving.

I looked closely as the rig turned and started across the farmyard.

Wearing bonnet and long skirt, Miriam was beside him.

The wagon was filled with vegetables, tomatoes showing. The farm stand was fifty yards south of me, same side of the road. I watched through the binoculars, and could see that Miriam looked somber, Victor, too.

Had she found out? Could Victor keep such a secret?

I sat and waited as the horse clopped toward me. They were fifty yards out when Victor saw my truck. He frowned, gave the reins a shake, and the horse moved to the far side of the drive. Miriam saw me, too, and looked serious and somber. Another shake and the horse picked up the pace, swung across the lawn behind the farm stand, and stopped. I got out of the truck and walked over.

They were unloading crates of vegetables: tomatoes, zucchini, corn, cucumbers. Victor put a crate of zucchini on the ground by the farm-stand tables, looked up at me.

"Hey, Victor," I said.

He nodded, turned, and started back to the wagon. Miriam came with a crate of corn, flashed a brief smile. She stepped behind the tables and started spreading the corn.

"Hi, Miriam," I said. "Abram around?"

"He's in the west field, digging postholes for a fence."

"Fence for what?" I said.

"To keep the deer out," she said.

"Hot work at midday," I said.

"Yes," Miriam said. "I'm sure he's tired."

"Late night?"

She looked away, rearranged the ears of corn. Victor came over with a crate of cukes, dropped it at her feet like a tribute. He paused, looked at me, and said, "The Bishop won't be pleased to see you."

"Why is that?"

"He thinks you're a bad influence. On Abram and us."

"Because I gave you a lift last night?"

"You're a disruptive presence, he says," Victor said. "As a people, we have the right to be left alone."

"Fair enough," I said. "I won't disrupt anymore. But I need to speak to Abram."

"The Bishop says you're drawing Abram away from God."

"Whoa," I said. "He overestimates my influence. By a lot."

"He says you are a nonbeliever and Abram shouldn't be listening to you."

"I've been doing most of the listening," I said. "And how does he know what I believe?"

"He just knows."

"Must be nice to be omniscient," I said. "Comes in handy, I bet, around us mere mortals."

Miriam looked at me, shook her head.

"Don't say that," she said. "The Bishop just wants us not to stray."

"I'm sorry, Miriam," I said. "I don't want you to stray, either."

I looked at her, felt like I could see through her shirt. I looked back at Victor.

"The Bishop wants us to stay with our own people," he said. "Mixing is bad because there are people who will try to lead us away. And if you stray, even for a short time, God may not forgive you."

"I thought Christianity was all about forgiveness," I said.

"There are limits," he said, looking at me steadily like he had some of the Bishop's power. " 'God spared not the angels that sinned, but cast them down to hell.' "

"There's some tough love," I said.

" 'The Lord knoweth how to deliver the godly out of temptations, and to reserve the unjust unto the day of judgment to be punished.' "

"I'm sure he does. You going to see Abram?"

"I guess I can."

"Would you tell him I'll meet him on the other side of the west field? I need to talk to him. It's important."

"Abram should stay on our side of the fence, I think," Victor said.

"I'll talk through it," I said. "Ten minutes."

I said good-bye to Miriam, and she gave me a shy smile as she laid cucumbers out in rows. I prayed that she'd never know what had happened. Victor seemed protective of her, maybe possessive, maybe even a little domineering. The junior Bishop. He and Abram. Semi and his two buddies. What was the likelihood that the secret would be kept? By the time I was in the truck, Victor was halfway to the bakery, the horse going at its steady single speed. I drove down the road a half mile, took a right, and continued on another half mile and took another right. It was a single-lane dirt road, woods on the right and fallow field on the left, then a field of cabbage, green heads with floppy outer leaves. I passed the cabbage patch lot, then came to another section of corn, uncut and eight feet high. I pulled in on the far side of the road, parked, and waited.

It was quiet on the edge of the woods, until you listened. I heard nuthatches, blue jays, acorns dropping from the trees, knocking on limbs as they ricocheted to the ground.

Minutes passed. Five, ten, fifteen, I thought about leaving but didn't. Ten minutes more and I turned the key in the ignition.

And then Abram appeared, slipping out of a corn row like he'd just escaped a maze. I got out of the truck as he approached and we stood by the front bumper, under the oaks. There was no fence.

"How you doing?" I said.

He shrugged.

"Not great."

"I understand. But I want to let you know that we talked to Semi."

His big eyes narrowed under his hat.

"About the video," I said.

"Yes?"

"He won't be posting it anywhere."

"He changed his mind?"

I hesitated. "Yes."

"But he still has it? He could do it later, if he changes his mind again?"

"I don't think so. He gave it up."

Abram looked at me.

"How did you get him to do that?" he said.

"We can be persuasive."

"We?"

"Yes, Clair especially. He knows how to reason with people, help them make the right choice."

A long pause, a longer look. An acorn fell from the tree and bounced off the hood of the truck, landed in the grass.

"Semi, he has some tough friends," Abram said. "They might—"

"That would be a very bad idea," I said. "I think Semi knows that."

"After your talk."

"Right."

"What did you talk about?"

"The Golden Rule," I said.

"Do unto others?"

"Yeah. I don't think Semi will be doing unto you anymore."

"And the video?"

"He had it on his phone and on his laptop."

"So what does that mean for Miriam?"

"I have his phone and his laptop now," I said.

"He gave them to you?"

"Well, sort of. Just for safekeeping."

"And the video?"

"It's gone."

"Did you watch it?"

"Yeah. We played it for Semi again, too, for discussion purposes."

"She doesn't know."

"You think Victor will keep his mouth shut?" I said.

"I think so. He cares for Miriam. He wouldn't do anything to hurt her."

"Glad to hear it. He doesn't like me."

"No," Abram said. "And he's not too pleased with me, either."

We stood. Looked up at the trees, across at the corn, down the road, at our feet. Then our eyes met again.

"Thanks for your help," Abram said.

"You're welcome," I said. "But we have another problem."

"What's that?"

"There's a record of the gun buys on Semi's laptop."

"Can't you get rid of it? Like the video?"

"It's evidence."

"Am I on there?"

"No. Not that I could see. You're not on his phone, either, seeing as you don't have one."

"So then it's okay, right? I won't do it anymore."

"Cops have seen you, I'm sure. And if they pick up Semi, he'll want to spread the blame around."

"Dang," Abram said.

"Yup, dang."

"So what do we do?"

"We?"

"Yeah. Well, you've been helping."

"Well, 'we' go in and talk to them. The whole story, start to finish."

I could see him running that through his mind. And I could guess the sticking points. Being charged. The Bishop knowing. Being let off. The Bishop knowing. Being called as a witness. The Bishop knowing.

He looked away, spoke without looking back.

"You'd go with me?"

"Sure."

He looked back at me. "I'll think about it," Abram said.

"I wouldn't think too long. If they have to round you up, it's going to go a lot harder."

Abram took his hat off, then put it back on. He squared his shoulders and held out his hand.

"Thanks," he said. "For what you're doing."

"No problem," I said.

And there was a thrashing in the corn, the stalks waving, and the Bishop came crashing out.

22

He came bounding toward us, fist shaking, hat nearly flying off. Abram stepped to the side as his father bore down on us. I stood my ground and he stomped to a halt in front of me.

Again

"I told you," he bellowed, sweat beaded on his forehead.

"Yes, you did."

"And still you persist in coming here. What is your interest in my son?"

I hesitated.

"Mr. McMorrow was giving me some advice," Abram said.

His father wheeled around.

"Him? He has no advice to give."

"Don't be so sure," I said. "Interview techniques. Narrative writing."

"A scoffer at the truth of God," the Bishop shouted, wheeling back to me.

"I'm not scoffing at all," I said.

"He hasn't scoffed," Abram said.

"Then what?" the Bishop said, wheeling back.

Abram hesitated.

"He wanted to bounce some ideas off of me," I said.

"What ideas?"

"Ideas about faith," Abram said. "And other religions and stuff. And what they have in common."

"What does he know about God? He drinks. He fights."

"But in moderation," I said.

"You think this is funny? I'll call the police. I'll tell them to stop you from interfering with my son."

"Not interfering. Having coffee."

"What are you?" the Bishop said.

"I was raised Catholic."

"A papist."

"Yes, but I just wish they'd invent a religion that united people instead of dividing them," I said.

"We are united. And we don't want to be bothered by the outside world."

"It has a way of making its way in," I said, thinking of Billy and Baby Fat and how they'd muscled their way into my life. "And sometimes people want to go out and see the outside world firsthand."

"I won't allow you to make your way in. This is a private road. You, sir, are trespassing."

"He was just talking to me," Abram said.

"He isn't allowed on this property," the Bishop said.

"But he wasn't—"

"I forbid you to have contact with my son. I forbid you to have contact with my daughter. I won't have him influenced by your tempting talk. I won't have her violated by your corrupting ideas."

"But, sir," Abram said. "Mr. McMorrow isn't—"

"—going to talk to you again," the Bishop said. "You are banned from this property, sir. If I have to involve the sheriff's office, I will."

"Not necessary, Mr. Bishop," I said. "I'll go."

I turned to Abram.

"See you around. Think about what I said."

"He won't," the Bishop said. "He's forbidden to do so."

I turned to the Bishop, held out my hand. He stared at it like it was a dead animal. I let it fall away.

"No hard feelings, sir," I said. "I know you're doing what you believe to be the right thing."

He softened, said, "I don't mean to be harsh."

"But there comes a time," I said, "when you just have to have faith in God, sure, but also faith in your kids—that you've done your job, that they're good people—"

I looked at Abram and added, "—that, given a choice, they'll do the right thing."

It was 1:35 p.m., school out at 2:05. I drove down from the ridge and northeast to the crossroad, then north. The sky was blue, the maples blood-orange on the shores of the marshes. It was harvest time in Waldo County—corn, vegetables. I passed a field of pumpkins, orange and yellow in the creeping carpet of green leaves and stalks. I wondered if the ATF thought of it that way: Plant the seeds, water the plants, swoop in for the harvest.

I shook my head, the Bishop's tirade replaying. I couldn't blame him. He was lashing out because he saw me as a serious threat to his kids. I was his Billy. It was only his religion that kept him from punching me out.

It was 1:50 when I pulled into the school parking lot, backed the truck underneath the oaks at the edge of the woods. There was nobody showing, just the usual minivans and SUVs, bumper stickers saying their kids had made the honor roll. No red Chevy pickup with black rims.

I sat back. Waited.

Saw the big Dodge flatbed roll into the lot to my right, Baby Fat at the wheel, Billy in the passenger seat.

Baby Fat wheeled around, the nose of his truck pointed at mine. Our eyes met and then he turned, threw the big truck into reverse, and backed it into a space in front of the main entrance.

Billy got out, sliding out of the cab to the pavement. He was wearing logging boots, jeans, a Carhartt jacket with his arm in a cast inside it. Looking across the lot at me, he reached back and pulled up his jeans, turned, and shuffled toward the door. He stood and waited, like he'd buzzed and was waiting for the doorman. And then a dad pushed out through the door, held it open as two kids tumbled out, a soccer ball flying before them. Billy grabbed the door as it slowly closed, turned to me, and smiled.

He was inside, the door closing behind him. I was out of the truck, at the door peering in, waiting for the next soccer dad to come out.

None came. I put my face up against the glass, shielding the light with my hands. Nobody in sight. I looked back. The truck was parked, Baby Fat still at the wheel. Where was Billy? What was he doing there? Where was Roxanne? Sophie?

I thought about breaking the glass, but then a woman, vaguely familiar, crossed the corridor. I knocked on the window with my fist and she turned, then walked slowly toward me. I smiled; she did, too.

She pushed the crash bar, and I said, "Picking up Roxanne," and I was in.

I managed a smile as I brushed past her, said, "I'm late," and hurried down the corridor. Sophie's room was at the far end of the building, and my walk turned to a jog. I saw kids in classrooms, the doors closed. A teacher at a chalkboard, another with his hand on the door.

And then a buzzer buzzed and doors clacked open. Kids streamed out of the classrooms, teachers calling after them, "No running!" They flooded the corridor like lava streaming from volcanoes. Backpacks. Soccer bags. Dodging each other. Swirling around me like I was a tree rooted in a swollen stream.

I was at an intersection, went left, and found myself going against the tide. Kids coming at me like snowflakes into headlights, moving left and right. I pushed through, and then saw Sophie's room ahead.

I broke left, got to the door. I peeked through the window. The kids had gone, but Sophie was inside, sitting at a table, Crayons strewn around her. I turned the latch but it was locked from the inside. I knocked. Sophie saw me and grinned, jumped up from her chair, and came running.

As I smiled back she opened the door, said, "Daddy!" I pushed inside, bent to take her hand, looked left and right. Salandra was lying back in a wicker-basket sort of chair, a book on her chest. Roxanne and Welt were sitting side by side at a table, a laptop in front of them.

They looked up.

"Jack," Roxanne said.

"Hey," I said, reaching back to make sure my shirt covered the butt of the gun.

Welt smiled, glad to see me.

"Hey, guys. Listen, have you seen the guy from the truck? The one at the farm, the smaller one?"

They shook their heads.

"He just came into the building."

Roxanne stood, hurried to Sophie.

"What's he doing here?"

"I don't know."

"Maybe he has kids," Welt said.

"I don't know," I said.

The girls were looking at us, wary now. I moved to the door and poked my head out and looked up and down the corridor. There were a few stragglers—a little girl trudging along, hugging a violin case, a boy dragging his backpack on the floor like a dead body. I came back in the room. Welt was standing beside Roxanne now, his hand moving away from her back.

"Lock this door behind me," I said. "Just in case."

I stepped into the corridor, closed the door, heard the lock snap into place. I went right, crossed the intersection, passed walls papered with kids' drawings, pictures of vegetables and fruits, the banner saying, "Seeds of Peace."

The corridor opened up to a sort of rotunda, glass-fronted offices to my right, the main entrance doors to my left. I slowed, looked into the offices, saw a gray-haired guy coming out of an inner door. He turned back—and Billy followed behind him.

They were talking. Smiling. And then I could see the top of a boy's head between them. The gray-haired guy bent and said something to the boy and the three of them moved to the corridor door.

The door opened. Billy stepped out, then the kid, eight or nine. He was chubby, with black hair like a horse brush, and sneakers that looked four sizes too big. I was standing along the wall to their right and Billy looked over, grinned.

"McMorrow," he said. "This is my nephew, Troy."

Troy looked at me, unimpressed.

"Mr. McMorrow is a newspaper writer," Billy said. "He's a friend of mine."

Troy gave me a sour look, then headed for the doors. Billy came closer, smiled, and said, in a quieter voice, "Doing a little scouting."

"That right?" I said.

"Yeah," Billy said. "There's just this one teacher. She's wicked hot. I'm thinking I should take her out on a date."

"You'll die trying," I said.

"Can't be everywhere, McMorrow."

"It's not just me."

Billy shrugged.

"You just seen how easy it is. Matter of time. A lot of country around here. Dark woods. Sometimes these teachers, they work late."

"I'll kill you. You know that, right?"

Billy smiled. The kid was at the door.

"Hey," the kid said. "Hurry up."

Billy looked at me and smiled. "Empty roads," he said. "Deserted. Dark. Nobody for miles. Nobody to hear you scream." And then he turned away, walked slowly across the corridor and out the door.

I waited outside the office until I heard Baby Fat's truck start and rumble across the lot and out.

I knocked on the classroom door. Roxanne opened it, looked at me for a clue.

"He's gone. Came and got his nephew."

"Welt was right, then," Roxanne said. "There was an explanation."

"He said he was scouting the place."

"For what?" Sophie asked as she came bounding up, waving a paper. "Daddy, I drew you and Pokey," she said.

I looked at Roxanne.

"We'll talk," I said.

I admired the picture, Pokey jumping a fence as tall as his head. A stick figure of me, watching from the fence. "Nice," I said. "Pokey's getting some air."

Salandra was at the drawing table and Sophie skipped back to join her. Welt was back at the laptop. Roxanne and I walked over to him and Roxanne said, "He was picking up his nephew."

"Who's that?" Welt said.

They looked at me.

"Troy," I said. "Big kid, gigantic feet. Third grade, maybe."

Welt looked at Roxanne. She looked back at him. I waited.

"He's got serious anger issues," Welt said.

"Comes by that honestly," I said.

"Difficulty accepting authority," Roxanne said.

"That, too," I said.

They were half listening, the visit having been explained away, Billy having a nephew somehow making him closer to normal. Roxanne moved around to the laptop, said, "We're rearranging the presentation. We decided to start with impact. It means a lot of rewrites, to still have it make sense," She added. "So could you take the girls to our house? We're going to need to work on this right up until meeting time."

"Here?"

Billy, how much in heat was he? Would he come back to the school?

"Actually, we'll be doing a run-through for Mr. Hanes. It's his building, so that makes it his program, too."

"The gray-haired guy?"

"Yeah," Roxanne said.

"In his office?"

"Yeah. Mr. Hanes and Sabrina Pinney, from Guidance, and Mr. Fisk."

Five of them, and then a school board.

"Strength in numbers," I said. "Call when you're done."

"We'll be fine," Roxanne said.

"Call, please," I said. "Promise me."

She did.

23

The girls rode side by side, chattering about Pokey, why horses ate hay. Sophie said it was because with their hooves they couldn't hold the bowls to make cookies. Salandra said it was also because horses didn't have ovens.

We were on the Dump Road, coming over the rise. I saw a van coming up fast behind us, but then it fell back and followed at a distance. When I pulled into the driveway, it swung in, too. Parked behind my truck. Sophie and Salandra turned in the seat to see who it was.

"Just some guys I know," I said. "You girls go inside. Get a snack."

They did, sliding out of the cab of the truck and trotting up to the house and through the door. I leaned down, pushed the Glock further under the seat. Then I walked to the van, stood by the driver's door, and said, "Long time no see."

"Think we met some friends of yours," Ramos said, from the passenger's side.

"Is that right?" I said.

"You tell us," O'Day said.

They got out and we stood beside the van. It was sunny and warm, one of those fall days in Maine that starts cool, heats up as it goes. They were in jeans and black T-shirts and boots, looked like bikers, except for the sidearms. I wondered if Clair and Louis would show up on armed patrol.

"I need to check on the kids," I said.

"Just want to run some things by you," O'Day said.

"Like this," Ramos said.

He held up his phone. There was a photo on it of a young black man. He was sitting on the curb by a highway, cars streaming past, police cars parked around an SUV. The SUV was the one from the party. The last time I'd seen the guy I'd put tape over his mouth.

"Know him?" Ramos said.

I looked more closely, buying time.

"It's a yes-or-no question," O'Day said.

"I've seen him," I said. "We weren't formally introduced."

"Seen him where?" Ramos said.

"Here."

"Here, where? At your house? In the woods?" O'Day said.

"How 'bout while you were conducting a home invasion in this very town of Prosperity, Maine?" Ramos said. "Where you abducted a man named Bates Cropley, who goes by the name Semi, as in semi-automatic."

I didn't answer.

"And the aforesaid home invasion was carried out with loaded firearms, namely a shotgun and an assault-type rifle," O'Day said.

"And the other occupants of the house were bound and gagged so as to prevent them from notifying authorities that a crime had taken place," Ramos said.

"Where'd you hear all this?" I said.

Ramos held up the phone.

"From one Errol Lloyd, of Dorchester, Massachusetts, aka Trigger. Who was arrested on Interstate 95 in Hampton, New Hampshire, this morning, along with Rodman Jones, also of Dorchester, aka, AJ. The two subjects are known to be members of the G-Block gang, a criminal organization that operates in the Dorchester area."

O'Day took over.

"A vehicle, a rented SUV, was stopped by New Hampshire State Police and federal agents. Lloyd and Jones, the occupants of the vehicle, were found to be transporting fourteen firearms and more than six thousand rounds of ammunition. As convicted felons, Lloyd and Jones are prohibited from possessing firearms. They are believed to have purchased or bartered for the guns in Maine, with the intent to bring them to the Boston area for use in criminal activities and/or for resale."

"Good bust," I said.

"Where's Semi, McMorrow?" Ramos said.

"I have no idea."

"Where and when did you last see him?" O'Day said.

"At his house. This morning."

"After you took him, you brought him back?" Ramos said.

I nodded.

"Was he alive?" Ramos said.

"Very much," I said.

"We went to the house. There was blood," O'Day said.

"May have been some bumps and bruises," I said. "But he was fine."

"Why'd you and your buddies grab him?" Ramos said.

"Long story," I said.

"Have to do with guns?" O'Day said.

"Yes and no," I said.

"What's the yes part?"

"I figured he'd been buying guns. For the two guys you busted."

"Semi was," Ramos said. "He's the straw buyer."

"Right."

"Were you planning on telling anyone about this?" O'Day said.

"I was going to tell thousands of people," I said. "When I wrote about it."

"And in the meantime, let how many people get killed with those guns?" Ramos said. "Kids and innocent bystanders and babies and ladies on their way to church. Good people, from my neighborhood.

Cape Verdeans. Made it all the way here, working their asses off to make it. And some kid shoots them dead. And you know what?"

"No, what?"

"Their blood will be on you, McMorrow."

"I'm a reporter, not a cop."

"I'm having trouble figuring out what the hell you are," Ramos said. "I know reporters. They call me up a lot. Sometimes I give them something good."

"I like to get my stories myself, not have them spoon-fed to me," I said.

"That's not a reporter," he said. "That's somebody who associates with and aids and abets criminals. Like the ones polluting neighborhoods just like the one where I grew up. Kids don't deserve to die."

"I agree," I said.

"We could lock you the fuck up," O'Day said.

Ramos moved and stood directly in front of me. He had his jaw thrust out, in my face. "What'd you do to Semi?" he said. "No more bullshit."

"Convinced him not to do something he was maybe planning to do."

O'Day stepped in, saying, "Plain English."

"He was threatening to hurt a friend of mine. We persuaded him not to."

"Who's 'we'?" Ramos said.

"Me and two friends of mine. Not the one who was threatened."

"They have names?" he said.

"Of course."

"You gonna tell us?"

"Not right now," I said. "But I will give you a couple of things."

They paused. I turned and walked to the house, the two agents hesitating, then catching up. When we got into the house, I heard *The*

Jungle Book on the television. There were footsteps, and Sophie came skidding into the kitchen, an empty bowl in her hand.

"I need more Cheez-Its," she said, then looked up. "Please."

She stared.

"Sophie, these are policemen," I said. "I'm helping them with a case."

"Huh," she said.

"What are you watching?" O'Day said. "Is that *Jungle Book*?"

Sophie nodded.

"With my friend Salandra," she said.

"That's fun," O'Day said. "My son likes *Jungle Book*. Mowgli and all those guys."

"And Bagheera," Sophie said, and then she looked at Ramos, back at O'Day.

"My mommy doesn't like guns in the house," she said.

O'Day smiled. "We won't stay long," he said.

"If your daddy helps us, we can leave sooner," Ramos said.

I handed her the Cheez-Its box and she turned and ran back to the den and Salandra.

"Cute little girl," O'Day said.

"Takes after her mother," I said.

I led them to the study. The phone and laptop were in a case on the floor beside my desk. I picked up the case, took the phone and laptop out.

"There are folders on the laptop: S-N-U-G is guns. S-E-N-Z-I-B is biznes."

"Rocket scientist," Ramos said.

"And phone numbers on the phone, of course."

O'Day took the laptop and phone from me and set them on the desk. He photographed them with his iPhone, then tapped the screen and spoke.

"Laptop computer and phone received from Jack McMorrow, September 9, 2015, McMorrow residence, Prosperity, Maine."

He held the phone out to me, recited the date and time, and said, "Identify yourself, please."

I did.

He asked if I was voluntarily delivering the two items, belonging to one Bates "Semi" Cropley, to the custody of Special Agent Terrence O'Day of the Bureau of Alcohol, Tobacco, and Firearms. I said I was. He tapped the screen again and slipped the phone into the pocket of his jeans.

"Don't say I never did anything for you," I said.

"You haven't done much," Ramos said. "Threw us a couple of bones to get us off your back."

"There's a list of the guns on there," I said. "Price paid, profit made. Numbers he's been calling, probably to your Dorchester guys."

"Maybe it's your info. Maybe you're the middleman. Maybe you're a straw buyer yourself."

"Not me."

"Okay, but even if you're not bullshitting us at this second, doesn't explain your involvement in this case. Rival organization? Falling-out among criminals?"

"No, it doesn't explain that."

"Gonna claim some sort of reporter's privilege," O'Day said, "because this is part of your story?"

"No," I said, "because it isn't."

They looked at me.

"Semi'll tell us," Ramos said. "Looking at fifteen years federal time, he'll spill his guts."

"Maybe," I said.

"Why wouldn't he?"

I smiled, didn't reply.

"What the hell kinda game you playing, McMorrow?" Ramos said.

"No game," I said.

"You lying?"

I didn't answer.

They said our conversation wasn't over, just paused. I said I understood. O'Day told me not to leave the area, and if I did, to call him and tell him my whereabouts. I said nothing. Ramos gave me a hard look. And then they were gone.

I walked into the den and saw that Salandra and Sophie were on the floor, drawing pictures. *The Jungle Book* was playing in the background. Sophie, without looking up, said, "Are those men still here?"

I said they'd left.

"Are they coming back?" she said.

"Sometime," I said.

"Before supper?"

"I don't know, Sophie," I said.

"They were mean policemen," she said, still coloring. "Are they going to take you to jail?"

"No, honey," I said. "They're not going to take me to jail."

"Don't worry, Sophie," Salandra said. "If your daddy goes to jail, my daddy will marry your mommy. And then we can all live at my house."

I bit my tongue. Salandra looked up from her drawing, a black outline of a building with bars on the windows. She smiled, a six-year-old provocateur.

Sophie reached for the sky-blue crayon, started coloring the space between the green trees and the gray clouds. The sky I'd never see in the slammer.

"Why did they have guns?" she said.

"In case bad guys try to shoot at them," I said.

"They would shoot them back?"

"Yes, they might."

"Would they shoot at you?"

"No, honey, because I'm not a bad guy."

"Mommy says guns are bad, and you have a gun."

"Just sometimes," I said.

"Are bad guys going to shoot at you?"

I smiled. "No, honey," I said, the lie catching in my throat. "Bad guys aren't going to shoot at me."

"Then why do you have a gun?" Sophie said.

"You'd make a good reporter," I said. "You ask good questions."

And she was waiting for an answer. Trying to figure out how the world works. Good and bad, Mommy and Daddy—how it all fit together.

"It's just that, sometimes you have to stop the bad guys from doing bad things," I said. "You have to take a stand."

"Nobody shoots at my daddy," Salandra said.

"No," I said. "I'm sure they don't."

The girls colored and the movie ended. Then they went upstairs to Sophie's room and made a tent on the bed and filled it with stuffed animals, like a miniature Noah's ark. I watched them for a minute, then went down to the kitchen and opened a beer. The Ballantines were gone. I grabbed a Shipyard IPA.

The gang guys had been busted and the ATF was off my back, for the moment. The video of Miriam was deleted, for the moment. Semi was chastened, for the moment. Clair and Louis were feeling like they'd done the right thing, for the moment. Miriam's secret was safe and Abram wasn't in jail, for the moment. Victor and the Bishop thought I was the devil's spawn, but the Bishop had softened, for the moment. Welt and Roxanne would be giving their presentation shortly, and then Roxanne would come home and Salandra would leave. We'd be a happy family again.

For the moment.

I hoisted the bottle and drank quickly, before the moment passed.

The beer was half gone when there was the faintest of footsteps, and then movement at the sliding door that led out to the deck. I got up from the kitchen table and went and unlocked the door and pulled it open.

"Hard day at the office?" Clair said.

I stepped out. Clair had leaned the shotgun against the railing. Beyond the railing, Louis stood by the edge of the garden, the AR-15 cradled in his arms, the dog sniffing the edge of the hosta bed. We moved down the steps and joined him.

"How you doing?" I said.

"Fine," Louis said, and for the first time since I'd met him, he sounded like he meant it.

"Thanks again for your help this morning," I said.

"No problem. Glad to put my meager skills to use."

"Just got in under the wire," I said.

I told them about the ATF, the bust on the interstate, giving the phone and laptop to O'Day and Ramos.

"Saw them roll in," Clair said.

"Semi's running now," Louis said.

"Unless they've caught him," Clair said.

"Think he'll rat out Abram?" I said.

"Maybe, but not the girl and the video," Louis said. "Not something you want tagged onto you in prison. Rapist. Only way you can get sex is to have the girl unconscious."

We stood, the disturbing image hovering. From the bedroom window we could hear Sophie's and Salandra's chatter, a jarring juxtaposition. The dog was finished sniffing and had crouched at Louis's side. I told them about Billy at the school and they said they'd be glad to do escort duty—just to call. And then they looked at each other.

"May be time for another session," Clair said.

"Overdue," Louis said.

"Billy won't scare like Semi did," I said.

"Almost everybody scares eventually," Clair said. "I've seen the ones who don't, and he isn't one of them."

Another disturbing image.

We were quiet for a minute. The sky was faded blue, like one of Sophie's drawings. A pair of mourning doves passed overhead, their wings whistling. They reminded me of the peace project, Welt and Roxanne. Probably getting ready to take the stage. Would he give her hand a good-luck squeeze? A lingering pat on the back? A hug afterward if the board approved? Would she hug him back?

I shook off the thought, told Clair and Louis I had to make dinner for the girls. They nodded and started for the woods, Louis and the dog going east toward the parking spot, and Clair taking the path toward his barn. I went back inside, put a pan of water on for mac and cheese out of a box.

No chèvre here.

From upstairs I could hear the girls' voices. The water boiled and I dumped in the macaroni, gave it a stir. Watched it as it cooked. It was 7:20; maybe they were mostly through with their presentation. I drained the macaroni and added the cheese, a little more from the fridge. Then I sliced up a zucchini to sauté, put butter in the fry pan. Got out another pan and dropped in four hot dogs.

The zucchini and hot dogs sizzled. The mac and cheese was warm and ready. I put three plates on the table, went to the bottom of the stairs to call the girls down.

And heard the siren.

It was on the main road, the sound wafting over the woods from the ridge to the north and west. The quick *whoop-whoop* of a state police car, not the slower wail of the sheriff, or the loping trombone of an ambulance.

I moved to the back of the house, slid open the door to the deck. The sound was getting closer and I felt a chill. I listened as the car approached the turnoff to our road.

And passed it, continuing on. I stepped out onto the deck and froze, listening hard.

And heard another siren, another trooper, this one approaching from the east. I was at the edge of the deck now, head cocked sideways, my right ear tilted to the woods. The second car followed the first. And then I heard a third, sheriff's deputy this time, the sound of the sirens moving fast.

My chest tightened. Roxanne.

I trotted to the kitchen, grabbed my phone, and banged Clair's number.

"I gotta go," I said. "There's cops, troopers, and Sheriffs. I could hear them, headed east, then north."

"Where is she?"

"School. Meeting with the principal."

"Secure?"

"Like a sieve. I should have stayed."

"What can I do?"

"Come and watch Sophie and her friend."

"Got it. Call me."

"Yup."

Clair was crossing the back lawn when I ran to the bottom of the stairs. I shouted up, said I had to go out for a minute, but Clair was here. A small *Okay* from upstairs. I went out the door, started the truck, spun the tires in the gravel, and was gone.

A minute to the main road, maybe two. I slid to a stop, waited for traffic to pass: a car with kayaks, an empty log truck. And then, coming around the bend fast, blue grille lights flashing, a state police SUV.

It flashed past, the cop in uniform, gray at the temples.

"Shit," I said.

I pulled out, put the pedal to the floor, and slammed through the gears. The car and the truck had pulled over for the cop and I whipped past them, trying to keep the SUV in sight. He was driving east, toward the center of town. The store. The school. I stayed with him, clenching the wheel as the g-forces pressed me sideways on the first turn.

And then he feathered the brakes, hit them hard. I slowed, saw him sling the SUV left and out of sight.

Not the school. Not Roxanne.

I felt relief sweep through me with a shudder, slowed and turned and followed, drawn like I was attached to the SUV by a rope. I breathed slowly as I ran through the possibilities. A shooting. A very bad car accident. I'd gotten only that far when we reached the next intersection, woods on the right, farm fields across the way. The cop wheeled left, headed west now, lights and siren still on. I rolled through the stop sign and followed, lost sight of him on the hard corners, picked him up on the straightaways.

And then there were more blue lights, and the SUV slowed. The lights were a sheriff's deputy, parked on the shoulder, standing by her car. She held her hand out, pointing to her left.

A back road, the one I took to the Mennonite farms.

An accident? With horses? Or someone abducted and taken here.

Roxanne.

The deputy saw me coming but I was past her, following the SUV before she could hold me up. I was twenty yards back, driving in his dust, when we came over a rise and the roadside was lit up.

Two blue cruisers. Two pickups with flashers on. Local EMTs.

The SUV slid to a stop and a big cop slid out. Sergeant at least. He put on his hat and strode into the woods. I parked and followed.

It was a narrow lane through the brush and then under the trees. ATV tracks with a tuft of dead grass in the center. The big cop was hurrying with long strides. I was a hundred feet back, deerflies circling my head. The path rose and fell, turned left and right. I was coming up a rise when I heard radios.

The sound was coming from the woods to my right. And then I could see a trooper meeting the big cop, clearly his superior. They exchanged a couple of words, the two of them wending their way through the trees.

I followed, my breath coming in short gulps, then not coming at all. And then I saw them.

The EMTs, guys from town, were standing together, hands at their sides, latex gloves still on. The cops were beyond them, all of them staring in the same direction, deeper into the woods.

I slowed.

Saw him.

It was the Bishop and he was on his knees, his forehead resting on his clenched hands. He was praying, a low murmur with the words *Savior* and *Jesus* emerging from the mumble.

I eased my way up behind the EMTs, looked deeper into the woods. A flash of an image, someone praying before a life-size crucifix. And then my knees buckled as I said, "Oh my God."

Abram was tied to a tree. His face and white shirt were black with blood. His mouth and eyes were open and flies whirled around him. The trooper turned and saw me and said, "Out."

The Bishop raised his head from his hands, turned, and said, "You," a strangled gasp, and as he sprang up from his knees, he bellowed, "You killed my son!" He was coming at me, pointing at my face with a long finger as though he could make lightning strike. "You are the Devil!" he shouted. "Sent from hell to live among us."

The trooper stepped between us, saying, "Easy, sir," but the Bishop kept coming, his face red and his teeth bared. "I told you, 'Stay away from my son.' "

The trooper had him by the shoulders, pressing his hands to the Bishop's chest. He took both of them with him, bulling his way toward me.

"This man drew my son into the darkness. This man took my son."

He was panting as he drew close to me. The trooper backed into me, stepping on my boots. He was shouting, "Calm down, sir." The sergeant was saying, "That's enough."

"I didn't hurt Abram," I said. "I liked him. I liked him very—"

"I told you to stay away," the Bishop wailed. "I told you to stay away."

And then he sagged as he said, "I prayed. God, didn't you hear me?"

Grief swept over him and he started to cry, a jaw-clenched spasm, tears streaming, his breath coming in jerks, no longer the Bishop, just a father who had lost his boy. A father who had tried to protect his son from the evils of the world, and failed.

For a moment we all stood as the Bishop wept. Over his shoulder I could see Abram against the tree, his hands bound in front of him, his expression frozen in sorrow. And then I saw something else.

The trooper turned to me and started to push me back, saying, "This is a crime scene," and I sidestepped him and took a couple of steps forward. As he grabbed me by the shoulder, I realized what it was. There were letters on Abram's forehead, dark gouges in his pale, now-bloodless skin.

As the trooper started to move me again I spun away from him, stepped closer. Cut into Abram's head, now showing as neat, scabbed lines, was a word.

RAT.

24

Clair listened to the story. We were standing on the deck in the deepening twilight, bats crisscrossing above us. Clair had given the girls dinner and now their voices trilled out of the bedroom window above us. I spoke softly and when I was done, Clair said, "Two things."

I waited.

"If you're going to kill somebody for being a snitch, why write it out? Anybody on the inside will know the reason. Pretty stupid to telegraph it to the cops."

"A lot of stupidity going around," I said. "Billy, Baby Fat, Beefy, and Semi. And these Boston guys seem to think they're invincible."

"Thing number two. This isn't your fault."

I didn't answer.

"He was in deep when you met him."

Still no answer.

"But if you do feel somehow responsible, there's only one thing to do."

I looked at him.

"Nail the ones who did it," I said.

"Right. And a third thing."

"You said there were two."

"I lied," Clair said.

"A lot of that going around," I said.

"Billy's not stupid."

"No."

"He's a sociopath. They're usually pretty smart."

"Yeah."

"Watch your back," Clair said.

"Not my back I'm worried about," I said.

Clair had been gone twenty minutes when the knock came. I trotted to the side door, kitchen towel still in my hand. Flung the door open and there was a detective standing there, a tall, dark-haired guy, pale skin and black eyes. Behind him was Deputy Staples, from the fight at Welt's farm. Both grim, their mouths flat lines.

"Mr. McMorrow," the detective said. "I'm Sergeant Robert Cook." I knew the name. Major Crimes Unit.

"You know Deputy Staples. She was at the scene. Offered to bring me here. Good time to talk?"

"Yeah, but I have my daughter and her friend here."

"That's okay," he said.

They followed me in, and we were standing in the kitchen when the girls came running in.

"Can we have ice cream?" Sophie said. And then she looked up, Salandra right behind her. They looked at Cook, then at Staples. They didn't say anything, just waited for me to spoon ice cream into two bowls.

Cook smiled at them and Sophie looked at him, then away. More cops in the kitchen. Ho-hum. And then the girls scurried out.

"How you doing?" Cook said.

"Not good."

"Abram Snyder was a friend of yours, I understand."

"Acquaintance," I said. "But yes, I liked him. A good guy."

"When did you last see Abram?" Cook said.

I thought.

"Today. Around one o'clock. At his farm."

"Did you talk to him?"

"Yeah. For a few minutes."

"About what?"

I hesitated.

"I'm trying to do a story on the Mennonite community here—
I'm a reporter—and I met him, some of his friends. Abram's father is
the Bishop of the district, and—"

"We know. How did Abram seem when you left him?"

"Okay. He'd got some things on his mind. The religion, his dad,
they were having some conflict."

"Why would he tell you about these things? If he was only an
acquaintance?"

"I don't know. It's what I do. I get people to talk to me. But I
think he also just wanted somebody to talk to. On the outside. He
was curious about things. So is his sister."

"Miriam."

"Right."

"Was anything else bothering him?"

"I'm not sure," I said, an uneasy feeling building.

Cook paused, like he didn't believe me. Staples, behind him and to
the side, shook her head almost imperceptibly, her lie detector going off.

"Okay," Cook said. "So you left him and went where?"

"I went to my wife's school. Prosperity Primary. She works there.
I brought my daughter and her friend home here because my wife
has a meeting at the school tonight."

The girls came trotting back in, Sophie yanking a towel from
the rack.

"We're cleaning it up," she said, and they trotted back out.

Cook smiled at the girls, then turned back to me, the smile gone.
"So tell me again about this conversation."

It was a tightrope now. A detective could smell lies like a blind man can hear. Hindering a homicide investigation? I could go away, Roxanne and Sophie left alone. Or worse. And whoever killed Abram, I'd do anything to nail him. Or them. But Miriam—if it all came out in court . . .

"I needed to see Abram," I said.

"Why was that?" Cook said.

The tightrope. I teetered. On one foot. Arms waving.

"He had a problem. I tried to fix it."

"What sort of problem?"

"Have you talked to the ATF agents who've been up here?"

"No," Cook said. "Should I?"

"Yes," I said.

"And when I talk to them, what will they tell me?"

He had his gaze fixed on me, unblinking. I was slipping now, Miriam falling with me. But her world was already shattered.

"They're investigating gun running that's been going on. Buying guns in Maine, driving them down to Boston."

"What's that got to do with Abram Snyder?"

I hesitated.

Took a deep breath. Heard Sophie singing along with the movie. And folded.

I told the truth. Abram buying guns with Semi. My conversation with Abram at the party, his wavering religious faith. The party itself, the Boston guys there. The aftermath, Abram and the video. Semi's interrogation session in the woods.

"Miriam doesn't remember any of it," I said. "I don't suppose there's any way . . . "

My words trailed off. I knew the answer.

"So the phone—the ATF has it. And the laptop?"

"Yes."

"The texts from the guys from Boston. What'd they say again?"

I told him, as closely as I could remember. *Delta fuckn force. Outta here.*

"We'll want to talk to Mr. Varney and Mr. Longfellow," Cook said. "But they didn't really know Abram?"

"No, they did it on principle. And for me."

"You haven't seen or heard from Semi since you dropped him off at his house?"

"No," I said. "He asked when he could have his phone back. And then he walked away. In his socks."

"How do you think he'd react to the news that his friends had been busted and he was in deep trouble? Blame Abram?"

"I think he'd run," I said. "Because we'd warned him not to bother Abram."

"Warned him how?" Cook said.

I hesitated.

"That if he bothered Abram he'd be dead."

"Had you given Semi any reason to believe that actually might happen?"

I paused. Cook waited.

"Clair and Louis," I said. "They've done this before. In their respective wars."

"Killed people, you mean."

"Yeah. Clair was Special Forces. Force Recon, Marine reconnaissance in Vietnam. Louis was in infantry in Iraq for one tour. Then he was a sapper next tour. Hunting IEDs and all that. Mosul. Sunni Triangle. He's pretty tough. Don't get me wrong; they're good people. The best. But with Semi, they—we—laid it on pretty good. So if you didn't know them, you might get the idea—"

"That they might kill you."

I nodded.

"And it would be no big deal," Cook said. "To them."

"Business as usual," I said.

He looked at me closely, as if he could glean more clues from my face.

"Kidnapping, criminal threatening, terrorizing, reckless conduct with a firearm—"

"Don't you need a complainant?"

Cook looked at me, started to say something, then caught himself. Took a breath and shook his head.

"I'd heard you played close to the lines," Cook said.

I shrugged.

"I think you may have just stepped over," he said.

"I'd do it again," I said.

"To help these Mennonite kids?"

"Yes," I said.

He looked at me, weighing what, if anything, to say. And then his cell buzzed and he stepped away. Deputy Staples looked at me, said, "How's your wife?"

"Okay," I said. "But they're still making threats. And one of those guys was at her school today."

"I'll talk to them, as soon as—"

Cook tapped his phone off and rejoined us.

"Who do you think could have done this, Mr. McMorrow?" Cook said.

He watched me, not as much waiting for an answer but gauging my reaction.

"I don't know," I said. "The gang guys?"

"They were in custody."

"Semi, then. Somebody else who was involved? The guys in the video?"

They watched and waited.

"Gun sellers? Maybe one was a regular, the beginning of the pipe-line?"

"Why would he kill Abram Snyder?" Cook said.

"I don't know," I said, rubbing my face with my hands.

"Did you kill Abram Snyder?"

I took my hands off my face and looked at him. His expression was calm, like he'd asked me if I'd come straight home from work.

"No," I said. "Why would I do that?"

"You were buying guns," he said. "You had the laptop and phone of one of the principals. Maybe he gave them to you to hide. Maybe this home-invasion abduction was part of some problems you were having with the group. Not getting your cut? Maybe this Semi was blackmailing you, too. "

"I write for the *New York Times*," I said. "The *Boston Globe*. I'm doing a story on private gun sales for *Outland* magazine. I don't sell guns to gangbangers."

"Maybe Abram there, he's getting a guilty conscience, decides to go to the police, rat out the whole crew."

"That's what I told him to do. Tell the ATF everything. Abram didn't know where the guns were going. He was just helping with the purchases. He thought Semi was selling them to out-of-state hunters."

"That's pretty clueless," Cook said.

"He's Mennonite, and not just Mennonite, but strict Old Order," I said. "It's not like he was watching *Law and Order* every night. He was naive. Gullible."

"I'm not," Cook said. "That's why I think it's quite a coincidence, you and your associates snatch one of the guys, beat him up. About the same time, ATF takes down a couple of the others. Four hours later, another guy involved in the ring is found murdered. He may have been talking to law enforcement, or believed to have been talk-ing. The killer appears to have thought so."

Staples watched me. She reminded me of Louis's dog. The stare.

"You're right," I said. "Those things must be connected. But I didn't kill him. I was trying to help him."

"Well, Mr. McMorrow," Cook said, "if that's the case, then it seems to me you haven't been very helpful at all."

25

I was sitting in the study, the chair swiveled around away from the desk, the same half beer in my hand. It was all playing and replaying in my head, and it always ended in the same way. Someone had killed Abram. I was responsible. I'd failed.

From there things got even darker, bleaker, heavier. Had he told them he wanted out? Had he told them, someone, that he was going to talk to the police? Had he been following my advice? If I'd never gotten involved, would Abram be alive right now?

And then it got darker still. Had I really cared about Abram, or had I just wanted to work my way into the Mennonites for the story? Had I been playing Abram just like Semi had? Had I gotten one guy killed and his sister publicly shamed?

I lifted the beer and finished it in three gulps. Went and got another and drank half of it down. And then I sat and pondered and took a last step downward, into the abyss.

What if the Bishop was right? His rants about heaven and hell and salvation and sinners. Did Abram die just at the time when he was questioning his faith? What if he would have come back to the church and Jesus and God and all the rest? And what if there really was a heaven and Abram had missed his chance? What if he was in the "lake of fire," or whatever the Bishop had called it? Joke's on you, bub. What if that was my fault, too?

It was deep dusk, the room getting darker with my mood. Sophie trotted into the kitchen looking for me, looked through to the study and spotted me. She came in and said, "Daddy, are you okay?"

"I'm fine, honey," I said.

"Can Salandra stay over?"

"Not tonight," I said. "It's a school night, and Mommy's out late."

Mommy. Roxanne. I looked at my watch. Reached for my phone and texted her. She texted back, said they were next on the agenda. I said I'd meet her.

"Oh, can't she, please?" Sophie said.

"Get your shoes," I said. "Time to go."

We sat in the lot and waited. There were cars, trucks, no big Dodge, none of the vehicles occupied. When people began to file out the door, I started the truck and pulled up close to the school. We waited there for fifteen minutes, the girls taking turns playing a game on my phone. Finally the lot was empty, just Roxanne's Subaru and Welt's pickup left. They were parked side by side.

I decided to give them one more minute before the three of us would go inside. And it was then that Roxanne and Welt pushed through the doors.

They were smiling, animated. I got out of the truck and the girls slid down, too, Sophie running to Roxanne and saying, "Clair was in charge and we had mac and cheese and hot dogs and ice cream and then there were police here and we watched *Jungle Book* and one of the policemen, he said his little boy likes *Jungle Book*, too."

Roxanne and Welt looked at me.

"Long story," I said. "How did it go?"

"Fantastic," Welt said. "The board is all in. Voted us another ten thousand for programming."

He beamed at Roxanne.

"She absolutely charmed them," he said.

Roxanne shook her head, said, "It wasn't me. It's the work we're doing. The antiviolence message just totally resonated with them."

"Good," I said. "I'm glad."

And with that we handed Salandra over. Sophie said she wanted to ride with her mom. I drove the truck over to the car as they got in, pulled the Glock out, and laid it on the seat.

It was nearly dark when we got home, a deep blue band showing on the western horizon, stars popping out overhead. When we pulled into the driveway, I saw Louis out back, the headlights reflecting in his eyes. He waved and moved into the darkness.

Roxanne said Sophie could have a quick tub in the morning, said she had to head for bed. Sophie gave me a hug and I kissed her good night and she trooped up the stairs in front of Roxanne, saying, "Head for bed" over and over in a singsong voice.

I stepped outside onto the deck, peered not at the stars, but at the blackening wall of woods. I walked down the steps and across the lawn, stopping every thirty feet or so and listening. I heard the night sounds—voles and moles rustling in the leaves—but nothing else. I crossed to the road and looked both ways. To my left, a quarter mile away at the top of the rise, headlights flared on.

I reached to my waistband for the gun, but the headlights swung away. The truck pivoted and taillights showed and then they disappeared.

Billy? Had he seen me? Just wanted to send his nightly message?

A sound behind me. Breathing. I whirled around. Clair and Louis were fifteen feet away, dark and silent.

"Could chase him down," Clair said, "but might just raise a ruckus."

"And there's enough going on," I said.

"Yes," Clair said.

"I'm sorry," Louis said.

"All over the news," Clair said.

I hadn't watched or listened.

"How much did they say?"

"Strangulation and blunt-force trauma," Louis said. "Found in the woods."

"Cops were here. What they're not saying is somebody tied him to a tree with his suspenders and carved the word 'rat' in his forehead," I said.

A pause, even from them.

"Thoughts on who did it?"

"I feel like I did, in a way. Tried to help him and got him killed."

Neither of them answered. A minute passed, the three of us standing there, and then Clair said, "You can wallow in that, or we can do something about it."

"Can't bring him back," I said.

"No, but you can make sure that the same person doesn't hurt somebody else," Louis said.

"And that evil acts are punished," Clair said.

"Seems a little late for that," I said.

"Never too late to make sure there are consequences," he said.

They melted away. I went inside and slipped the gun into the drawer of the study desk and locked it. When I went upstairs, I could hear pages turning in Sophie's room, saw the light on in ours. I pushed the door open. Roxanne was in a sleep shirt, sitting on the bed with her laptop open.

She looked at me.

"It's on Twitter. *Bangor Daily.*"

"I'm sure."

"It's not your fault, Jack," she said.

"You don't know," I said.

"But I know you cared about him."

I shrugged.

"For what that's worth," I said.

"I have no idea what's going on in your head these days," Roxanne said.

I didn't answer.

"I rest my case," she said.

I went over and sat on the edge of the bed. I looked over at Roxanne's pretty legs, her bare feet, her toenails painted red. I wondered if Welt liked the same view.

"I'm glad your presentation went well," I said.

"Thanks. Me, too."

There was a long silence, until I said, "Do you think bad things come in threes?"

"I don't believe in any of that," Roxanne said.

"I don't know. There's Abram. There's Billy and Baby Fat. What's next?"

"I just said I don't believe in that."

"I do," I said. "And other things, maybe."

I told her about my theory—that maybe Abram had died at the exact wrong time, when he was feeling doubts about God and all, and that he'd never had a chance to get his faith back. And what if the Bishop was right and we were all wrong.

"Don't take this all on yourself, Jack," Roxanne said. "Abram's God will understand, if there is one. If there isn't, then that part of it doesn't matter."

I thought that was an easy way out but I didn't say so. Instead I said, "I don't want the third thing to be us."

Roxanne put her hand on my arm, but only for a touch, and then took it off.

"I don't, either," she said. She didn't tell me not to worry.

Eventually the night would end, I knew, with me staring at the ceiling in the dark. But not yet.

Roxanne went to bed and I went downstairs, took another beer out of the refrigerator, opened it, and brought it to my desk. I held up the bottle, said, "Abram. I'm sorry." And then I drank. Then I put the bottle down and took out a legal pad, started to scrawl. The players. The sequence.

Party . . . Roust Semi . . . text from Lloyd or Jones. Lloyd and Jones arrested in NH . . .

I stopped. Went back and drew a line from the word *text*. The phone was gone, so I tried to recall the exact words. Slick. His bitch. Maine, the woman said, is Appalachia. Her street name: Gucci.

If Slick and Gucci weren't with Lloyd and Jones when they were arrested, where were they? It had been something about him saying it was time to load up and leave. Time for Lloyd and Jones to load up. Where was he?

And what had Semi said? Something about G-Block.

I flipped on the laptop, Googled it and Boston gangs. G-Block was a gang in Dorchester. The *Globe* story said G-Block was feuding with the Keith Street gang. In July a guy named Randall "Juicy" Luce had been shot and killed in a park there. Three guys with him had been wounded. Luce was seventeen, with Keith Street. The Boston PD gang interdiction unit was investigating, along with Boston Homicide.

A few more mentions, all connected to shootings. In 2011 a twelve-year-old boy had been shot in the head on his way to choir practice, also in Dorchester. He was expected to survive. Cops said he was an innocent bystander, hit by a round from a .45 caliber handgun fired on the next block. "The G-Block–Keith Street feud is a threat to public safety," an assistant police commissioner said.

And still was.

Slick. Gucci. Where were they now? I Googled them, and Dorchester, and gangs, and got nothing. I looked at the page, illuminated by the glow of the laptop screen. Flipped back to e-mail, opened the photo of the list of incoming calls to Semi's phone. Among the various area codes were a few Maine numbers, probably cell phones, probably Semi's buddies, like the guys from the party and the video. I could text them, say I was a buddy of Semi's, got another live one, way hotter than the Amish chick. Want to hang out?

See if we could invite them to the party. The party could be me, Clair, Louis, and one dirtbag at a time.

Would they have killed Abram? To accomplish what? Keep him from talking about the video? Would they even be ashamed of what they'd done? With Semi on the run, would they respond to a stranger?

I looked at the numbers more. A few exchanges I recognized, one number that looked familiar. I took my phone out and compared them. Three of them were gun sellers, Semi and Abram and I making the same rounds. Had they called Semi to confirm an advertised gun was available? Called to say there were more guns to be had for the right price?

And then there was another number, 338, the Galway exchange. Three calls in two minutes, all received. Then another an hour later, for sixteen minutes. Making up? Someone who would know where Semi would go underground? How fast would the detectives track these numbers down?

I pictured many interviews with many Mennonites before they got to this level. So I tapped the number in. Waited. It rang. And then a click:

"Waldo Street Hotel," a woman's voice said, cheery and eager. "This is Celeste. May I help you?"

Galway. Boutique hotel. Expensive.

"Hi," I said. "I'm looking for a friend of mine—hope he's still there."

"Yessir," Celeste said. "Who would that be?"

Another image. *Where is he? He can't just leave me here in this hick town. Put him on. Don't you hang up on me. I know he's there.*

"Well, I don't know what name he would have checked in under, but he goes by Slick. His girlfriend is Gucci. They're from Boston. They were just up for a few days, you know, a romantic getaway sort of thing. I hope I haven't—"

"The rapper, you mean," she said.

"Right," I said. "Is he still there?"

"I'm sorry, they checked out this morning."

"Oh, shucks," I said. "Just missed them."

"Yeah, he had some meetings with producers."

"Slick's a busy guy."

"Yeah," Celeste said. "He was sweet, though. Treated the staff real nice."

"Yeah, he's very generous."

"I'll say. That's why I didn't mind when she called."

"Gucci?"

"Yeah. Is she a friend of yours?"

Wariness in her tone.

"I've met her a couple of times is all."

"Yeah, well," Celeste began, the caution gone, "she's lucky we liked her boyfriend so much."

"Why's that?" I said.

"Well, her sunglasses? Yes, I'll mail them to her, but she ought to know better. What goes around, comes around, you know?"

"Gucci can be a little snooty."

"I guess to heck. Which is fine, if you don't need people. But sometimes you need something, and they remember."

"She needed her sunglasses?"

I was tapping the keys softly.

"Mailed to her. Overnight. She said they cost four hundred and eighty dollars and they're discontinued, and they're her favorites of all time, and, and, and."

I called up the Dorchester map. Picked a street.

"You mailing them to Slick? At the Geneva Avenue address?"

"No, to her. Except she isn't Gucci on the mail. She's Deloris Franklin."

"On Geneva Avenue, right, thirteen-eighty?"

"No, she wanted them to go to her."

"Oh, I thought she was living with him," I said.

"Well, her fancy sunglasses aren't. They're going to six-eleven Intervale Street, number three."

"Uh-oh," I said. "Sounds like trouble in paradise."

She paused.

"They did leave together, in this big shiny black SUV thing, but last night? I thought we were gonna have to call the police."

"No kidding. Well, Gucci, she does have a temper."

"I guess. I mean, she was calling him every name in the book. You could hear it on the whole second floor. And she doesn't think much of Maine, either."

"She was mad because he brought her to Maine?"

"I can't really say," Celeste said.

I waited, knew she would.

"One of the girls, she said they were arguing about another woman. She was texting him, and Gucci, whatever she calls herself, she saw the texts."

"Whoops."

"I guess there were pictures."

"Double whoops."

"And besides," Celeste said, indignant now. "Appalachia, at two-fifty a night? Taittinger in your room at check-in? And it costs us, like, twenty-five bucks a bottle, and that's by the case. Heated towel racks? Lobster omelets? If this is Appalachia, I'm, like, signing up."

"He said he was glad to have some privacy," I said. "Just kick back."

"I know. He wouldn't even tell us his rapper name at first," the young woman said.

"Which one did he give you? Slick Fitty?"

"No, Slick X."

I could hear her fingers on a keyboard.

"Are there more under Slick Fitty, 'cause I could only find two for Slick X. Him and all his friends, dancing around with guns and bottles of liquor and big stacks of hundred-dollar bills."

"Yeah, that's Slick all right."

"Are you one of the guys in the videos? You don't sound black."

"Black Irish," I said. "Celeste, you have a good night."

And that's exactly what Slick X was doing in the videos on YouTube. He was a muscular guy, big smile under his Phoenix Suns ball cap, jeans held up by the big G buckle of his Gucci belt. He was rapping in the courtyard of a project, surrounded by his buddies, everybody flashing wads of cash, drinking Courvoisier out of the bottle, pulling guns from their waistbands and aiming at the camera.

A beat-up TEC-9 machine pistol, a long-barreled .357 revolver, a snub-nosed .38, a Glock with a thirty-round clip. The words mostly had to do with what would happen to anybody who messed with them, what had happened to people who had. "Putting steel to your grill, head shots we pull."

I sat back in the chair. So this was the destination for the guns Semi bought in Dixville and Davidson, Monroe and Newburgh. I wondered what the sellers I'd met would think of seeing their guns waved around like toys. Was this what Abram had been killed for? Street gang had met Old Order Mennonites and the gang had won.

For now.

If Gucci wanted her sunglasses sent down to Dorchester, and they had come to Maine together, then they were back home. I doubted Lloyd and Jones would flip on him, the rap videos full of scorn—and death—for snitches. They'd sell out Semi in a second, but Slick, the guy calling the shots, would walk.

Had he stuck around to tie up a loose end? When he got word that his boys had been arrested, did he go after Semi? When Semi couldn't be found, had Slick killed Semi's Amish friend?

Headphones on, I watched the video again. With all the guns, the gun talk, wouldn't Slick have shot Abram? A blunt instrument, Louis had said, possibly a gun butt. Maybe Slick had walked Abram into the woods at gunpoint, realized the shot would be heard, and decided to hit him on the head instead.

And then leave his message.

But like Celeste had said, what goes around comes around. I finished the beer, closed the laptop, shut off the light. And then I crossed the room, stood by the sliding doors to the deck. Stepped out into the night. Took a long, deep breath.

"I know how you feel," a voice said.

Louis. He moved out of the shadows under the lilacs.

"How would you like to go to Boston?" I said.

26

The girls overslept, left the house in a rush of sneaker-finding, blow-drying, and *Did you brush your teeth?*

I hadn't noticed the time because I was online again, studying the street view of 611 Intervale Street, rotating to see across the street, up and down the block. Roxanne sped across town, raced up the drive-way to the school. I sat in the truck as she and Sophie trotted across the lot and through the door.

It was 7:15, teacher arrival time. I took out my phone. Tapped in a number, waited.

"Sergeant Cook."

He was driving.

"This is Jack McMorrow."

I said I had some information for him. Slick and his girlfriend, Gucci, how they stayed in Galway. That he was some sort of superior to Jones and Lloyd.

"Uh-huh," he said.

"So he could have done it, after he heard his boys were busted."

I heard the sound of traffic.

"Well?" I said.

"A step ahead of you, Mr. McMorrow. The subjects you're speaking of were interviewed last night. They say they never heard of any Mennonite, that they were in Maine on vacation."

"Says who?"

"Says both of them, including Miss Franklin. She said she couldn't get out of Maine fast enough."

"Maybe she left separately?"

"Doesn't have a driver's license," Cook said. "Said she's never learned to drive at all. According to her, they had an argument and she demanded he take her home ASAP."

"Could have cut through Prosperity on the way home."

"Could have, but they say not. At this point we have no information tying him or their vehicle to Prosperity. Not like the town is filled with video surveillance. And now he's lawyered up."

"So what do you do now?"

The sound of the car slowing, then stopping, the motor shutting off.

"Continue our investigation in other directions, Mr. McMorrow. And speaking of that, I was going to call you."

"Oh, yeah?"

"Yeah. Bishop Snyder. He told me that he warned you not to speak to his son or his daughter. That you were a bad influence on them, that you were known to be a violent person and he didn't want you associating with Abram or Miriam."

"His opinion," I said. "Not Abram's."

"But Abram—the circumstances of his death might suggest that his father was right."

"Or that he should have been warning somebody else off," I said.

"We'll be talking," Cook said.

"No doubt," I said.

I met Louis and Clair at the restaurant, the two of them in a booth at the far end of the room, looking out at the view to the west. Belle was behind the counter and she said good morning, then gave me a searching look.

I moved closer and she said, "Awful about your friend."

"Yes. He was a very good guy."

"Seemed it. But he would be, being a Mennonite, right. Awful for his family."

I didn't answer.

"Word around town this morning is it was guys from out of state," Belle said. "Been having parties up there in the woods."

"I don't know," I said.

"Feds have been up here."

"Really."

"Yup. Hope they catch whoever did it and lock them up."

"For a long time," I said.

"Oughta bring back the death penalty," Belle said.

"I don't think the Mennonites would go for that."

"Yeah, well, maybe somebody oughta stick up for them, if they won't stick up for themselves."

She was breaking eggs in a big metal bowl.

"Heard Semi was looking pretty beat-up," she said, without looking up.

"Ran into a door," I said.

"Funny how that happens," Belle said.

"They say most accidents occur in the home."

She turned and poured the eggs onto the grill. They sizzled and steamed. She poked at them with a big spatula, then turned back.

"What can I get you, Jack?"

"Scrambled, home fries, whole-wheat toast, and tea."

"My treat today," Belle said. "You and Clair and your friend."

"Then I'll have sausage, too," I said.

She looked at me, her cheeks rosy from the heat of the grill.

"You break Billy's other arm, steak and eggs on me."

We ate first, talked after. Belle refilled their coffees, brought me a second pot of tea. They listened as I told them about Slick and the Galway hotel, Sergeant Cook and their denials, their alibi.

"Might be worth asking him ourselves," Louis said.

I pulled up the street view of the tenement on Intervale Street, held up my phone, told them about the sunglasses.

"Six-eleven Intervale, number three," I said.

"Ground floor would be easier," Clair said.

"In a perfect world," I said.

"She lives there with him?" Louis said.

"I don't know," I said. "They were fighting at the hotel. I guess another woman was texting him pictures of herself. The G-Block gang is based at a project a half mile away."

We paused as two older men sat at the next booth. They looked like farmers: ball caps, dark blue Dickies, ruddy faces. Belle came with coffee and one of them said, "How you doin' today, dear?"

Boston gangbangers and Prosperity, Maine. Drugs and guns: the common denominators.

"Need to do some reconnaissance," Clair said.

"But not you," Louis said to him.

Clair nodded.

"I stay," he said. "If something went wrong up here, Billy and the boys, it wouldn't be enough to have—"

"Me alone?" I said.

"No offense," Clair said.

"Not that you're not capable," Louis said. "For a reporter."

"Thanks—I think."

"The girl first," Clair said. "Just talk to her. See if that leads to the boyfriend."

"Get there fast," Louis said. "While she's still pissed-off."

I looked at my watch. It was 8:10. Three hours to Boston.

"Need a rental," Louis said. "Can't roll with a Maine pickup truck. In Iraq, the Special Forces guys drove old beat-up minivans. Blended right in."

That would add an hour, with a stop at the Portland Jetport for the car. Leave now, be in Dorchester by noon. I looked at Clair. He was gathering himself up, taking a last drink of coffee.

"You sure?" I said.

"Sure as shooting," he said.

We took Louis's Jeep, the dog in his place in the backseat. Louis was quiet, his eyes fixed to the road as we sped south out of Waldo County. We drove seventy on the back roads, swerved left to sweep by slower cars and trucks. Coming into Augusta, Louis concentrated like a race-car driver as he passed on the left and right, slipped into spaces between cars, rode on their bumpers until they pulled over.

"We'll get there," I said, as he wove his way through traffic on the approach to the interstate.

"Once you know your mission, your job is to execute and get out," Louis said. "We miss this lady by five minutes, we're making it up from that point on."

"We're making it up anyway."

"Not me," Louis said. "Plan's broken down into steps. Execute each step and we achieve our objective. We improvise when there's a busted play. We don't improvise to start off."

I didn't answer. We merged onto the interstate and Louis hit the gas, the Jeep winding up to eighty. The dog got to his feet on the seat and Louis opened the back passenger window six inches. The dog stuck his nose out and sniffed.

"He knows," Louis said.

"Knows what?" I said.

"It's almost time to rock and roll."

"What's his job?"

"Intimidation," Louis said.

We drove the thirty miles to Brunswick in twenty minutes, nobody speaking, the dog back on the seat. Just north of Freeport I said, "You don't have to do any of this."

"Don't have to do anything," Louis said.

I waited. Five miles. Ten miles, the Jeep eating up the miles, big tires whirring.

"Thing is," Louis said, as though there had been no pause in the conversation, "messed up as that war was, and they all are in their own way, it was the most alive I'd ever felt."

I looked at him, his dark brooding eyes still fixed on the road, one hand on the top of the wheel.

"Connected to my squad like I'd never been connected to anybody before. Any day you could die, and some people did. But if you made it, it was like all of the crap was scraped away. The purpose of life was to survive, help your buddies make it, kill anybody who stood in the way of you living another day."

"Life stripped down to its core," I said.

"Because what is the purpose of it?" Louis said. "To make more money? Buy a bigger car? Lie on a beach someplace and stare at the water? Is that what we're here for?"

He didn't expect a reply.

"My grandfather, he was CEO of a company that makes wire. Still does. From tiny filaments to the copper wire inside big electrical cables. He made wire and he made money, a real lot of it, and he went to meetings about how to make more and better wire and more money, and meetings about more meetings."

"What did he do for fun?" I said.

"I just told you."

"What about your grandmother?"

"She waited for him to get home. And to retire."

We were north of Portland now, the traffic heavier, cars moving in a sixty-mile-an-hour procession, clouds building on the southern horizon like mountains. Louis looked lost in thought, or maybe he was done.

"Your dad a lawyer, your grandfather a CEO. What did they all think when you joined up?"

"Thought they'd failed. How'd a Longfellow turn out to be such a screw-up. Boarding school, where my dad and grandfather went. A couple years of bad grades in a fancy college. Because I couldn't buy that any of it mattered. Why was I doing this? Was this all that life was? Another paper? Another exam? Get good grades so I could get a job, make money, go to meetings, buy a bigger house, a bigger car, wait to retire, retire and die? They said I was depressed, but I wasn't."

"So, you enlisted?"

"Me and the other square pegs."

"But you liked them."

"I loved them. I'd kill for them and them for me. And we did."

"Hard to match that in civilian life."

"Impossible," Louis said. "But this comes close."

We parked the big-wheeled Jeep in the Portland Jetport lot and Louis and the dog waited as I walked across to the car rental lot. The young guy behind the counter had his hair flipped up in front and smelled like cologne. I told him we wanted an SUV, a big one, with privacy glass.

He searched on his computer, typed a lot, finally looked up.

"I have a Chevy Tahoe," he said. "It's got the privacy package. Like the Secret Service uses. Except we can't get you the bulletproof glass."

The guy grinned.

"Too bad," I said.

I didn't grin back.

The Tahoe was white with Florida plates, the windows blacked out. I parked by the Jeep and Louis loaded in an army duffel, which he'd packed. Then he went to the glove box of the Jeep and took out a small black rectangular thing, like a cell phone. A stun gun.

He got in and said, "Cell phones off."

I looked at him.

"Trace you by the towers."

I powered my phone off and drove, the dog sniffing the new seat, circling to get comfortable. Traffic was light south of the city and the truck was big and fast and quiet. Louis was quiet, too, all the way to Portsmouth. We looked out from the bridge, saw powerboats on the Piscataqua River, their wakes showing like contrails behind jets.

I felt like I was worlds away from Prosperity, Maine, but, oddly, not from Abram, murdered and defaced. It was like I was plunging headlong into a place where that sort of atrocity was conceivable, committed in the name of business or revenge.

Coming down off the bridge, I said, "So tell me about this plan— the one with the steps."

Louis did.

27

Dorchester is south of the city center, where it hugs the shoreline along Route 1. With Louis reading directions off of his phone, I swung off at Columbia Road and continued south. It was mostly triple-deckers, with restaurants and hair salons, pharmacies and liquor stores sprinkled here and there. Intervale Street was one-way, the wrong way, so I went three streets down and took a right, backtracked, and took another right.

Louis watched the rain, the wipers slapping. The street numbers climbed and Louis said, "Slow," and we approached No. 611, rolled past.

It was a three-decker with porches on the front, pale green with cream trim. The paint was peeling, and there was a sign on the post by the front door that said POSTED—NO TRESPASSING. The yard was overgrown and there was a drive to the side with a gated chain-link fence. At the back of the driveway two cars were parked, both small sedans. One looked like it had been there for months.

No Toyota SUV.

"Let's go," Louis said.

I stopped the truck and backed up. Turned into the driveway and pulled through the gate. I parked to the side and we got out, the dog whining out the cracked windows at being left behind.

The first-floor windows were covered with security bars. There was an entrance on the driveway side, one on the front porch. We walked to the side entrance, opened the metal door, and stepped in.

There were two mailboxes, junk mail scattered on the floor beneath them. One box said FRANKLIN APT. 3. The staircase was to the rear, and we walked up to the second-floor landing and paused. There was a television on there, a game show in Spanish. We moved quickly but quietly up the next two flights and stopped.

There was a sign that said TAKE OFF YOUR SHOES, and they had. There were work boots, Air Jordans, running shoes, and tall pink rubber boots you would wear in the rain. They were all neatly arranged. Fastidious. We moved to the door and listened. Heard another television, this one in English. A talk show.

I looked at Louis. He nodded.

I knocked. We waited.

There were footsteps, a woman's voice saying, "Who's that?"

I said, "My name's Jack McMorrow. I'm from Maine. I'm looking to speak to Gucci."

No response, and then we heard a chain rattling and the door opened, the chain still on.

A young black woman looked out. She was very pretty, hair straight and parted on the side. Wary but curious.

"Who are you?" she said.

"I'm Jack McMorrow. This is Louis."

"What are you, cops?"

"No," I said. "We're not cops. I'm a reporter."

She looked at me, then at Louis.

"What's he?"

"My assistant," I said.

"What do you want?"

"I need to talk. To Slick."

"We aren't together anymore," Gucci said, and started to close the door. I held it open and said, "That's okay. We don't need to talk to you. But we need to see Slick."

"I have nothing to do with him," she said.

"Oh," I said. "I thought you were together, that you stayed with him in Galway, Maine."

"How do you know that?"

"I'm from there. Somebody told me."

She looked doubtful but I kept talking.

"Things went south? While you were in Maine?" I said.

She hesitated, looked closer. "You could say that. Is this for some story?"

"No, just very deep background. Totally off the record, I absolutely promise. So where is Slick now?"

A long pause, Gucci sizing me up—the situation, the possibility for revenge versus the risk of ratting him out.

"He's with her," Gucci said.

Yes, I thought.

"If he wants to go with some piece of trash, that's his problem, you know what I'm saying? I'm taking my boards for RN. As in registered nurse. And I'm Keisha in the hospital, not Gucci, by the way. That girl, she's a crackhead. In a coupla years she's gonna look like you hit her with an ugly stick. You seen those people. Before and after?"

"Right. Does a number on you," I said. "Can't understand what he's thinking, I have to say. A crackhead or you? Man, his mistake."

Gucci rolled her eyes.

"But, listen, would you mind taking the chain down? Can we just talk?"

She hesitated, then closed the door. The chain rattled and she opened the door and stepped out onto the landing. She was wearing yoga pants and a T-shirt that said MASS GENERAL 10K, 2014. Built like a ballet dancer and looked like Halle Berry. She could play the nurse in a movie.

"So what do you want to know?" Gucci said.

"I really need to talk to him. Did you guys come right back here?"

"I did. Grabbed the bus in Portland. No offense, but Maine gave me the creeps. Nothing but woods, and at night it's pitch-dark and cold, and that town, there's, like, nothing open after nine o'clock, and people looking at me like maybe I'm Beyoncé, hard to tell because all black women look the same."

"Yeah, well, Maine's not for everybody," I said. "So Slick didn't come back with you?"

"Not with me. I didn't want to be in the same car with that lying sack anymore. I told him, just let me off here. What do you want to talk to him about?"

"AJ and Trigger."

She looked at me, then at Louis.

"You sure you aren't cops?"

"Not even close."

"Well, okay, but like I told the real cops, I don't know anything about those guys. Or him, really. Thought I did, but turned out I was wrong. You know he's a smart guy, underneath the thug life. You sure this isn't gonna end up in some story?"

"I'm sure," I said.

"Why should I believe you?"

She nodded toward Louis.

"Or him?"

"Because I don't lie," I said. "And he doesn't either."

Gucci looked at us, from one to the other. Back again. She ended with her gaze locked on mine. Waited and then said, "Okay. First time we went out, he's talking about poetry and history and all this, people like Ralph Ellison and Richard Wright, stuff from English class, you know? And he's comparing them to Tupac and Akon, Lil Wayne. I said, 'Your crew know about this, mister college professor?' He said, 'No, I'm telling you about my secret life, stuff goes on in my head.' "

"Interesting," I said.

"You know what Slick's problem is?" she said.

"No."

"He won't buckle. Won't bend for nobody, ever, not for a second. Not in school, not on the street, nowhere."

"Running drugs and guns isn't bending?" I said.

"For Slick, it's looking out for your own. His crew. He says he's got responsibilities."

Gucci shrugged. "But hey, turns out he thinks with his you-know-what, like most guys."

She paused.

"You know what? You should just call her. That's where he'll be. With his hooker crackhead and her naked selfies."

"She disrespected you," Louis said.

Gucci looked at him, like she was surprised he could talk.

"She was texting him pictures and she knew we were together. On a vacation. I mean, have some class."

"You hate him?" Louis said.

"Oh, yeah. Cheat on me, you get some serious hate."

"Then shoot him a text," Louis said. "Say you want to give him something back. A piece of jewelry or something."

"I'm not giving him shit," Gucci said.

"You won't have to," I said.

Gucci crossed her arms over her chest.

"You guys are cops."

"Nope."

I took out my old *Times* ID and held it up. Louis dug in his jeans and took out his wallet and fished out a tattered Marine Corps ID.

"And now you work for him?" Gucci said, nodding toward me.

"Sometimes," Louis said. "If I like the story."

"Louis is a researcher," I said.

She looked at him. "What kinda research you want to do on Slick?"

"Just ask him a few questions," Louis said.

She paused. Looked at both of us. Then reached to the back of her T-shirt, took a phone out of the waistband of her yoga pants.

"Is he gonna even get here? To this apartment?" she said.

"No," Louis said.

Gucci pondered it, then raised the phone, started to text, reading aloud as she tapped.

"Hey. You want any of this shit you better get your sorry cheatin' ass over here. I'm tossin' it. Some homeless person gonna be wearing a twenty-four-carat gold chain from Neiman Marcus."

She pressed SEND.

We watched while she stared at the phone and waited. Then the phone buzzed and she squinted at it and said, "Done."

"What'd he say?" Louis said.

"I'm a crazy-ass bitch, and he'll be right over."

"What's he driving?" I said.

"An X-Three. Silver. She rented it for him. Texted him a picture. Her on the hood of the car."

"Huh," I said. "Thanks."

"Payback's a bitch," Gucci said, and she shut the door. The chain rattled as she slipped it back into place.

We sat in the truck at the curb in front of the next house up. The motor was running and the AC was on, the dog starting to pant. I was watching the mirror and Louis was watching the front.

We'd been there fifteen minutes when Louis said, "We're on."

The silver BMW was approaching, a guy at the wheel, black with a blue-and-white baseball cap, nobody else showing. We looked away as Slick passed, slowed, swung left between the gates and into the drive. Louis was out of the car, moving fast, a low sort of trot. I had the Tahoe in reverse, backed up, swung through the gates.

As I came out of the truck, Slick was reaching for his waistband, saying, "What the—," but Louis was on him, jabbed him with the stun gun. Slick stumbled as I ran up, and we each got a hand under an arm, dragged him to the truck, yanked the door open, and slung him in. The dog, in the cargo compartment, barked and jumped in place. Louis was leaning over Slick, turning him, fastening his hands behind his back.

A length of tape over his mouth and we were gone.

He'd been reaching for a knife, had decided not to carry a gun with the ATF all over him.

We knew this because Slick told us. He was in the backseat of the Tahoe, which was parked in a pullout across from some tennis courts in Franklin Park, a couple of miles west of Gucci's house. Louis found the spot on Google Earth, then checked it out on street view. They used satellite maps a lot in Iraq, he said. This location was private and deserted, and the rain-spattered windows were like a double layer of privacy glass.

The three of us were sitting in the backseat, Slick in the middle. Louis was holding a KA-BAR commando knife. The dog was standing up behind Slick. He was growling, his warm breath on the back of Slick's neck.

Louis had ripped the tape off but, unlike Semi, Slick hadn't made a peep. He just looked at us, hands still fastened behind his back, and said, "Who the fuck are you? What the fuck do you think you're doing? Do you know who the fuck I am?"

"We're from Maine," I said. "We have some questions. About Trigger and AJ and what happened up there."

"You have some questions?" Slick said. "I'll tell you the question you should be asking. Am I gonna die today or tomorrow? Are they gonna shoot me in the head once, or shoot the whole fucking clip? Those are the only questions going on here. Those are the—"

"Enough," Louis said.

Slick looked at him and said, "What is this? Some fucking gonzo white Maine militia? Crawling around the woods with fucking shoe polish on your face? Well, baby, you ain't in Maine now. My boys, they'll blow your goddamn face off. I mean, are you serious? Two crackers come down here and—"

Louis waited again. "We ask," he said. "You answer."

"Listen," I said. "What's your name? Your real name, I mean."

"My gov'ment? What you want that for?"

"I like to know who I'm talking to."

"You're talking to Thomas Lincoln Pierce. As in Paul."

"Okay, Thomas," I said. "Abram Snyder. He's Mennonite, but they call him Amish."

"I don't give a shit what they call him."

"Your boys up in Maine were buying guns from a guy named Semi. Amish and Semi were buying the guns. Now Abram is dead. Somebody killed him yesterday, carved the word 'rat' in his forehead."

Slick looked at me.

"And this Amish guy's some friend of yours. And you're out to get revenge."

"I want to know who it was," I said.

"And this guy here is your psycho muscle? Dragged some whack job outta the woods? Take him down to the 'hood, beat the truth outta some gangbanga?"

I didn't reply.

"How'd you find this house?"

"Hotel. In Maine. They had this address."

"You get Gooch to text me?"

I shook my head.

"Just sat on the house. Figured you'd show up."

He looked at me. "She's work, but she's worth it. You know she's gonna be a nurse? A real nurse, not some CNA shit. You in the hospital, wake up with her staring down at you. You say, 'If this is heaven, let me in.' That chick's beautiful *and* smart. Even got me thinkin' maybe I'll go into the medical field. Physical therapist, maybe. Got my GED. All I need is—"

"Abram," I said.

Slick looked at me, then at Louis, then back at me.

"You think I capped some Amish? Didn't cap no Amish. Didn't cap no white boy up in Maine, neither. Carving stuff into people's heads? What do you think I am—a fuckin' savage?"

"Why should we believe you?" I said.

" 'Cause anybody wasted Amish, they got it wrong. R-A-T on his head? That's bullshit. Rat bitches got Trig and AJ busted, they ain't in Maine. They're here. And I know who those bitches are."

"How do you know the snitches are from here?" I said.

"My team picked it up."

"From where?"

"The bricks."

"Inside?"

"Them rat bitches running their mouth, thinking I won't know? Confidential rat-bitch informant? Yo, there ain't nothin' confidential. Confidential informant, that's an oxy fuckin' moron."

I looked at him.

"So what happens to them?"

"Hey, natural selection, baby. Charles Darwin. I loved reading that in school. Liked biology. All the science shit. But Darwin, that dude had the big picture. You a weak rat bitch, you get cut out of the fuckin' herd. You strong, you survive. Natural selection, baby. Going on all around us, all the time."

We sat. The dog yawned. Slick said, "Your smelly dog ain't droolin' on my back, is he?"

"What about Semi?" Louis said. "You saying he killed Abram?"

"Semi? I barely know that motherfucker's name. He's the help, you know what I'm saying? Some hillbilly the boys bring in to move some drugs, buy some guns. That's it."

"You don't think he'd kill Abram to keep him from talking?"

Slick shrugged. "Ask him."

"So why did you go to Maine?" I said.

"Hey, I don't go, something goes wrong, we got nothing to show. This way, two vehicles, they get a couple of boys, the load. They don't get the money. They don't get the other fourteen hammers. You don't put all your eggs in one basket. And the old lady, her boards is coming up. She needed a vacation."

"And you didn't kill Abram?"

Slick shook his head, smiled, rolled his eyes.

"Kill him? I barely heard of him. Never met him. Never touched him. Never spoke to him. There's levels in this business, you know? Ain't you ever watched *The Wire*? I thought all white people watched *The Wire*. Think it gives them the real thug life. After a few episodes, they go around saying 'motherfucker' all the time. It's pathetic. But you seen it, right? You think the managerial level is down there chitchatting with the shrimps on the street? Shit, no. There's a hierarchy, you know what I'm saying? Some gun picker in Maine? That's nothin'."

I looked hard at him and he stared back.

"Who you judging, looking at me like that?" Slick said. "Piss me off. White folks create this fucking prison for black people to live in, keep us locked up in it last hundred years, then shake their heads when we do what we have to do to survive."

He looked at me, gave a snort of disdain.

"You try walking in my skin. Try living in my world."

I didn't answer. He kept on.

"Been on my own since I was fuckin' eight. Father hauled off to prison. You know for what? Standing on the corner, Bronx, New York.

Hunts fuckin' Point. Cop driving by, he stops, says, 'What you doing? Selling drugs? Move your ass outta here.' My father says, 'I have a right to stand here.' He's like Rosa Parks on the bus. He ain't budgin'. The cop, he starts pushing him. My father stands his ground. He always said, 'Be peaceful. Obey the law. Respect everyone. But if someone puts a hand on you, send him to the cemetery.' "

"Malcolm X," Louis said.

We looked at him.

"Yo, an educated cracker from the Maine wilderness," Slick said.

"Did a paper on him," Louis said.

"Get you a medal."

"He was talking about striking back at whites," Louis said, "not black kids in your own neighborhood."

Slick gave him a long, cold stare. "I love you white people," he said. "Run this apartheid country for three hundred years, keep throwing us crumbs, fenced in the fucking ghetto, falling-down houses, falling-down schools, crap everywhere, cops rounding us up when we go off the reservation. It's like, shut two of us in a fucking cage with food enough for one, then say, 'Whoa. Look at them darkies. They're killing each other. What's wrong with them people? Guess we better lock their black asses up. Getting paid by the head, get them cattle in the pen.' Well, fuck that."

He paused, then looked back at me.

"The cop whacks my daddy with a baton and then he puts a hand on him. My father fights back, thank you, Malcolm X. The cop pepper-sprays the shit out of him, then gives him a beat down. Charge my daddy with aggravated assault because he won't buckle, ain't gonna grovel, say yessir, nossir. Never did. Never got out, either. Killed a man in prison, defending himself, shipped him off to fuckin' Ohio. Me and my mama moved up here, be near her aunt. But my daddy, he stands his ground. Won't kneel for no man."

He paused.

"And you won't either?" I said.

"Not for you, not for nobody."

"You kill Amish?" Louis said.

Slick snorted.

"I told you. Besides, I respect those buggy people. Telling the rest of the world to fuck off."

Their eyes locked and they stared, like they were searching each other for clues. And then Louis looked at me and said, "He's right. And he's telling the truth."

"About time you crackers wised the fuck up," Slick said. "Now you better start running for home, while you still got time."

28

We'd crossed the Tobin Bridge and were heading north on Route 1, silent since Dorchester. After a couple of miles of fast-food and liquor stores, Louis said, "What's that leave?"

"Semi," I said.

"Scenario?"

"Abram decides to push back about Miriam. He won't be black-mailed. They argue and get in a fight, and maybe Abram is getting the best of him. He was a strong guy. All that farm work. So Semi reaches for something, whacks him and kills him. He panics and does the thing with the R-A-T, makes it look like the gang guys did it."

"He was the first one to go for the gun in the woods," Louis said.

"Dumb and violent," I said.

"So what next?"

"Go home. See if he shows up."

"You think he'll come back?"

"It's all he knows," I said. "The same twenty square miles his whole life."

"They usually come home?"

"Find them in the back of their sister's closet. Under their grand-mother's bed."

"Cops'll be sitting on those places," Louis said.

"And mine," I said.

We were quiet for a few more miles. I swung off of Route 1 onto the interstate and continued north. There was farmland filled with trailers, signs showing the way to more fast food. I felt the same urge that Semi would feel, the need to get back to my own little sleepy hollow, familiar roads and trees and barns, all leading to Sophie and Roxanne.

Louis looked over at me, then away.

"How's she about all this?" he said, like both he and the dog had a sixth sense.

"Not happy," I said.

"You could just let it all go. I mean, you've got a nice life. Nice wife, cute little girl, house in the country."

"Haven't gotten around to building the picket fence," I said.

He didn't reply.

"Fence could keep out the psychopath sex pervert," I said. "Or the guy who kills someone and then carves words in his head. Or the trust-fund goat farmer who's hitting on my wife. Or the Mennonite Bishop who hates my guts, or would if it weren't a sin."

"Pickets with razor wire, maybe," Louis said.

"Electrified," I said.

"With surveillance cameras."

"And a guard dog."

"Got that covered," Louis said.

We dumped the Tahoe, headed north. It was a little after five when we swung off the highway in Augusta, a straight shot up Route 3 to the northeast, forty miles from home. Ten miles north—thinned woods running up a ridge on the left, a lake glimmering through the trees to the right. I remembered my phone, took it out of the door holder, and turned it on.

It was booting up when Louis, at the wheel, said, "Billy."

"Yeah."

"He's a felon."

"I'm sure."

"What if he got guns from Semi? What if Abram found out and didn't like it? Possession of a firearm by a felon, that'll get you a couple of years. And Billy's capable of killing, carving the letters. Any of it."

"We can tell Cook," I said, "make sure he has him on the—"

A buzzing, like a snake. My phone.

I picked it up and looked. Three missed calls. A message. Roxanne. I listened, her voice fading in and out.

She'd been at school. She'd had a meeting, and now Sophie and Salandra wanted pizza. Sophie and Salandra. That meant a foursome. They'd be home late, after six. She'd told Clair.

Her tone was businesslike, like she was calling her admin with an updated schedule. She didn't say good-bye.

We were in Vassalboro, twenty minutes out. I called Clair, but we were in a dead spot, a valley between wooded hills, and the call kept dropping. I asked Louis to drive faster and he did.

Nobody spoke as Palermo passed. Wooded hills with squares of pasture. Sinking farmhouses, trailers swallowed up by brush. Louis blew by trucks stuffed with camping gear, cars festooned with bicycles, coast-bound tourists searching for the last pure place. Good luck.

Past Lake St. George, we swung north into Montville, climbed the long hills, passed crossroads named for dead people, the road like a winding and overgrown cemetery. No crossroads for Abram.

It was twilight when we wended our way into Prosperity from the south. I called Clair, got voice mail. I told him about Roxanne and the pizza, asked if he was on it. Our ETA at my house was four minutes.

And then we were there, Louis slamming the Jeep over the potholes, lifting over the rises. He turned and slid into the dooryard. Stopped and we both looked.

The house was still. We sat for a minute and it remained so. Goldfinches were fluttering in the thistle and goldenrod. We sat another few seconds and the dog whined.

"Has to pee," Louis said. "Just be a minute."

I got out, reached under the seat for the Glock. Louis and the dog got out on the other side and the dog made for the lilacs, started to sniff. "Hurry it up," Louis said. I went to the shed door and stepped inside, fumbled for my key to unlock the door to the kitchen.

The door creaked open and I stepped inside. The air was cool and still. It smelled like cigarettes.

I froze. Sniffed. Cigarettes and body odor. Not mine.

I turned back to see if Louis was behind me, to warn him, could hear him talking to the dog. I looked back to the kitchen, took a step in. Another. Slid a round into the chamber, the click reverberating in the stillness.

And then it was still again.

I moved through the kitchen, looked through the study to the sliding-glass door to the deck. It was broken open, the glass cracked, the metal frame bent at the lock. I turned, sniffed. The odor was fainter here. I backtracked, moved silently through the center hall. Heard Louis calling to the dog, closer now.

I kept moving.

The living room was empty. The dining room, too. Nowhere to hide in either.

I moved to the base of the stairs, looked up. Sniffed.

He'd been here.

I put one foot on the first stair, weighting it gradually. No creak. Another step and a pause. I listened. Heard the palpable stillness. My own heart. Stepped again.

A loud creak, three-quarters of the way up. I waited. Listened. Sniffed. Kept moving. From outside I could hear Louis. He was calling the dog. They were closer.

I was about to go back down when I heard a scratch. Boot on the wooden floor. Our bedroom.

I raised the gun, softly squeezed the trigger. Took the last three steps and pressed against the wall outside the closed bedroom door. Inhaled slowly, smelled his smell, stronger now.

Swallowed. Listened. Turned.

Wheeled into the room, gun swiveling left and right.

Nothing.

I eased my way into the room, around the end of the bed. Nothing on the floor. I turned. Looked at the closed closet doors. They slid both ways, Roxanne's stuff on the left, mine on the right. I sniffed, the smell still there, the body odor stronger now.

I raised the gun, took two steps, started to extend my left arm.

Smack, a hole the size of a half-dollar had shattered in the closet door.

I dove to the right, rolled, came up, and fired two shots at the hole, black spots in the painted wood. Another blast from inside, a foot to the left of the first. I fired once, hit an inch from the big hole, lunged to the bed.

Heard clunks inside the closet, him moving.

"Give it up," I shouted, and moved left. He fired at the sound of my voice, the bullet pocking the wall to my right.

And then there was scrabbling on the stairs, the dog showing first. Louis stepped in, gun raised. A shot from behind the door, a pock in the doorframe next to his head.

He moved two quick steps, wheeled, and fired. A yard left of the big holes, then a yard to the right. Then closer, the shots coming fast, the rifle barrel swinging. Six shots, then three more, the holes patterned like dots on a graph. When they converged at the center Louis stopped.

The room reverberated. And then it was still.

Louis moved quickly along the wall to the end of the closet, looked at me and nodded. I raised the Glock and he slipped his fingers inside the crack of the door, shoved it hard. It caught on the splintered wood. Louis gave it a hard kick with his boot.

Billy fell out.

He landed face-first, the gun, a big revolver, hammering the floor. There was a bloody softball-size circle between his shoulder blades. Blood pooled under his neck, then ran over the first floorboard and into the crack. The dog watched the blood.

"Did a lot of doors in Iraq," Louis said.

There were cops at the house, a crime-scene van in the driveway, yellow tape over the doors. Louis was sitting in the front seat of an unmarked car, talking to a detective. I got out of the Jeep and Cook came out of the side door, saw me, and waved me over. Clair watched from the side of his truck.

We sat in Cook's car. He was tall and lanky and he had the seat cranked back but his knees still stuck up, like somebody crammed in a basket. He took notes on a yellow legal pad, either shorthand or taking down every fifth word.

"Where were you today?"

My turn to hesitate. Louis and his cell-phone towers.

I wavered, then told him the truth.

"What sort of discussion?" he said.

"An animated one," I said.

"What did you want to know?"

"If he killed Abram Snyder."

Cook looked up.

"What did he say?"

"He denied it. Emphatically. And we believed him."

"We?"

"Me and Louis."

A pause, while Cook decided whether he was ready to switch gears. And then he did.

"So you came home. How did you know someone was in your house?"

"I could smell him," I said. "Cigarettes. We don't smoke."

"And then what?"

I told him the story. The shots from inside the closet. Me returning fire. Louis stepping in and finishing it.

"I guess there's a technique," I said. "He learned it in Iraq."

"Acquire some valuable skills in the military," Cook said.

"Yes," I said.

Cook said the police found a backpack under the bed. It contained duct tape, rope, a hunting knife, handcuffs, and a leather hood, and what Cook awkwardly described as "a sex toy."

"Wife and daughter okay?"

"Pretty shook. I haven't seen them yet. Went to stay with friends."

"Pretty darn lucky."

"One way to look at it," I said. "What about Billy?"

"What about him?" Cook said.

"Will he make it?"

"I'm no doctor, but I doubt it."

"Good," I said.

Cook wanted to talk more about Boston. I asked him if I could go see my wife and daughter first, and we could talk later. He hesitated, then said that was okay. "But we're not done."

As I walked to my truck, Louis was getting out of the cruiser. I fell in beside him and we walked to the driveway. We stopped and I reached out and clasped his shoulder.

"Thanks," I said.

He shrugged.

"I mean it."

"I know you do," Louis said.

"He was waiting for Roxanne."

Louis looked away, didn't answer. Then he took a long breath.

"His luck ran out," he said softly. "I guess it was meant to be that it was me."

"I'm glad you were there," I said.

Louis turned to me with the same fixed stare he'd had when we first met. A lost look, the rest of him trapped deep inside. He shrugged, looked away.

"It's still a life," he said.

29

The rain had been run off to the east, a ridge of dry, cool air coming in from the northwest. The clouds were still visible, somewhere out over the coast, the sun hanging just above western mountains. It was like it was a new day, Billy gone to hell or prison, Baby Fat way less of a threat on his own. Especially now that he'd seen how it paid to go up against us.

But I didn't feel much better. Not yet.

If Billy died and he'd killed Abram, he'd take that secret to his grave. There would be no justice, except maybe the Bishop's kind—the eternal lake of fire.

Screw the fire. I wanted more justice. I wanted it now.

I thought this as I sped over the back roads to Welt's farm. The truck bounced over the ruts, jumped the crests. When I got to the farm, I braked and downshifted, half skidded onto the gravel drive. Up ahead I saw Roxanne's Subaru parked beside Welt's truck. For a moment it seemed like a premonition, but I parked and, with goats watching me, trotted for the door.

The entrance was on the side, a big veranda with railings and flowers. I knocked and pulled the screen door open, found myself in a mudroom, wellies lined up against the wall. They had names written on them, Welt and Salandra among them, Roxanne and Sophie on the end.

I called "Hello, hello," heard voices deeper in the house. I moved through a door into a big farm kitchen. A young woman—college age, tanned, and blonde, very pretty—was standing on a chair hanging bunches of plants from hooks. Herbs?

She turned and I said, "I'm Jack. Are Roxanne and Sophie here?"

"Oh, my God, I'm so sorry about what happened," she said. "It's like—oh, my God—so terrible. They're on the porch."

She pointed and I left the kitchen, walked through a big parlor, out onto a screened-in porch on the back of the house. Sophie and Salandra were sitting on the wooden floor playing a board game. Chutes and Ladders. To my right, Welt and Roxanne were sitting on a wicker couch. They were drinking wine. Roxanne looked like she'd been crying. Welt had his hand over hers.

He jumped up, said, "Jack. So glad you're here. It's been"—he searched for the right word—"difficult."

Roxanne got up, too, putting the glass down on a metal tea table, moving to me, putting her arms around me. I held her tight and she held me, too, and we stayed that way for a long time, saying nothing. And then we broke apart slightly, and I said, "Thank God you're okay."

And then I heard the sound of bare feet on the decking, turned as Sophie jumped for my arms. I hugged her, too, and then the three of us hugged, and Roxanne started to cry again.

Sophie slid down and said, "Daddy, there was a bad man in our house, but Louis came and the bad man was hiding and he had a gun and he didn't know Louis was a soldier and Louis shot the bad man and now he might die."

Welt looked down at Sophie sadly. "It's a terrible thing, honey, but we can learn from it. You know what we said about violence, how it—"

"Yes, Soph. It just shows that bad things happen to bad people," I said. "And you don't have to worry, because Clair and Louis and all of your friends, and Mommy and Daddy—we're all looking out for you."

"And Salandra and Welt," she said.

"Right," I said.

I turned to Roxanne. She was wiping her eyes with a tissue.

"Jack," Welt said, remembering his upbringing. "We just had sandwiches. Panini, with organic wheat bread that this friend of mine bakes over in Waldoboro. And turkey from this farm in Belmont. They're free-range, no chemicals or artificial enhancers. And my cheese, of course. Are you hungry? Heather can grill up a couple for you."

"No, I'm good."

"Then can I get you a beer? We have Shipyard, Geary's, some really good ales from Portland Beer Company. They're excellent. Won all these international awards. The red ale, it's—"

"Sure, anything," I said.

Welt hurried off, his Birkenstocks flapping. Salandra called Sophie back to the game, and I took Roxanne's hand and we moved through the screened doors and down the steps and out into a garden where cascades of fall perennials were blooming, spilling over stone walls, reds and yellows, the colors choreographed to the seasons.

"You okay?" I said.

She shook her head.

"It's awful," Roxanne said. "What if I'd walked in there?"

"You would have smelled him."

"But what if I hadn't? He was waiting for me. And he had ropes and things, and he would have . . . and Sophie. My God . . . "

She trailed off.

"Thank you," she said.

"He's gone now. No matter what, he's not coming back. He'll never bother you again."

"Where were you? I tried to call."

"I had to go talk to somebody. In Boston."

"Boston? Why didn't you tell me? I thought you were around here."

"It was a last-minute decision. Somebody the police linked to Abram. It's a long story, but—"

"If you had been with us and Clair at home, he probably wouldn't have gotten in," Roxanne said.

"I figured you'd be at school. Clair would be here until we got back."

"We?"

"Louis came with me."

A pause, and then Roxanne said, "Oh. One of those."

Sadness fell over her and I took her hand. She gave me a half-hearted squeeze, her mind somewhere else.

"Being with Clair—you couldn't be safer than that," I said.

Roxanne walked across the lawn, past the first wave of flowers to a wrought-iron bench. She sat and I sat beside her. She was looking straight ahead, seeing nothing. I waited, felt something building inside her, the words forming.

"I know you feel responsible for Abram. Or fond of him. Or like you're the one who has to get even."

"It's not just that. Whoever killed him is still here. Unless it was Billy."

"No, Jack. It's about vengeance and getting even and this idea you have. Clair has. And Louis. The answer to violence is more violence."

"That's not true. I don't—"

"I know. I'm thankful that Louis was there. And you. I always am. I'm glad you stopped that man. I am. But where does it end, Jack? This spiral. They start it. You end it. But it doesn't end, Jack. It just keeps going."

"That's the world we live in," I said.

"But it doesn't have to be."

She turned to me, beautiful and sad and terribly discouraged.

"Look around you. This place. The flowers, the animals, the—I don't know what you call it—the tranquillity."

"But this isn't reality. Or it's one reality. The other one is out there, whether you like it or not. You can't pretend, like Welt does, that—"

"He's not pretending, Jack."

"But you can't just let things like Abram dying, Billy coming to hurt you—you can't let them go unanswered. There have to be consequences."

"For them?" Roxanne said. "Or for us? For Sophie?"

She reached to her eyes and held her hand there and tears slipped from under her fingers. I put my arm around her shoulder and she felt small and tired.

"I'm sorry," I said. "I'm sorry for all of it."

She wiped her eyes and pulled herself up. Took a deep breath and said, "We can't stay there."

"I know. I'll get cleaners to come in. Get another door."

"But we can't sleep there. Not in that room. I mean, how could we now? It was our place, Jack."

She broke down, fighting back a sob.

"It was where we made love. It was where you held me and I held you and we talked and Sophie climbed in bed with us in the middle of the night. It was ours, and the rest of the world—all the horribleness—it couldn't bother us there. It was the one place."

"I know. And it will be that way again."

"It won't be. How can it? That horrible man and the shooting and—the world found us, Jack. The world found us, and it's all ruined."

I held her as she cried, felt the tears wet on my neck.

"We'll put it back together," I said. "We won't let anybody ruin it."

Roxanne sat up and wiped her eyes.

"Welt said we can stay here. The three of us, I mean."

"That's okay. We can—"

"He has this big house and it's just him and the interns. And Salandra is here for Sophie, to take her mind off of it. He really wants to help. To help all of us."

I didn't answer.

"Sounds like your mind's made up."

"It's the best solution."

"For how long?" I said.

"I don't know."

"Will you go to school tomorrow?"

"Yes. Sophie needs normal. And I do, too."

"You'll need stuff from the house," I said.

"Can we get in there?" Roxanne said. "Isn't it, I don't know, a crime scene?"

Roxanne was silent during the ride across town. Her face was drawn and pale and her eyes were red-rimmed and swollen. When we pulled up in front of the house there was a cruiser in front, a state police crime-scene truck parked in the driveway. We got out and walked across the lawn, a trooper rolling out of the car, approaching us with his hands hooked in his belt.

"I'm sorry, folks. You can't—"

"This is our house," Roxanne said. "We need our clothes. And toothbrushes and makeup. And my hair dryer. And my daughter's stuffed lamb."

The cop said, "Well, I suppose I could talk to—" but Roxanne was already next to him, bending under the tape.

She collected the things, taking a tote from the kitchen closet and going to the second-floor bathroom. I went to the bedroom door, looked in to see two crime-scene techs packing up. There were adhesive tags on the bullet holes in the closet door and on the far wall where two of Billy's slugs had ended up. His blood smelled like rancid meat.

The crime-scene techs stepped out, booties still in place.

"Will that blood come up?" I said.

"Floor, yes," he said. "Carpet's toast."

They padded along the hall and started down the stairs. I looked up to see Roxanne standing at the bathroom door, pale and wide-eyed.

I followed, and when I got outside, bent under the yellow tape. We climbed into the truck and she sat beside me and stared straight ahead.

I started the motor. The seat-belt chime tolled. I waited and it stopped, and Roxanne said, "I don't know if I can come back here, Jack."

"We can decide that later," I said.

"I can decide," she said.

We drove in silence, the ten minutes feeling like an hour. Roxanne was very still, unseeing. She'd retreated somewhere deep inside her head.

"You okay?" I said.

She blinked.

"It will get better. I promise."

She didn't respond at all.

I saw three deer, white tails flashing as they crossed the road and bounded into the woods. On the main road, I went right, drove a couple of miles, then slowed for a Mennonite horse and buggy, eased around it, and looked to see if I knew the driver. I didn't.

"I wonder when the funeral is," I said.

Roxanne said nothing.

And then we were approaching the entrance to the farm, and I reached across the console and took Roxanne's hand. A last chance before we entered Weltville. She gave me a limp squeeze and then her hand slipped away.

I pulled into the yard, parked between Welt's pickup and the intern's Volkswagen. Shut off the motor and looked at her. She was already climbing out, reaching behind the seat for her bag. I followed, dreading the night, said, "What do we do now? Sit around and watch TV?"

"I don't know about you, Jack," Roxanne said. "But I'm going to bed."

She did, taking Sophie with her to a room on the second floor at the rear of the house. I followed, saw that the room had a double and a single beds, flowers in the vases. Roxanne got Sophie's nightshirt from the bag, helped her put it on. Sophie got in the twin bed and Roxanne tucked her in. Roxanne kissed her on the cheek, then it was my turn. I leaned down and said, "Love you, pumpkin."

"Love you, too, Daddy," she said.

I kissed her and she gave me a hug, pulling me down toward her for another kiss. "Don't you worry," I said. "Mommy and Daddy are with you."

She looked at me.

"But not all the time," Sophie said.

"Yes, all the time," I said.

Roxanne had stepped out of her skirt and pulled off her sweater, was slipping a nightgown over her head. A glimpse of her back, her breasts—I felt an odd shimmer of desire. And then she got into the big bed and pulled the sheet and blanket up under her chin and turned to the wall.

It was 9:05.

I stood for a minute, heard Sophie start to snore, the faintest rasping sound. It was the sleep of the innocent. I went to the door, opened it, and stepped out, closing the door behind me.

The rear section of the house was above the kitchen, and I could hear the intern talking, Welt presumably there and listening. I went around the railing and down the stairs, and when I walked in he was pouring glasses of wine for Heather and another young woman. Welt's glass was on the wooden harvest table.

"Jack," he said, turning, bottle in hand. "This is Maria."

Maria—dark curly hair, pretty Latina features—smiled sympathetically, like I was sick.

"How are you all doing?" she said.

"Okay," I said.

"How are they doing?" Welt said.

"Okay, considering," I said.

"Anything you need. Anything at all. Just shout."

"Yeah," Heather said. "Cheese and crackers?"

"I just made hummus," Maria said.

It was awkward. What do you say to somebody who had a sexual predator hiding in his closet? What do you say to someone whose friend just shot the predator dead?

"I'm going to go back to the house, pick up some stuff, check the pony," I said. "But thanks anyway."

"Jack," Welt said. "I don't think violence is ever justified, but I have to tell you, this was as close to an exception as I could ever make."

A psychopath sex fiend waiting for my wife, Welt's latest crush. And it was tough for him to make an exception. He smiled, like he'd gone the extra mile and was proud of himself.

"I'll see you in a while," I said, and I left.

On the drive back to the house, I realized I hadn't eaten since breakfast, but I wasn't hungry. The blood. I'd barely slept, but I wasn't tired. I was wired, a hound back in the pen but ready to hunt. But who?

Semi on the run. AJ and Trigger in jail. Slick in the clear. Billy, dead or dying. Who did that leave?

I drove down the road, the light almost gone. A porcupine waggled into the ditch to my right and disappeared. I slowed and peered into the black woods after him but he was gone. The woods were dark and deep, but they weren't lovely—not tonight.

The trooper was still parked out front, lights off, the interior filled with the gray-blue glow of his laptop. I rolled by slowly and continued on to Clair's, turned in, and saw the lights on, the house and the barn. I parked and walked down the drive past Clair's truck, Louis's Jeep, Mary's Honda. I touched the hood of each and they were cold. My bodyguards were in for the night.

I went to the barn door and pushed it open. Stepped in. The music was on, Mozart's Requiem, chorus and symphony. The lights were dim, just a small work light glowing on the bench. I peered into the gloom and finally spotted him. He was sitting on a folding chair in the far corner. I walked over, saw the whiskey bottle on the wooden floor.

"Hey," I said.

"Hey," Louis said.

"Taking a break?"

"Yeah. Had some dinner. Broccoli soup. Clair and Mary are playing Scrabble."

"She'll whup him."

"No doubt."

We paused.

"How you doing?" I said.

"Fine."

He held out the bottle of whiskey. Jameson Black. I took a swallow. Louis raised his glass and sipped.

"How are Roxanne and Sophie?" Louis said.

"Asleep."

"You'd better take extra good care of them," he said.

"Trying," I said.

He sipped. I swallowed.

"Remember this time outside of Ramadi. Humvee takes an IED, the truck's on fire. Me and the radioman, we pile out into the smoke and make this alley, zigging and zagging. We're sitting there, he's all blood, trying to get backup on the radio, and we hear the bastards coming. They go by us full run, carrying AKs and launchers, wanted to get there and watch us roast like marshmallows."

Louis held out his glass. I poured. We drank.

"And then this straggler comes up, skinny kid, AK looked too big for him. He stops right in front of me and bends down to get a rock or something out of his sandal. And then he turns and looks me right in the eye. Starts to open his mouth to yell, and I clamp my hand over him, he's biting me, trying to get his finger on the trigger. I yank the gun away, and now he's got two hands on mine, clawing and scratching and kicking. Like trying to give a cat a bath."

Louis paused.

"He screams, we're dead."

Another swallow for both of us.

"So I hold him, get my other hand on his throat, and he's looking at me, right in the eyes. And there was this moment where he knew. That it was the end. That his life was over. That was all he was getting. And we just stared at each other until after a minute or two, he wasn't really looking anymore. He was gone. Died in my arms, sort of."

I waited.

"So, McMorrow, I been thinking, compared to that one, this thing today was easy-breezy. But, still, takes a toll on you."

"I'm sure," I said.

"Woulda been a toll on you, if you'd hit him," Louis said.

"I'm sorry I missed."

"You say that," he said. "But you don't know."

Louis smiled.

"Don't get me wrong. That bastard was evil, and I'd kill him with my bare hands before I'd let him hurt your wife or your daughter. But it's interesting. He wasn't born evil. Something set him down this path. And it ended here. With me."

"And me," I said.

I held out the bottle. Louis hesitated, then clinked his glass against it and we drank. The Requiem chorus sang, a soaring passage.

"Clair would be proud of us, don't you think?"

I looked at him.

"The music, I mean," Louis said.

I drove back up to the house, waved to the cop, and he waved back. I parked in the driveway and walked back to the cruiser and told him I had to get a couple of things.

He nodded, went back to his typing.

I went inside and into the kitchen and the house seemed cold, already uninhabited. I stood in the darkness and listened, heard the hum of the refrigerator. I opened it and rummaged around and found a last Ballantine, in the back behind the juice. I took out a beer and packages of sliced turkey and cheese.

At the counter, I flipped on a light and made a sandwich. The bread was from the supermarket. The turkey was from some turkey processor someplace, probably the Midwest. The cheese was made by a company that was a subsidiary of a conglomerate. I slapped it together and took a bite, washed it down with ale brewed in Texas by the tanker load.

Take that, Welt.

I stood and ate and drank, finished the sandwich, and made another half. When that was gone I considered making another but decided against it. I put the food back in the refrigerator and, with half a beer left, walked across to the study.

At the desk, I pushed the chair aside, flipped up my laptop, and, still standing, waited for e-mail to load. There was a note from the *Times*, asking me for an update on the "Mennonites in Maine" story. Two from *Outland*, one asking how things were going, another forwarding a story about some legislator in Massachusetts pushing for stiffer penalties for illegal gun possession when a gun was used to commit a felony.

Would Slick start looking for alternatives? Capping people with a crossbow?

A crossbow. Were they legal? I decided to make a note of that for the story. I reached for a pen from the mug, dropped it, and it rolled across the desktop and onto the floor at my feet.

I bent.

The window exploded.

30

A slap and a boom.

I fell to my knees. Felt glass under my left hand and moved it. Dropped to my belly and started crawling for the kitchen. I was almost there when the next shot came.

More glass-shatter, a *thunk* in the wall above me.

And then I was in the kitchen, raised to a crouch. As I made it to the shed door it banged open, the cop from out front pointing his gun at me.

"Two shots," I said, standing. "Through the sliding-glass door to the deck. Rifle."

"What's out there?" he said.

"Woods," I said. "For miles. A trail that leads north, branches out different places along the way."

He backed out and ran, talking into his radio. "Shots fired . . ."

I ran after him, said, "Wait."

He slowed and I trotted with him.

"Two friends of mine. Clair."

"The neighbor?"

"Yeah. And Louis."

"The guy with you in the Jeep."

"They might go out there. To find the person. Don't shoot them."

"If you see them," he said, "tell them to stay put."

And then he was on the radio again, saying, "Two friends of the subject targeted . . . "

I turned around and trotted to the truck, got the Glock from under the seat. Racked a shell into the chamber. I was backing out of the truck when I heard a scratch, a boot on gravel.

"He's running," Clair said.

"You heard it?" I said.

"Two shots from a deer rifle. But you know what I didn't hear."

"A car or truck starting."

"He's on foot in the woods. Louis is driving around to the main road, see if he can see something parked."

"The cops will want to talk to me," I said. "I can't chase him."

"Not gonna run him down, not in the dark," Clair said. "Only chance is to cut him off before he can get out of the woods."

"Cops will bring a dog."

"They won't go in there," he said. "Not at night. Sitting ducks."

We stood, listened to the voices on the radio in the deputy's cruiser. Cops calling in. Motors roaring. Sirens. A dog barking.

"How close?" Clair said.

"Very," I said. "I dropped a pen. If I hadn't bent to get it . . . "

"Second shot?"

"Just over me. I was on the floor."

"Lights on in the room?"

"Yes."

"Like shooting fish in an aquarium," Clair said.

"Baby Fat? Revenge for Billy?"

"Be my first guess."

"What's your second?" I said.

"Semi's back."

"Payback for being humiliated?"

"And maybe he thinks you're the rat. The one who twisted the kid's arm. The one funneling info to the cops."

"Interesting theory," I said.

"A lot of people have been killed because of theories," Clair said. "Interesting or not."

Clair jumped in his truck as the sirens approached, hit the throttle, and was gone when the first cruiser slid to a stop, killed the lights.

It was a trooper and he went to the trunk, popped it, and started getting into SWAT gear. Body armor. Rifle. Helmet. Night vision. Camo.

He looked at me, then trotted to the deputy, who was on the radio by the car. The deputy pointed to the house, said a few words, and the SWAT guy trotted to the left of the house and disappeared into the darkness.

Another cruiser, then a state police SUV, then a second one, a dog barking inside the truck. They parked in the road, shut off their lights. The guy in the first SUV was the same sergeant from the scene of Abram's murder. He slipped out of the car, strode over to the deputy. The third guy joined them and they turned in unison and looked at me. I started over and we met in the middle.

"Sergeant Rousseau," the older guy said. The name tag said his first name was Kevin.

"Jack McMorrow," I said.

"I know," he said. "Start at the beginning."

I did. Finished at the end. It didn't take long.

The cops turned and gazed at the woods. As they stood there, the first trooper came around the end of the shed. As he joined them, he said, "Black in there. Can't see shit."

"His story fit?" Rousseau said after I repeated myself.

"Two shots through the window. Consistent with a high-powered rifle."

"Distance?"

"Pretty heavily wooded. I'd say he was in close."

"Isn't anymore," Rousseau said.

"I'd say not."

They looked at me, then at each other.

"Contain him," Rousseau said, and to me he said, "How far does this tract go?"

"All the way to the main road. Two miles. East to west, four miles."

"Access?"

"Trails run through it. Four-wheelers. My walking trails."

"Access points from the main road?"

"In the four miles? A couple you could put a four-wheeler on. Two or three more you could do on foot."

"Show us," Rousseau said. He nodded to the second trooper and said, "Take him."

I sat in the front seat, the trooper, a big, rangy kid who looked like a Boy Scout in the wrong uniform, swiveling his laptop out of the way. He whipped the cruiser around, took off up the road to the east. At the first rise I said, "My friends are already there, looking for somebody coming out."

"What friends?" he said.

"My neighbor and another friend of ours," I said.

"What are they going to do if they see somebody?"

I hesitated.

"I don't know. Maybe apprehend him."

"They'd better leave that—"

He looked at me.

"What did you say your name is?"

I told him.

"And your friends?"

I told him that, too.

"I've heard of you," he said. "So who's armed?"

"Everybody," I said.

"You call them," he said, not a kid after all. "Tell them to stand the hell down. I see somebody with a firearm, they don't want to be that person."

So I did and Clair answered. I passed the message on and he said he'd call Louis. They'd covered the trailheads, driven the four miles twice.

"Nothing," Clair said.

"So he's still in there?" I said.

The trooper listened.

"Or covered a lot of ground in a hurry," Clair said.

By the time we hit the main road, there were blue lights coming from both directions. By the time we pulled in behind Clair's truck, it was turning into a strike force. Waldo County Sheriff's Office, times two, the second a K-9 unit. A game warden coming from the west, blue lights flashing in the grille of his truck. And then Rousseau, pulling up, getting out, taking charge.

We all got out, faces illuminated by the strobes. Rousseau went directly to Clair, said, "Mr. Varney. What was your time on scene?"

"Nine minutes from shots fired," Clair said.

"And nothing showing?"

"Nothing."

"That's four-minute miles through the trees carrying a rifle in the dark," Rousseau said.

"Look for the guy in the track shorts," I said.

"He's still in there, most likely," Rousseau said. "We'll contain him, hit it hard at first light."

Another trooper arrived, a grim-faced woman who joined the circle. They nodded to her and Rousseau started giving orders, establishing the cordon. He asked who had night vision and my trooper nodded. Rousseau told him to park at the main trailhead. Two others were to head back to the house. The game warden said he'd move into the woods by the secondary trail and wait.

And then they dispersed, tires spinning in the gravel, radios squawking. Moths flailed at Clair's headlights, like they were wound up about it all, too. Clair said, "I'll get Louis up to speed."

We both turned to the wall of trees, a twisted weave of shapes and shadows. There was the soft crackle of stuff moving in the undergrowth: mice, voles, moles, snakes. Then a snap, a branch cracking. A rustle of leaves.

Clair moved to the truck, killed the lights, and pulled his shotgun from the scabbard behind the seat. I slipped the Glock out.

"Don't shoot," a voice said. "It's me."

A shape materialized out of the blackness like an apparition, and then Louis was standing with us, a rifle at his side, muzzle down.

"Anything?" Clair said.

"A couple of broken branches where someone came through," Louis said.

"So he did beat us out?" Clair said.

"Or maybe got this far and saw us and turned back in. But he's big. Stuff was up high." He put his hand across his throat. "I'd say well over six feet."

We looked at the black woods, then up and down the road. To the east we saw headlights reflecting off the trees, a pale flicker in the dark tunnel between spruce and firs. And then the headlights came over the rise. We moved back, guns kept low as we waited for the car to pass. But it slowed, blue strobes blipped in the grille, and it swung in, slid to a halt beside my truck.

State police. Unmarked Impala. The door popped and Cook climbed out.

He strode around the front of the car, directly to me. Clair and Louis stood stock-still, like a general had just walked into the room. Cook looked at them, the firearms, and said, "Put 'em away. I've got enough going on."

They looked at him, then started walking back to their vehicles. I started to turn, too, and Cook said, "Not you, Mr. McMorrow. It's time for us to talk."

I stopped, turned back to him, and said, "I thought we had been talking."

"We've been dancing around each other. We're done with that."

"Whatever you say."

"I say how 'bout you come with me. Voluntarily, of course. We'll go where we can start at the beginning and get to the end."

"Doesn't appear like the end is in sight," I said.

"Now, Mr. McMorrow," Cook said.

"I have to call my wife."

"Call her from the car," he said, so I did.

31

Roxanne answered on the first ring.

"I didn't wake you?" I said.

"I couldn't sleep."

I heard footsteps, not hers.

"Where are you?"

"Where am I? In the kitchen. Welt was up, too. He's making tea."

Pajama party.

"How is Sophie?"

"Out like a light. Where are you? At the house?"

I glanced at Cook, from the backseat. He'd turned down the radio when I took out the phone, but it still made a faint scratchy hiss.

"With the police," I said.

"Still?"

"Something else happened."

"What?"

I hesitated, felt like our life was being buried and this was another shovelful of earth. I let it fly.

"I'm fine. They missed."

"What? Where?"

I told her.

"Did they catch him?"

"No. It's dark and there's a lot of woods out there. They're trying to contain him, drive him out in the morning."

"So—"

"So I'm going to meet with them, tell them what I know."

"Okay. When will you be done?" Roxanne said.

"I don't know. It depends."

"Depends on what?"

"On what they think about what I say."

"Jack," Roxanne said. "They don't think—I mean, you're not some kind of suspect or something, are you? That's crazy. We're the victims here, for God's sake. A madman in our house, somebody shooting at you—"

"I'll text you. So I don't wake Sophie."

A pause.

"Yeah, text me. That would be better."

I put the phone down. Cook didn't turn the radio back up. I turned to the window, watched the woods flash by like the side of a subway tunnel. When I turned back I could see he was watching me in the mirror.

"Your wife okay?" he said.

"Not really," I said. "It's been a bad day."

"Could've been worse. That dirtbag wasn't in the closet to watch somebody get in their pj's."

"No."

"One bad dude," Cook said.

It sounded funny coming from him. Dude. Like a dad trying to be cool.

"Yes," I said. "But he got his comeuppance."

He glanced at me in the mirror, that word probably sounding funny coming from me.

"You and your family have a place to stay? Got family around here?"

"No. But a friend of my wife's has a big house. We'll stay there. She's there already. My daughter, too."

"The farmer," Cook said.

My turn to glance.

"Yeah."

I looked out the window again, then back.

"Big spread," he said. "Nice vehicles. A new tractor. Not like any farmer I know around here. He have a pile of cash or something? Can't imagine there's that much money in cheese."

"I don't know. Family money would be my guess."

"Not that I care. I just notice that sort of thing. I've got four kids, my oldest starting to look at colleges. I mean, we do okay. My wife's a nurse-practitioner. But, still, we've got every dollar spoken for."

I started to say something about Welt, then stopped.

"What's with the small talk?" I said.

"Just chatting," Cook said.

"If I didn't know better, I'd think you were just softening me up."

"Gotta talk about something, Mr. McMorrow," Cook said.

"And we already talked about how there was a twisted psycho pervert in my wife's closet."

"Oh, we're going to want to talk more about that. And the rest of it. But I thought we'd better wait."

"For what?"

"For everybody to be there," Cook said.

Everybody was there, sitting around a conference table in the back of a stripped-out Airstream trailer. The trailer was called a State Police Mobile Command Center, or so it said on its aluminum side, and it was parked in a gravel lot just off the entrance to Abram's farm.

Cook was there, along with a trooper/detective named Carmello who was taking notes on a yellow legal pad. O'Day and Ramos from ATF. A deputy investigator from the Waldo County Sheriff's Office named Karl, which was either his first name, or his last. Sheriff's Deputy Staples. They were drinking coffee from white Styrofoam cups. I asked for tea and Staples got me Lipton.

"Every time we think this is over, something else happens," Cook said. "And when we make a Venn diagram of all these things that keep happening, you're right in the center of it."

They looked at me.

"Who do you think took a shot at you?" Cook said.

"Two shots," I said. "And I don't know."

"If you had to guess."

"Semi. If he's alive and he's back."

"Why him?"

"He lost considerable face."

"Second guess?"

"Beefy Rowe, maybe?"

"What's his problem with you?"

"We got in a scrape with them—Beefy and Billy and Semi and Baby Fat. Well, that's what we call him. Wesley Junior. Ran into them in the woods. They were cutting illegally. They came out on the short end of it."

"Christ, time to cut the crap, McMorrow," Ramos said.

"Nobody here believes you're just a reporter," O'Day said.

"We think you know way more about this guns-for-drugs thing than you're saying," Ramos said.

"And now we've got a homicide," Cook said. "And another probable fatal shooting. And a missing person. And an attempted homicide."

Carmello was to his right, still taking notes, the first page almost full.

"And then we have you," Cook said, the words spewing out of him. "Hanging out with a guy who is part of the gun ring, who later is killed. Doing some sort of Iraq-style interrogation of the soon-to-be-dead guy's partner, now MIA. Going to Dorchester, and doing something either to or with the head gangbanger."

"And accompanying you as you carry out these various missions," O'Day said, taking over, "are your buddies, these military veterans who act like the war never ended. And are heavily armed. And take on the locals and the Boston gangs, and one of them shoots a psychopath who happens to be in your bedroom closet."

"What was he supposed to do?" I said. "Shake his hand?"

"The point," Cook said, "is that you know more than you're telling us. And this is your chance to come clean, or become what we could call adversarial."

I looked at him. I looked at O'Day. I looked at Ramos, who said, "Cough it up, McMorrow. Spit it out."

I smiled.

"Sure," I said. "It started with a story I was writing. . ."

They listened as I ran through everything that had happened since I started making the rounds of the gun sellers. The only time I paused was when I talked about Miriam and the video. It was like I'd been hoping that if I didn't talk about it again, they'd forget that I'd ever mentioned it. But I kept going, Carmello scribbling away, and then I was done. I picked up my Styrofoam cup and leaned back and took a sip of tea. It was cold.

"That's it?" Ramos said.

"Yeah," I said.

"That's still bullshit," he said.

O'Day put his hand on his partner's arm and said, "You're telling us that all of this started with this story about guns."

"Yeah."

"And that's the sum of your involvement?" Cook said.

"Right."

"Oh, come on. You're up to your eyeballs in this shit," Ramos said. "You roam around this place with your freakin' Navy Seals, march into Dorchester, and roust a guy who'll kill you soon as he'll look at you. Beat the ever-loving crap out of some guy who's now disappeared, blow away some other dirtbag, and when some other shithead takes a potshot at you, your boys are out with shotguns and rifles, containing the perimeter."

He wiped at the spittle on his chin.

"And you say it was all because you don't want some freakin' Amish girl to be embarrassed by her homemade porn video?"

He remembered.

"Old Order Mennonite," I said. "And embarrassed is an understatement. Mortified. Devastated. Humiliated. Destroyed. Crushed—"

"Bullshit, bullshit, bullshit," Ramos said. "You barely know this kid."

"It's not the kid," I said. "It's the principle."

"People don't do stuff like this out of principle."

"I do," I said. "And my friends do, too."

And I looked at him, held his gaze.

"True fact," I said.

It was Deputy Staples who drove me back to my truck. Her orders were to pick up Clair and Louis, too, and bring them back to the command center for the same sort of debriefing.

"Clair will be glad to do it," I said. "Louis will be gone."

"Why?" she said.

"Because he doesn't trust authority."

"Who does he trust?"

"His dog," I said. "And Clair Varney."

"Not you?"

"Sometimes," I said.

My truck was parked on the roadside, camouflaged by the darkness. Staples pulled up, threw the gearshift of the cruiser into PARK. I reached for the door handle, but paused, waited.

"McMorrow," she said.

"Yeah."

"Between us, I sort of believe you."

"Good to know."

"But if you're lying, even lies of omission, and it comes out, you're seriously screwed."

I turned back.

"If you'd like to say something, but don't want to talk to Cook or the ATF guys, call me."

She handed me a card. I took it, nodded.

"In case it's a mano a mano thing," she said. "Guys backing each other into a corner."

I nodded and got out of the car and she pulled away, the taillights fading and leaving me in darkness.

Except it wasn't. As my eyes adjusted, the blackness turned pitch blue, with shimmers of green and black and brown in the wall that was the edge of the woods. I stood for a minute and watched and listened. There was woods noise, a constant crackle and rustle. The trees seemed to be moving, the branches undulating in the breeze. I turned to the truck and took a couple of steps and stopped. Behind me I saw the same shimmering shapes, heard the same scratch and snap.

And felt surrounded.

32

It was 12:45 a.m. The side door of Welt's house was open.

"What the hell?" I said, as the knob turned. What if they knew where she was? Just walk in and—

I caught myself. It was Roxanne's choice to be here, not mine. But still. Lock the friggin' door.

I stepped through and snapped the bolt shut behind me. Turned and listened. Again.

This time there were house noises. Creaks. Hums. A faucet dripping. A thump.

I tensed. A black cat came around the corner from the dining room, looked at me, and cried. The cat rubbed against my legs but I sidestepped it and started for the back of the house. There was a nightlight on in the kitchen, its glow showing wineglasses and coffee mugs in the sink, a half-empty bottle on the counter. I walked through, saw a folder on the table, and stopped. I flicked my phone light on and leaned closer.

On the cover were the words *Welt and Roxanne*, circled with a flourish underneath. I opened the folder, read the top page. It was a letter to a school district in Maryland, an offer to put on a program for them.

I flipped to the next page. It was a pitch letter with a handwritten note affixed. *Hi, Alan. Thought you might be interested. Hope all is well with you and Nancy.* The letter described the peace program and offered to put it on for students in primary- and middle-school grades. Welt and his partner, Roxanne Masterson, MSW, were available for $750 per day, plus expenses.

The next page was a list of school districts, check marks beside a few of them. Above the check-mark column it said LETTER MAILED.

Roxanne and Welt were planning to take their show on the road.

I closed the folder, turned off the light. Felt a pang of jealousy ripple through me, then another. In a flash I saw hours in airports, elbow to elbow on planes, chatting in rental cars, celebrating afterward when a presentation went well.

Toasts.

High fives.

A congratulatory hug.

A good night at the hotel-room door.

"Jesus," I said.

I shook it off, left the kitchen, and started up the back stairs. The room was the second on the left, and I eased along quietly. I felt like an intruder, the Glock wedged into my waistband. I reached back and adjusted the gun outside the closed bedroom door.

I stepped in, closed the door carefully behind me. Turned.

Saw Sophie splayed on the big bed. Alone.

I looked to the twin bed. It was empty.

I checked again, moved to cover Sophie with her sheet and blanket, ease her stuffed lamb closer. Looked at the empty bed and backed out of the room.

Billy in the closet; shots through the window; Welt down the hall.

Pick your poison.

I walked slowly toward the front of the house. There was an open door, some sort of study or office. Empty. A closed door across from it. I paused. Listened. Heard nothing.

Another door just down on the right. I paused there, too. Heard heavy and regular breathing, the sound of sleep. I listened closely, to see if I could differentiate two people sleeping. I couldn't, and I kept on walking, past an open door to another bedroom, empty, and a third door, with a hand-lettered sign saying PRINCESS SALANDRA'S CASTLE.

A last door, beyond the central staircase. It was closed, and this time I could hear someone breathing, a half-snore. And then the creak of a bed, someone turning over.

The snoring didn't pause. Two people.

Welt and Roxanne? Welt and one of the interns? The intern and Salandra, come to find someone when she was scared? Or was my imagination running unchecked?

I stood for a moment, then backtracked to the stairs. The treads were carpeted, some sort of Oriental, and I moved slowly down, then across the silent living room to a set of French doors that led to a screened-in porch and then to a deck.

The door was unlatched, one side slightly ajar. I felt for the Glock, kept my hand on it as I pulled the door open.

The night breeze came in, carrying the smell of flowers. I stepped out, looked left and right. There were wicker chairs, a couch. Empty. I crossed to the screen door that led to the deck. Opened it and took a step out.

The deck was L-shaped, extending into the garden to my right. I squinted into the darkness. There were Adirondack chairs arranged in pairs and I started toward them, heard a sound.

Movement. Behind me, to my right.

I swung around, saw the glint of a knife.

"Jack," Roxanne said. "It's you."

"I couldn't sleep. I felt like I was just lying there, waiting for something to happen. So I came down here. There's a door to the ell right there, and I left it open, the bedroom window, too. I figured I'd hear somebody coming."

"You didn't hear me," I said.

"No," Roxanne said.

"I put her covers back on," I said.

"She was asleep?"

"Out."

Roxanne was huddled under a blanket. The knife, a ten-inch butcher blade from the kitchen, was across her lap. I sat beside her, took the Glock out of my waistband, and put it on the bench beside me.

"Look at us," she said, shaking her head. "Is this what we've become?"

"Better than a victim," I said.

"I think we're victims already," Roxanne said.

"I know."

"It's worse now. Louis stopped that horrible man, but now there's another one."

"Yes."

"And we don't know who it is. And he could hide out there in the woods and shoot you, anytime. Or me. Or Sophie."

"The police will get him," I said.

"Don't patronize me, Jack."

"Okay," I said. "The police may get him. Or Clair and Louis. They're watching the road."

"Aren't you the optimist," Roxanne said.

"One way or the other, he's done."

"Who is it?"

"I don't know," I said. "We're working on that."

There was a puff of breeze out of the east and it carried a fragrance from the gardens.

"What's that smell?" I said.

"Mock orange," Roxanne said. "It blooms late."

"Nice."

"The gardens are beautiful. It's like a magazine. Welt has an intern who worked with Martha Stewart. She has this way of pruning that keeps them blossoming."

"Is that one of the ones who's here now?"

"No," Roxanne said. "Heather works in the cheeserie. Maria works with the goats. She wants to be a vet. They're a couple."

"Ah."

We smelled the mock orange. A bat flitted past over our heads, then back again.

"So you have no idea?" Roxanne said.

"Possibles."

"Like who?"

I told her. She said she'd never heard of Beefy Rowe—not by name.

"He hasn't been much of a player. Not since the fight. He went to jail for something. Then he got out."

"The one in the woods."

"Yeah."

"As opposed to all of the other ones," Roxanne said.

"I suppose."

We sat, hands at our sides. The breeze blew and the fragrance from the bush was lovely.

"The house is wrecked," Roxanne said.

"We can fix it. Some glass. Some plaster. New carpets, some closet doors."

"I think it might be ruined for me."

"Don't think that," I said.

"Welt said we can stay here as long as we like."

"I'm sure."

Roxanne didn't reply, so I said, "Are you going away with him?"

"What?"

"I saw the stuff on the table in the kitchen."

"You snooped?"

"It's what I do."

"You shouldn't have."

I didn't answer.

Roxanne waited and then said, "It's all in the planning stages. We don't know if anyone will want to hire us. Who knows if we can make a go of it."

"A go of what?"

"The consulting thing," Roxanne said. "Welt figures it might turn into something. If not, you're not out much. Some postage."

I swallowed, hesitated, then said, "I saw that he describes you as his partner."

"He means business partner."

"I know," I said.

"But you don't," she said. "Not entirely."

"No. I'm worried that we're going in different directions. I'm worried that we'll just keep getting further apart and you'll end up with him."

I hoped she'd say I was ridiculous, crazy, overreacting, paranoid.

"You don't make it easy to go in the same direction as you," Roxanne said. "I don't want to carry a gun. I don't believe in fighting. More and more, I abhor violence."

"But you've got a ten-inch butcher knife on your lap," I said.

"That's to protect Sophie."

"That's what I'm doing."

"Getting in a fight with these loggers is protecting her? Chasing gang guys around Boston?"

"We didn't chase him. He came to us."

"Whatever you did with that guy out in the woods. Was he bothering Sophie? Don't use her as an excuse to wreak some sort of havoc."

"I'm making sure that the world she grows up in hasn't fallen apart. That it's not okay to abuse a girl and put pictures of it on the Internet. That there are consequences."

"There are police to do that," Roxanne said. "Call 911."

We paused. The flower fragrance had become cloying and sticky. Late-season mosquitoes had found us, and one was buzzing around my head. I didn't move to swat it.

"I am what I am, Roxanne," I said.

"I know," she said.

Carrying our weapons, we walked through the house and up to the bedroom. Sophie had kicked off the covers and was asleep on her back, her arms and legs stretched out like that da Vinci drawing. Roxanne leaned down and straightened her, then said, "I'll sleep here with her. In case she wakes up."

"Fine," I said.

We got undressed and climbed into our beds. I took the clip out of the Glock and squeezed it under the mattress on the wall side. The gun I put under my pillow. In the dark I didn't see what Roxanne did with the knife.

And then we were lying there, both of us awake.

"Tomorrow," I said quietly.

"Yes."

"Are you going to school?"

"It's the safest place I know."

"I'll follow you over," I said.

"And then what?" Roxanne said.

"The search will be under way," I said. "Of the woods. And there's the funeral in the afternoon. For Abram."

"Are they going to want you there?"

"No," I said.

Roxanne didn't answer.

Sunrise was at 6:15. I was out of the house at 5:45, Heather and Maria coming into the kitchen as I finished making tea and filled my mug for the ride.

They were chipper, like they were trying to cheer me up. I said I'd be back by 7:30, and was out the door.

It was cool, everything wet with dew. The goats were milling against the gate that led to the pasture, and they bawled at me but I ignored them. I drove down the drive to the road, remembered Billy and Baby Fat parked there, yanking Billy out of the truck, Welt hanging back.

Was that what Roxanne wanted? Police had a term for it, the cop who's the last to join in when there's a brawl. Last man in.

I ran through our conversation of the night before, couldn't find any angle that made it anything but bleak. Yes, we were going in different directions. No, it wasn't easy for her to stick with me anymore.

I drove south, descending the ridge in zigs and zags. In brief glimpses I could see morning mist hovering over the facing hills, the pink-seeped sky creeping up to the east. It was beautiful, the tableaux anyway, until you started zooming in, like you were clicking the PLUS button on Google Earth.

Mountains and rivers. Click. Roads and houses. Click. Cop and criminals. Click. Perverts and snipers.

I made it home in eleven minutes, including a stop to let a flock of wild turkeys cross the road. As I approached, I could see the assembled police: cruisers and SUVs parked in our driveway, in front of the house, K-9 handlers corralling their dogs, snapping on leads. Cops—troopers and deputies and at least two game wardens—were tucking their trousers into boots, slinging semiautomatic rifles and shotguns over their shoulders.

As I got out of the truck the dogs bounded around the side of the house, straining against their leads, pulling the handlers along. I walked over as the wave of searchers followed, guns out. In their wake were a couple of troopers, a Warden Service officer, and the state police sergeant, Rousseau. He looked up as I approached, then back down at a map, spread out on the hood of his SUV. He kept his head down as I joined them, nodded to the troopers.

"Mr. McMorrow," Rousseau said, without looking up. "Describe to me the trails on the property, which ones would be the best traveling for somebody trying to escape."

I came around to the side of the truck and looked at the map. He gave me a pencil and I traced the trails on the map. One was wide enough for an ATV, hard enough for a mountain bike. But it petered out a half mile in, dumped off at a swamp that was bordered by a stream. There was no trail on the far side. To reconnect, you'd have to go upstream for a quarter mile and know exactly where to climb the far bank, cut through the brush, and rejoin the next trail. That trail, narrower and rougher, eventually merged with another that led to the main road, but not directly. To make it all the way out, you had to take a right-hand turn and backtrack for a couple of hundred yards. Then take a left and head north.

They listened to my explanation, the Warden Service guy making notes on the map. He then got on the radio and relayed much of the information to whoever was coordinating the search in the woods.

"Thanks," Rousseau said.

"Sure," I said. "Did they tell you what my friend Louis saw? Twigs broken off six or more feet up? Close to the road?"

"Could be a moose browsing," the Warden Service lieutenant said. "With that bog in there, this area is chock-full of moose."

"One of the possibles is six six, six seven," I said.

"Even a deer will browse way up high," he said.

"So you think he's still in there?"

"Have to run like a deer to get clear before we set up the cordon on the road," Rousseau said. "We'll flush him out. A night out in the woods, he'll be cold and hungry. Hopefully, he'll come out peacefully."

"Yes," I said.

We all knew what the alternative was: a shoot-out in dense woods, potential for all sorts of injury.

"He'll either surrender or we'll take him down in the woods," Rousseau said. "Or he'll pop out on the road, trying to run. We've got that covered, so it's just a matter of time."

He waited with a couple of troopers at the rear of the lawn. The dog handlers went in first, three abreast, about fifty yards apart. They were flanked, ten feet back, by eight SWAT guys in camo with rifles and shotguns. There was a swishing sound of cops and dogs moving through the brush at the edge of the woods, then that diminished and they were gone.

We waited. Listened. I turned to the house and eyed the bullet holes in the window, turned, and tried to picture where the shots had come from. Had he been on his belly on the grass? Standing in the underbrush? Why hadn't he charged in to get me at close range?

Because I would have shot him? Or because he didn't want to kill me at all?

I heard a yelp, a hushed voice on the cop radio, looked to Rousseau. He murmured something into his shoulder mic, then asked if everyone had it.

"What?" I said.

"Stickley and Blaze," he said. "His K-9. They're on the track."

"Does the dog get body armor?" I said.

"No. His life is on the line."

"Him, too, huh?"

We stood and listened. Somebody following Stickley was reporting his position. There was thumping in the background, the dog and cop at full run on a trail. Then thrashing.

"Back in the woods," Rousseau said, then, "Forty-five, forty-eight, stay in a line. We don't want him flanking us, or getting between you and Stick."

"Where are they?"

"Quarter mile from the road, due north of here."

"They see him?"

"No, just tracking."

More waiting, listening hard to every word and sound from the radio. A small plane passed overhead and the pilot said something and Rousseau said, "Roger that."

"For when he pops out?"

"If he pops out," Rousseau said.

We waited, more back-and-forth on the radio. And then, after a half hour, the camouflaged cops started popping out of the woods. First to our left. Then to our right. We heard voices from the center, then Stickley and the dog came pushing through the brush. Blaze was back on his lead, head and tail high, hyped and proud.

"Good track," Stickley said. "Right to the road. Then gone."

And then there was a new urgency with the police, Rousseau hurrying away, the cops conferring. Rousseau came back around the shed, stopped in front of me.

"Your gun guy, the one who's MIA," he said.

"Semi," I said.

"You know his truck?"

"Sure. Older Chevy. Red, with black spoke rims."

"They just found it."

"He's not with it?"

"Hard to tell, McMorrow," Rousseau said. "It's underwater."

"Huh," I said.

"You know where Turner Pond is?"

"Sure," Clair said. "Five miles east, off Route 137."

"Come with me," Rousseau said. "You, too, McMorrow. Just so I can keep track of you."

He turned and started walking and we fell in beside him, one on each side.

"Your perp in the closet," he said. "He's hanging on."

"Aren't we all," I said.

33

It wasn't really a pond, not in September. By then it had dried up into more of a cattail swamp. There was a two-wheel track through the woods, scraggly grass three feet tall in the middle. The track went for a hundred yards and then stopped. There was a big field pine, the ground underneath it glittering with broken glass, the blackened embers of an old campfire at the center.

A sloping bank.

And the top edge of a tailgate poking out of the pea-green water.

Rousseau said they didn't have a diver available, the closest ones looking for a drunk who tried to swim to an island in Hermon. But there was no need. The wrecker driver, a skinny, barely bearded kid, backed his truck up to the clearing, got out, and yanked the winch cable off of its spool. Holding the cable, he waded into the water up to his waist. Reached into the murk and hooked the cable onto the rear bumper.

He waded back out, stomping muck from his boots. Went to the side of the truck and pulled a lever. The truck motor idled up and the spool began to wind. The cable tightened, the winch motor whined. The pickup lurched and then started to emerge, the tailgate coming out of the water.

Then the wheels, the black spoke rims. And the cab of Semi's truck, the driver's window shattered, two bullet holes in its center.

"Is it his?" Rousseau said.

"Yes," I said.

The truck was draped with weeds and coated with green scum. Water ran from inside the cab and back down the slope into the swamp. The whole thing smelled like muck and algae. And then it started to smell worse than that.

We moved closer as the wrecker driver stepped to the driver's door. He looked to Rousseau and Rousseau nodded and the driver grabbed the door latch and yanked the door open.

I saw boots. Legs. And when I moved closer, Semi slumped on the seat, most of the back of his head gone. Another guy in the passenger seat, his head thrown back like he'd fallen asleep. His neck gaped open, white flesh spilling from the gunshot wound, the skin gnawed by turtles.

It was one of the guys from the Miriam video, the one who had touched her face with his penis.

"Know him?" Rousseau said.

"Yeah," I said.

"Who is he?"

"Friend of Semi's. He was at the party."

Rousseau stared at the sodden bodies.

"Too bad, huh?" he said, then looked at me.

I shrugged.

There was only the one lane in, so the vehicles stacked up. Rousseau's cruiser. The wrecker. The crime-scene guys' SUV. The coroner's Suburban. Cook's unmarked Impala. Deputy Staples's brown Charger. She walked over as the crime-scene guys leaned into the still-dripping cab. I was off to the side with Clair—no clear role, but no way to get home.

Staples sidled up, looked at the pickup, and wrinkled her nose. "Been there a while."

"Probably since he went missing," I said.

"Two shots, two kills. Not exactly spray and pray."

"One in the head. Other one in the neck."

"These boys play rough," she said.

"Somebody sure does," Clair said.

"Boom, boom, then put the pickup in neutral and give it a shove," Staples said.

We stood there, picturing how it would have happened.

"I wonder why they didn't get out of the truck?" I said.

"Because they never saw it coming," Staples said.

"Arranged to meet somebody here, were waiting for a car to roll up behind them," Clair said.

"But it didn't," she said. "If it had, they would have seen a gun and tried to get out, you would think. I think somebody stepped out of the trees and popped them."

"Park on the road and walk in?" I said.

"Or just know the woods," Clair said, because he did. "Come in from another direction."

We turned and looked past the pine. The clearing gave way to bushes and brambles, some poplar and birch, small pines and hemlock scattered here and there. Rousseau was still poking his head in the truck cab so we walked away, past the big pine to the edge of the thicket. There was a hint of a path, a trail where deer had walked down to drink.

"Could be the way in," Staples said.

She was cheerful, familiar. Like we were buddies. Good cop, bad cop. And a third who pretends to be your friend?

I turned back from the path, walked back toward where the cops were gathered. Clair lingered, looking into the trees. Staples stayed with me. When I stopped to watch, she stood beside me.

"You think they deserved it?" she said.

I hesitated, then said, "The death penalty? Probably not."

"How 'bout your friends? They seem to take things to a different level."

"They aren't murderers," I said.

"Is it murder if you consider it just another war?" Staples asked.

I looked at her, looked back at Clair, still standing at the edge of the woods. Thought of Louis, suddenly MIA, and fought back the words *What the hell have we done?*

It was Staples who drove us back to my house, pulling out as the first TV news truck rolled up. It was from Bangor, and the reporter, who had covered arsons in Sanctuary, recognized me as we drove past. I turned around to see her writing in her notebook.

Great.

It was me and Clair in the back of the cruiser, me wondering if this was prescient. Staples turned out to be into horses, so we talked about Sophie's pony, the difference between a pony and a horse, different places around the world where ponies were used for work.

And then we were home and she let us out. There were no cops.

"See you later," Staples said.

"No doubt."

She drove off, and we stood for a minute, somber and distracted.

"Well," he said.

"Execution-style. My guess is Boston hired it out. And his buddy there was in the wrong place."

"How would Boston know about that cart path?" Clair said. "You'd have to be very local."

"Maybe Semi's idea of a place for a meet. Set up by Boston as another drug delivery. Shooter gets there early. Semi and Nub pull in and park. And bam."

"Pretty cold-blooded."

"And your point is? These gang guys'll kill you for talking to their girlfriend. Losing two guys, a dozen guns, and bringing the ATF down on their heads—that's gotta be worth the death penalty."

Clair looked at me.

"I hope not."

"I didn't rat them out," I said. "ATF was already here."

"The computer? The phone?"

A sinking feeling.

Clair said he'd head home, see if Louis had shown up. I said I'd go back to see Roxanne and Sophie.

"How are they doing?" Clair said.

"Sophie's okay," I said.

He looked at me.

"Stay with her, Jack," Clair said. "Don't let her go."

"Trying," I said.

"Try harder," he said.

Clair started up the road. I slipped under the crime tape and went into the house and upstairs to our room. It looked like pictures of places where civilians had fled a war. What was the saying? With the clothes on their backs. The bloodstain was black and crusty, but the smell had dissipated some. Drawers were still open where I'd gotten Roxanne some clothes. I wondered if she'd ever come back for more, or just buy new.

I went to the bureau and took out a pair of khakis, then to the closet, stepping over the stain, sliding the bullet-riddled door open wider. When I pulled the clothes aside, I saw blood spatter on the back wall, drips on the closet floor. Four of the shots had gone clean through, and the slug holes were marked by numbered tags on the wall.

Flipping through the shirts, I wondered if Baby Fat was worried, if he'd go underground. He didn't seem to be part of the gun ring, but neither had the kid from the party. Had Semi talked in the woods? Had Baby Fat been the snitch? Worse for him, would some-body else think so?

The thoughts still circling, I took out a blue Oxford cloth shirt, reached for a dressier belt from the rack. I looked at my shoes, lined up against the wall. There was blood on my dress loafers, so I picked up a pair of well-worn desert boots.

What did one wear to go *near* an Old Order Mennonite funeral?

Grabbing socks from the drawer, I gathered up the clothes and headed downstairs. The kitchen was silent, the glass still on the floor. There were two more tags on the wall of the study—same house, dif-ferent crime. I looked at the big slug holes in the wall, a .30-30 bigger than Billy's .25, the rifle slugs mushrooming.

What had been used to kill Semi and Nub? Something big, by the looks of them.

I took the clothes and a small duffel from the closet, stuffed them in as I went down the stairs. In the hallway, I went to the closet, pushed boxes aside, and reached down a box of nine-millimeter ammo—eighty rounds. If that wasn't enough, we were in serious trouble indeed.

On the way to the truck I called Roxanne.

It buzzed, then went to voice mail. I texted her, said I was on my way back to the farm, be there in fifteen.

No reply.

I called Clair and he answered.

"Any sign of Louis?"

"No," he said.

"He's probably back home, walking the woods with the dog."

"Yes," Clair said. "Trying to think things through."

"Like the rest of us," I said.

"Like the rest of us."

A pause.

"You get hold of Roxanne?"

"Not yet. On my way."

"Remember what I—"

"I did. And I am. And I will," I said.

I powered through the gears, jumped the potholes, clung to the turns. There was no reason to think that the person or persons who killed Semi would keep going. Message was sent. The remaining loose end of the team after Abram.

Payback complete.

If they were rational.

If there was order to their vengeance.

If there was a limit to their need to even scores.

If.

On the cutover road, I passed a Mennonite horse and buggy, saw a family in white shirts, long skirts, white bonnets on the women and girls. Headed for the funeral?

And then I went right and left, saw another buggy up the road in the direction of the Bishop's farm. I felt an urge to follow, but I went right, sped down the main road, and then swung off, the tires slinging gravel as I slid onto Welt's road. I came in from the west, saw Roxanne's car as I came up the long drive between the maples. The intern Heather's car was there, too, and a Mini with Pennsylvania plates. Maria?

Welt's truck was gone. A goat auction? A wine tasting? A peace conference?

I pulled in and parked, was tucking the ammo and Glock under the seat when Heather came out of the pole barn, goats trailing behind her. She waved and Maria came out of the barn and tried to shoo the goats back.

I went over and said, "Hey," and Heather said, "Hi, Jack," and Maria smiled. They were pretty as a picture, like Welt recruited out of J.Crew catalogs.

"Jack, I have an idea," Heather said. "Sophie's pony. If you're going to, you know, be here for a while, why don't you bring him over. There's lots of room in the barn, a nice box stall. Horses are social animals, you know. The herding instinct. He'd probably like having all the goats around."

"I don't know. I'm not sure how long we'll be here."

She kept on.

"Sophie could get him out on the trails. With someone with her, I mean. Maria and I were out this morning, and we saw these trails out off the north field. There were hoofprints, so people are already riding them."

"It's pretty out there," Maria put in. "Trails go for miles."

I said I'd think about it, asked where the girls were.

"They went to the corn maze," Heather said. "The one in Monroe. They have pumpkins and apple picking and cider."

"When did they go?"

"Ten minutes ago. I think Welt thought they needed a break, go in to school later."

"The four of them?"

"Yeah. The girls were excited about a hayride."

"Oh, good," I said.

The happy family. I smiled.

They turned back to the goats, Maria telling me to have a good day. Really? I went back to the truck and got my bag. As I walked to the house I looked out at the north pasture, thinking that moving Pokey here would be another nail in the coffin.

"Over my dead body," I said, then thought that, yes, it would have to be.

The house was quiet, flowers on the kitchen table, two empty wine bottles by the sink. I went through to the back and upstairs to our room. There was a note on the neatly made double bed. Roxanne had written, *Went with W. and the girls to a hayride place in Monroe. See you around 2.*

No sign off, no Xs and Os. And what about school being the safest place? Well, maybe better to be unpredictable.

I put the note on the bureau and went back and closed the door. Then I changed into my funeral clothes, left my jeans and shirt folded on the bed. I paused and turned.

Looked to the closet door. Walked over, hesitated, then yanked it open. It was empty. Of perverts. Just Roxanne's clothes: a dress, a skirt. Sweaters in a neat stack. Shoes in a row.

It was like she'd moved in.

I closed the door, left the room, and walked down the hall. At the top of the stairs, I looked to the end of the ell. There was a window that faced north, across the lawn and gardens and onto the pastures.

I went and looked out. The field was green scrubby grass, the goats grazing everything short. There was a fringe of woods on the far side, and I could see a marker at a dark break in the trees.

Trails go for miles, Maria had said.

Both ways, I thought. And I pictured Welt. The smarmy smile. The peacemonger, never an angry word. But what was he really? Teachers turn out to be molesters. Public do-gooders embezzle from nonprofits. The pillar of the community abuses his wife. Ministers cavort with hookers. Welt, the preacher of nonviolence. What was he underneath?

I went back and down the stairs and outside. Maria and Heather, in their overalls and wellies, were herding the goats across to the pasture gate. Like a catalog shoot—life in the country, where everyone was beautiful and life was good.

Unless you got your head blown off.

I drove out of the long drive, went right, and made my way west, along and then up onto the ridge. At the road to Abram's farm, I slowed to a stop. Took a long, deep breath and then turned and started in. It was a dirt road and dusty, and the truck left a faint plume. The hayfields were ready for cutting, the flowering grasses showing tan against the green.

Beyond the fields and the trees the sky was blue with clouds moving fast, west to east. It was a pretty early-fall day, and it made me think of everything Abram was missing. The farm and fields, horses and equipment, his friends and family. Even the grappling with his faith was something powerful and alive. And now he was gone, and I hadn't saved him.

As Sergeant Cook had said, I hadn't been much help at all.

I approached the long road to the farm, slowed, and turned. I let the truck roll, then barely touched the gas. Ahead of me was the big house where Abram's family lived, big barns out back. Windmill rotors turned in the breeze and cows raised their heads from the grass and eyed me as I passed.

The road widened and I came to the house and looked over. There were flowers in boxes on the edge of the big open porch, herbs drying in upside-down sheaves. I kept driving, past an equipment shed, then a paddock where horses leaned over clumps of hay.

And then the church.

There were six buggies standing off to the side, horses still hitched. One buggy had a flatbed and it stood by the front steps of the church, awaiting the trip to the cemetery. A boy, barefoot and dressed in black and white and a straw hat, was putting out pails of water for the horses. He looked up at me and I nodded. He put the pail down and stared.

I parked the truck beyond the church, along the fence. And then I got out and stood on the far side of the drive across from the church and waited.

There was singing coming from inside the church. I caught the words "My God and I," something about heavenly plans. I wondered what plans Abram had. I hoped to God they were, in fact, heavenly.

The singing stopped. I could hear a man's voice, the Bishop presiding at the funeral of his murdered son, an assignment worthy of Job. He was talking about sin. God's message. Walking in the light.

And then there was more singing, the Bishop starting them off. "A heartache here is but a stepping-stone . . . " And then the congregation joined in, and I lost most of the words, but heard the melody. It was mournful but serene, and I supposed it provided some solace to Abram's family, gave them something to think about other than the harsh reality—that he'd been bludgeoned, tied to a tree, defaced, and left to die.

And then they were quiet. There was a shuffling and the two pine doors swung open. Two bearded men in hats stepped out, saw me, and frowned. But they stood on each side of the door as more men followed. They were carrying a pine coffin, and they moved slowly through the door and down two steps. More men followed, then women. The men were grim-faced. The women were crying or fighting back tears.

And then the Bishop came out with a tall, angular woman who must have been Abram's mother. She looked exhausted, all cried out. She was holding hands with Miriam, who was sobbing. Behind Miriam came Victor, like he was part of the immediate family, a son-in-law. He looked over at me and glowered.

I didn't blame him.

They proceeded deeper into the compound, past my truck, and then turned through a gate into the pasture, the procession starting to sing as they approached a cemetery plot.

I followed at a distance, saw the white-painted rail fence, two or three stone markers. And at the side of the plot, a raw piece of ground, showing red-brown in the grass. Abram's grave.

I stayed outside of the gate. The Bishop said a few words, and then there was another song. I caught "Remember, child, I love you," and something about being alone.

And then they lowered the coffin in. A shovel was passed and I could hear the sound of earth hitting the wooden box, a hollow sort of *whoomp*. And then a prayer of some sort, and the sound of sobbing.

I backed off as the group approached the gate, walked over to my truck. They glanced at me as they swung back toward the church, but the Bishop, the bearded doormen, and Victor veered off and walked in my direction. I waited.

They formed a line as they got close, the Bishop at the center. When they were eight feet away, they stopped.

"I want to give you my condolences," I said. "I didn't know how else to do that."

"I accept your condolences, Mr. McMorrow," the Bishop said, his voice low and measured. "Please go now."

"Just go," Victor said. "Leave us alone."

"I thought a lot of Abram," I said. "He was a fine young man."

The Bishop nodded, his face drawn with grief, held together by his role. The two doormen stared at me stonily. I wondered if they wished their religion would allow them to beat me up and throw me out into the road.

"You don't belong here," Victor said, his voice cracking. "Get out. Get off this property."

"I'm going," I said, and then to the Bishop, "I didn't want you to think I didn't care about Abram."

"He didn't need you to care about him," Victor said. "He didn't need you for anything. So leave him alone. Do that much at least."

I looked at him, his eyes moist with sorrow or rage, or both. And I nodded to them, turned to the truck.

"Please wait to start your truck until we are back in the church," the Bishop said. "The sound will disturb the prayer and conversation."

Fair enough.

They walked away without another word, only Victor turning back to glare. And then they went inside. I started the truck and idled past the church, the sheds and the big house, and the cows and horses, all of it gleaming in the noontime sun. The horses lifted their heads from the hay and watched me. Abram and his horses. Abram working the fields with the team. I wondered if they noticed he was gone.

A gang guy is killed, somebody moves up to take his place. A Mennonite guy is killed, another guy takes the reins.

I pulled out onto the road and took my phone off the seat. I checked for messages, and there were three. I tapped the numbers and listened as I drove.

Clair: "Give me a call back. Important."

Ramos, from the ATF: "McMorrow. Call me ASAP."

Roxanne: "Hope you're doing okay, as okay as can be." A pause. "At something like that, I mean. Sad. Anyway, we're going to stop and get the girls—and us—an ice cream. Won't be too late. Welt says help yourself to beer or whatever. There's cheese and prosciutto in the fridge." Welt in the background: "Not just any prosciutto. It's San Daniele prosciutto. It's from northeastern Italy, and it's almost impossible to get in this country. These friends of mine—"

The call ended.

I dialed Clair. He answered. I heard the clank of a wrench.

"Hoses. Sick of losing fluid on the skidder."

"But that's not why you called."

"No."

"What?"

"Ramos. And Cook. They were here."

"What do they want?"

"You."

"Dang," I said.

"Dang?"

"Abram. His worst curse word. I just came from his funeral."

"Then I'd start danging like crazy," Clair said. "They were all business."

"I don't know any more than I've already told them," I said.

"They don't believe that," Clair said. "They think you know who killed Semi and—"

"Nub. But I don't. And Louis doesn't know, either. I mean—"

"We don't know what he knows, Jack. He was gone a lot, out all night. Out in the woods."

"You don't think—"

"I don't know what to think. He hasn't been here. I tried his cabin in Sanctuary. Nobody. Cops went there, too."

"Good luck with that," I said. "He's got three hundred acres to hide out in."

"And he's good at it."

"If they find me—"

"They bring you in for questioning."

"I can't leave Roxanne," I said. "Not now."

"She won't be alone," Clair said. "I'll be here. And she's got—"

"I know," I said. "It's not just him. It's everything else. I feel like it's all closing in."

"That's because it is, Jack. It is."

34

I went into the house, bounded up the stairs to the bedroom. I put my jeans and T-shirt back on, my old belt and boots. I felt more capable dressed like that, less vulnerable. Which made no sense; but then, all the stuff going on around me made no sense.

That much was clear.

I went down the hall, this time made my way to the front of the house. The front hall window looked out on the fields and the driveway, all the way to the road. If Ramos and Cook came back, I'd at least have some warning.

To collect my thoughts. To leave a note for Roxanne. To tell her to call a good lawyer.

Dang.

I grabbed a beer, sat down, and went through everything again, all of it flowing through my mind in a torrent.

A lawyer, for a trial? It would suck us dry. Charged with kidnapping, a Class A felony? For rousting a gang leader? Was that a crime? But wouldn't it all go away when they realized I knew nothing more, and neither did Louis?

Would Slick flip if he'd ordered the hit on Semi and his buddy? Was this his way to deflect suspicion about that? What about Gucci providing Slick's alibi? Wouldn't she retract her story?

And if Slick and G-Block didn't kill them, who did? I started at the beginning, which seemed like months ago, but was only a week. The gun sellers. Which of them had something to lose if he was connected to moving guns to gangs out of state? Were any of them felons? The weirdo in Bangor selling his father's shotgun—he had to have a record. Maybe he was on probation; if so, a violation would put him back inside for two or more years.

But was he crazy enough to whack two guys at point-blank range? Sure, if they couldn't shoot back. If he could slip into the woods and crawl back under his rock.

I watched the driveway. Went over the same ground, over and over. I'd tell the cops about the guy in Bangor. I'd tell them about Semi and Abram. I'd tell them again about the party in the woods, Miriam on the video, the gang guy in bed with the woman at Semi's house.

I'd lead them right through it from start to finish, not leave out a minute. But would it convince them that I hadn't killed anybody— that I wasn't capable of it? Or would it just pin the whole thing on Louis, the hardened combat veteran who, like Clair, had been trained to be a walking, talking lethal weapon?

That couldn't happen. Shouldn't happen. Or should it?

What had Clair been intimating? That maybe we didn't know Louis well enough? That maybe we'd pushed him over the edge?

Louis was interesting. Thoughtful. Intense. But he wasn't—

I'd seen him with Slick. The knife at his throat. The way he turned it off once he decided Slick was telling the truth. Like flipping a switch. But did it flip just as easy the other way?

I watched the driveway. Heard a car start, a diesel, and saw Heather's VW go down the driveway. Two women in it, Maria, too.

Another fifteen minutes, almost 1:30. I fingered the cops' cards. Watched the road. Went through it again and again. Finished the beer. Saw a truck flashing through the trees from the east. Brake lights coming on.

Welt turning in.

I could see Roxanne in the passenger seat, talking to him as they drove up the drive. They parked by the barn and got out, crossing paths as they passed the back of the truck. Welt reached out and gave Roxanne's arm a squeeze. She gave him a weary smile.

They got the girls out of the back. Salandra was asleep, and Welt picked her up and carried her to the house. Roxanne had a bag of apples and Sophie was carrying a squash. Sophie was chattering away and Roxanne turned to her to listen.

Their world, about to change?

There were footsteps downstairs, then on the staircase coming up. I was partway down the hall when Welt came up, still carrying Salandra. He saw me, whispered, "A tummy ache," and eased past me to put Salandra in her room. I went downstairs, came into the kitchen as Roxanne and Sophie did, too.

"Hey," I said.

"Daddy," Sophie said, and she came running, the squash in front of her. "It's an acorn, because it looks like one. Me and Mommy are going to make a pie. Or we'll just cook it in the oven. Welt has a good—"

She turned to her mother.

"Recipe," Roxanne said.

"Recipe," Sophie said.

She turned and put the squash on the table.

"Where's your truck?" Roxanne said.

"At the side of the barn."

She looked at me.

"It's a long story," I said, and she put the apples on the counter with a resigned expression. Weren't they all.

"Salandra got sick," Roxanne said. "They had candy apples. She threw up at the farm and then she fell asleep on the way home."

"Daddy, can we bring Pokey here?" Sophie said. "Heather says he needs a herd."

"Of goats?" I said.

"They're—"

Again, looking to her mother.

"Social animals," Roxanne said.

"I don't know, Sophie," I said. "Pokey likes his barn. And he gets to see Clair and Mary. And now Louis. He might miss them if he was here, and—"

"He'd have the goats and Heather and Maria and us guys, and I think he'd like it. I think he misses me."

I looked to Roxanne. She was putting the apples in a bowl, her back to me.

"I need to make a picture of Pokey with the goats so he can see what it will be like," Sophie said.

And she was off, trotting to the staircase, Roxanne shushing her, saying Salandra was asleep. "Close your door," she said. Sophie kept going, but more quietly. I heard her tell Welt to shush as they passed on the stairs.

And then it was the three of us. Welt went to the wine cupboard, looked at me, and said, "I don't know about you, Jack, but a day at a corn maze makes me ready for glass of wine."

A corn maze. Was that what this all was? I gave him a half smile. He pulled out two bottles, inspected the labels. "The 2011 sauvignon blanc from Twiddling Thumbs. Four stars from *Wine Spectator*."

He went to the drawer for a corkscrew. I moved to Roxanne, gave her a nudge. She looked up at me, said, "Is everything okay?"

I started to say, *Sure*, but stopped. It was enough.

Roxanne's eyes widened and she turned to me. I nodded toward the sunroom, and we walked out of the room as Welt turned the screw into the cork.

We stood on the deck. Clouds had moved in from the south and the temperature was dropping. Roxanne shrugged her sweater up over her shoulders and said, "What is it now?"

I took a breath, looked out at the flowers, and said, "You remember Boston."

"Yes. You went to talk to somebody. With Louis."

"Yeah, well, that guy. He's in a gang in Dorchester. The one getting the guns from Semi."

"Yes."

"The cops want to talk to me about it. I don't know what that guy is saying—"

I stopped.

I was looking across the field. There was someone on a horse coming out of the woods, crossing the field toward us. The person was riding hard and fast, pressed to the horse's neck like Paul Revere.

And then he veered and went out of sight behind the flower sheds and the barns. I stood up, watched for him to reappear.

"Heather said they saw hoofprints out there."

"So the guy in Boston," Roxanne said.

"I don't know, but—"

"Oh, Jack. They aren't going to charge you with something?"

"I don't know. I haven't talked to them. They came around looking for me, and Clair said—"

"Happy hour," Welt said, coming out on the deck with a tray holding the prosciutto and cheese, crackers. Two glasses of wine, a can of ale for me, and a frosted glass. We turned.

Roxanne smiled, said, "The service here is certainly—"

"Put it down and put your hands up."

The voice was behind me. I whirled around, Roxanne already saying, "Oh my God."

There was a guy in black wearing a ski mask coming up the steps.

A sawed-off rifle pointed at my head.

35

———～———

He came onto the deck, stopped ten feet away. He had the gun at his hip and he moved it from me to Welt to Roxanne, then back to me. Welt carefully put the tray down on the table. We all raised our hands.

"Keep them up," the guy barked.

And I knew.

The hectoring tone.

Victor.

"My wallet's in the kitchen," Welt stammered. "And if you want drugs, there's OxyContin in the upstairs bathroom. From when I tore my ACL. I think there's some Oxycodone, too. I'll get it for you if you—"

"Quiet," Victor said.

He stepped closer, pointed the gun at my chest.

"On the floor, all of you. Hands behind your heads."

Roxanne hesitated, eyes fixed on the mask, then dropped to her knees. Then to her belly.

"Come on," he said. "Move."

Welt did, falling prostrate to the deck like he was paying homage.

"Hands behind your head, I said."

Then the gun turned back to me.

"Didn't you hear me?"

"Heard you loud and clear, Victor," I said. "Also know now who took a shot at me and then got through the woods so fast. The horse."

He stiffened.

"I'm not Victor," he said. "I'm Abaddon."

"And I'm Captain America," I said. "We can play games, but you really should put the gun down. Put it down and then tell me what you want."

"Revelation, nine-eleven," he said, barking the words. " 'They have over them as king an angel of the abyss. His name is Abaddon.' "

He raised the rifle, pointed at my face. Just like Semi's last moment on Earth. His buddy's, too.

" 'He cast upon them the fierceness of his anger, wrath, and indignation, and trouble, by sending evil angels among them.' "

"You're not an angel, Victor," I said. "You're just a young guy from an Old Order Mennonite community in a small town in central Maine. A good guy who's lost his best friend in a horrible way. It's very upsetting, I'm sure. Hard to make sense of it."

" 'And the Lord said to Gabriel, proceed against the bastards and the reprobates, and against the children of fornication.' "

I saw Roxanne flinch and then tense.

Sophie.

"He said it to Gabriel, Victor. He didn't say it to you."

"I'm Abaddon," he said. "Now get down."

I stayed standing, moved a third of a step closer. Then another.

"So what do you want, Abaddon?" I said. "Anything. Just tell me."

He seemed to relax his shoulders and neck.

"The computer and the phone," Victor said.

"What computer? What phone?"

"His," he said. "Semi's. The ones with—"

He stopped, unable to say it.

"The video of Miriam?"

"Yeah."

"Why do you want them?"

"To destroy them. I'm the destroyer, the angel of judgment."

"Okay, but I don't have them," I said. "I gave them to the police."

"Liar," Victor spat. "Semi, he said you had them. He said you were using them to make him give you money."

"He was lying, then," I said.

"He wasn't. He was telling the truth. You tell the truth when you're about to fall into the abyss. You tell the truth to try to save yourself from the eternal fire."

He'd killed twice. He'd kill again. And the Glock was in the truck. I looked at him and smiled.

"I guess he thought you were bluffing," I said. "But good for you. You weren't."

"I'm presiding over the tribulation," Victor said. "I am the minister of death. Where are they?"

"I can get them," Welt said, lifting his head from the deck. "Let me go and get them for you."

Victor hesitated, then shifted the gun to Welt.

"No, please," Welt said. "God, no."

"Don't take the Lord's name in vain," Victor said, his mouth contorting behind the cloth.

"Okay, okay," Welt said. "But listen. I have nothing to do with this. I just let them stay here because their house got messed up, and the police were there and everything. It was a Christian thing to do, right? Kind of like the Good Samaritan. They needed a place to stay, and—"

"Quiet," Victor said.

He put the gun back on me. Welt began backing away, scooching his way toward the shrubbery.

"Where are they?" Victor said.

"I told you. Sergeant Cook, Maine State Police."

He lifted the gun to my face. His finger massaged the trigger.

"You do that, you'll never get them."

"I'll send you to hell," Victor said. "You made all this happen. You brought us to that party. You told them it was okay to go. It was you."

"I just gave you a ride so you wouldn't get hit by a car," I said.

"And now Miriam, if they see it, those guys putting themselves on her, stripping her naked like a harlot—"

"They won't, Victor."

"Because Abaddon will stop you."

"And you'll go to hell," I said.

"I'll burn in the fires of damnation for all eternity to save her." He was trembling, the end of the gun barrel shaking. "I've decided. That's my choice."

Welt was up on his elbows. Victor turned to him and moved fast, pressed the gun barrel to the back of Welt's head.

"And the Lord said to Gabriel," he said, panting, "proceed against the bastards . . . and the reprobates. He cast upon them the fierceness of his anger, wrath, and indignation. Proceed—"

"No," Welt said. "Please, no."

He started to cry, his head jerking up and down with his sobs.

And there was a footstep at the screen door to the house. A whisper. Sophie.

She was standing there with a piece of paper in her hand. Her picture. Pokey and the goats.

"Mommy?" she said softly. "Daddy?"

"—against the children of fornication," Victor said.

He turned to the door, started walking. "Hi there," he said. "What's your name?"

He had the gun lowered, aimed at her small center. I started to move and he said, without looking back, "Don't, McMorrow. I'll do it."

I froze. He pulled the screen door open. Reached for Sophie and, taking her by the shoulder, guided her out onto the deck. He kept her in front of him and moved back to us, stopping six feet from me.

"Now you choose," he said. "The computer and phone or your little girl."

"I want my mommy and daddy," Sophie said in a small voice.

"Choose, McMorrow," he said.

"Stop it," Roxanne said.

The masked head turned slightly.

She was getting up onto her knees.

"Stay down," Victor said.

"There is no God," Roxanne said. "It's a fairy tale. There is no Abaddon or whatever the hell you're playacting at. There is no Gabriel. There is no heaven and there is no hell. When you're dead, you're just gone."

"Reprobate," Victor cried. "Unbeliever."

"Do you think if there was a God he'd let your friend die the way he did?" Roxanne said, easing to her feet now. "Smashed in the head and tied to a tree? He was a good person. Would God let that happen?"

"Abram deserved it," Victor said. "He allowed it to happen to her. If he hadn't—"

He caught himself. The pause hung in the air.

"You killed him," I said. "You killed him because of Miriam."

"Abram had fallen. I stopped him from taking any more of us with him. From taking her to hell."

"And carved his forehead?"

"The defilers must be defiled."

"And you needed time."

"The Lord sent me to save her. Protect her. I needed time."

"Miriam."

"To keep her pure. To keep her from knowing that the Devil tried to possess her."

"So she's good enough for you?"

"I'm on this Earth to protect her. It's God's will. She loves the Lord. It was one night when she was tempted. They drugged her and tried to seduce her. But Abaddon avenged her."

"Victor," I said. "Would Abaddon hurt a little girl?"

Sophie was still, her face pale, the picture still in her hand. It fluttered in the breeze. And Roxanne started to move, almost imperceptibly.

"You're not an angel," I said. "You're a pathetic little coward. Hit Abram from behind. Shot the other two when they were unarmed and defenseless. Because you wanted to be the hero. Because you have some weird sexual repression, obsession thing."

Roxanne was turned. Lowering ever so slightly.

"You're a backshooting little worm, Victor. A freak. A sinner if there ever was one."

"No. It's not a sin. It's ordained. It says it. Revelation, nine-eleven."

"Killing in the name of religion," I said. "Hey, I admit it's a long tradition. The Inquisition. The Crusades. Maybe you ought to move to the Middle East and lop people's heads off because they read a different version of the Holy Book."

"No," Victor said, spittle showing at the mouth hole of the mask. "Stop."

The gun came up, the raw edge of the sawed-off barrel showing in front of my face.

And Welt ran, breaking from the floor like a sprinter, tumbling off the deck. As Victor spun toward him, Roxanne launched through the air. I dropped and got under the gun, grabbed Sophie, and swung her aside. The picture flew into the air, was floating when Roxanne hit him, the boom deafening.

The shot went high, over my shoulder, and Roxanne was on him, Victor trying to backpedal. He had his hand on the bolt, yanked it back, started to push it forward, rack another shell. Roxanne dropped down and sank her teeth into that hand. Victor screamed and she kept biting, her jaw clenched, blood running. I wrenched the rifle from his hand and flung it aside.

Roxanne was up now, clawing the mask off. She raked his face with her fingers, nails clawing his cheeks, his forehead, his eyes. Victor was writhing, trying to get loose, but she was astride him, both hands slashing, leaving pink-flesh gouges. He got his hands up, tried to get them around her throat, but she was quicker, had her hands clenched around his neck, squeezing, the muscles in her arms taut.

Victor choked and sputtered and his hands fell off of her. His face was bloody and then it was turning dark blue under the red and Roxanne stayed locked onto him.

I moved to her, said, "Enough. Enough." A flash of déjà vu, pulling Louis off of Billy. And then she relaxed her grip. Took her hands off his throat.

"It's okay," I said.

And Roxanne raised her right arm, made a fist, and drove it into Victor's face.

"Don't you ever—"

Smack.

"—threaten—"

Smack.

"—my child."

Smack.

She raised her arm, then stopped. Her knuckles were gashed and bloody, Victor's face, too, blood streaming from his broken nose and open mouth.

Roxanne got off of him, wiped her hands on her jeans, and moved quickly to Sophie, picked her up, and trotted down the steps to the lawn. I rolled Victor onto his stomach, yanked his arms back. Unbuckled my belt and yanked it off and cinched his wrists tight. "If you try to get up, I'll let her kill you," I said.

And then I went and picked up Sophie's picture and brought it to her. The three of us stood on the grass in a family embrace. We were quiet, not crying, not talking, just pressing ourselves together like we wanted to become one. Again.

And then Sophie said, her voice muffled against Roxanne's shoulder, "I don't think Pokey will like to live with goats."

We stood for a minute and then heard a sound on the deck. Salandra was standing over Victor, a puzzled look on her face. Roxanne handed Sophie to me, ran to Salandra and picked her up and brought her to us.

Salandra looked at us and said, "Where's my daddy?"

36

Welt was upstairs, came running down and back out onto the deck. He skirted Victor, lying in a pool of blood, and hurried over to us, grabbing his daughter and swinging her up into his arms.

"Daddy," Salandra said, squeezing him tight. "Where were you?"

"I was looking for you," he said.

"I woke up," she said. "I was looking for everybody, and then I came outside and saw that man lying there."

"It's okay," Welt said. "Daddy's here."

He looked to us and said, "I called the police. They should be here shortly."

We turned and walked away.

Roxanne collected our stuff from the room. Welt was in the kitchen with Salandra. I waited on the deck with Victor, who lay there for ten minutes without speaking.

"I was just trying to save her," he said finally.

"Good job," I said.

"If I go to hell, that's okay," he said.

"You're on your way," I said.

37

It all made sense, so much so that we wondered how we'd missed it. Victor lost
in the sway of two forces that were most irrational: love and religion.

"He forgot about the 'thou shalt not' part," Roxanne said.

"Happens," I said. "In the end, Abaddon just wanted to get the girl."

We threw out the bloody rug, repainted the floor where Billy had fallen. I patched the bullet holes in the wall, and Clair and Louis hung new closet doors. Roxanne and I painted the walls mocha and the trim off-white. And then we rearranged the furniture, swapping the bed and the bureaus and the overstuffed chairs. We hung a framed photograph of the three of us. With Pokey.

And then we stepped back and surveyed our work. I held Roxanne and we waited for the bad karma to infiltrate the room like gas. It didn't. The curse was lifted.

That night, we brought our suitcases from Clair and Mary's house, Sophie between us with her stuffed lamb, its fleece hugged off.

We were home.

I had called the *Times*, said there would be no story on the Old Order Mennonites in Prosperity, Maine. I'd called *Outland* and said there would be no story on the Maine gun pipeline. The editors understood. They'd read the stories about the Prosperity homicides, the guy who had killed his best friend. They'd read that Sergeant Cook of the Maine State Police said the motive was a dispute about a girl. He declined to elaborate.

And then we sat on the couch, the three of us, and watched *The Jungle Book*. Sophie concentrated, not speaking, holding my hand, and Roxanne's. It wasn't easy for Mowgli—the tiger, Shere Khan, almost got him—but he made it home, too.

And then Sophie slept on the couch between us, her mouth open and her breath coming in small, delicate strokes, like a violin being played very softly.

"Thank God," Roxanne said.

"That fairy tale?" I said.

"I was praying the whole time, until I started screaming at him."

"Me, too. No atheists in foxholes."

She looked away and said, not to me but to herself, "All the killing."

We sat and Sophie's hands fell away and I reached over and took Roxanne's in mine.

"I believe in it, you know," she said. "The nonviolence. The peace project. I still do."

"And I didn't not believe in it," I said. "I just didn't believe in him."

"Welt believes in it, too," Roxanne said. "He's just—"

She searched for the word. I waited.

A womanizer, I thought.

"Flawed," she said.

A coward, I thought.

"I told him I was through with working with him. He got all huffy and hurt and said he'd find another partner if I wasn't interested. I think he expected me to change my mind. When I wouldn't he said he needed to get away, go where people were way more chill."

"Napa?" I said.

"To go stay with his ex-wife or wherever. He ran."

I smiled inside.

"Nonviolence," I said. "It isn't for the faint of heart."

We sat and watched Sophie for a minute, maybe two. She rubbed at her nose and then fell back asleep, the lamb clutched to her chest.

"A lot of what I said, it still stands," Roxanne said. "About the example we set for her. About what she sees."

"I know. I'll keep it in mind."

"I'm not expecting you to turn into—"

She paused.

"Him?" I said.

"Oh, Jack. I don't even really expect you to change much at all."

"I'm an old dog," I said.

She smiled at me.

"Not that old," she said.

So I carried Sophie upstairs and we tucked her in, one of us on each side of her bed. And then we went to our room, which smelled of paint and scoured wood and the new rug. There were fresh sheets and blankets and we turned them back, took off our clothes in unison, and climbed in. We pulled the covers back up and, in the dark, quietly made love. And when we fell back, my arm around Roxanne's shoulders, her head on my chest, we didn't speak.

There was nothing to say, nothing that wasn't understood, nothing that we could keep from each other, even if we'd tried.

POSTSCRIPT

We gave statements, each of us. This was in Bangor, at the attorney general's office, up by City Hall. Cook was there, and an assistant AG, a young woman who listened hard and asked good questions. When I was done they looked at me, then at each other. Hit the button to turn off the recorder and leaned back.

"Pretty much the same as the kid told it," Cook said.

"I don't think he thinks he did anything wrong," I said.

"I go to church every Sunday," Cook said. "Thou shalt not kill. As far as I know, that's still in there."

"Victor found a loophole," I said. "The Book of Enoch."

"Hey," Cook said. "Once you're prepared to die and go to hell, it really opens up your options."

Clair had been wrong. Billy lasted fifteen days before succumbing to an infection that lodged around his heart. Rousseau came to the house to tell me that he had "expired," that no charges would be filed, that the AG's office had ruled the death justified.

"Good riddance," I said.

He stood there in the doorway and said, "I know. Some are more regrettable than others."

"Have you told Louis?"

"Been trying," Rousseau said. "Haven't been able to locate him. A lot of woods down there."

"He'll be glad to hear it," I said. "He took this kind of hard."

"Shouldn't," the cop said.

"Easy for us to say."

"Yes," Rousseau said. "I suppose it is."

We stood. There didn't seem like there was much left to say, but Rousseau lingered.

"You know," he began, "you're not what I thought. Not dirty."

"Thanks," I said.

"But you're still not squeaky clean."

I shrugged.

"The way I see it, you won't leave well enough alone. You're the kid who always wants to give the wasp nest one more poke with the stick."

"Some people don't deserve to be left alone," I said. "They deserve to be punished. 'All that is necessary for the triumph of evil is that good men do nothing.' "

"Someone said that, right?"

"Edmund Burke. Smart guy."

"Well, good luck to you, Mr. McMorrow. I have a feeling our paths will keep crossing."

"No doubt," I said.

"Watch that you don't go too far. You or your friends. Because the law is the law."

"Right."

"And that's what we enforce. Not some battle between good and evil."

"Understood," I said.

He shook my hand and we looked each other in the eye. Neither of us blinked. When he'd left, the last police car gone down the road, I walked to my truck. I started it and pulled out and drove north and then west. I stopped by the field, where the horses were pulling a harrow. The Bishop held the reins.

I climbed the fence and crossed the furrows and stopped six feet in front of the horses. He tugged the reins and the horses pulled up, dropping their heads. I walked around them and up to the side of the harrow.

"We love our children," I said. "We want to protect them."

"Sometimes that's not God's will," the Bishop said.

"So I'm assuming somebody loved Victor," I said. "How did he get so far off track?"

The Bishop looked away, his expression softening.

"His father and mother left the community. They made Victor choose. He chose to stay. He remained with his faith."

"And when the others started to question, he was threatened," I said, understanding. "If they were right, he'd chosen wrong."

"They weren't leaving," the Bishop said. "They were coming back."

I didn't reply.

"All violence comes from fear," he said. "Victor was afraid of his own weakness. He was afraid he wasn't worthy of my daughter. He was afraid of being abandoned again."

"So he had to take on this other identity. This alter ego, like Spiderman."

"Abaddon, the angel of darkness," the Bishop said.

"Darkness," I said. "He got that part right."

I looked at the Bishop, thought to hold out my hand, but didn't.

He nodded, snapped the reins, and the horses lurched forward. Then he yanked the reins back and the horses paused and he turned back to me.

"I pray for Abram every day," he said. "I pray for you, too."

And he snapped the reins again and the horses ambled away, furrows trailing in their wake.

It was colder, the days shorter, maples flaring orange over our heads, the leaves illuminated like lanterns by the midday sun. We were dropping the trees, then limbing them, leaving the crimson and yellow bouquets strewn like colorful clothes stripped from a corpse.

Clair was skidding the logs out. Louis and I were cutting. We fastened the cables and stepped out of the way as the diesel roared and the logs were lifted, and then they were dragged down the trail, the ground gashed in their wake.

Louis had been gone for a couple of weeks, then had shown up without warning. We'd told him the Boston cops had backed off, that the threat of charges from Dorchester was just a way to pressure us to talk about Semi and the guns. Now there was nothing more to say.

Louis had said, "Okay. Let's get to work."

So that day we were working, a selective cut on more of the Hoddings' lot, another payment due for the nursing home. Clair and the skidder disappeared down the trail in a plume of blue smoke, and Louis and I walked to the truck, and lunch.

Friend, the dog, looked up from his bed in the back of Louis's Jeep and wagged.

"McMorrow," Louis said, sitting on the tailgate, opening his lunchbox.

"Yeah."

"I let you down."

I shook my head.

"Nobody knew what was coming."

"I left before the job was done," Louis said. "Started to head into a dark place in my head and had to navigate it alone."

"I hope you sorted things out."

He took a bite of sandwich and chewed and swallowed. Then he said, "I've got to know the triggers," Louis said. "Spent a lot of time making them full automatic. Had to be, to survive over there. A second slow and you were dead. But now I have to learn to put the triggers on manual, keep the safety on."

He looked at me.

"I was changed by all of it," Louis said, "and now I have to change again. Not back to what I was, but into something new. Anyway, my problem. I'm sorry I wasn't there for you."

"That's okay," I said. "I had serious backup."

He opened his water bottle, tipped it back, and drank. Held it out and dribbled some on the dog's tongue.

"Don't get between a tiger and her cub?" he said.

"Exactly," I said.

"She's a keeper, Jack."

"Yes."

"You know I mean that in a good way."

"I know," I said. "And I agree. She is."

Clair rumbled up on the skidder, shut it off, and climbed down. He went to the truck and took his lunch basket from behind the seat, then sat beside Louis on the tailgate of the Jeep.

Louis finished his ham-and-cheese sandwich. I had peanut butter and jelly, which Sophie had made for both of us that morning. Clair opened a thermos of Mary's vegetable soup.

A pair of crows flew over, circled back in case we might be deer hunters, leaving offal behind. Louis broke a piece of his sandwich off and tossed it a few feet away. He looked at the dog and waited, then said, "Okay." The dog bounded off the truck and scarfed the morsel down. Then he stood and raised his head, sniffing the air.

We looked through the trees, saw nothing. Then, from the distance, we heard a chain saw start. It sputtered, stalled, started again, and revved up.

"How far your friends own?" Louis said.

"That direction? All the way to the marsh," Clair said. "Two miles north and almost as far to the south."

The saw slowed, the chain biting into a log, then the motor wound up again.

Louis looked at us and waited. I looked at Clair and he looked at me.

"It's only trees," he said.

"They'll grow back," Louis said.

"And it's only one guy cutting," I said. "How much could he take?"

A second saw started.

"Then again," Clair said, "there's right."

"And there's wrong," I said.

"We could talk to 'em," Clair said.

"I suppose," Louis said. "Talking never hurt anybody."

ABOUT THE AUTHOR

Gerry Boyle is the author of a dozen mystery novels, including the acclaimed Jack McMorrow series, and the Brandon Blake series. A former newspaper reporter and columnist, Boyle lives with his wife, Mary, in a historic home in a small village on a lake. He also is working with his daughter, Emily Westbrooks, on a crime series set in her hometown, Dublin, Ireland. Whether it is Maine or Ireland, Boyle remains true to his pledge to send his characters only to places where he has gone before.